DON'T MISS THESE EXCITING
TIME PASSAGES ROMANCES, NOW
AVAILABLE FROM JOVE!

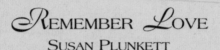

ℛEMEMBER ℒOVE
SUSAN PLUNKETT

A bolt of lightning transports the soul of a scientist
to 1866—and into the body of a beautiful Alaskan
woman. But her new life comes with a price: a
maddeningly arrogant—and seductive—husband...

𝒜 𝒟ANCE 𝒯HROUGH 𝒯IME
LYNN KURLAND

A romance writer falls asleep in Gramercy Park,
and wakes up in fourteenth century Scotland—in
the arms of the man of her dreams...

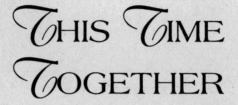

THIS TIME TOGETHER

Susan Leslie Liepitz

JOVE BOOKS, NEW YORK

THIS TIME TOGETHER

A Jove Book / published by arrangement with
the author

PRINTING HISTORY
Jove edition / December 1996

The Putnam Berkley World Wide Web site address is
http://www.berkley.com/berkley

ISBN: 0-515-11981-4

A JOVE BOOK®
Jove Books are published by The Berkley Publishing Group,
200 Madison Avenue, New York, New York 10016.
JOVE and the "J" design are trademarks
belonging to Jove Publications, Inc.

PRINTED IN THE UNITED STATES OF AMERICA

10 9 8 7 6 5 4 3 2 1

To Don Phillips —

My own six-foot-six, blond Flynt Avery
A gentleman in the truest sense
My best friend
My husband

I love you.

Special thank-yous to:

GRACE M. HARRIS, my seventh-grade English teacher, who not only sparked my interest in writing while on the *Wildcat* newspaper staff, but also gave me a copy of the *Dunsmuir Centennial Book 1886–1986,* which sparked the idea for this particular story.

My appreciation extends to everyone who contributed to the Centennial book, especially the editors—Reva Coon, Grace Harris, Patricia Girard, and Flora Wintering—who brought the history and people of Dunsmuir back to life.

PETER M. KNUDTSON, author of *The Wintun Indians of California and Their Neighbors.*

LOUZANA KAKU, writing as "Christina Dair," who loaned her name and gave her invaluable writing advice.

STEVE WRIGHT, the guy who single-handedly keeps dozens of romance writers writing because of his computer expertise!

JANET CARROLL, of the former Book Emporium in Long Beach, California, who suggested years ago that I write a time-travel romance. I'm glad I finally listened to her!

PATRICIA TEAL, my friend and my agent. I have the best of both worlds with Pat and I dearly appreciate her love and support.

JILL MARIE LANDIS, a sister not by blood, but by love. You believed in me when I had yet to believe in myself. Since then, you have taught me to expect and accept the best possible outcome to my prayers. *Mahalo nui loa!* (Many thanks!)

VERA MAE LIEPITZ, my mother. God bless you, Mom.

Do you not believe that spirits sometimes come back to the world to fulfill some work that lay near their hearts?

—EDWARD BELLAMY
Looking Backward

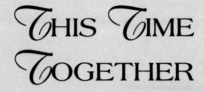

THIS TIME TOGETHER

Chapter 1

THE DREAM STILL haunted her.

In the early morning hours, Katherine had awakened in her motel room, still aware of the distinct aroma of meat roasting in its juices. Such virtual reality in her sleep was a new and strange experience for her. Perhaps her longing for a simpler time had stirred her imagination. It made sense. What didn't make sense was the very real smell of cooked meat.

Not that she believed dreams had any prophetic value. On the contrary, she viewed them more as mental scrapbooks with familiar faces and the surroundings of everyday life. Usually they were so uneventful that she rarely, if ever, recalled them in the morning.

Until now.

Sitting alone in a booth near the door of the diner, she held the white stoneware mug with a two-fisted grip, staring out the plate-glass window toward a highway overpass that blocked the view of the snow-crested Mt. Shasta. Even though the caffeine had cleared the cobwebs of sleep from Katherine's brain, it couldn't clear her head of the peculiar dream. She dropped her head a bit and rubbed the back of her neck. These few days of rest would do her good. If nothing else, it might erase the disturbing dream from her mind.

"Need some aspirin?" asked the waitress as she delivered the heaping breakfast plate, placing it next to the empty mug.

Katherine glanced at the spreading puddle of melted butter on top of the English muffin, dribbling down the sides like gravy over a slice of roast. . . . The dream again. Why wouldn't it go away?

When the question about aspirin finally registered in her brain, Katherine looked up at the waitress. "That's thoughtful of you, but more coffee will do just fine."

The blond girl shrugged it off with a smile and turned to leave, then hesitated. "Are you a model?"

Startled by the question, Katherine resisted the urge to laugh at the absurdity of such an assumption. Fast approaching thirty, she had clients who would have smirked at the idea of their attorney prancing down a runway or mugging for the camera.

"Actually, I'm an attorney." She held back the rest—that she was an attorney in the entertainment industry with her own talent agency. The girl would probably start to audition, she thought wryly, then chastised herself for putting this waitress in the same league with the starving actresses who served tables at restaurants near the big studios.

"Lost that bet," sighed the blond.

"I take it you don't lose very often."

"Nope." She gestured at the crowded roadside cafe. "We get a lot of tourists stoppin' here. But they're pretty much average-lookin' people. Now as soon as we saw you gettin' out of that Lexus out there, Hank—he's the one at the grill— says that you're an actress. But I told him, 'Naw, she's got to be a model.' "

Katherine let her pancakes get cold. The small-town friendliness of her talkative waitress was simply too charming to ignore. Maybe she'd leave a couple extra dollars on the table to offset the lost bet. Then suspicion leapt into her thoughts, condemning the girl for suckering another tourist for a big tip.

Mentally shoving aside the cynical attitude that seemed to pop into her head a lot these days, she extended her appreciation for the compliment, adding, "I hope you didn't bet your paycheck."

"Worse—I've gotta fork over my recipe for blackberry cobbler." The girl laughed, shaking her head. "With the way you're dressed, I figured it was a sure bet."

After a quick glance around at the jeans and cotton shirts, Katherine noticed the stark contrast of her boxy linen jacket and long gauze skirt. Accustomed to the eclectic fashion of Los Angeles, she belatedly realized her own casual tastes translated a bit differently in this rural environment. The fascinating thing was that the girl was so refreshingly candid about it.

"Orders up, Jan," Hank-the-grill-guy hollered over the murmur of multiple conversations by the dining customers.

"Comin'." The waitress scribbled on her order pad, ripped off the page and laid it on the table. "You just passin' through then?"

"Actually . . ." Katherine had started to say yes but the word seemed caught in her throat. "I think I'll stay a few days."

Now that she'd said it, she didn't think it sounded like such a crazy notion. After all, she had no destination in mind. No deadlines. No meetings. This tiny railroad town in the mountains of Northern California was as good a place as any to spend some time rethinking her life.

"There's not a whole lot to see around here," Jan explained with the apologetic tone of a country kid who dreamed of big-city excitement. "But if you're into history stuff, you can check out the fountain up the road. And there's the museum down in town. Of course, you can stop and ask just about anybody for directions. . . ." Her words trailed off behind her as she hurried toward the plates of food waiting for her attention.

After Katherine squared her bill at the Hitching Post Restaurant, she checked out the fountain, then drove south on Dunsmuir Avenue until she located the museum in the heart of town.

Losing all track of time among the memorabilia, the lawyer in her perked up at an old yellowed newspaper headline: WRONG MAN HUNG FOR MURDER. Curiosity drew her eye to the finer print. It seemed the poor guy turned out to be an eccentric millionaire from San Francisco who lived as a recluse south of town. The real murderer was discovered after the innocent man was strung up.

Bureaucratic bumbling never changes, Katherine thought to herself as she left the museum.

She walked the length and breadth of the historic business district—a short stroll, to say the least. Nestled in a deep canyon, Dunsmuir appeared to have seen better days when the railroad first laid tracks along the headwaters of the Sacramento River. Only the Rostel brick building remained from a fire that had destroyed most of the original main street down by the train depot. Yet small retail shops had revitalized some of the older stores. Nowadays, the bank and a few stores and bars lined the old "back street" up the hill from the tracks, creating a new main thoroughfare. As time passed, the town boundaries pushed outward in the only two directions possible—north and south—until Dunsmuir resembled the long, narrow ribbon of water running along its length.

By early afternoon Katherine had learned just about everything imaginable of the town's one-hundred-plus years. After a brief lunch stop in a converted old railroad car, she drove past the granite spires of Castle Crags, choosing an old highway road rather than the four-lane freeway carved high into the west wall of the canyon.

Savoring the scent of pine and the sound of the rushing river somewhere beyond her sight, Katherine hooked her elbow lazily on the open window frame—a luxury she never indulged while driving alone in the city.

Turn here.

Startled, Katherine hit the brakes. Her seatbelt locked across her chest. Had she actually heard the command? She couldn't be sure. To her left was a dirt road just like a dozen others she'd passed, most of which had been blocked by rusty chains with pockmarked metal signs. Scanning the knee-high weeds and blossoming berry bushes, she couldn't see any posted warning of private property.

Curiosity prodded her to turn the steering wheel. She wouldn't go far. Just a few feet. That's all. After a quick look, she could easily back her car out and be on her way.

The front end of her Lexus dipped slightly as the wheels crossed from the asphalt into the shallow ruts worn into the dirt. Satisfying her curiosity may not have been the wisest decision she could've made, especially if it meant bottoming out her car or scratching the white finish on thick brambles at the edge of the road. But the sedan cleared the center hump between the ruts with no problem. Same for the thorny bushes. The sound of the rushing water grew louder, tempting her to venture further than she'd intended. She continued until the road dead-ended at a breathtaking view of the river and the bank beyond.

In the shade of tall pine trees, Katherine stood at the crest of a slope above the muddy bank, allowing the sounds and scents to rush over her like white water frothing over the rocks and boulders. The raw beauty was a soothing change from the rush-hour congestion of L.A. freeways, which is where she would have been at that moment had it not been for her sudden need to put her life on hold, to simply take off for parts unknown. To run away. Granted, this was probably the most spontaneous thing she'd done in her entire life. But she was long overdue for some much-needed soul searching. At least that was the excuse she'd given her partners from the pay phone at a rest stop outside of Fresno. Neither of them asked her reasons why. They both knew.

Katherine chose her footing carefully as she worked her way down the embankment, which was covered in dead oak leaves and pine needles. Her suede boots and filmy gauze skirt were the furthest thing from rock-climbing attire in her wardrobe. But her impulsive departure on her way to work yesterday morning had kept her from returning to her condo for a suitcase full of clothes. For once, reliable, predictable Katherine had done something . . . well, spontaneous. Any needs that arose could be solved with any one of a dozen credit cards. And at the end of a few days, she would head home—hopefully with some answers.

Eyeing the muddy bank, she dropped her bulky purse at the foot of a thick tree trunk. After slipping off her jacket, folding it and placing it on top of her purse, she sat down on the makeshift perch and removed her boots. Using a little ingenuity, she reached between her knees, grabbed the back hem of her skirt and tucked it in at the waist in front. Though the effect made her look a bit like an Italian grape-stomper, it would be sufficient to keep the wispy material from dragging in the mud.

As Katherine ventured down the embankment, pebbles in the wet soil dug into the tender soles of her feet. Years of cushioned shoes had softened the tough skin from her days on the sandy beaches along the Southern California shores. Now she was forced to step gingerly, cursing her cushy lifestyle until she reached the water's edge. Choosing a large, smooth rock that was partially submerged, she sat down on the sun-warmed granite and plunked both feet into the river.

With a gasp, she yanked her knees to her chest. Despite the warm spring weather of late March, the water was colder than ice itself. Dangling her toes in a refreshing mountain stream certainly wasn't anywhere near as appealing as she'd imagined.

Nothing in your life has ever turned out like you'd imagined, taunted a now-familiar voice in her head. The voice hadn't always harassed her. But after her marriage soured two years earlier, and a couple of legal deals turned ugly, she had felt as if her usual optimism were slipping through her fingers like sand. No matter how hard she tried to regain her positive perspective, the cynical voice intervened. It had seemed like a losing battle.

Until two days ago.

As she rubbed the chill from her toes, the sound of a train coming up the canyon distracted her. She heard the echo of the lonely whistle growing louder as the diesel engines came into view on the other side of the river. The rhythmic clatter of the wheels rolling over the rails lulled her. The rush of water mesmerized her.

Memories of her two business partners, Sunni and Michael, drifted into her mind. Except for a few years after college, the three childhood buddies had been inseparable. Katherine had spent those few years in a rocky marriage to a fellow lawyer who was eager to climb the ladder to the Hollywood high-wire acts. She, however, had been content to join her Aunt Lillian's talent agency as a contract specialist. When her aunt died in the midst of the ugly divorce, Katherine nearly lost the Meridian Talent Agency to her ex-husband until her two friends signed on as her partners. Both Michael and Sunni proved to be savvy agents in their own right, leaving the legal paperwork to Katherine. Things had been looking pretty good until Michael dropped a bomb two days earlier. With the same flippant attitude he displayed under every circumstance, he'd asked Katherine to marry him.

"And ruin a perfectly good friendship?"

"We'd make a great team."

"At the office, yes."

"I mean in the bedroom," he had answered, in a quiet sincerity that replaced his jovial tone. Katherine loved Michael like a brother. Next to Sunni, he was her best friend. When she'd sworn off the male species after her divorce, Michael playfully fretted about changing his sex to meet her newly established criteria for friendship.

Imagining Michael as her lover was darn near impossible. To be fair, she herself wasn't exactly seductive temptress material, based on her own limited experience. The thought of being intimate with a man again scared the hell out of her. And yet, Michael wasn't just any man. Maybe she was looking at this all wrong. The one reason why she kept turning him down might be the one reason why she *should* give him a chance. Could best friends make the best of lovers?

Still lost in the memory of that afternoon, Katherine stared at the end of the train as it disappeared up the grade. Once more, the disappointment of Michael's kiss enveloped her. In a way, she wanted to believe that a marriage between them would be as great as their friendship and business partnership. Falling in love with Michael would solve the complicated game of finding Mr. Right. But that romantic spark just wasn't there.

Asking him for a few days to decide, Katherine later dreaded going to the office the following morning, imagining awkward glances and tight smiles. Halfway to Century City, she realized she couldn't work alongside Michael, knowing that he was waiting for her to accept his proposal. Within moments, she maneuvered her Lexus to the nearest off-ramp and rerouted herself back to the northbound lanes of Interstate 5. She didn't stop until she was outside of Fresno, and only then to make that quick phone call so Michael and Sunni wouldn't worry. Afterward, she drove to the point of exhaustion, forcing herself to pull up to the motor lodge in Dunsmuir.

Now the midafternoon sun descended toward the western rim of the deep canyon, rays of light pierced the treetops like brilliant theatrical spotlights focused on the narrow, fast-running river. The sparkling water seemed to dance with life. Mist from the rapids downriver reflected tiny rainbows of color, capturing Katherine's interest. She felt as if one blink would make the beautiful illusion disappear.

She imagined herself living here in these mountains, away from the crowded streets and city crime. Away from the nameless neighbors and high-powered Hollywood deals. *What would it have been like to live a hundred years ago in some tiny mountain town, where life was centered on the town hall and quilting bees?* If she had been the girl next door and Michael had been the boy who used to dip her pigtails in the inkwell, Katherine would have undoubtedly stepped up to the altar of some rustic little church without any of her present-day turmoil of doubt and experimental kisses.

With a sigh born of wishful fantasies that could never be, Katherine stepped off the rock onto the muddy bank. Her self-imposed solitude by the river seemed to stir up more longings in her imagination than she cared to entertain. She'd come here to contemplate her future, certainly not dream of the past.

Dream. The word had become a nemesis. Maybe this silent reflection wasn't a good choice after all. She'd been better off distracted by the tourist-type sightseeing in town. Determined to steer her mind into a more productive direction, Katherine marched up the bank to where she'd left her boots and jacket, and put them on. Releasing the hem of her skirt, she let it drop into place.

A sudden breeze cut through her thin jacket. Rubbing her arms at the sudden chill, she glanced up from the darkening canyon to the pale blue sky. An eagle caught her eye. A magnificent bald eagle, its wings spread wide, soared high above in the air currents, then dipped into a graceful circular descent. She watched, fascinated at the bold swoop of the white-crested bird as it passed only a few feet above the white water and landed on the boulder she'd been sitting on. She remained still, trying not to make a sound that might scare it off. Moments ticked by while the eagle perched motionless on the rock, poised like an exquisite sculpture carved in marble. Then slowly his white head pivoted.

Yellow eyes looked directly at her. She held her breath. The air grew colder. Her skin prickled with goosebumps. A rustle in a bush startled her. She glanced at the noise. It was a gray squirrel scurrying up the trunk of an oak tree. When she glanced back at the boulder, the bald eagle was gone.

The temperature seemed to be dropping steadily by the

second, reminding her why she chose the warmer climate of Los Angeles. Mountain weather was too unpredictable for her tastes. She grabbed her black purse from the ground and hooked the strap over her shoulder, then started back up the slope.

When she reached the top, she paused for one last look at the river and saw that the bald eagle had returned to the rock below. He cocked his head. She gave a single nod to say good-bye, then turned back toward her car.

And stopped.

Six feet in front of her stood a luminescent apparition of a young woman in a dress of beaded white leather. Katherine's heart pounded wildly as she noticed the faint outline of trees beyond the translucent image. Her gaze locked onto beseeching dark eyes. The girl lifted her arms, her palms upturned as if beckoning Katherine.

The air grew cold as ice. One by one, tiny snowflakes began to drift out of nowhere, floating around and through the vision of the young Native American girl.

It's another dream, Katherine told herself, unable to force her muscles to move. *I'm tired and stressed out. That's all. This can't really be happening.*

The woman slowly closed the distance between them. Katherine remained rooted to her spot. She looked down at the small hands reaching out but not quite touching her sleeves. She saw perfect crystal snowflakes settle on her jacket. In the silence, she lifted her gaze and suddenly understood the plea in the girl's eyes.

"I—I can't go with you," she barely managed to whisper, surprised by the eerie echo of her words. A shiver rippled through her, setting her teeth to chattering. She clenched her jaw shut. An icy wind swirled around them.

She had to get away. Panic goaded her legs to finally

move. Stepping back, she realized her mistake as her body fell over the lip of the riverbank in a strange sort of slow motion. The impact with the ground knocked the wind out of her as she slid, head first, down the needle-slick hillside.

Not the water. Please let me stop before I hit the water.

MARCH 27, 1892

Flynt Avery heard a woman's scream as he stepped off the abandoned train. His horse Sasti spooked, tugging nervously on the reins looped over the iron handrail. Though the snow-locked canyon was silent now, save for the rush of water below, he was certain the cry came from the opposite bank. Hampered by the falling snow of the late-season storm, he could not even see the steam engine beyond the next railway car, let alone a few hundred feet across the river. With a touch of his gloved hand, he calmed Sasti, then swung himself into the saddle.

As his roan horse labored over the familiar mountain terrain, Flynt allowed Sasti to find footing, confident in the animal's instincts. Had this been December or January, the flurries would have dusted the winter pack with a light powder. But the late-season warmth had created a wet, burdensome snow, hampering the animal's progress.

Deep snowdrifts and raging water doubled the time it would have normally taken to ford the river, already swollen from the first spring thaw. By the time Flynt caught sight of the woman lying facedown at the bottom of the bank, he held little hope of finding her alive.

Leaving Sasti on higher ground, he waded through thigh-high drifts, working his way down the steep slope. Snowflakes had already accumulated on the woman's cloth-

ing, shrouding her in white. Her head and shoulders lay in
the shallow waters. The only movement was her long dark
hair floating in the ripple of the current. As he carefully
lifted her limp body and turned her over in his arms, he
glanced from the ghastly blood-washed bump on her forehead to the smooth granite stone in the water. It seemed the
rock on which she'd hit her head had also saved her from
drowning. Yet he had no indication that the blow itself had
not caused irreparable harm.

Mindful of further injuries, Flynt moved back from the
water's edge and lowered the woman onto the snow. Kneeling at her side, he gently packed a handful of snow on her
forehead to stem the flow of blood and bring the swelling
down. If the gods were with her, she would have only a
nasty bruise and a devil of a headache. But that remained to
be seen. He dropped his gloves to the ground and withdrew
a clean handkerchief from inside his fur cloak. Careful not
to disturb the lump of snow, he smoothed a strand of wet
hair from her cheek, inspecting for broken bones.

His gaze traveled over the sable hair framing her delicate
features. She appeared to have the face of an angel if not for
the garish cosmetics. Unnatural shades of brown powder
colored her eyelids. Evidence of painted lashes had left a
black smudge beneath each eye. And with full lips a curious
shade of dark pink, she looked every bit a whore, though the
strange costume was more of a gypsy.

Forcing his mind back to her present needs, he lightly
grasped her arms to check for injuries, cautiously pressing
his fingertips through the sleeves of a jacket far too large to
be called her own. The soiled pink cotton had absorbed a
great deal of dampness from the snow and river, darkening
it to the shade of her lips. Soft, inviting lips. His gut knotted. With a mental reprimand, he continued his inspection,

working his way down to her wrists and hands. His brow furrowed at her torn and broken fingernails, all the more grotesque from the strange red paint on them.

A slight moan escaped her lips, though she didn't move.

"You've taken quite a fall, ma'am," he told her, in the event she could hear him. "As soon as I determine you haven't broken a limb or such, I'll get you in out of this cold."

He quickly finished his careful survey, pressing her ribs lightly with his palms as her breasts rose and fell in a reassuring rhythm. If a rib had broken inward and punctured a lung, she'd certainly have shown signs of distress, he assumed.

With the blank canvas of white snow beneath her, the outline of her black stockings were easily discernible through a skirt that was more like a gossamer underslip of purple and green and black. The odd attire was potently disturbing if not absolutely scandalous. He worked his fingers down thighs that should not have aroused him. Or at least he should not have allowed it. But his body betrayed him.

A few inches below her knee, the supple leather of her boots made it unnecessary to remove them to inspect her slender calves and ankles. Confident there were no broken bones in need of a splint, Flynt retrieved the blanket roll from his saddle and returned to her side.

Though there was little wind, the snowstorm hadn't let up. If anything, it seemed to have worsened during the time it had taken to minister to the unconscious woman. In the few moments he had spent away from her, freshly fallen snowflakes had dusted her lashes, melting as they settled on her skin. He brushed the packed snow from her forehead, hoping he still had time to get her into town.

Lifting her once more into his arms and carrying her up

the embankment to where Sasti waited, Flynt mulled over the fate of the strange woman he'd found across the river from the abandoned train. Once again, the snow drifts on the rails had made the steep grade impassable. No doubt the station in Dunsmuir had been alerted by the delayed train and volunteers had come in search of it. Yet by the time Flynt came upon the Oregon-bound train, any sign of the passengers' footprints had been long since covered by the snow. As he mounted up and settled the woman across his lap, he pondered one question—how could she have crossed the swollen river without being swept downstream? All practical explanations escaped him while time passed slowly in his arduous struggle against the mounting snowstorm.

Flynt gazed down at the woman he carried in his arms. In addition to his own size, her weight made the journey all the more difficult. His horse struggled with each step. To reach his cabin was all he could ask of the animal. Continuing the extra distance into town would be sheer cruelty. He had no choice but to take the mysterious lady home with him.

The scent of wood smoke and cooked meat tugged Katherine from her contented sleep. Regretfully, a fascinating dream faded from her mind. Something about a man . . . and snow, of all things. He had wrapped her in something to ward off the chill, then picked her up and carried her. Cradled like a baby, she drifted in and out to a gentle rocking motion. Trying to recapture the fantasy, she turned on her side to snuggle further down into her bed.

Intense pain slammed into her temple. Where the headache had come from was not as important as how fast she could grope to the bathroom for some aspirin. As she cautiously opened her eyes, the unmistakable flickering light of fire seeped through the haze of pain and the hangover of sleep.

Her condo was on fire!

She gripped the bedcovers to throw them aside, then gasped, startled by the soft, thick fur beneath her fingers. This wasn't her bed. And this wasn't her condo.

Determined to wake herself from this nightmare, Katherine squeezed her eyes shut. In the dark void behind closed eyelids, her mind grasped for some small memory, only to see bits and pieces of a river. A squirrel. Falling. Fear. Then blackness. She reached up and pressed her fingers to her temples to try to block the pain. Discovering the outrageously large lump dead-center above her eyes didn't come as a surprise. But could it be causing her to actually hallucinate?

"Of course," she breathed, content to settle on any explanation—rational or not. No doubt she was in an emergency room imagining all this.

She opened her eyes once more. Despair replaced her small attempt at practical reasoning as her gaze darted around the room. It was anything but a hospital. The fire that had scared the living daylights out of her was safely contained in an enormous stone hearth, where a soot-smudged cookpot hung on a large black bracket. A safe distance from the sparks, her boots sat on the floor. Above them, her muddied pink jacket hung over the back of a chair, apparently drying by the heat of the fire.

The stark reality of her surroundings stirred recollections of her wistful daydream at the riverbank. . . . *What would it be like to live a hundred years ago in some tiny mountain town, where life was centered on the town hall and quilting bees?* Were those momentary thoughts the source of this delusion? Was she deep in a coma or caught in a drug-induced dream?

The deliciously familiar aroma of food cooking drew a profound complaint from her stomach, further confusing the question of her present state of consciousness. Was this real or imagined?

Another stab of pain urged her to scan the four rustic walls for a bathroom where she could find some aspirin. Nothing. She groaned, which made her head pound all the harder. With one objective in mind, she put off worrying about how or why she'd ended up in a cabin that didn't even sport indoor plumbing. All she wanted at the moment was to take care of an urgent need for something to ease the torture.

Gritting her teeth, she forced herself to muscle aside the animal pelt and drop her feet off the edge of the bed, a bed she realized was nothing more than four shaved logs, some rope and a mattress that looked more like a huge flat sack stuffed with God only knew what. As she pushed her hair out of her eyes, her fingers caught in the damp, snarled ends. She stared at her toes, which barely touched the dirt-packed floor. Whoever had brought her here had the good graces to leave her clothed and otherwise unharmed, she realized, sending up a quick prayer of gratitude that she'd not become another statistic for a newspaper headline.

She hoisted herself out of the sagging mattress. The effort made her woozy. Steadying herself, she braced one hand on the flattened top of the bedpost, her fingers curled over the edge. When some degree of lucidness returned, she shuffled to the chair where she was forced to pause once more as her surroundings blurred from the agony inside her head. Stinging tears pooled behind her eyes. If only she could find. . . .

A muffled thump drew her attention around to the door.

Its thick wooden bar was the width of her arm and twice as long, clearly strong enough to keep out any intruders. Just as she'd convinced herself of her safety, the bar lifted and the door opened.

A brilliant white light pierced the room like a laser. Katherine stumbled backward, shielding her eyes with her hands.

Chapter 2

WITH HIS BACK to the reflective glare of sun and snow, Flynt paused in the doorway while his eyes adapted to the shadowy interior. From the manner in which his guest retreated, she appeared to be as startled by his sudden arrival as he was surprised to discover her awake and standing barefoot—and dangerously appealing—in the middle of his cabin.

"Ma'am," he greeted with a nod, then stepped inside. With practiced agility, he balanced the firewood in his arms, kicked the door shut and set the bar. When he turned around, he saw for a brief instant the image of his wife before he realized it was only his eyes playing tricks on him. Little Deer had been gone for eight years, and no woman had set foot inside his cabin since. Until now. It was reasonable to expect a moment of confusion, he rationalized. Even still, it disturbed him.

"I promise I won't bite," he grumbled, making his way

past her in the narrow space between her and the chair. "There's really no need for you to be afraid."

"I'm not." But when he accidentally bumped the table and upset a mug, she took another step away from him. "Who are you? And what am I doing here?"

The soft huskiness of her voice should not have made him think of sultry nights and warm bodies. Not here. Perhaps in the city. In his hotel room overlooking the bay where he could be with a woman without being haunted by the memories of his wife. Facing those same memories now in the primitive surroundings of the log walls and dirt floor, he felt guilty about the way his body involuntarily responded to this mysterious lady.

"Flynt's the name and you're here because I found you lying facedown in the river." Kneeling next to the flat stones of the outer hearth, he stacked the firewood, careful to shake the snow off each log. Out of the corner of his eye, he watched her inch forward to the only source of heat in the room. "My question to you, ma'am, is—who are you and how in blue blazes did you manage to get yourself on the other side of the river?"

"Why didn't you take me into town?" she asked, clearly evading his inquiry.

"Too far. I found you about a mile from here," he explained without looking up from his task. Snowflakes fell from his fur cloak to the floor around his feet and melted into the packed soil. "With this storm blowing in as it did, you should consider yourself lucky anyone found you at all."

He looked up to see her staring into the firelight, her ashen features softened in the glow of yellow and gold. Her contemplative gaze fell upon him for a moment and he saw a flicker of vulnerability before she looked away.

"I don't consider myself lucky to be holed up with Grizzly Adams."

"Avery," he corrected. "Flynt Avery."

"Mr. Avery," she amended in a weary tone, "I fail to see anything good about waking up in a stranger's cabin that doesn't even have indoor plumbing—especially when there's a full-blown blizzard outside, though God knows where it came from." Katherine tried to focus past the pain. During client interviews at the agency she was a master at reading people. But now it was impossible to see through this bearded mountain man with the deceptively genteel British accent. She shook her head, then winced. Her hand darted to her forehead. As she swayed, Avery shot to his feet and grabbed her shoulders to steady her.

"Don't—" Katherine rasped. Her fingers sank into the deep brown fur of his coat as she tried to push away. "Please . . . I'm okay. Really."

"It does not appear that way to me." The quiet concern of his voice seemed as out of place as his regal accent.

She was not accustomed to looking up to men—figuratively or physically. But she guessed this Englishman was at least six foot six, perhaps more. Another startling discovery was the color of his eyes. Though she didn't expect beady black eyes glowering at her from beneath the fur hood, she wasn't quite prepared to see deep blue eyes. Gentle eyes. The realization was unsettling.

"I appreciate your concern." Moving out of his reach and gripping the back of the nearby chair, Katherine slowly lowered herself onto the wooden seat as she bit back the pain. "I . . . can manage."

"Are you certain?"

She only nodded, rubbing her temple, cautious of the tender lump at her hairline. When her rescuer walked briskly toward the door, she couldn't hold back a feeling of panic. Being secluded in the cabin with the stranger was not the best of circumstances, but it was a darn sight better than being left alone to helplessly battle this mother of all headaches.

"Where are you going?" she demanded, anxiously perched on the edge of the chair.

His head snapped around. "Nowhere in this storm." He sounded agitated with her domineering tone. Yet his expression softened as if he saw the fear she tried so hard to hide. "Worst bloody snowfall we've had in years, coming this late as it did."

Stopping behind the closed door, he shrugged out of the long overcoat, revealing dark blond hair that fell well below the broad shoulders of a navy blue flannel shirt. Hair that looked too soft, too touchable for the bearded giant. Catching her misguided thoughts, Katherine sternly warned herself that this man was still a stranger, still potentially dangerous.

"There was no sign of a storm when I was at the river," she pointed out, realizing that her bewilderment sounded more like an accusation against Avery's credibility.

Coat in hand, he glanced back at her with a puzzled frown. "Blew in quick."

"I didn't mean to imply you were lying." Uncomfortable under his glare of scrutiny, she resisted the urge to squirm in her seat like a scolded child. Instead, she averted her gaze toward the divided window pane and the steady snowfall outside. "Obviously it's not an illusion, though for the life of me I wish it was."

"Fair to say that it nearly *was* 'for the life of you'." Gripping the shoulders of the long coat, he reached up and hooked the collar on a high peg beside the door. His buttoned cuffs strained at his wrists, tugging the full sleeves taut along generous biceps. The shirt yoke cut a horizontal line beneath his upraised arms, marking the width of his shoulders with breathtaking clarity. Below the seam, generous gathers in the dark cloth were pulled into long vertical ridges by the snug fit of his belted jeans.

Her gaze followed him to the hearth where he used an iron poker to swing the hanging kettle away from the fire.

From the thousands of publicity glossies that passed through her hands at the agency, Katherine sensed that Flynt Avery had more income potential in the fashion or entertainment industry than any model or actor on her client list. He was undeniably well proportioned for someone of his size. No lanky arms and legs. Except for bumping into the table earlier, he didn't appear to be the least bit awkward. On the contrary, he moved with a fluid elegance that conveyed a natural ease in his body.

Her professional appraisal shifted to a sudden awareness of her clammy palms and tingling skin. Refusing to believe she was experiencing her own primal response, she blamed her sweaty hands and goosebumps on her exposure to the freezing water. The only rational explanation she could accept was an out-of-whack internal thermostat.

"There's a bit more stew in this pot than I'll be able to eat," Avery stated flatly, snatching a couple of faded rags from one of several iron hooks pounded into the thick wood mantel. She watched him set the kettle lid aside. Steam curled upward, floating away into the stone chimney.

"It smells wonderful," she lied, certain her opinion would have been different if a knot of nausea hadn't lodged in her throat. "But I'll pass."

As Flynt stirred his supper he pondered the deathly pale woman who seemed as odd as her exotic clothing. The inflections in her voice were distinctly different than any he had heard in San Francisco or among the mountain folk. Despite her occasional sharp remark or question, there was a bit of a lazy quality to her speech pattern that smoothed her words like hot buttered rum.

He peeked over his shoulder at the strange woman with her elbows propped on his table. She'd bowed her head as she massaged both temples, her face concealed by the curtain of her long damp hair. She had been quick to demand answers, yet not as forthcoming with a response to his own questions. The only explanation that made any sense to him was that her memory had been affected by the blow to her head.

"You need food in your stomach if you expect to feel better." Flynt rose to his feet and walked past the table.

"I'm not very hungry."

"Nonsense."

Without looking up, Katherine heard a clatter of wooden bowls at the sideboard, then the muffled thump of his footsteps on the dirt floor. A hiss and sizzle from the fire accompanied the dull clunk of metal upon metal.

She forced her eyes open as he set the wooden bowl in front of her, along with a large soup spoon. He scooped up the overturned mug from the table, then grabbed another from the array of dishes. After pouring a dipper of water into each from a wooden barrel beneath the workbench, he placed them on the table, dragged a crude stool from out of a dark corner and sat down to eat.

Staring down at the steaming bowl of stew, she felt the moist heat on her face. The aroma triggered a distant memory that wavered just beyond recognition. Her eyes watered, blurring the vision of meat, carrots and potatoes that should have made her stomach grumble from hunger. Instead, she fought the nausea with a difficult swallow. It didn't help.

Bolting from her chair, she fumbled with the wooden crossbar, yanked open the door and managed a couple of steps before her knees buckled.

When the woman unexpectedly fled the cabin, Flynt nearly choked on a large chunk of venison. As the unmistakable sound of retching came through the unlatched door, he dropped his spoon and charged outside. Seeing her on her hands and knees, he cursed his insensitivity. The minute he'd found her up and about, he should have put her back into bed straight away. A blow to the head was serious enough without the added strain of weathering freezing temperatures. It wasn't any wonder she'd been overtaken by dry nausea.

"Is there anything I can do?"

"Leave me alone," she snapped without looking up at him.

"I could be of some assistance."

Her snow-dusted shoulders shook as if she were laughing to herself. "How about assisting me off this mountain and back to where I belong?"

"This snow is too heavy, too wet. Look what it's done to your clothing in the few moments you've been out here. You can't possibly expect to survive an hour—" Flynt stopped himself when he realized she was caught in the throes of another retching convulsion.

He was torn between leaving her and leaning down to cradle her forehead in his hand. But he had the distinct impression that she would just as soon bite him as let him do anything so merciful. Shaking his head, he went back into the cabin and returned with his mug.

He found her still on her knees but sitting upright with her feet tucked under her. Her head tilted back with her face to the falling snow, as if in divine supplication. The vision of her tore through him once again with memories of another time, another woman. He pushed them aside and offered her the mug.

"Drink this," he commanded, perhaps more sternly than he'd meant. As she accepted the drink, the brush of her fingers against his declared a silent truce. Short-lived, however. She cast a suspicious eye at the orange-tinged water, then sniffed it and wrinkled her nose.

"It smells like rotten eggs."

"It's exactly what you need to calm your stomach," he assured her.

She took one sip and spat into the snow, spilling the soda water from the mug. Frantically, she scooped up a handful of snow and wiped it on her tongue like a bar of soap on a washboard.

"Is this your idea of a joke? I'm dying here and you hand me sulfuric acid to help me on my way."

The idea was tempting, Flynt mused, suppressing a smile. Her caustic tongue could cause even the most tolerant of men to contemplate such extreme measures. "It happens to be mineral water from the soda springs."

"It's certainly not Evian."

"No . . . it's Ay-ver-ee. Flynt Avery." Flynt was baffled by her inexplicable reason to discuss his name.

She stopped, stared ahead for a moment, then squinted up at him, studying him with the most perplexed expression. "I *know* your *name*."

"Then you have me at a distinct disadvantage," he prompted, yet she offered no name—first, last or otherwise.

When she started to push herself to stand, he silently extended his hand. Merely a reflex of his gentlemanly upbringing, he told himself, refusing to make more of it.

She stared at his hand disdainfully as if it were a centipede, then looked up at him and deliberately shunned his offer by plopping the mug into his palm. Though it would have been easier to accept his help, she struggled to her feet, then offered him a self-satisfied smirk. At the doorway, however, she paused and turned her head to one side. Without looking directly at him, she addressed him over her shoulder.

"Katherine," she said with a quiet dignity that matched her aristocratic profile. "Katherine Marshall."

After she stepped out of sight he puzzled over the half-dressed dark-haired woman he'd carried home from the river. The name of Katherine seemed more suitable to a stiff-postured, tightly laced governess. Hardly the description of his unexpected guest. No, she was far more like a strong-willed Kate.

Katherine went over to the hearth and placed a stick of wood on the glowing embers. If Avery had a lick of sense, he'd take a hike until she was done fuming over that mug of foul-tasting mineral water. He was probably standing outside right now having a great laugh at her expense.

She jabbed the burning log with the iron poker, wishing she were venting her frustration on the man himself. It didn't help. Still, if she were forced to admit it, the effervescence of the soda water had cleaned the repulsive aftertaste of nausea from her mouth.

She heard Avery enter the cabin. Keeping her back to him, she squatted and sat on her heels with her arms wrapped around her knees. An involuntary shiver shook her from head to toe. Suffering in silence, she tightened her grip around her legs to stave off the chill.

"It will not do your health a bit of good to stay in those

dirty, wet clothes," he commented casually. "Would you care to take them off?"

Katherine craned her neck around so Avery could get a clear look at her not-on-your-life glare.

"I'm fine, thank you." But another shiver betrayed her, bringing a disbelieving arch to his thick eyebrows.

"I cannot fathom which it is that clouds your good judgement—pride or ignorance."

"Neither, I assure you." Katherine turned back to stare at the growing flames, refusing to say more that would draw her into his argument. She wasn't about to defend her good judgment to Flynt Avery. His opinion meant nothing to her.

"Very well." She heard him settle down at the table behind her and continue his interrupted meal. "Your supper is still waiting for you, if you choose to eat."

Considering his preference for sulfur-scented mineral water, Katherine grew skeptical of his stewed concoction of meat and vegetables. There was no guarantee that this man knew anything about wilderness survival. For all she knew, he could be a British refugee from a heavy metal band with nothing more than passing knowledge from old Disney episodes of Daniel Boone.

The chilly dampness on the back of her damp skirt and blouse prompted her to turn her back to the fire. Her head still pounding, she watched in agonizing silence as Avery ate with surprisingly good manners, given the Neanderthal image she had of him. Averting her eyes from the sight of food, she dropped her gaze to her cold toes. The feet of her pantyhose were wet from her trip outside and now muddied from the dirt floor. Resigning herself to the discomfort, she tried to take a deep, relaxing breath but managed only a shaky, shallow one. Her second try was a little more successful.

"Something isn't right, Mr. Avery."

"Flynt," he corrected again. "And I couldn't agree more."

"I don't know anything about concussions but I think I need a doctor." Keeping her head down, she stole a glance to gauge his reaction. "You don't have to take me all the way into town. If I can just get back to my car, I'll take myself. . . ." Her words drifted off as she watched those blue eyes narrow.

"Too easy to get lost," he said after swallowing, impatience laced in his words. "Besides, it will do no good to return to an empty train, I assure you."

Train?! Katherine's stomach muscles tightened. "I don't want to return to a train—empty or otherwise. I wasn't even *traveling* on Amtrak."

He looked at her as if she had rocks in her head. "What, may I ask, is an . . . 'Amtrak'?"

In her experience as an attorney in the industry, she'd developed an instinct for hard-edged tactics when challenged. One hell of a headache didn't exactly sweeten her demeanor, either. She didn't bother to hide her sarcasm as she explained, "Amtrak . . . you know that long, silver passenger train with a big diesel engine."

"You must mean a steam engine."

He was dead serious. Katherine felt the blood drain from her face. Her head pounded harder. Her heart slammed against her rib cage.

"It may take several days before the storm clears and the tracks are opened. But I think I can deliver you to the depot in plenty of time to continue your journey. In the meantime, I'm afraid you have no choice but to tolerate my hospitality and limited cooking skills."

"I don't have a few days," she said emphatically, marching up to the table. The sudden move brought another intense wave of pain and nausea. She braced both palms on the smooth wooden surface and formed her words through clenched teeth.

"If you won't take me, I'll hike to town if I have to." *And find a sane human being to help me.*

"Not in this storm," Flynt answered distractedly, leaning across the narrow table. Taking her chin in his hand, he turned her head so the firelight illuminated most of her face. If she'd appeared pale earlier, she was now undeniably white as the blanket of snow outside his door. Virtually clean of her superficial cosmetics, she appeared considerably younger than when he'd first found her. Smooth skin. Long lashes. Slender nose. Lips the color of a dark rose. Her natural beauty was far more alluring than the painted image he had looked upon at the river.

Careful not to bruise her jaw with the firm pressure of his fingertips, Flynt gently coaxed her face toward him. He stared into her eyes, deep green and vulnerable, and felt an overwhelming need to take care of her.

"You are in no condition to go anywhere. From the look of you, I'd say it's best if you crawled back into bed."

Katherine batted his hand aside, annoyed as much with his hypnotic mannerisms as with her own lulled response. "How many times do I have to tell you—I'm well enough to travel."

The man was articulate, she'd give him that. But he was no genius when it came to comprehending her determination to get back to civilization. With each passing moment, she had the distinctly uncomfortable feeling that Avery was intent on keeping her. Preferably in his bed, according to his last comment.

"Point me toward the road. I'll thumb a ride into Dunsmuir."

He looked puzzled. "What do you mean by 'thumb'?" He held up his own, examining it as if it were going to sprout horns.

"Forget it," she groaned, shoving herself away from the table. One way or another, she was getting out of there. She didn't have a chance against him if she tried to run from the cabin. First she had to find a way to get outside without him being suspicious of her intention to escape. Lord only knew what she'd do once she got that far.

"What the devil are you doing now, woman?"

"Putting on my boots, Mr. Avery. And as soon as I get my jacket, I'd like you to tell me where I might find a bathroom."

"If you wish to take a bath," Flynt informed her dryly, "You needn't go looking for another room—you are standing in it."

"I don't want to *take* a bath, I need to *use* the bathroom." She rolled her eyes at his stymied expression. "You know . . . nature calls."

"Indeed. I think you must mean—"

"Just tell me where it is, okay?"

"As you wish," he answered, with as much nonchalance as a butler granting a request for a brandy—which she could use right about now. If not the liquor, at least the bottle so she could knock him out cold and make a run for it.

After being escorted to the one-hole outhouse beyond the stable, Katherine was repulsed by the primitive facilities, yet relieved to discover the obnoxious mountain man had enough decency to build anything at all. It could have been worse, she realized. He could have led her behind a snowbank.

Closeted in the dank wooden box, she banged her elbow,

then her head as she struggled with her wet pantyhose and cursed the filmy gauze skirt that wouldn't cooperate with her efforts. For a few minutes, her bare backside froze while she listened to the muffled squeak of footsteps pacing back and forth in the snow.

Avery may as well have been a prison warden the way he kept watch over her. It looked like her hasty plan to get outside and escape into the woods was destined to fail unless she could think of something. She would have to convince him that she was going to take longer than expected and that he should go back to the cabin.

"Mr. Avery?"

His pacing stopped but he didn't answer. Perhaps it wasn't him outside. If he'd walked away during her noisy attempt to undress she wouldn't have noticed. Then who—or what—had been moving around out there?

"Mr. Avery?" she called out again with a flutter of apprehension in her voice. Still no response. Where was he? Certainly he wouldn't have left without telling her. He must be close. Close enough to hear her scream and come running.

"Flynt!"

"That's more like it."

"You've been here all along!"

"Guilty."

"I don't find your joke very funny."

"Yes, well . . . perhaps you could hurry up a bit so we could continue this discussion inside."

"You can't hurry these things, Avery. Go on without me. I'll get back by myself."

"I'd rather not, if you don't mind."

"I *do* mind," Katherine argued, feeling utterly ridiculous talking through the thin walls of an outhouse. "Despite what you might think, I can manage walking thirty feet from here to the cabin without getting lost."

She held her breath for a moment, hoping he would comply. The silence stretched out until the Englishman finally spoke.

"Very well. But try not to be too much longer."

The challenge of pulling up her damp pantyhose proved more difficult than taking them off. The more she hurried, the clumsier she got, which only slowed her progress. Finally finished, she stumbled from the outhouse.

Through the white filter of falling snow, she could barely make out the only clear path that led away from the cabin into the dense forest. Gray clouds hovered low, obscuring the top half of the trees. As far as her eyes could see—which wasn't far—there was nothing but a lumpy, sound-deadening blanket of white. She couldn't tell a bush from a rock. Despite the ominous weather, she pulled her jacket collar around her neck and followed the parallel line of boot prints.

Pounding headache and all, she had to find her way back to civilization. If she was to get out alive, it would be totally up to her. Michael and Sunni didn't know she'd spent the night in Dunsmuir, let alone that she'd been taken in by Grizzly Adams. It could be days before her disappearance would be investigated.

At the edge of the clearing, the trail led into the pine trees and dipped to the left, following the steep incline of the mountainside. Above her head, a green canopy of pine boughs had caught much of the current snowfall. But freezing temperatures had left slick patches in the old snowpack. She slipped and slid in her high-heeled boots.

With no other choice but to slow her pace, she managed to gain some traction by digging her heels into the hard-packed snow. Her progress was a joke, as was her stomping, arm-waving duck-waddle down a slope that would be better used as a bobsled trail. Concentrating on her balance was made more difficult by the hammering going on inside her head.

Suddenly a hand grabbed her wrist. She cried out as her feet slipped and her body weight pulled mercilessly against her captured arm. In the next instant, she was whipped back around, then caught about the waist by a strong arm.

This is it. I'm going to die.

Chapter 3

WITH HER FEET dangling off the ground, Katherine was practically nose to nose with the giant Englishman. From the tip of his blond shaggy beard and bushy mustache to his blue eyes squinting at her in anger, he looked like a golden boy gone bad. A shiver of fear rippled down her spine.

"Put me down!"

To her astonishment, he relaxed his hold and set her down firmly on her feet, bracketing her waist with his massive hands.

"How do I know you will not take off running again?"

"Listen, mister . . ." Offering him a strained yet polite smile, she removed his hands from her body with exaggerated slowness and carefully lowered his arms to his sides. "I have friends who would not be too happy to learn I'm being held against my own will. In fact, they probably have the local search-and-rescue teams looking for me right now. Why don't you make it easier on yourself by taking me back to where you found me. I'll get my car and keep this little misunderstanding to myself."

"I'm afraid I can't possibly let you go," he argued in that rhythmic cadence of a Brit. The seemingly sympathetic tone of his voice was almost convincing. But she wasn't going to buy it. Rescuer or not, the man had no business keeping her in this wilderness.

"It's not like I don't appreciate all your help but I think it's time for me to be moving on."

Flynt watched the crazy woman mince away from him, convinced that her fear of him drove her to the wild-eyed notion that she'd a better chance of survival in the forest.

Had it not been for the severity of the storm, he would have allowed her to attempt a witless trek through the woods. He still had half a mind to turn his back on the ungracious Katherine Marshall. But he couldn't stoop to such barbaric indifference—despite his local reputation otherwise.

He shook his head. "Why are you so hell-bent on freezing to death out here?" His arm made a wide sweep to emphasize the frigid wilderness surrounding them. As he watched her eyes flicker with uncertainty, he enjoyed a small amount of satisfaction that he might finally be getting through to her.

"Why can't you understand that I must get back?" she demanded in exasperation. Dropping her gaze, she pressed her fingertips to her temples, paused for a moment, then tried to rake them back through her hair. When the tangles thwarted her efforts, she dropped her hands. As she lifted her chin in defiance, her eyes appeared filled with renewed determination.

"I can't stay here. Not in these mountains. *Especially* not with you." Her emphatic declaration might have been more successfully executed if she had had a door to slam in his face. As it was, her dramatic departure failed when, in her haste, she spun around in the narrow trench of snow, caught her foot and unceremoniously plopped down on her backside. Given her own height and the three-foot depth of old snow, Katherine looked as though she were seated in a chair. Her scowl said otherwise.

Flynt cocked one eyebrow in silent acknowledgment. Perhaps this latest demonstration of her questionable capabilities would prove his point. Never mind the snow, the precarious trail, the bear or wolf or cougar. Her bullheadedness was going to be the cause of her own undoing.

When she tried to lever herself out of her predicament, he offered his assistance once more. And once more she refused, choosing to stand up on her own accord.

"You are still adamant about continuing," Flynt stated with controlled politeness.

"Yes." Her wary gaze told him that no amount of gentlemanly tenderness was going to placate her until the storm passed. For her own safety he was forced to use less mannerly tactics.

"So be it," he sighed. He made as if to leave, then bent over and grabbed her about the legs. Catching her off guard, he hoisted her onto his shoulder and headed home.

Pounding her fists against the back of his hairy overcoat, Katherine put up the best struggle her limbs would allow, especially after her arm had nearly been yanked from its socket. It was bad enough that he'd slung her over his shoulder like a side of beef, but he also managed to bump every tree bough they walked under, dumping its ice-cold snow onto her upside-down head.

Incensed more than humiliated, she continued to fight him all the way back to his isolated cabin. Futile as it seemed, she refused to give up. She'd make him regret bringing her back. Blizzard or not, she'd make him so miserable that he'd volunteer to dig a snow tunnel through twenty-foot-deep drifts just to get rid of her.

When he dropped her to her feet in the middle of the dim, squalid room, she vented her anger with a slap across his face. His blue eyes registered surprise as his head whipped to one side. The foolishness of her action belatedly entered her mind. For all the good it did her, she may as well have batted the nose of a bear.

Then she saw the small trickle of blood. Oh, Lord—now she'd really done it. Her ragged fingernail had left a tiny scratch just below his left eye.

He kept his disbelieving gaze locked on her while he slowly reached up to touch the cut. She braced herself for the worst. Lowering his gloved hand, he studied the bit of blood on the leather. Her imagination ran amok with frightening images of the man in full rage. Yet he only shook his head and turned away.

Leaving her standing in the middle of the room, he wordlessly removed his coat and hung it by the door, then took a large enamel pan from beneath the trestle table. As he placed utensils into the pan, Katherine grabbed the opportunity to call a truce, however tentative. Her footsteps made no sound on the dirt floor in the three short strides she took to pick up their two wooden bowls from the dining table.

"What should I do with my stew?" She hadn't meant to sneak up on him. But he practically leaped out of his buckskin boots. Or so it seemed.

His head snapped around with a force that tossed that long hair over his shoulder. Faced with his steely glare and unkempt beard, she immediately erased her earlier image of a muscle-bound model. Her assessment was further confirmed when he gruffly snatched the bowls from her hand with a muttering of reluctant appreciation—a meager attempt at civil behavior, but one that still amazed her. He was a puzzle. A contradiction of himself. One minute gentle, the next rough. One minute talking like some kind of educated Englishman, the next muttering in monosyllables like a caveman. Completely unpredictable.

Perhaps unstable. Possibly even deranged.

The headache that had begun to fade was building once more. She was foolish to forget so easily that she was in one hell of a mess. Giving him plenty of room to work without being in his way, she planted herself in the chair at the far corner of the hearth. Allowing herself to be lulled by the warmth of the fire, she stared at the undulating red glow of the burning logs.

His unintelligible muttering continued as he emptied the cookpot, refilled it with water and swung it back over the fire to heat. Of course, he didn't have hot and cold running water to wash the dishes, she reminded herself. Only civilized people lived with indoor plumbing. That thought brought to mind the disgusting outhouse. Good Lord, she couldn't wait for this nightmare to be over.

After a while Avery passed behind her and walked to the back of the shadowy cabin. She heard a click of metal and a thump but she refused to give him the satisfaction of asking what he was up to.

"Gypsy fool," he groused. His deep voice was barely a whisper, but still audible over the crackle of the fire and occasional hiss of snow falling in through the chimney. "Hasn't the foggiest notion of proper dress." Katherine imagined he was accustomed to talking to himself, being out here alone and all. He probably wasn't even aware that his words had been spoken aloud.

"She's fine, indeed. Just touched."

Katherine's mouth dropped open. *HE thinks I'M touched? At least I'm not the one talking to myself.* She stood up with a ready remark on the tip of her tongue. But when she faced him the words died. In the corner beyond the bed, the mountain man was kneeling in front of an enormous open trunk. Hidden in the shadows, the old battered trunk hardly stood out from the dark log walls. Now, however, the lid was up and colorful pieces of cloth spilled out over its sides and into piles on the ground.

Avery paused, then reached down and lifted something carefully from the trunk. Katherine stepped closer, curious to see what he treated with such reverence. His hands held up a white leather dress, the bodice elaborately decorated with tiny shells and beads. Though similar to ones she'd seen at the Southwest Museum, it looked brand new. Katherine knew very little about Indian artifacts, but she suspected that an authentic dress in such perfect condition was probably worth a lot. Perhaps Flynt Avery was an anthropologist who studied Native Americans. At least that might explain why he was holed up in this isolated cabin.

Then she pushed aside the need to rationalize the man's behavior. After all, defending the stranger wasn't going to explain why she was holed up with him. Or how she was going to find her way home. Home. She closed her eyes, fighting off the foreboding tightness in her chest.

Another chill swept down her spine. Rubbing the damp sleeves of her arms, she glanced down at the soggy material, then at Flynt Avery. He was right about one thing—she had to change out of these wet clothes. No matter what her plans were to get home, they wouldn't do any good if she came down with pneumonia.

"Here we are," he announced, rising to his feet. She expected to see him turn around with the squaw dress in his hands. What she didn't expect was the floor-length yellow gingham gown he held out for her inspection. The long straight sleeves were puffed at the shoulders. A hint of lace at the high collar was duplicated in two parallel lines down the front of the wide cotton panel in the bodice, which ended at the gathered skirt.

"You want me to wear that?" Katherine asked incredulously, then realized he was dead serious. With a placating smile, she offered, "Certainly there's something else in there."

She stepped around him and surveyed the array of musty clothing, picking up pieces and examining them. There were black wool pants and a matching coat, two slightly yellowed shirts, socks and black leather boots—all of which seemed large enough to fit a man the size of Flynt Avery. She also found a white cotton nightgown, another dress, a lace-up corset and other old-fashioned lingerie, each beautifully detailed with fine stitchery. Unlike movie costumes with Velcro or hidden zippers, these were designed with buttons or ribbons to look every bit like the real thing. Holding a red calico dress to her chest, she rubbed the material between her fingers. It didn't feel worn out from years of use. Nor rotted from age. It felt crisp and new.

A strange uneasiness came over her.

"Wear that one if you prefer," Avery suggested, his voice indicating he'd moved away to the fireplace.

Her eyes were glued to the tiny pattern of white daisy bouquets on the crimson background. Goosebumps prickled her skin. Her practical mind rejected the unreasonable anxiety. Her reaction was more likely the result of her headache and dry nausea. Avery probably had a perfectly logical story behind the unusual collection in his trunk. But something kept her from asking. Fear, perhaps. Fear of an answer that would only sound like all the rest of his responses that didn't make any sense.

"I know beggars can't be choosers and all that," Katherine said, turning to face him. "But if I try to squeeze myself into either of these dresses, I know I'll bust a seam." *Or pass out from lack of oxygen.* "And I'd hate to ruin these antiques when they're in such perfect condition."

"Antiques?" He gave an indignant snort. "I'm afraid that knot on your head has muddled your mind. I purchased that clothing new for—" He cut himself off. "Let us just say that I purchased them new in San Francisco eight years ago."

New? Eight years ago? So much for the practical explanation. His blue eyes narrowed, warning her that the subject was closed.

"I have to feed the horses," he informed her, striding over to his coat on the wall. "When I come back I want to see you in that bed or I'll strip you down and put you there myself."

Inside the small enclosed livestock shed several paces behind the cabin, Flynt stroked the snow-white blaze of his chestnut mare, Yola, the Wintun word for snow. She was due to foal this spring. The indifferent sire was his roan, Sasti, feeding on the hay he had put out for the two animals. His hand paused as he stared at the vacant corner where the milk cow had once stood next to his wife's pony. He'd gotten rid of both eight years ago, two months after Little Deer's disappearance.

The mare lifted her head beneath his motionless hand. He glanced toward the cabin, wondering if Kate had followed his orders and taken to bed. The image of Little Deer in that same bed tugged at his memory. The first time he'd seen her, she was but a girl of thirteen. The second time, a woman nearing twenty. And the last time she was his wife, carrying their child.

His mind filled with recollections of his fruitless search for her, then his mournful return to London to settle his father's estate. The events that had unfolded during those few months in '84 convinced Flynt that his home was no longer in England. Then, as now, he was drawn back to live in the shadow of Castle Crags. Though he never learned the fate of his wife, he could not say for certain when the pain gave way to resigned acceptance.

There had been a time when he couldn't bear to gaze upon the clothing that his wife had never seen. Yet the sight of Katherine holding the calico had not been as disturbing as he would have thought. The generous curves of the dress should suit her well, which was more than he could say about her own choice of baggy, mismatched clothing.

Flynt gave Yola one last pat and extinguished the hanging oil lamp as he walked out. Whether Kate was ready or not, he didn't wish to dawdle while the cold crept into his bones.

The heavy snowfall hadn't let up. Through the haze of white he could barely make out the curl of smoke rising from the stone chimney and disappearing into the low gray clouds. A week earlier the dogwood had been blooming under the warmth of the spring sunshine. At the time, SnowEagle had passed through on his way to the mineral springs. The Wintu holy man had warned that he saw on the horizon a fierce wind of disharmony. Flynt now wondered if the shaman's prophetic dream had signaled the coming of the unseasonal blizzard or the discovery of the injured Katherine Marshall.

He touched the cut at his temple. She could certainly be considered a tempest with a wallop. And "disharmony" couldn't begin to describe the tangled mess of thoughts re-

garding her. She confused him, angered him, even drew a
moment of sympathy from him. But, most assuredly, she
aroused him.

And that put him in one hell of a spot.

Especially when that spot happened to be his bed.

Katherine had dropped the dress into the trunk as soon as
Avery left, his threat still ringing in her ears. She hadn't
doubted for a second that he would carry it out. As she
snatched the man's pants and shirt from the pile on the floor,
she pictured herself in a useless struggle against the brawny
mountain man. Fear roiled in her stomach. Her head
throbbed. She slipped out of all but her underpants and bra,
nervously glanced at the door, then stripped them off as
well. The fire did little to ward off the chill quivering
through her body. If he walked in now, she was done for.

As quickly as her aching muscles could move, she pulled
on the billowy shirt, then the trousers. Though the white cotton shirt was soft and yellowed from wear, the wool of the
pants scratched her bare skin. As an afterthought, she
grabbed the lady's drawers and put them on instead. After
she tied the drawstring at her waist and lowered the long
shirttail, she felt sufficiently covered up. Now if only she
had something for her bare feet.

She gathered up her damp clothing, padded across the
cool damp dirt and did the best she could to arrange the
clothes to dry. Everything but her underwear was muddied
to some degree. But there wasn't much she could do about
it. By the time she was done, her bra and panties were hanging over the lip of the open trunk. The blouse lay at one end
of the table. Her jacket was hooked over the back of the
chair, the chiffon skirt on the bedpost. On the hearth, her

boots drooped sadly to one side. And her black pantyhose hung from the mantel like an X-rated Christmas stocking.

Katherine groaned at her results. The inside of the tiny cabin looked like the morning after a wild night of abandon. She hoped it didn't give Grizzly Adams any ideas. He was wild enough as it was—especially when he wore that woolly mammoth coat. His shaggy beard fit the image, as well. She wrinkled her nose in disgust as she returned to the trunk, pointedly ignoring the bed.

Changing out of her clothes was one thing. But she couldn't bring herself to obey the second half of Avery's order. No matter how rotten she felt, she wouldn't crawl back into his bed. The weather may have given her no choice about staying with him, but she still had a choice about sleeping arrangements. And she wasn't about to volunteer to buddy up.

Setting her mind to repacking the trunk, she knelt in front of it and scooped out a wad of clothing, dumping it onto the pile on the floor. The last piece lay almost forgotten on the bottom of the trunk. Katherine assumed it was nothing more than a remnant left over from material cut for a shirt. But when she picked it up to refold it, her chest tightened.

The infant gown was only as long as her arm, with six tiny buttons down the front. She clutched it to her breast as her gaze turned toward the door, trying to fit the image of the man who'd stormed out earlier with the image of a tiny baby in the soft white gown. As new as the dresses, it couldn't have been an old family heirloom. But why did Avery have it in his trunk? Was it for his own child? Katherine pictured the wild and woolly Flynt Avery as a new father, cradling a small bundle in those massive hands.

Impossible. She was unable to fathom the belligerent beast as anything but a male chauvinist who probably looked upon birth control as a woman's responsibility and babies as a woman's mistake. From his backwoods lifestyle, she doubted he even knew what "safe sex" meant, let alone practiced it.

The reminder of yet another complicated aspect of searching for the right man brought a sigh of resignation. She considered Michael's proposal as she held the tiny gown at arm's length, easily imagining him rocking a baby in his arms. With his gentleness and sense of humor, he'd be a great dad. Marrying Michael would be a sensible decision. But she'd made sensible decisions all her life. Even her early marriage during law school was logical at the time. When their goals had changed, the divorce itself had been a rational choice, despite the ensuing settlement fight.

For once, just once, she'd like to be caught up in the thrill of the moment instead of first weighing the outcome. She folded the white gown and reverently laid it on the bottom of the trunk, relegating her own dreams to the dark recesses of her mind.

As her fingers released the folded material, the back of her hand brushed against something that didn't feel like soft material. Katherine craned her neck over the lip of the trunk and peered down inside, spotting the long rolled up paper. To reach it, she stood up and leaned in, bracing one hand on the edge.

When Flynt pushed open the door, the last thing he expected to see was the woman's upturned buttocks clad only in white pantalettes. His first response was lust. Pure and simple. He couldn't fault himself for a natural male reaction. Nor could he do a damn thing about it—not as long as she would rather claw his eyes out than remain caged with him in this cabin.

"What the bloody hell are you doing?" he demanded as he

slammed the door. Kate bounced up like a startled jaybird taking flight. When she pivoted to face him, the gentle movement beneath her shirt caught his eye. Her unbound breasts draped only in the white cloth were nearly his undoing. Clearly the woman had no shame in her half-naked state. His sweeping gaze took in the enticing sight of her scattered clothing around the cabin. Her brazen appearance suggested a woman of seasoned sexual experience.

"I was just putting some things back in the trunk," she answered defensively—with her hands behind her back, the shirt pulled tighter against her breasts, outlining their fullness.

"It appears as though you put too much back. Or am I to assume you plan to wear this . . . outfit." He stamped his boots to rid them of snow.

"Your treasure chest isn't exactly bulging with fleece-lined sweatshirts or stonewashed jeans. These happen to be the only comfortable things I could find." Like a queen, she squared her shoulders, a gesture that jostled her breasts. When Flynt shook his head and muttered an oath, she glanced down at the focus of his gaze, then raised her head to look him square in the eyes. Her chin tilted up in wordless defiance.

Judging from her silent stance, Flynt couldn't ascertain whether she was inviting him or warning him. A burning log shifted, sending up a burst of sparks that momentarily brightened the room. She didn't move. Her breasts rose and fell with each breath.

He cursed himself—and her—as he forced his eyes off her shamelessly half-clothed body, pegged his coat and marched over to the hearth. Whether the fire needed tending or not, he used it as an excuse to keep himself busy. He didn't want to chance another look at her until he could trust himself not to lose control. Glaring at the sheer black stockings dangling before his eyes didn't help the ache in his groin. He tried to tell himself that her behavior could very well be the result of the blow to her head. After a good night's rest, she would no doubt awaken greatly embarrassed by this afternoon encounter.

And if not? If she were truly a whore? Mindful of the misadventures leading up to this moment, he envisioned her enticing him into bed only to scratch his flesh to ribbons. More and more he wished he'd never heard her scream at the river.

Katherine quickly replaced the paper scroll and finished with her own task, thankful that each of them had something to distract them. She'd come a little too close to losing the battle of wills with Flynt Avery. All it took was one jiggle under her shirt and the man practically came unglued. Yet she'd nearly lost it herself when those blue eyes of his locked with hers. For a brief instant, she caught another glimpse of a gentle soul buried beneath that gruff veneer. The image was so fleeting that when the log fell in the fireplace and the firelight lit up his narrowed glare, she was sure the shadows had played tricks on her mind. Convincing her body was another thing altogether as it responded on its own to his heated gaze drifting down the length of her, burning a white-hot trail to the apex of her legs. By the time he'd turned away, her knees were ready to give way. She'd had to grab the nearby bedpost to keep from wobbling.

Now as she slammed each piece of clothing into the trunk, she mentally chided herself, welcoming the throbbing pain in her head as justifiable punishment. How could she have gotten aroused by that grizzly-faced animal? She needed a brain scan. Obviously she'd short-circuited something when she hit that rock in the river.

Katherine took her underwear from the edge of the trunk, closed the lid, then draped the bra and panties over the top. In a natural reflex, she glanced down at her wrist to check the time. Her watch was gone. It was useless to try to remember when the thin leather watchband might have fallen from her arm. She'd been too busy falling down mountains, escaping a Neanderthal and imitating a sack of potatoes over his shoulder!

"What time is it?" she asked automatically as she stood and stretched the kinks out of her legs and back.

"Late afternoon."

"How late?"

He paused at the long side table where he was working with his back to her, then shot a puzzled look over his shoulder. With a shake of his head, he went back to work. But his answer was loud enough for her to hear.

"It is after noon. When the sun first sets, I call it 'evening,' after which I find the darkness aptly named 'night time.' At dawn, it's 'morning.' Any more questions?"

"Yes . . . what time is it?"

He cocked his head as if in contemplation as he looked out the window. "Difficult to judge with this storm," he finally said as she approached and gazed over his shoulder at the fat white flakes drifting to earth.

"Don't you own a clock?" she asked in exasperation.

"Why? Are you late for an appointment?"

"I'm simply trying to carry on a civilized conversation but I suppose that's asking too much of you."

"I can be quite civilized . . . given the proper company."

She stepped up next to him and planted one hand on the worn wooden side table. "Are you saying I'm not proper?"

As Avery nonchalantly flung the towel over his shoulder, Katherine snapped her head back to avoid being hit. He swung around, leaned one hip against the table and folded his arms over his massive chest.

"I'm saying that a proper lady does not prance around in front of a gentleman wearing little else but a man's shirt and a thin pair of drawers. Unless she wishes to be intimate with him. But I must say that I am more than a bit tempted by your offer."

Chapter 4

"HOW DARE YOU!" Katherine snarled, barely believing his insinuation let alone her own absurdly melodramatic response. Somehow her words didn't pack as much punch as she thought they would. Nothing like the slap she'd doled out earlier. "If you'd get your mind out of your shorts, you might have listened to me when I told you that the other clothes weren't comfortable."

"Hardly sufficient reason not to wear a dress."

"That dress would've fit me like a second skin and not given me an inch to breathe!"

She took one step back and held her arms out. "You would've had a hell of a lot more to ogle in that dress than what little you can see beyond this baggy shirt and bloomers."

"Those are not bloomers, Katherine."

Flynt eyed the bounce beneath the material and itched to remove the flimsy cotton. But he kept his arms folded, digging his fingernails into his sleeves. He was an honorable man, despite what the residents of Dunsmuir said otherwise. He was also a man of great patience—more than most might have displayed given the same circumstance. But he'd come to the end of his rope with this woman whose crude slip of the tongue and blatant display of inhibitions prompted him to call her bluff. If she was a prostitute, he wanted the cards on the table.

"How much?" he asked, unbuttoning his shirt.

"What are you talking about?"

Impressed with her ability to act puzzled, he pulled his shirttail free of his waistband. She played the innocent so well that he could imagine she made good money convincing her gentlemen callers of her naïveté. A pity she wasted her talent on him. He could see right through her ploy even as she feigned wide-eyed fear and stepped backward.

"I confess I have never had reason to call on a woman such as yourself . . ." The edge of the table blocked her retreat as he approached.

"What are you doing?" Her gaze skittered down his chest to where his hands paused on his belt buckle. She jumped when he flicked the end of the belt free.

"Come now, Kate," Flynt warned, growing testy with her continuing ruse. "Quit playing me for the fool. I am prepared to pay you five dollars for your services, unless you can prove you are worth more."

"You pompous a—"

Flynt caught her wrist before her palm smacked his face, then grabbed the other when she tried again. She struggled and swore like a Liverpool longshoreman, but to no avail.

Although he no longer had any intention of teaching her a lesson, Flynt didn't dare let her go and risk serious injury. Instead he held tight until she finally settled down, which didn't take long.

"If you so much as kiss me," she warned, her voice lowered into a deep rasp, "I swear I'll bite so hard my teeth will go right through your lower lip."

The corners of his mouth twitched with a suppressed smile as he contemplated her threat. He was tempted to challenge her but thought better of it. "You win," he conceded.

"Win *what?* Round one?"

He dropped her arms, then watched her rub her wrists and noticed the reddened skin caused by his own hands. It seemed each time they'd gone to battle in the last few hours, he'd come away feeling like a bastard, which wasn't far from the truth anyway.

There was little option but to apologize. "Forgive my behavior. I wrongly assumed . . ." His voice trailed off, uncertain how to explain the conclusion he'd derived from her own outlandish conduct.

"You assumed from the way I was dressed that I wanted sex?" she asked, followed by a derisive snort. "For money?"

Still holding her wrist, she shoved herself away from the table with a thrust of her hips, then skirted the corner and went to the hearth. Facing the fire, she seemed unaware of the light piercing her clothing, outlining her body with breathtaking clarity. As Flynt studied her for a long moment, it became equally clear to him that the woman was completely oblivious of her suggestive gestures. Where in heaven's name had she been raised? A brothel?

"Considering that you can curse a blue streak and blithely toss about such a word as 'sex,' I think you should hardly be offended by my mistaken assumption."

She turned sideways enough to reveal a tantalizing angle to the silhouette. Damnation, she was going to drive him to drink. And he wasn't even a drinking man.

If her pointed glare had been a dagger, he'd have taken a

lethal blow directly between the eyes. "I'm genuinely flat-
tered, Frank."

"Flynt."

She shrugged. "Right."

"Kate—"

"Katherine." One eyebrow lifted in warning. " 'Kate'
sounds like a name *you'd* give a hooker."

"Well, 'Katherine' sounds like a priggish, straitlaced governess. Sensible and practical."

"That's right . . . Katherine Marshall, attorney-at-law and
predictable person at your service." Her mouth clamped
shut. "Scratch that last part," she amended.

Flynt stifled a grin, unwilling to jeopardize the tenuous
rapport between them. If he was lucky, this truce might last
a bit longer than the last one. But he wouldn't stake his life
on it. "A lady lawyer? How . . . progressive."

"Don't worry. I won't sue you for assault as long as you
don't try something like that again."

He chuckled to himself as he held up his hands in surrender. "That, my dear *Katherine,* is a fair deal."

"Speaking of deals . . ." She walked over to the table feeling a little more steady on her feet than a few minutes earlier when she'd had her confidence knocked out from under
her. "We need to work out some kind of sleeping arrangement. I didn't climb into bed earlier—"

"As you were told."

She ignored his interruption. "Because I didn't think that
I'd be in a position for negotiating territory." She held up her
hand to silence any smart remark. "And after what nearly
happened a couple minutes ago, I can see I made the right
decision. But I'm about to keel over from exhaustion so I'd
like to know where I can crash."

" 'Crash,' you say?"

"Sleep."

"You will sleep in the bed, of course."

"And you?" she asked.

"The bed is large enough to accommodate two."

"No way. I'm not getting in that bed." She shook her head, then winced from the lingering pain. "Just give me a couple of blankets or buffalo pelts or whatever you mountain men use up here. I'll just make up my own little bed on the floor."

"Buffalo?" His laughter ping-ponged off the log walls.

"Oh, *please,*" Katherine groaned.

"You can hardly blame me for my response," he defended. "Wherever did you get such a notion as buffalo being in these mountains?"

"I *know* they aren't here. Everyone knows they're practically extinct."

"Indeed."

"I said it because of your looks." Katherine pointed to his beard. "Big as a buffalo and shaggy as one, too."

His tapered fingers stroked the long dark blond whiskers covering the lower half of his face. "I prefer my appearance. It tends to keep strangers at a distance." He looked her up and down. "Until now."

"This particular stranger had no choice in the matter," Katherine reminded him, quelling the trepidation caused by the glint in his eyes. "About my bed—"

"Ah, yes."

"Just give me some extra blankets."

"I have no extra blankets. As you can see, I have neither a second storage trunk nor space to store one. And before you suggest I hand over the few on the bed, I should warn you that you will certainly freeze before the night is over. I, on the other hand, will have advantage of the mattress beneath me and the bearskin over me. The only trouble I will encounter is the disposal of your frozen body before I eat my breakfast."

"Spare me the theatrics." Katherine pivoted on her bare feet and marched over to the bed. There was no way in hell he was going to get her in there, even if it meant freezing to death. She yanked back the woolly bearskin, retrieved the two sorry excuses for blankets, and went over to the fireplace. Doing the best she could to tuck the scratchy wool around her as she sat cross-legged, she could feel his eyes on her, watching her stubbornly stick to her decision, no matter what it cost her. She didn't dare glance over her shoulder. If she did, she had a feeling she'd see that scruffy beard split with a dumb, ugly grin, which would only make her want to hit him again.

What she would give for some aspirin.

Flynt stared at her straight back, awed by the rigid display of morality that had appeared as unexpectedly as the unseasonal snowstorm. He was not about to bodily throw her into his bed. But when he saw her shoulders sag and her fingers rub her temples, he knew he wouldn't sleep one wink while she played the martyr.

"Your head still hurts."

Her hands darted back under the blanket. "I'm fine."

"I could brew something for it."

"Suit yourself."

Flynt worked around her in silence. When he put a kettle of water over the fire, she asked if he'd used that disgusting soda water, and seemed relieved when he told her he hadn't. He selected a combination of sweet herbs, blending in two teaspoons of the bitter-tasting powdered root that would ease her discomfort. His knowledge of the healing plants had come from SnowEagle, who had taught Flynt not only about Wintun medicine but about the Great Spirit in the white mountain. Right now he could use a bit of advice about dealing with one very stubborn woman in his tiny cabin.

Several minutes later he brought the herb tea over to Kate, and hunkered down next to her to offer the mug. Her heavy-lidded eyes stared into the flames. The heat of the fire and her own exhaustion had lulled her almost to sleep. It wouldn't take long for the *all-heal* to take effect.

"Kate . . ." When he touched her shoulder to gain her attention, she blinked slowly then turned her head and looked up at him. All the spit and vinegar had left her. In its place was a doe-eyed softness that stirred up the same puzzling feelings he experienced when she had been on her hands and knees outside his door.

"Here," he ordered, handing off the mug, then abruptly stood. With one hand braced on the edge of the mantel, he stuffed the other in his back pocket and glowered at the embers alternately radiating red and white. Once again the enticing sight of the woman's sheer black stockings did not help his present state of confusion. He could ill afford to investigate the strange response she stirred up inside him. Once the storm passed he would be escorting her into town, after which she would disappear from his life as quickly as she'd entered it. Satisfied that he had shut the door on his own irrational behavior, he pushed his hair back over his shoulder and gazed down at Kate, who sipped quietly.

The lump on her forehead didn't look any smaller and had begun to take on a deep purplish color. As the firelight flickered over her features, he also noticed the dark shadows of fatigue under her eyes. The sleep she so desperately needed would be difficult indeed if she intended to sit upright all night. He envisioned her drifting off and flopping forward like a rag doll. No doubt she would strike her head on the rock hearth and wake up with a headache far worse than the one she had now. And he knew that somehow he would be blamed for it, as well.

He shook his head and strode over to the bed. A glimpse of white atop the chest caught his eye. Upon closer inspection, he could only imagine that the lacy items were her feminine foundations. Yet they appeared to be of no supportive value like a strong boned corset. Odd, indeed.

And devilishly hedonistic. Provocative observations seemed to meet him coming and going, no matter what diversions he used to dissuade them.

He hefted the bearskin into his arms and carried it over to Kate. As he spread it behind her, she shifted around to observe his actions.

"What do you think you're doing?" Her low, tired voice was feminine yet husky. The sound of it played down his spine in such a way that reminded him of rumpled bed sheets and sated lovers. Cursing himself, he banished the image from his mind as he bunched the skin to form a ridge for a pillow.

"I am making a place for you to sleep."

"I told you I won't sleep with you."

"You told me you won't sleep in my *bed*."

"And what about you?"

"We will sleep in shifts. It will be several hours before I retire. By then you will have had sufficient rest that I can retrieve my bedding and fall asleep without worry that you will tip over into the fire." He hoped his explanation was delivered with enough arrogance to convince her that he was not doing her any favors. He merely wished to spare himself any further inconvenience regarding the woman. "Are you finished with the tea?"

"Yes," she handed him the empty cup. "Thanks."

He nodded and moved to the chair at the table, placing the mug in front of him as he settled back to wait. He watched Kate scoot backward onto the brown fur, draw one side of it over her body, then lower her head tentatively to the makeshift pillow. After a brief moment, she rose up on one elbow and looked straight at him, then squinted as if to bring him into focus. The pain-killing potion had started to take effect.

"You'll wake me?"

"I promise not to take your bed from under you without a word of warning first." Flynt chose his words carefully, knowing that tomorrow he would be called upon to defend them. "Sleep well."

Within a short time he heard her steady breathing and knew that the herb would rid of her discomfort by morning. He, on the other hand, had nothing to rid himself of the discomfort caused by the woman herself.

It would prove to be a long night. A long night indeed.

Katherine awoke with a start. Her eyelids flew open. Once again she'd awakened to find her body drenched in perspiration. Once again she could remember the smell of roasted meat. But this time she remembered a little more than before. Glancing around, she now realized that the dark cabin had been in that same disturbing dream she'd had in her motel room. She stared at the crude rafters and remembered the same flickering light and shadows. The soft, textured fur beneath her was also familiar.

How was it possible to have dreamed all of this up in her mind before her accident at the river? She touched her forehead. Though the headache was gone, the bump was as big as ever. If only she could talk to a doctor, preferably one who specialized in head injuries. Maybe the trauma to her brain had scrambled her memory like a tangled necklace, causing her to *think* she'd had the dream the previous night. And yet she realized not even her theory of a tangled time-line held up when she could mentally check off the chrono-logical order of everything else she'd done over the last forty-eight hours.

Quit grabbing at straws, Katherine.

But I know there's a logical explanation.

Growing up in the midst of the Hollywood entertainment industry had taught her that every fantasy, every fairy tale was nothing more than a theatrical illusion. There was a practical explanation for everything. Until now. She had dreamed of this cabin, the meat that still scented the air, the bearskin on the dirt floor. And more. She didn't yet know what it was, but something had happened to her in this rus-tic setting. She sensed it in her gut, as if her body—not her mind—held the memory locked inside. She knew it from the sweat on her skin, the rapid beat of her heart. If only she could remember . . .

Propping herself up on one elbow, she craned her neck in search of Avery, prepared to give up her place beneath the cozy bearskin even if it wasn't quite time to switch. He was slumped over the table, his shaggy coat draped over his shoulders for warmth.

"Avery?" she called softly. He answered her only with a gentle snore. After a louder call, then another, she realized he was not going to respond unless she crawled out of her bed and coaxed him into it. Before she went to his side, she added two logs to the dying fire so she wouldn't need to dis-turb him while he slept in front of the hearth.

She stepped forward. His bulky frame brought to mind a hibernating bear; she prayed he wouldn't behave like one when she tried to rouse him. As a precaution, she moved to the opposite side of the table.

"Wake up, Avery."

She reached out and jostled his right elbow, prepared to jump back if he made a sudden swipe at her across the table. "It's Katherine . . . You can have the bed . . . It's your turn."

Still no response. The longer she tried, the colder she got from the perspiration cooling her body. Finally, she gave up and retreated to the shelter of the fur. Although she wanted only to fall quickly back to sleep, the dream crept back into her thoughts, tormenting her with its shadowy imagery.

As the added wood finally ignited, the fire flared to life, brightening the world behind her closed lids. She opened her eyes and rolled onto her back, thankful for light. Studying the roof timbers, she decided to lie awake until morning rather than succumb to the heart-pounding phantoms of that damn dream.

The heat from the fire grew stronger, lulling her like a hot bath. She wished she were home in a soothing tub of scented water—her favorite way to relax after a long day at the office. Closing her eyes to her rustic surroundings, she pictured her own personal sanctuary—her feminine bathroom with two dozen candles strategically placed and potted plants thriving on the humidity. Allowing herself to drift with the wonderfully soothing memory, she mentally went through the ritual of pouring the perfumed bath oils in anticipation of a long, leisurely soak. As she slid down into the inviting water, she welcomed the heat curling over her body. With each passing moment, the temperature seemed to rise another degree. Steam rose from the surface.

It's hot. Too hot.

She needed to add cold water. Lifting her hand, she reached for the faucet at the other end of the tub, but it was too far. She stretched, yet the knob was still beyond her grasp.

It's getting hotter. I've got to do something.

Shifting herself onto her knees, Katherine leaned forward, extending her hand toward the shiny chrome. She was almost there when something yanked her backward. Frightened of being pulled back into the scalding water, she tried to lunge away but the assailant gripped her shoulders. Blinded by terror, she found herself on her back, lashing out at her attacker without seeing him.

"Enough," he bellowed, capturing her wrists in his massive hands. Evading her frantic kick, he pinned her body beneath his. She squirmed beneath him as the last remnants of energy drained from her limbs. "I have no intention of hurting you."

"Avery?" Katherine blinked to clear her vision, her labored breathing matching his own.

"What were you thinking, woman?"

She glanced over at the fire, then at the thick brown bearskin beneath her arm. Despite his firm grip on her wrist, she uncurled her clenched fist until the backs of her fingers pressed into the animal pelt.

"It's only fur," she said in awe, unable to drag her eyes from the reassuring touch of reality. "I thought it was water. And I thought you were trying to drown me."

His long fingers slid up to her sensitive palm, then splayed out over her own fingers. "When I woke up, I saw you kneeling on the hearth. You were about to put your hand in the fire." He cupped the back of her hand in his own and stroked the thick pad of his thumb over her fingertips.

"Thank God I grabbed you before you were burned. Whatever possessed you to something so foolish?"

"I thought I was reaching for the faucet," Katherine managed, distracted by his tender inspection—as intimate as it was innocent. The caress rippled down her body like a seismic tremor. "My bath water . . . it was hot. Too hot. I was trying to turn on the cold water."

"It was the *fire* that had grown too hot," he corrected, drawing her gaze back to his bearded face. "Not only did you use too much wood, but you added to your own discomfort the closer you moved toward the flame."

"How could I have imagined—" She broke off, suspicion creeping into her thoughts. "It was the tea, wasn't it?"

"No." He shook his head and his long blond hair slipped from his back and over both shoulders. The shimmery waves of burnished gold brushed against her temples and the sides of her cheeks. "The herbs I chose and the amount I used were only enough to concoct a mild sedative, and something for your pain. Nothing more, I assure you."

"I wish I could believe you."

"You can. As I said before, I won't hurt you." In contrast to the intimidating mask of his full beard, the sincerity in his midnight-blue eyes seemed to slip past her defenses, and reach into her soul. Something in the way he studied her compelled Katherine to tell the truth.

"You . . . could be lying," she explained cautiously, aware of the great risk of showing her fear. Every intake of breath pressed her breasts into his chest, reminding Katherine of her minimal amount of clothing—hardly a sufficient barrier against a mammoth mountain man who had endured one too many lonely nights. "From the looks of you and your reclusive lifestyle, you can't blame me for being . . ." *Scared,* she almost said. " . . . reluctant to trust you."

"Despite the fact that I could have left you to die at the river? Or to freeze to death when you tried to run away? And what about right now, Kate, when I saved you from the fire? What more proof do you need before you realize I will not harm you?"

Flynt saw the fear in her eyes and damned his inopportune arousal. Their scuffle had left a flush on her cheeks, a delicate pant in her breath, and a quickened heartbeat that fluttered against his ribs.

"Maybe you'd be more convincing if you weren't on top of me with my arms pinned down," she said quietly. Her beseeching gaze warred with the primal need inside him. Unable to discern the heat of the roaring fire from the heat of his own flesh, he shifted his body to the floor beside her and rolled onto his back. The muscle in his jaw twitched as he stared at the ceiling, his forearm propped behind his head as a pillow.

"I have never taken any woman against her will," he assured Kate, his low voice far more controlled than he felt. "Nor have I ever been refused by any woman, even if my present appearance leads you to believe otherwise. When this storm lifts, I promise to take you to Dunsmuir. Until then, you are safe—even with me."

As he turned from her and began to push himself to his feet, she caught his sleeve. "Don't go."

He paused, surprised by her change of heart, then glanced back at her. When his expression betrayed his thoughts, her eyes widened.

"I didn't mean I would, or *we* would—" She hesitated, then scrambled to her feet and pointed down at the rumpled bear hide. "It's yours. We agreed. If it's okay with you, I'll just borrow your coat and sit at the table."

"Nonsense."

"I beg your pardon?" The challenge in her green eyes amused him, though he guarded his thoughts more closely this time. Careful not to further provoke her, he could not help but feel the slightest hint of enjoyment.

"To put it simply, Kate, I don't trust you." Without allowing her the satisfaction of face-to-face confrontation, he gathered the bedding from the floor and returned it to his bed.

"I couldn't care less whether you trust me or not, I'm not going to climb into that hammock with you. And quit calling me 'Kate.' "

"Imagine you are me, if you will—" Flynt perched on the edge of the timber bed frame and shucked his boots, dropping them on the earthen floor with muffled thumps. "Which do you suppose poses the greater threat—allowing my accident-prone and injured houseguest to roam unattended while I sleep, or insisting she stay close enough that I can keep my eyes on her."

"It's not your eyes she's worried about," she remarked, reaching for his coat, which had been left in a forgotten heap on the ground when he'd rescued her from the fire. The weight of the garment surprised her, nearly buckling her knees. "Lord, what's it made of—lead?"

Flynt was behind her immediately, taking the coat from her before it dragged her to the ground. "It is heavy, but you are also weak from your ordeal yesterday."

"I may have gotten hit in the head," she snapped, "but I still remember everything . . . I think . . . most of it, anyway."

Before he realized it, she had slipped her arms into the sleeves and shrugged into the hooded coat, pulling it from his grasp. Letting out a startled gasp, she teetered backward from the cumbersome weight.

Chuckling to himself, Flynt caught her shoulders before she slammed against him. She was undoubtedly a menace to herself as well as everyone around her. When the crown of her head brushed the underside of his beard, he reached up to smooth the wisps of her dark hair—a gesture that struck a strong chord in his memory. His hand stilled as he recalled Little Deer, her back pressed against his chest as he'd stroked her ebony hair, then slipped his arms around her waist to feel their child move inside her growing belly.

"Avery?" Kate twisted around to look up at him. "Are you okay? You look sort of . . . pale."

Though he met her penetrating gaze, his bittersweet memories momentarily disarmed him, revealing the dull ache he had tried to bury over the last eight years.

Chapter 5

"I AM PERFECTLY fine." Mentally arguing against his own inexplicable need to talk about Little Deer, Flynt gently moved Kate to one side where she could lean on the table if she was still intent upon wearing the voluminous coat.

"You're not fine," she insisted, the fire in her eyes replaced by compassion. "What's wrong?"

Although he should have been relieved to have abandoned yet another argument, he was not the least bit pleased to find himself the object of her concern. He wanted the woman in his bed, to be sure, but not ensconced in his life.

"There is nothing to be gained by probing into my mind, especially when it's the middle of the night and I'd rather sleep." He strode to the bed, unbuttoning his shirt. "Why else do you think I choose to live in isolation up here in the mountains? I like my solitude." Failing to hide his irritation, he peeled off the flannel and hooked it over the end post of the bed. "I'll never know why in blue blazes I saved your sorry hide and brought you back here. From the moment you woke up, you've been nothing but a pain in my backside."

He unbuckled his belt and stripped off his pants, leaving only his drawers. "The minute I opened the door and saw you standing in the middle of my cabin, I thought—" *You were my wife.*

"Thought what?" she prodded.

Flynt glanced up, startled to see Kate rooted to the spot where he'd left her, the bottom of his coat pooled at her feet. From the manner in which she clutched the front of the coat together with both hands, as well as the wary expression in her eyes, she was obviously concerned with his state of dementia, if not her own safety.

"I thought . . ." He conjured up a suitable excuse for his behavior. " . . . your injury did not seem as severe as I had originally imagined. What you saw just now was my own annoyance with myself for not taking you to Dunsmuir," he lied, throwing back the covers and dropping into the bed. With his back to the fire, he heard Kate shuffle across the room, certain she was dragging the bottom of his coat over the packed dirt.

"That's not what you were going to say, Avery."

He stared at her tall shadow cast against the wall. "Can you read my mind?"

"No."

"Then this discussion is closed." After a long moment in which he heard only the sound of the cracking fire, Flynt finally felt the movement of Kate slipping under the covers. He smiled in spite of himself as he felt the bulky fur against his back. If she felt safer wrapped up tight like a cocoon, so be it.

*   *   *

The following morning, Katherine feigned sleep while Avery got up and dressed. She felt certain she hadn't slept at all. Watching him undress earlier, she had initially worried that he would strip off everything and sleep naked. But when she saw his gray one-piece union suit, she didn't know whether to feel relief or panic.

From her ties to the movie industry, Katherine knew about film companies hiring Civil War enthusiasts who were devoted to reenacting battles in full uniform and armament. The Renaissance Faire was famous for its reenactors wearing their own creations of Elizabethan costumes. But even if Flynt Avery was a reenactor of the Old West, why was the man wearing authentic underwear out in the middle of the wilderness? Wasn't he taking authenticity a bit too far for someone who lived alone?

Those questions and others had remained on her mind the rest of the night. Every time Avery had stirred, her entire body went on red alert. Her muscles tensed, and she held her breath, remaining still until she was reassured by his mild snore that he was sleeping.

Now that he was out of the bed, however, she could let down her guard and relax. His movement about the cabin was quieter than she had expected for a man of his size who was accustomed to being alone. Hearing the cautious creak of the wooden door as it opened and closed, she was vaguely aware of his coming and going, and assumed he was getting wood or tending the animals. By the time the fire had taken the frosty chill from the air, Katherine grew restless and finally decided to give up any hope of falling back to sleep.

Cradled deep in the center of the crude mattress, she was lying on her side when she opened her eyes, giving her a startling view of a muscular male torso, bare to the waist and bent over a shallow tub of water on the table. With his hair pulled back in a ponytail, Avery had shed the top half of his long johns, leaving them to hang from his slender hips. As Katherine silently watched him lather a yellow bar of soap and wash his face, she secretly hoped he would take a razor to the beard. Without the unkempt facial hair, his appearance wouldn't seem so primitive, so deranged.

Given this rare opportunity to study him without being noticed, she imagined him clean-shaven. His profile would likely be one of classic elegance. She saw it in his high forehead, the set of his eyes, the slope of his nose. If he got rid of the whiskers, she wouldn't be surprised to see a strong jawline, maybe even a dimple when he smiled.

Her gaze followed his large hands scooping water and rinsing his face, then moving downward to his broad chest. The intimacy of observing his bathing ritual created an odd, unfamiliar sensation inside Katherine. Flynt Avery was a stranger and possibly dangerous. Yet she watched him with a fascination that mystified her as his fingers spread soapsuds through dark blond hair that defined an inverted triangle from his collar bone to his navel.

He wet a cloth and gave it a light squeeze. Starting at his right shoulder, he began to wipe off the soap in a circular motion that gradually slowed. Katherine felt a distinct uneasiness tighten her shoulders.

"Here now, what's this? A voyeur? I'm surprised at you, Kate," he remarked, his British accent stronger, earthier than his normal aristocratic tone.

Her head bobbed up. The glint of amusement in his eyes brought a flush of warmth to her cheeks. She hadn't meant to stare but now that she'd been caught, there wasn't anything she could say in her defense. Perhaps an apology was in order, though he hardly appeared offended.

"You don't have to look so smug," she grumbled, meeting

his gaze. "You're not showing me anything I haven't already seen hundreds of times."

"Really now?"

"Don't look so surprised." The muscles of her left leg complained as she hooked her foot over the bed frame and struggled to pull herself out of the crater. Realizing that the bulky coat hindered her progress, she took a moment to take it off. Her battered and bruised limbs ached with each movement.

"Am I to assume you view gentlemen *au naturel* as a normal, everyday occurrence?"

"Not completely nude. And not every day. Lord, that would be a bore." With an indelicate grunt, she managed to make it halfway—lying on her stomach, straddling the edge of the bed, one leg in and one leg out. Exhausted from the effort, she contemplated rolling right back into the sack until her strength returned. Before she made a decision, she felt a firm grip around her waist.

"What are you doing?" she demanded, though it was evident before her question was finished. He was simply trying to help her out the bed.

When both her bare feet touched the dirt floor, his hands remained in place as if he were afraid she'd fall over without his assistance. Turning in the circle of his arms, she intended to scold him for scaring the living daylights out of her . . . again. But her words evaporated as she stood at eye level with his bare chest. The scent of fresh clean soap filled her nostrils, prompting her to take a deep breath, inhaling his subtle masculine fragrance. Her spontaneous reaction was too obvious to go unnoticed by Avery, she realized to her chagrin.

"Well?" he asked, as if seeking her approval.

Trying for her own sake to be disinterested, she looked up

at him and answered him with a casual shrug. "You smell good."

"That's all?"

"What else do you want?" Quick to see the predatory glimmer in his eyes, she instantly braced her palms against him. "Every time I open my mouth, you twist my words all around and wind up with that look in your eyes."

Behind his thick beard, one corner of his mouth tilted up in a leer that had been menacing the previous day, yet no longer held the same threat. Now Katherine found herself wondering about the man beneath the whiskers, rather than truly fearing him.

His right hand left her waist and reached up to her forehead. With a feather-light touch, he inspected the swelling of the scraped lump. "There is so much about you that puzzles me."

"Ditto."

"See?" Glancing down at her, he chuckled. "What ever in the world does 'ditto' mean?"

"It means I feel exactly the same. Everything about *you* puzzles *me*."

"Ah yes, I suppose it does." His teasing smile faded. "And yet . . . somehow, I sense we are not altogether different, you and I."

As silence stretched out between them, Katherine grew increasingly aware of her hands still braced against the wall of his chest. Feeling the caress of short blond curls, she slowly realized it was her own fingertips moving ever so slightly, stroking the soft hair on his pectoral muscles. Mortified, she started to yank her hands away, but Avery caught them.

"Please . . ." The husky timbre of his voice quivered down her spine. "Don't be afraid to touch me."

Allowing him to raise her hands, she thought he would place them on his chest. Instead, he lifted them higher, cupped them in his own and kissed them with a reverence that stunned her.

Though the moment was gone in a heartbeat, Katherine would remember it with perfect clarity—the way his head had bowed, the way his eyes had closed. The gentle strength of his fingers, the warmth of his breath, the press of his lips. And the unexpected softness of his beard. For reasons she didn't try to understand, she extended her fingers and touched his mustache where it had brushed her skin.

"It's soft," she marveled to herself.

"Did you expect a porcupine?" He guided her open hand to his whiskered cheek, which moved with his smile. "You see, Kate? I am not a beast—real or imagined. You are safe with me, understand?"

When she nodded, he turned his head slightly and kissed her palm. A strange sort of electrical current hummed through her veins, flowing up her arms with a pleasant warmth. As the heat crept closer to her core, she felt her pulse race and knew she had to stop the direction her thoughts were taking her.

Silently, she inched her hand away. "I'm grateful for all you've done for me. I realize now that I wouldn't be alive if not for you." Her mind groped for words that could not be misconstrued as an insult. "But I can't give you anything more than my gratitude. I'm only going to be around another day or two, at the most. Right? So I'd like it if we could just be friends. Good friends. Like brother and sister."

"As you wish," he replied amiably, acceptance evident in his dark blue eyes. Turning from her, he finished dressing, then dumped his bathwater outside, returning as she donned her boots for a trek to the outhouse. "After we eat, I should have enough water heated for you to bathe, if you so choose."

"Thanks, I'd like that." She reached for her jacket.

"Wear my coat."

"But it's too big. I'll trip on it."

"Probably. But it is a far sight warmer than that scrap of cloth you consider outerwear." He scooped the fur coat from the bed and met her at the closed door, holding it up by the shoulders.

"What if I fall down and can't get up?"

"At least when I finally come to look for you, I'll find a warm body inside my coat rather than a frozen icicle wrapped in pink cotton."

"If it'll make you happy," she conceded, reluctant to admit he was more than a little right. Without removing her jacket, she allowed him to assist with the mammoth overcoat, then stood aside as he opened the door. Stepping past him, she swayed under the excess weight and grumbled, "Oh, for the love of Pete."

"Flynt. The name is Flynt," he amended before the door closed behind her.

The late-season snowstorm lingered far longer than Flynt had anticipated, though he could not find it within himself to be eager for the clouds to lift and the warmth of spring to return. A week had passed since he had rescued Kate from the river and brought her to his cabin. After that hellacious first day together, he was only too glad to settle on a peaceable agreement between them. It seemed that one of the conditions they had silently agreed upon was to avoid questions of a personal nature. He could only assume Kate had come to her decision based upon his earlier remark regarding his solitude.

Although he also refrained from satisfying his curiosity, her odd behavior and strange speech pattern continued to bewilder him. On the other hand, the less he knew about the mysterious woman, the better off he would be when she was finally gone. He had already grown too fond of her.

Even now as he rode Sasti back from Sweetbrier Creek, he should not have been looking forward to her exuberant welcome. He was well aware of the fact that she anxiously awaited his return because of her fear of being abandoned in the wilderness, not because of her concern for his own safety and well-being. Yet he liked to think otherwise. The notion of Kate caring for him was absurd, he knew. He did not need anyone to tell him so. His own common sense hounded him daily to find an excuse to leave the cabin, to get away from the woman, if only for a few hours.

While Sasti plodded through the deep, wet snow, Flynt rebuked himself for dwelling on Kate. He needed to remember why he had gone fishing today, and hunting yesterday, and something else the day before. It did him no good to run away from the temptation if he spent the hours daydreaming of her.

His gaze fell to the forest trail ahead. No new snow had fallen in the tracks Sasti had left behind earlier. Peering through the pine boughs, he could see that the clouds had lifted considerably. Time was running out. By tomorrow morning, the sun would return. By the following morning, Kate would be expecting him to fulfill his promise. He should have been more than happy to get her off his hands and back on the northbound train. He should have been glad to get his life back the way it was before she came into it. He should have been.

But he wasn't.

*   *   *

Katherine paced the dirt floor, checked the window, then went back to sit at the table. Working by lantern light, she inspected her dismal attempt to mend a ragged tear in her chiffon skirt. Ripped by an exposed nail in the door frame, the sheer material had proven that it couldn't withstand the rigors of daily life in a rustic cabin. Katherine felt the same way about herself. Lowering the mending to her lap, she thought about the dresses in the trunk, which were much more practical than her own clothes. The cotton drawers and man's shirt were no longer an option. Even though she wore them while trying to fix her skirt, they were currently serving as her pajamas—a more suitable purpose that met with Avery's approval.

Her gaze turned toward the window again, then to the door, listening for the sound of his boots as he stomped the snow off them before coming inside. Still, she heard nothing but the crackle and spit of the fire. Avery had been gone longer than usual. Or so it seemed. She went through this every day.

Waiting.

Initially, she had welcomed the privacy, appreciating the opportunity to bathe, wash her hair, rinse out her clothes. By the time Avery returned after his first afternoon away from her, she felt as good as could be expected for someone who had fallen down a hill and slapped her forehead against a rock. Unaccustomed to idle time, she ignored his insistence upon rest, pestering him for some work to keep her occupied—which led to her first lesson in cabin cooking.

In the days that followed, the two of them settled into a comfortable coexistence, with Avery playing his role of teacher with remarkable patience, and Katherine playing her role of incompetent student. A quick study she wasn't. At least he acknowledged her efforts, which—oddly enough—pleased her. Despite her often disastrous results, she tried to cook and clean and wash.

And mend, she reminded herself, picking up the chiffon skirt one more time. Using the point of the sewing needle, she began the painstaking task of removing each stitch of the black thread, which was in extremely short supply. Anything was better than just waiting.

Waiting.

Waiting for Avery to come back was almost worse than waiting for the storm front to pass through. Sometimes the least little noise could make her jump a foot. She hated being so jittery—it wasn't like her at all. But then again, she had never been so completely out of her element. This was his world. Not hers. Give her a traffic jam on the L.A. freeways, and she could maneuver her way around it on surface streets without so much as looking at a map. In the city, she knew where to go and how to get there. She took it for granted that a meal was as close as the phone or a market or a restaurant. Not here.

Looking up from her work, she glanced around the now-familiar dark interior, lit only by the fire in the hearth and the lantern on the table. Beside it lay the book Avery had been reading nightly. Whether it was his only reading material, she didn't know. As it was, she hadn't a clue what corner of the sparsely furnished little room could have been hiding it. From the moment it first appeared, however, it had remained on the table, waiting for him.

Like her.

Snap out of it, Katherine. He's coming back.

"What if he fell off his horse?" she asked aloud, gently coaxing the thread free. "What if he's hurt and he can't get back?" Even though the questions fell within the realm of possibility, she also knew that he was as likely to fall off his horse as she was to wake up from this nightmare. It had gotten to the point that she didn't know which she dreaded more—the dream at night or the reality of day.

A sound outside brought her head up.

"Well, it's about time, Avery." She plunked her skirt on the table and stood up as the door opened. "What took you so long—" Seeing the short, dark-skinned old man startled her, yet he posed no visible threat. "Who are you? What are you doing here?"

"SnowEagle. Flynt is my . . . friend." Shuffling into the cabin as if it were his own, he closed the door and shrugged out of a jacket of tanned leather. He draped it over the back of the chair on his way to the hearth. "Where is he?"

"I'm not exactly sure," she answered honestly. She felt no reason to be less than candid with the stranger now warming himself in front of the fire, his weathered hands outstretched as if summoning the heat into his body.

Katherine took in the knee-high leather moccasins, beige slacks and plaid cotton shirt—a contrast in cultures. He bore a striking resemblance to an Alaskan Eskimo by the roundness of his face and almond eyes. Although his collar-length hair was pure white and his bronze skin was creased with deep lines, his square shoulders and straight spine gave him the posture of a younger man.

"He will return soon." The statement lacked the inflection of a question, yet she answered it anyway.

"Yes . . . yes, I expect him any minute."

"You are here for Flynt," he stated as a fact rather than a question.

"No. Actually, it's the other way around—Avery has been here for me." She explained his role in saving her at the river and sheltering her during the snowstorm.

"You are here for Flynt," he repeated, hunkering down in front of the flat stones and leveling his gaze on the flames. She shrugged, realizing the uselessness of her disagreement.

"Maybe so, but he's promised to take me to Dunsmuir when the weather clears, which ought to be any day now." He didn't nod. He didn't agree. He simply kept looking at the fire. "What makes you think I'm here for Fl—Avery?"

After a long silence, she assumed he was reserving his conversational skills until Avery returned. Straightening to his full height, which was at least six inches shorter than her own five-seven, he turned and studied her, his closed mouth forming a kind smile.

"It was told to me," he explained, which didn't begin to explain anything.

"By whom?" Inside her head, a lightbulb flicked on. "Don't tell me—Avery's been hanging out with you every afternoon. Is he the one who told you?"

"No. *Bohem Puyuk*—Big Mountain."

"Big mountain?!" *Good gravy, this guy is crazier than Avery.* Grizzly Adams may have eccentric taste in clothes, but at least he didn't claim to communicate with mountains.

"You know not where you are."

"Not exactly," she hedged, mentally downshifting to follow his sudden right turn in the conversation. "I know we're somewhere south of Dunsmuir." His expression remained unchanged. "I know this is the Southern Cascade mountain range." Still no response. "Northern California." He shook his head, gazing at her with sympathy in his dark eyes as if she were a naïve child. "Now I *know* we're in Northern California."

"You have seen the white mountain?" he asked.

"It's been snowing for a week—they're all white."

"It stands alone with a smaller one at its side."

His description brought back the memory of her first morning in Dunsmuir. She had walked out of the Hitching Post after breakfast and stood by her Lexus, mesmerized by the view of the mountain. "The dormant volcano . . . and its cinder cone."

"Bohem Puyuk."

"I thought it was called Mt. Shasta. And the shorter peak . . ." Thinking to herself for a moment, she snapped her fingers. "Little Shasta? No, Shastina."

"That is what your people call it—the name of Chief Sasti of the *Wai-yuki*—the Shastas. Some say it is the lodge of the Great Spirit."

"But not you?"

He shifted his stance and folded his arms over his chest. "All things—all mountains, rocks, plants and animals—all are one with the Great Spirit, with *Olelbis*. All have a voice."

Piecing together this information, she concluded, "You're trying to tell me Mt. Shasta or rather this *'bo-hem poo-yuk'* is a run-of-the-mill mountain spirit that's told you I'm here for Flynt?"

He nodded. "Your eyes do not believe me. I understand. Few know the secrets of the mountains as my people have known them."

"Who *are* your people?"

"*Wintun*—it is our word for 'people.' We who live in the north are called *Wintu*. To the south are my brothers of the *Nomlaki* and the *Patwin*. But we are all the Wintun, the People. There are whites who call us 'Digger Indians' because we forage with digging sticks. But it is not said kindly. It is meant as an insult."

"Sorry, I've never heard of any Native Americans with any of those names."

His shrug conveyed the attitude that he knew who he was and it really didn't matter to him whether she believed him or not. Still, she couldn't help wondering if he and Avery were kindred lunatics acting out their delusions of timeless historical figures.

A familiar thump of boots outside the door made her heart leap with unexpected joy. Avery entered the cabin with a string of fish dangling from one gloved hand, and looking every bit as huge and woolly as the first time she saw him. Now, however, she recognized the smile hidden in his beard, the subtle laugh lines at the outer corner of his eyes. Without exchanging a word, she felt his warm hello before his attention was drawn to his visitor.

"SnowEagle," acknowledged Avery, clearly delighted. "Too many days have passed. I began to worry."

"No need. I was prepared for this." His hands gestured gracefully to encompass his surroundings.

Avery nodded in comprehension as he moved toward the workbench with his catch. "Ah yes . . . the 'fierce wind of disharmony' of which you spoke several weeks ago."

Katherine met him halfway. "Let me take those for you." Responding in a manner she'd never have expected of herself a week earlier, she reached for the slender rope in his grip. When their eyes locked, his puzzled expression dissolved into an appreciative nod of approval.

"They're heavy," Flynt warned, holding out the string of plump brown trout. He took her free hand and placed it over the rope as well, curling his fingers over hers to tighten her grip. "Are you sure you have it?"

His gaze lifted to luminescent green eyes watching him intently. He might as well have placed her hands around his heart and squeezed until it broke in two. It was his own fault for taking the liberty of touching her, yet he couldn't seem to resist. Damning his failure to maintain a mere friendship, Flynt reminded himself of her determination to leave. Brusquely turning away, he removed his coat, hooked it on the peg and approached SnowEagle.

The old man observed Katherine working at the side table, her back to them. In his native tongue, he stated, "The woman has replaced Little Deer."

"No, she is not my wife," Flynt responded in English.

Chapter 6

HESITANT TO SHUT Katherine out of their conversation by speaking Wintu, Flynt was also reluctant to let her learn of his feelings for her. Her head turned to one side, listening. "Weather permitting, I am escorting her to Dunsmuir the day after tomorrow." When she turned at the waist just enough to look at him, he felt his insides twist into a knot. "Will that be quite all right with you, Kate?"

She nodded solemnly. "Yes, of course."

Watching her return to her work, he realized she was preparing to clean the fish by herself for the first time. He also noticed another first—she had refrained from correcting him with her full Christian name. Before allowing himself to construe hidden meaning into a simple oversight, he pulled his attention back to SnowEagle.

"She is called Kate?"

"She prefers the name of Katherine," he explained, certain she would reward him with another glance, perhaps even a smile. She did not disappoint him.

Realizing his own oversight, he promptly made the proper introductions between Katherine Marshall and the Wintu holy man, then invited him to share their meal.

"No, I must go to the spring."

In all the years he had lived in the Cascades, Flynt had grown accustomed to the twice-weekly visits, never once having been refused his standing offer. "It is too late for you to walk there and return to your lodge before dark," he pointed out. "Take the water you need from my barrel."

SnowEagle wrinkled his nose in disgust.

"My sentiments exactly," Katherine interjected.

Flynt chuckled, shaking his head and glancing over at an equally amused SnowEagle, who spoke slowly and eloquently. "Flynt knows of *Olelbis* as well as I now. It is time he talks the stories. It is time for me to listen."

"As you wish," Flynt replied with a reverent nod. Feeling unworthy of the tribute paid to him by his own spiritual teacher, he still considered himself but a student of the mystical Wintu. Yet to refuse this honor would be an act of disrespect.

"The sulfur taste is not his objection, Kate," he began. "Wintu believe that the mineral water comes from the spirit of the earth. To drink fresh water from the spring is to drink the essence of life in its purest form."

"He hikes to a mineral spring every day because he actually believes it's the fountain of youth?"

"You might say so . . . yes."

Her curved dark eyebrows arched, conveying her disbelief. "The exercise alone probably does more for his health than anything he drinks."

"It is hard to deny what you see with your own eyes. I know for a fact that SnowEagle is as old as eighty years, perhaps more." The old man proudly squared his shoulders, a mild grin on his round face. Clearly, he had no intention of joining the debate.

"I admit he's fit, but Willard Scott sends birthday greetings to lots of people who've reached one hundred."

"Preposterous," Flynt scoffed. "No one lives so long. And who is this Scotsman? I've never heard of him."

"Aw, come on, Avery. You can't tell me you've been dug in up here so long that you haven't ever seen *Today.*"

"Why of course I have seen today. Gather your wits about you, woman. You are not making a blinking bit of sense."

Silence fell between them when the quiet voice of SnowEagle claimed in the rhythmic cadence of Wintu, "She knows not where she is, my son."

Despite earlier deference to Katherine, Flynt answered humbly in the language of his elder. "Please excuse her behavior. And mine, as well. I fear the blow to her head causes her to talk nonsense at times."

"Be patient with her," he advised, his dark eyes filled with ageless compassion. "Listen to her. Then listen here." He touched his chest. "I must go now. While you are gone, I will stop on my way to the spring to feed the mare."

"The trip will not be that long."

SnowEagle silently studied him, then glanced at Katherine before he walked to the chair and picked up his jacket. "I will come by anyway. If you are here, I would be pleased to accept the meal I refused tonight." Bidding Katherine farewell in English, he slipped into his coat.

Following him, Flynt lifted the wooden bar and pulled open the door. Although a handshake was not the Wintu custom, SnowEagle had learned it many years earlier among the miners and trappers and used it until it became second nature, as did the language of English and French spoken by the first white strangers.

"Remember my words," he said, his grip firm as he inclined his head toward Katherine. "She knows not where she is."

"I shall remember, wise one. Travel safely."

"Always." The old man smiled knowingly, then departed.

"What did he say to you?" Kate asked after he closed the door. Her voice had returned to the familiar husky tone that he found so appealing. Dwelling on this thought delayed his reply, causing her to prod him. "I know you two were talking about me, so spill it."

"Very well, I shall—as you say—'spill it.' After I apologized for our rude outburst in front of our guest, he claimed . . . you know not where you are."

"He told me the same thing. What's he talking about?"

"SnowEagle is not the most direct person I've ever met."

"Then you don't understand him either?" She cocked her head to the side. When he shrugged noncommittally, she released a sigh of disgust, then abruptly stopped, listening. "Did you hear that?"

A distant train whistle blew long and short sequences as Kate stood with her head tilted back, her eyes gazing at the ceiling as if searching for the source. The forlorn sound, muffled by the blanket of snow throughout the river canyon, seeped through the walls and roof.

"The tracks have been cleared," he explained, captivated by the lift of chin accentuating her slender neck. "The railroad must have had men working round the clock long before the snow stopped this morning. Do you still believe you were not a passenger?"

Unaware of him watching her, she drew a shaky breath. "I've already told you—I wasn't on a train."

"Are you absolutely certain that you did not become lost, perhaps during the rescue?"

"We've been through this before," she complained, turning her face toward him. "How many more times do I need to tell you before you'll believe me?"

Be patient with her. Listen to her. Then listen here. In his mind's eye, he saw SnowEagle touch his chest. But how could she be believed?

Katherine went back to the workbench, muttering in disgust, "I can't wait to get back to the *real* world."

Masking his disappointment, Flynt was once again reminded how much she wanted to leave. And he couldn't blame her—not when he looked around at the squalor of her surroundings. He couldn't blame her one bit.

Throughout the remainder of the evening and on into the next sun-filled day, Katherine had noticed a sullenness growing in Avery. It was pretty easy to figure out the reason. He was tired of having her around, of showing her how to do the simplest things, of butting heads with her on every subject of conversation. During their final dinner together, he had barely spoken a word, except to say she'd done a fair job of roasting the rabbit—the charred rabbit. Afterward, he left to tend the animals and didn't return until she went to bed.

Before dawn of her last morning at the cabin, she was aware of his movement as he climbed out of the bed and dressed. Standing over her, he quietly asked for his coat, claiming he had to answer nature's call. Half asleep, she relinquished it. When he didn't return, she tried not to worry. Instead, she wondered why he couldn't stand being near her anymore. Her presence had chased him from his own home during most of the day, and now chased him from his own bed at night.

Her body shivered involuntarily. Sure, she was cold. *Who*

wouldn't be? she asked herself. Without the human heater lying next to her, she didn't have a chance of getting warm again. But she tried. Lord, how she tried, curling up into a fetal position deep under the heavy covers, rubbing the goosebumps on her arms. But worse than toes that felt like ice cubes, worse than a nose that felt like an icicle, she hated the cold loneliness of his empty bed. The realization struck her harder than the smack she had gotten in the forehead— she missed him.

"Damn you, Avery."

"What did I do now?"

Poking her head out from under the bearskin, she spotted him kneeling on the hearthstones. Still dressed for the weather, he stacked wood on the cold fire. "When did you sneak in?"

"Just now," he said, continuing his task without looking at her. "I'm not surprised you didn't hear me. You were too busy burrowing in your den."

"You don't have to make it sound like I'm some sort of rodent."

"I was thinking 'badger,' actually." He rose to his full height as a small flame took hold. Taking his sheathed hunting knife from the mantel, he fit it snugly in his right boot— a ritual she'd noticed prior to his leaving the cabin every day. "Ornery little devil, the badger, when it gets its dander up. Sharp teeth." Turning around, he touched the faint scratch next to his eye. "And claws that'll rip—"

"I get the picture," Katherine growled, shoving back the covers and climbing out of bed. She padded barefoot to the trunk and gathered her clothes draped across the closed lid. "When are we leaving?" she asked, fingering the puckered stitches of her repair work.

"After we eat." Unlike other mornings, Avery didn't immediately excuse himself so she could dress in privacy. "I know you will do what you please, in spite of my advice. But may I suggest you wear one of the more modest dresses today?"

"You may suggest it, but my own clothing is just fine."

"I must disagree."

"Go ahead—you always do." Plopping the pile on the thick bear fur, she picked through each item. The chiffon skirt was snagged in several places, threads dangling from the hem. The black pantyhose had more runs than the Dodgers had all season. The shell top was wrinkled but wearable. "These may not be in the best of shape, but no one can expect me to be impeccably groomed after ten days in the wilderness."

"I only mean to give you a fair warning, Kate."

"Warning? Get to the point, Avery."

"You may as well know now that I have never set foot in the town. Several years ago, miners and trappers became suspicious of me due to . . . my reclusive nature, I assume. By the time the railway came through in '86 rumormongers had me sighted as a mysterious half-man/half-animal. SnowEagle heard their talk. Fear spawns hatred, even out of the best law-abiding citizens. When we ride in together, I am concerned their fear of me will be directed at you, as well. Especially if you arrive half-naked in that patched underslip, showing all the world your legs and talking about things that make no sense whatsoever. You'll likely end up in the state home rather than your own home."

His impassioned speech left Katherine dumbstruck. The man was certifiably crazy. Miners and trappers? It was entirely possible that a few starry-eyed weekend prospectors or illegal poachers still poked around in these woods. But it was absolutely impossible that Flynt Avery was the cause of frightful rumors during the previous century. Yet he was worried that *she* would be sent to an institution! That was a laugh.

Staring at the bearded giant, she struggled for several moments to find her voice. "When is your birthday?"

"Fifteenth of July. What does my date of birth have to do with this?"

"Year."

"Here you go with your odd twist of the conversation. I won't allow you to drag me into it again." Throwing his hands up in the air, he bellowed, "Wear what you want. It matters not to me whether you are befriended or beheaded."

"Dammit, Avery. Tell me the *year*." His angry stride chewed up the distance to the door.

"Eighteen sixty-two," he answered, reaching for the bar.

"That's impossible!"

He raised his hand and smacked his palm flat on the center board. Katherine cringed at the sound. When he spun around and headed in her direction, however, she held her ground. In the short time she'd spent with him, she'd learned at least one truth about Avery—he was a gentleman in every sense of the word, even if he did get his hackles up every once in a while. So if he wanted an in-your-face shouting match, she wouldn't back down. Squaring her shoulders, she took a fighting stance as he closed in on her . . . and marched right on by.

Her shoulders sagged in relief. Shaking her head, she turned to see him ransacking the trunk, garments flying in every direction. The stiff-boned corset flopped onto her shoulder.

"Hey," she yelped.

Oblivious to her protest, he snatched something from the bottom, straightened and held it up for her to see. Her gaze

darted from his smug expression to the familiar roll of paper
in his grasp. When he took it over to the table, she was hot
on his heels. Standing beside him, she watched in fascination as his long, tapered fingers tugged at one end of the pale
blue ribbon until the bow gave way. When he smoothed out
the tight scroll, she realized it contained several buff-colored
papers in various sizes. He pulled one of the largest ones
from the bottom of the stack, placed it on top and held it
down for her inspection.

Bordered in pastel flowers and a pastoral scene at the top,
the large bold script proclaimed the document as a certificate of birth of Flynt Cromwell Avery in London, England,
on the fifteenth of July in the year of our Lord eighteen hundred sixty-two.

"Your great-grandfather's," she reasoned, a prickling sensation crawling up the back of her neck.

"Mine."

Her gaze leaped from the page to his dark eyes filled with
grim determination. Slowly, she shook her head. It was in-
comprehensible. There wasn't even a remote possibility that
this man—who was clearly in the prime of his life—was
born over a hundred years ago.

"I don't believe—"

"Look at it," he gently demanded, picking it up and handing it to her. When she accepted it, he walked off, pacing between the hearth and the far side of the table.

To appease him, she studied it for a moment, then laid
it next to the other papers, which had rolled up on their
own accord. "Anyone could have documents falsified to
look like the real thing. Why I even know some people
who—"

"But it *is* the real thing!"

"I'm no expert, Jack." Planting her fingertips on the edge

of the weathered table, Katherine leaned forward to address him as he paused opposite her. "But even I know that these don't look over a century old, any more than you do."

"My name's not Jack. It's Flynt—precisely the same as on that certificate. And I assure you that it is far from one hundred years old."

"My mistake—" She did a simple mental calculation. "One hundred *thirty*."

"Blast it, woman!" His fist came down on the table next to the rolls with such force that the paper bounced. "What in bloody hell will it take to convince you?"

"Of what?" she fired back. "That you're crazy? You're doing a damn fine job of it."

"*I* am not the one who cracked her skull on a rock."

"If you're saying I've got brain damage—you're wrong. My mind is as clear and sharp as ever."

"Not from what I have witnessed," he said, bending closer, his arms braced on the wood. "Your manner of dress. Your language. Your lack of basic knowledge which any woman your age should know."

"At least I don't pretend I'm living in the nineteenth century."

"Pretend, you say? It *is* the nineteenth century, by God. Eighteen ninety-two." Nose to nose, he challenged her with narrowed eyes. "If you believe otherwise, you have proved my point—there is but one sane person in this room. And it is I, not you."

Taking a cautious step backward, she put up her hands to stop the futile argument. "Okay, have it your way, Avery," she offered, realizing it was pointless to provoke a man who had lost touch with reality. And yet, she wished sadly that her initial instinct hadn't been right. "Let's just forget this whole conversation. Now if you'll excuse me, I'd like to get dressed . . ." *So I can get out of here.*

"Of course." Instead of heading for the door, he went over to the scattered clothing, scooped up the red calico dress and deposited it on top of her things as he walked by the bed. "Wear it over your slip . . . rather, skirt. For warmth, if nothing else."

Once alone, Katherine picked up the dress and glanced at the door. His final comment made some sense, she'd give him that much. Riding on a horse through five or six miles of snow-covered terrain was not going to be comfortable or warm. The heavy cotton would be marginally better, though not nearly as good as thick fleece sweatpants. For a brief moment, she considered the trousers tossed on the dirt floor. Wearing them would only set Avery off again.

Holding the dress up by the shoulders, she shook her head in dismay. Her resolve weakening, she grudgingly admitted to herself that appeasing the man was wiser than defying him at this point. After all, she only had to wear the thing for one day. With a sigh of resignation, she placed the dress on the bed and began unbuttoning her shirt.

The midmorning sun had long since cleared the crest of the mountains behind the cabin when Flynt brought Sasti around to the front door where Katherine waited, her long dark hair tied back with a ribbon she'd found in the trunk. As he drew nearer, his steps slowed. She wore her pink jacket over the snug red dress that had captured his attention earlier, distracting him from his breakfast. The rest of her clothes were in a neatly tied bundle held tight against her bosom, as if she were afraid of losing the last of her belongings.

For all she had been through, she was a strongly independent woman, determined to mask her vulnerable side. As she faced him now, he wondered if he was not doing her a disservice by taking her into Dunsmuir and abandoning her with strangers. She had no baggage, no currency—though he intended to remedy that situation with the small pouch of coins inside his coat. Worse yet, however, she had no idea of the wrong impression her clothing made on the wrong kind of men. Without his protection, it pained him to think of her fate.

"Ready?" he asked, holding the reins. Sasti dipped his head and brought it back up. She leaned back, eyeing the animal with some apprehension. Flynt grinned, stroking the white blaze on the face of the roan. "You have never been around horses, I may assume."

"Never."

"An hour from now, you will feel much more at ease with him, I assure you. Now, allow me to help you into the saddle."

"Where are you going to sit?"

"Behind you."

"If you don't mind, I'd rather take the backseat."

Another unique choice of words, he thought, suppressing the urge to shake his head in amazement. "Much of the trail is shaded by trees, which means it will get quite cold. With you in front of me, this coat is large enough to keep us both warm."

"Fine," she sighed. Despite her acquiescence, he suspected quite a bit more had been left unsaid.

After Flynt got her settled, he moved her boot from the stirrup, slipped his own into it, and swung himself onto the horse's broad rump. Opening the front of his coat, he brought it around her, suggesting to her that she lean against him. Her silent obedience surprised him, but not nearly as much as his own hidden response to her closeness. Sweet pleasure it was to feel her slender back pressed against him, to have her nestled between his arms as he took the reins from her delicate hands.

How could he endure such splendid torture for the entire ride?

Leaving the clearing behind, they started down the gentle slope which zigzagged through the forest until it reached the canyon floor. The snowmelt of the previous day had frozen again overnight, creating a thin layer of ice over the packed trail. In the relative quiet of the blanketed landscape, a rhythmic crunch sounded with each step of a hoof.

The scent of pine mingled with Katherine's feminine scent, drifting around him as it had every night when she lay bundled in his coat. The safety barrier he'd once thought ridiculous had been a wise decision after all. Considering his present state of arousal, he could imagine the great control that would have been required of him if her half-dressed body had lain next to him.

While both of them had been avoiding physical contact for days, he saw a strange irony in the unanticipated intimacy of riding double. Despite their best efforts, they were now forced to live out the next hours closer than they had dared to be in the last several days. The irony was not lost on Flynt, with his dry sense of humor.

"What's so funny?" she asked when a small chuckle got the better of him. Passing under a pine bough, they each ducked low, bringing Flynt closer to her fragrant hair.

"Nothing you want to hear," he said in her ear before straightening his spine.

She twisted her head around and looked up at him with a quizzical expression. "Oh, really?"

He failed to suppress a grin. She was absolutely enchanting—radiant eyes, glowing skin, and lips which gave him the strongest desire to kiss her. Dismissing the foolhardy notion, he motioned ahead with a lift of his chin. "Watch the trail."

Within the hour, they reached the river. Following it north until Flynt found a suitable crossing proved a challenge. Already the water had risen from snow melting along the bank as well as the innumerable streams, which fed the headwaters of the Sacramento. Often, the rugged terrain forced Sasti to higher ground, beyond view of the river though not beyond the constant sound of the water rushing over rocks and boulders. They would be faced with more of the same obstacles unless they reached the old stage road along the western wall of the canyon.

Above, in the bare branches of an oak tree, a small racket ensued between a bushy-tailed squirrel and a bold bluejay, each as determined to win as the other.

Katherine mused, "I wonder what that's all about."

"Squabbling over a cache of acorns, I would wager."

"Bizarre."

"To fight over food?"

"No—a cute, passive squirrel arguing incessantly with a noisy bird."

Rather like you and I, Flynt mused.

She went on, oblivious to his thoughts. "It seems odd to me. Like a meek David taking on a bully like Goliath. Well, maybe not in actual size."

" 'Tis nature, Kate. If you try to fit the survival instinct of forest creatures into a moral code of good against evil, you may find yourself greatly disappointed."

"Wouldn't be the first time," she remarked with a bite of bitterness.

"Are you a student of animal behavior? I thought you were involved in law."

"Both are surprisingly similar fields of interest, I've discovered."

"I don't believe I follow."

"Attorney humor," she tossed back over one shoulder. "As I was saying—it wouldn't be the first time I've been disappointed. And I know it's not the last . . . not by a long shot."

Katherine didn't notice when her body had finally relaxed. Long before the river crossing, she'd grown weary of trying to hold herself stiff while Avery seemed wrapped around her in every sense. His muscular arms inside the sleeves of his bareskin coat pressed against her own arms as he held the reins. Since he was using the stirrups, his long legs extended beneath hers, thigh to thigh, his knee caps rubbing the back of her knees.

The slow gait of his horse rocked them in unison. After a while, they moved together like a hand in a glove. The implied intimacy was comfortable in an odd way, much the same as his huge coat wrapped around her at night. Though she couldn't say when it had actually happened, she realized his lingering scent on the garment had become synonymous with her growing sense of security.

It was no longer the coat that made her feel safe but the man who wore it. The thought roared through her head like the deafening sound of the nearby rapids. Now was not the time to romanticize the long-haired British recluse. She knew better than to allow gratitude to cloud her judgment, mindful that he still considered himself a throwback to some sort of frontier knight in shining armor. As soon as they reached town, she wondered how he would try to explain away all the modern-day conveniences. This time, he would be on the receiving end of that smug expression of self-righteousness. And she planned to enjoy every minute of it.

Chapter 7

BY LATE AFTERNOON, Katherine decided Avery had chosen the most obscure backroads for their journey. Of course she hadn't expected him to take Interstate 5 on a horse, but she also hadn't expected to travel so long without seeing more than the quaint buildings of a snowbound resort they'd passed near the crags. When asked, he had identified it as Castle Rock, a popular summer retreat. Although she couldn't remember seeing it during her meandering drive prior to the storm, she realized that the few landmarks she might have recognized were significantly hidden under a white blanket of snow. If she hadn't known better, she never would have thought a multilane freeway actually existed somewhere beyond the trees, high up on the mountainside. Apparently, the insulating snow cover and the noise of the river kept the sound of the cars from reaching them.

"How much longer do you think?" she asked, aware of a drop in temperature now that the western rim of the canyon blocked the warmth of the sun.

"Not long. Quarter of an hour, perhaps." His estimate had to be wrong. Fifteen minutes by horse would place them in the lower end of town at least. Yet there was still no sign of civilization.

"I meant to ask how long before we reach the center of town, not the outskirts."

"Yes, I know."

Several minutes had passed when a frame house came into view. It was small with white clapboard siding, and snow from the roof was mounded in front of the porch. Long icicles dripped from the eaves. A crude snowman squatted in the front yard. Until now, they had followed a road covered with a pristine layer of white. As they passed the house, however, the snow showed signs of more activity, trampled by footprints of man and animal.

But no tire tracks.

Was that so strange? she wondered, realizing that her own concept of rural life came from the celluloid of Hollywood. She shouldn't have been surprised to see that someone had used a horse to get into town rather than a car, especially when it looked as if the snowplows hadn't managed to reach this end of town yet. Clearly, someone had used a little ingenuity. Nothing wrong with that, she surmised, her gaze following the hoofprints ahead of them.

As Sasti brought them to a crest in the road, Katherine lifted her eyes. Railroad tracks. Not just one set, but several ribbons of steel ran north and south in a rail yard that extended across the flat plateau next to a train station she'd seen only in museum photos. Recoiling in shock, she instinctively drew back against Avery.

"Kate?" With a tug of the reins, he stopped his horse, and leaned around her until she saw his face out of the corner of her eye. "What seems to be wrong?"

"Everything," she said vaguely, her voice quaking in her throat. "It's all wrong—the steam engines, the depot, the town."

"I had assumed you had been here previously. You don't recognize it?"

"No. Yes. I mean, it's . . . not right."

"We have had a long ride. Perhaps you simply need a good rest." Flynt pressed his knees against the horse, setting Sasti into motion again. "Where do you wish me to take you?"

"It's a motel north of town."

"*Motel*, you say? A man by the name of Mannon runs a *hotel* at Upper Soda Springs."

"No, that's not it." She let out a frustrated groan. Passing by several Asian children playing outside a home, they approached the main business district of Front Street, which faced the train tracks and the light beige station building. Along the first block, several men loitered at the doors of saloons, some at the railing, all staring at Flynt and Katherine. One ducked inside and emerged with a number of women in dance-hall costumes of various jewel tones.

The next building was a mercantile where a grandfatherly figure cast a suspicious gaze, nodding and conversing with a younger gentleman. Next to them, a towheaded boy in knickers seemed to be listening to every word the old man spoke, then took off like a shot.

"Hey, everybody! Come look—it's the wild man," the child shouted, glancing back over his shoulder. He ran the length of the raised boardwalk, down its steps and back up the next set of steps. Into each doorway he passed, he loudly announced, "It's Sass-Kwatch! He's ridin' into town. An' he's got a woman!"

Flynt found the erroneous identification quite humorous,

though his size and bearskin overcoat certainly added to the similarity between him and Sasquatch, the mysterious mountain creature. Although he had never come face to face with such a being, he could not deny the legend, not when he knew that this small pocket of the Cascades held far more mystical secrets than most people could begin to comprehend.

Soon a bevy of children joined the little town crier, as well as more adults. The crowd began to follow them, gawking, pointing, whispering. Katherine grew more agitated, muttering to herself, though he could only feel the vibrations against his chest rather than actually hear her words.

At the end of the long block, Flynt turned Sasti up a road which was more of a gully between Gongwer's Saloon and the Mt. Shasta Hotel. SnowEagle had spoken fondly of two sisters who ran the Walker Boarding House on Back Street. The old man had befriended the ladies six years earlier when they had followed the northern expansion of the railroad. If these two women could welcome the Wintu to their dinner table, Flynt felt confident they would help Katherine get back on her feet and continue her interrupted travels.

Ignoring the curious townspeople trudging up the hill, he glanced to his right where a Chinese laundry spouted steam from its roof. Directly across the street stood the jail, and next to it a livery stable and blacksmith shop. Flynt turned his attention to his left, spotting the boarding house on the southwest corner, diagonal to the laundry. People flocked through the muddied center of the street as Sasti crossed to the front steps. They formed a wide circle as he dismounted. Aware of their audience, Flynt kept his eyes on Katherine, reaching up to help her slide off the horse.

Her face was as colorless as the first day he'd found her.

"Take me back, Avery," she pleaded, clinging to the saddle horn, her bundle of clothes squashed between her arms.

"To the cabin?"

She nodded emphatically. "Now."

A baritone voice with a French accent spoke loudly enough to be heard over the murmuring crowd. "Sasquatch, *mais non*. He is the squaw-man from Sweetbrier Creek. He took a Wintu child as his bride. *Oui*, Squaw-man?"

"Hey, mister?" asked an adolescent boy whose polite inquiry brought Flynt's head around. "Was yours the Indian wife I heard about long time ago when I was a kid? The one that disappeared? Real mysterious-like, folks say." Many people nodded in agreement with the inquisitive young man.

"Yes. Now if you would please excuse us." Flynt fixed his gaze on Katherine.

As someone remarked in surprise at his fancy speech, she glanced nervously at the small throng of people, then back down at him. "What's happened to me? What's going on?"

"Perhaps it would be best if we continued this discussion in private." He beckoned her with a gesture of his hands.

"No . . ." A shiver shook her body.

"Look, she is afraid of him," erupted the taunting voice again. "*Bon raison*, she has—Good reason, indeed."

"The cold is doing you not a bit of good, Kate. Come down so we can step inside. No harm will come to you, I promise."

"Is that what you told the Injun girl, *monsieur?* She trusted you too much I think. For where is she now?"

The chill in the air sent a second quiver through her. Katherine leaned over, allowing him to grasp her about the waist. With one hand clutching her wad of clothing, she braced her other hand against his shoulder for support as he gently lowered her from his horse and set her on her feet in front of him. After he wrapped his coat around her, she grasped the front of his shirt in one fist, tugging him down toward her. The pleading gaze in her eyes tortured him.

"I'm sorry for everything I said to you," she whispered frantically, her hushed words tumbling out as fast as a rabbit with a bobcat on its tail. "If you take me back, I'll make it all up to you. I swear. I'll do anything. Anything you want." Shaking her head, she pleaded, "You can't leave me here, Avery. Something has happened. Something terrible. When I left here there were cars and trucks and street lights and—"

The circle tightened around them as a woman speculated, "I don't think the lady wants to go inside, do you?"

"*Pardon moi, madame.* Open your eyes. She is no more a lady than he is a gentleman, in spite of his eloquent dialect. After all, he bedded a Digger girl, *n'est-ce pas?*"

"Mr. LeBouche!" the offended woman exclaimed. "There are children present."

"She's right, Blackjack," another man said. "Why don't you go on back to the saloon and finish your game?"

With the attention momentarily diverted, Flynt seized the opportunity to quietly nudge Katherine ahead of him. As they mounted the steps, he realized to his dismay that their exit had not gone unnoticed by the Frenchman.

"*Très bien, mes amis.* You are all ignorant fools if you stand around in the street while this man rents a room in this fine establishment for his whore."

Flynt paused on the top stair, then turned slowly. His gaze settled on the tall, wiry man with a thin black mustache and an arrogant tilt to his chin. Dressed rather plainly in black trousers, wrinkled white shirt and satin vest, LeBouche appeared as he was—a small-town gambler with a big mouth.

Katherine wrapped her fingers around his upper arm and tugged him toward the door. "Don't listen to him, Avery."

Though reluctant, he let her lead him away. It would do neither of them a bit of good if he landed in the jail across the street. Despite her nonsensical gibberish, she was his responsibility for the moment. His primary concern was to help ease her torment over the strange happenings she'd just told him.

"*Monsieur,* did you tell your white woman the fate of your squaw?" he called after Flynt. "*Mais non,* you would never admit to murder."

Wresting his arm from Katherine, he swung around. The milling crowd scrambled back, leaving his accuser alone at the foot of the steps. He strode to the edge of the porch and launched himself toward LeBouche.

"Avery, *no—*"

Katherine was drowned out by a guttural roar from the mountain man. The two men went down into the snow and mud, rolling and striking one another with blows that should have knocked them both unconscious. Avery was heavier and a few inches taller, which had led her to expect a one-round boxing match. In truth, she feared her gentle giant might actually kill the Frenchman. But Blackjack had turned out to be as tough as his larger opponent.

The mothers with children in tow hurriedly shielded innocent young eyes, dragging the little ones away from the scene. Other ladies without similar responsibilities lingered at a safe distance while older boys and men shouted and cheered.

Dropping the bundle and shrugging off the cumbersome bearskin coat, she started down the steps. "Somebody stop them," she pleaded.

"Are you nuts, lady? I got a twenty-dollar gold piece ridin' on that man of yours."

"He's not my man. And I don't give a damn about any bet," she shouted back, trying in vain to gain the attention of the enthralled mob. "Do I have to stop them myself?"

"Try it and you'll wind up dead."

"Is that a threat?"

"Ain't no threat, just the truth. None of us are willin' to be at the receivin' end of them fists. Like I says—you try it and you'll be gone to heaven 'fore you hit the mud."

She watched helplessly as the fighters grunted with pain from each strike to the face or punch to the stomach. One minute they were standing, the next they were staggering across the street. It seemed endless and hideous. Yet the circle grew larger as more men ran from all corners to see the spectacle. Katherine was pushed and jostled, cut off from the scene by a sea of warm, sweat-stained work shirts.

Amid the chaos, a deep voice yelled, "He's got a knife!" Other shouts sprang up.

"Where'd it come from?"

"Watch out!"

"Let me through," Katherine demanded, elbowing her way to the front of the spectators. The moment she emerged into the fighting circle, a collective groan rippled through the crowd as the kneeling giant clutched his bleeding stomach and slumped to the ground.

Standing over his victim, the swaying figure of the exhausted gambler clenched the knife in his hand. Nearly the full length of the long blade was coated red, dripping blood from the pointed tip.

"*Avery,*" Katherine cried out, darting past Blackjack, who was claiming the mountain man had pulled the weapon from his boot. She fell to her knees and carefully rolled Avery onto his back, vaguely aware of her unquestionable strength. The abdominal wound pulsed dark purplish blood that became crimson red as it poured down his sides. He was bleeding to death and she couldn't do a damn thing about it. Not here. Not in this time warp of the Wild West. There were no telephones to call 911. No paramedics.

"Hang on, Avery," she pleaded into midnight-blue eyes that searched her face. She leaned close so only he could hear her words. "I need you. Now more than ever. SnowEagle was right. . . ." Tears fogged her vision as she swallowed hard to keep from crying.

His hand reached up and touched her bruised forehead. "You know not where you are," he recited with great effort.

"Yes," was all she could manage before a sob broke loose from her tight throat. His fingertips caught the first tear. He gazed at it, then slowly rubbed the droplet with his thumb. When he looked at her again, it was with an expression of profound sadness that tore at her heart.

"I'm sorry. . . ." His voice drifted off as his eyes slowly closed.

"Avery? Avery?! You're not bowing out on me, dammit. I won't let you."

Flynt knew he was dying.

While Katherine cried over him, he closed his eyes, feeling nothing of the pain or the frigid snow beneath him—only a sensation of his body becoming lighter and lighter until he expected his arms and legs to lift on their own accord, floating off the ground. It was quite pleasant, really. Not at all as he thought death would be.

He found himself walking alone in the forest along a path of fallen leaves. Coming upon a timbered ravine, he spied a small creature lying motionless far below. As he descended the steep trail, he became more and more certain that the animal was a spotted fawn which had probably lost its footing and fallen from above. Within a few yards of the young deer, a sound drew his attention to the ridge.

Kate? He glanced over his shoulder. She wasn't there. But when he turned back to the trail, the forest was also gone. Only blackness remained.

Somewhere behind Katherine, an authoritative female voice spoke up. "Someone fetch Dr. Gill. Sheriff Murdock, too."

"Already done, Miz Louzana," answered a bystander.

Katherine's downward gaze slowly rose, taking in the black high-top shoes, black skirt and white high-collar blouse. Except for a silk shawl in brilliant purple that was draped around her shoulders and tied casually across her ample bosom, the mature blond woman looked and acted like a schoolteacher, a person clearly respected by the crowd.

Silhouetted by the fading light of the late-afternoon sky, the woman called Louzana presented a formidable figure. Over her shoulder, a distant bald eagle soared in the thermal air currents sweeping up the canyon. Yet the serene picture did nothing to alleviate Katherine's anguish over the mortally injured man lying in front of her.

Another onlooker offered further information about the doctor. "One of Manley Brown's boys already lit out as soon as Blackjack pulled out the knife."

"*Mais non,* I tell you he pulled it from his own boot," LeBouche interjected in his own defense. "I only took it from him to save my own life."

Louzana silenced all talk with an abrupt wave of her hand, then announced to no one in particular, "When the doctor comes up the hill, send him over to my rooming house. Pete? Willy? Sam? Pick out three more as strong as you to carry this big fella into the kitchen. Go around back. Miss Rita will be ready and waiting."

As the men stepped forward, Blackjack casually pointed with the bloodied knife in his hand, motioning toward the still form of Avery. "Surely you are not going to save the life of this murderer."

Katherine rocketed to her feet. "You dirty bast—"

A firm grip on her shoulders held her back. "Don't you have a lick of sense, child? It'll do your man no good to get yourself killed defending his honor. Let the law handle him."

At that moment, the crowd parted and a man wearing a badge approached LeBouche. "I see you've got everything under control, Miss Louzana. I'm surprised you didn't disarm the gentleman yourself."

"I do believe that's what the good citizens of Dunsmuir expect you to do, Henry," the older woman remarked with sweet sarcasm before turning Katherine toward the Walker Boarding House on the opposite side of the street.

Leaving their audience behind, they walked through the mud and slush behind the men carrying Avery, three on one side and three on the other. Trying to banish the image of pallbearers from her mind, Katherine appreciated the older woman's comforting arm around her shoulder.

"Watch your step with him, fellas," Louzana warned. "Too much jostling and he'll bleed all the more."

After they rounded the three-story building and climbed the slope to the back porch, they entered a warm, spacious kitchen. Though daylight was fast receding, soft light spilled from a red oil lamp with a white milk-glass shade suspended from the center of the high ceiling.

A dark-haired woman of similar size and attire to the blond Louzana greeted the solemn entourage without making a single comment about the blood dripping on her clean wood floor. Introductions could wait. Instead, the aproned woman quickly moved aside and gestured toward the long dining table beneath the lamp.

"Over there," she said calmly. "Two of you fetch some wood for the fire. You other four need to strip those wet clothes off him—two on each side—while I take a look at the damages. Be quick but avoid moving him. Cut his shirt and trousers, if need be. Scissors are on the counter."

With Louzana still at her side, Katherine watched from a far corner as Avery was lifted onto the eight-foot table, his full height taking up all but a small space at either end. The two men closest to the door insisted upon being the wood brigade, bumping into each other in their hurry to leave the room. The remaining male crew glanced nervously at the three women, then at one another.

"Quit hemming and hawing, boys. Lou and I took care of wounded soldiers before some of you were ever born. And I don't think the little lady has any objections to seeing her man naked. So let's get to it." She opened the bloodied flannel shirt. "Land sakes, it's a wonder he's even alive."

Katherine flinched, bile rising in her throat. Squeezing her eyes shut, she turned her head toward Louzana, who wrapped her arms around her.

"Perhaps we should leave Rita and the boys to do their work. We can wait in the parlor, dear."

"Give me a minute and I'll be okay." But would she? What if Avery died? Except for his few attempts to teach her the basic elements of cooking and cleaning, she didn't know the first thing about how to survive in this antiquated world of female subservience. Without so much as a birth certificate, she couldn't even claim she'd been born in this century, let alone practice the only profession she knew—law.

Avery moaned. Forgetting her own concerns about the future, she pulled away from Louzana and quickly moved to the end of the table, being careful to stay out of the way of the others. She leaned her head over his, stroking his temples in a meager attempt to soothe him. As the last of his clothing was removed by the men, her gaze remained on his closed eyes and the fringe of dark blond lashes. To venture further would risk another glimpse of his torn flesh, as well as her first look at the lower half of his anatomy—both of which would be disturbing in their own way. And she didn't dare get caught staring at "her man"—as they insisted on calling him.

After he was covered with a heavy blanket from the waist down, Katherine didn't know who was more relieved—her or the four men. Thanked for their help and dismissed, they made a quick but quiet exit. On the heels of their departure, the other two delivered the firewood and beat a hasty retreat as well.

Alone in the presence of the two unusual women, Katherine felt a definite drop in the anxiety level in the room. Considerably more at ease, she gave her attention back to Avery. His long blond hair had come loose from its leather thong during the fight and was now a wet, tangled mess. Of the little she could see of his face above the beard, he looked pale.

Didn't skin turn gray or blue when there was extensive blood loss and lack of oxygen? She tried to recall a medical drama that had starred one of her clients. If his color was bad, he would need a transfusion, wouldn't he? And a respirator? Neither of which were available in this makeshift emergency room.

Avery moaned again as Rita finished wiping the blood from his skin and discovered several slashes and yet another puncture, though not as ghastly. Without looking up from her work, she spoke to her sister. "Lou, get this girl some of that Winterbloom steeping in the kettle."

Katherine declined the tea. "I don't need—"

"It's for him. Stops the internal bleeding."

"But he's unconscious. He'll choke on it."

"Not if Lou shows you how to help him swallow."

As Louzana filled a delicate china teacup, Katherine grew concerned. "Shouldn't you wait for the doctor?"

"Rita is only doing what needs to be done until he arrives." Bringing a demitasse spoon with her to the table, she set about demonstrating the proper procedure of administering the folk medicine. "Considering the healing talents of my sister, however, I truly doubt his services will be necessary."

"Enough flattery." Though not angry, Rita appeared decidedly uncomfortable with the praise. Picking up the pan of water, she deposited it on the counter behind her. "It is merely the plants of Mother Nature which do the work, not me. Soon you will have—What *is* your name, by the way?"

"Katherine."

"As I was saying—soon you'll have Katherine here believing I'm a medieval sorceress." She returned to the table with a smaller bowl in the crook of her arm, stirring the contents into a spongy paste.

"Perhaps you are," offered Louzana with a wink to Katherine, who was caught off guard by the comment.

Dropping her gaze, she asked tentatively, "Do you think it's possible to come from another time?"

For a flicker of a moment, there was a silence between the sisters. With a light, feminine chuckle, Rita responded, "Of course not."

"This shaggy beard is a nuisance," Louzana groused, reaching for the shears used to cut off the wet clothing. "If

I'm going to see to it he's swallowing properly, the long whiskers have to go."

The quick trim was anything but neat, leaving his facial hair untouched above the jawbone yet chopped ragged beneath the chin. Katherine had a distinct feeling that Avery was going to hit the roof when he finally came to and saw the hack job. No doubt, she'd take the brunt of his anger, too. Right now, she didn't care, as long as he came through this alive.

Rapid footsteps on the back stoop were followed by a rap at the door. "Miss Rita?" announced a youthful voice breathlessly. "I got a message from Mrs. Gill, ma'am!"

"Then get yourself in here, son." The herbal poultice hid the wounds from view as Rita began to bandage Avery with torn strips of white muslin.

When the young boy burst in, flushed and panting, his gaze dropped to the blood on the floor, then darted along the trail to the red pool beneath the table. Between gulps of air, he asked "Is he dead?"

"Not yet, he isn't."

As he stepped further into the room, he snatched his wool cap from his head and crunched it in his hands. "I went for the doctor but his missus told me that he's gone up the tracks on his four-wheel cycle to see some folks at Shasta Springs. She says if he's not back by nightfall, he probably won't start home 'til mornin'."

"You did good, son," Rita answered, then nodded to a freestanding cupboard with decorative punched-tin doors. "You get yourself a pie out of there and take it home to your mama for supper. Tell her she's raising a fine boy."

"Yes, ma'am." His wide eyes stared at the table as he cautiously crossed to the pantry, keeping his back close to the wall. "I never seen no murderer before."

"And you still haven't." Louzana threw a sideways glance at Katherine.

"I heard talk that he kilt an Injun girl. Some folks say she was his own missus."

"And some folks should know better than to circulate vicious rumors," Rita mildly reprimanded, unfolding the top of the blanket and draping it across the bandages. Her hand paused on the bare shoulder as she gazed down on her patient. "Flynt Avery is no murderer."

"You *know* him?" Katherine asked, stunned.

Chapter 8

"I CAN'T SAY I know the man personally," Rita explained. "Over the years, we learned about him through a Wintu gentleman who shares my interest in medicinal herbs."

"His friend, SnowEagle," Katherine recalled, then noticed the sisters exchanging a puzzled look. "Is there something wrong?"

Rita shook her head, and turned to the boy at the pie cupboard. "You best hurry on home, son, before you catch the devil for being late for supper."

"Yes'm."

After the door closed, Louzana offered the cup and spoon to Katherine. "It's high time you tried your hand at doing this, dear."

Though Katherine didn't feel the least bit ready to take over, she gave it her best shot.

"Lord o' mercy, child, your hand is shaking like a willow leaf in a windstorm."

Louzana closed her fingers around Katherine's hand and

gently slipped the spoon from her grasp. "This whole ordeal has been far more taxing than you care to admit. Let's get you settled in the parlor while Rita finishes with your Mr. Avery."

"But I *need* to be with him—"

One blond eyebrow lifted. "Not another word."

As Katherine was led into a shadowed hallway and past a grandfather clock, she heard a chuckle from Rita in the center of the kitchen. "Once a schoolmarm, always a schoolmarm. When her time comes, she'll no doubt stare down St. Peter at the Pearly Gates."

"Pay no mind to my sister," Louzana clucked, entering a room charmingly cluttered with porcelain knickknacks and furniture upholstered in floral patterns. Even the air smelled of lilac and roses. "Rita is the sweetest thing in all the world, but she does go on at times—especially at my expense. Not that I truly mind. After all, she's family."

Flynt had heard Kate as well as other voices, which puzzled him. At some point—though he could not say exactly when—he finally realized he was not dead, but most assuredly close to it, if he were to believe the talk around him. He wanted to tell them he had every intention of being up and about by the morning, but he could not seem to open his eyes, let alone speak. It was rather odd, yet not disturbing. He could hear perfectly well, which was a comfort in itself, especially when Katherine spoke with that familiar husky softness.

Acutely aware of her presence, he waited anxiously for each word from her, wishing she would talk more, needing the reassurance that he had not somehow passed on into a different place, a place where he might finally open his eyes only to realize he would never see her again. He heard someone moan, then realized the sound had been his own response—not to physical pain, however.

Indeed, there was no physical sensation throughout his entire body. As far as he could tell from the conversation, he had been carried into a kitchen, stripped naked, and had his wound treated. Yet, he had not felt a single touch of a hand.

Perhaps he had been entirely too optimistic. Perhaps he was truly dying. As a distinct feeling of buoyancy came over him, the darkness behind his eyelids slowly gave way to a shadowy fog and finally to the forest where he had been taken earlier. Yet when he lowered his gaze, the image of the dead fawn blurred, then transformed before his eyes into the elongated form of a naked man.

Without a flicker of hesitation or fear, he instinctively knew he was looking upon his own body.

Katherine watched Louzana pick up a crocheted afghan from the rolled arm of a rose-patterned sofa.

"I want you to rest your head on those pillows," the woman instructed, unfolding the turquoise and pink throw. "And put your feet up while I go brew a pot of tea. How does that sound?"

"I'll ruin your couch." Slipping off the pink jacket, Katherine held out her arms to show the soiled skirt of her dress, mud-stained from the knees to the hem. Her suede boots were even worse. Suddenly, she remembered the bundle dropped on the porch. "My clothes!"

"Your clothes will be just fine and so will my furniture."

"I meant my own clothes, not this," she explained, plucking at the skirt. "Avery had it stored in a trunk and insisted it was more suitable for the weather." *And for this century,* she realized, a chill rippling down her spine. Understanding finally dawned on her about his bullheadedness over the red calico dress. "*My* clothes were tied up in a bundle. I dropped them outside, along with his fur coat."

"Well then, I'm sure they are still there." The older woman reached up to Katherine's shoulder and gently pressed her down onto the cushion. "If you promise to lie down and rest your eyes a bit, I will see that your things are put in a room for you upstairs."

"A room?" Her dire circumstances hit her square in the face. Without a penny to her name, she couldn't even afford a roof over her head or a bed to sleep.

"This *is* a boarding house, dear."

Pushing aside her pride, she swallowed hard and admitted the truth. "I don't have any money to pay you."

"I'm sure Mr. Avery anticipated the cost of room and board."

"I don't think so," she remarked, shaking her head. "He talked about getting back to his cabin as soon as he dropped me off in town."

"To be perfectly honest, I am about as confused as a rooster crowing at a full moon." Louzana's cheerful expression quickly faded as she sank onto the couch and set the coverlet aside. "You can tell me to mind my own p's and q's, but I have a feeling you are carrying a mighty big burden. Care to share a little of it?"

The invitation tempted Katherine. She needed to talk, to let everything spill out—down to the last detail in this bizarre nightmare. Dropping her gaze to her lap, she flexed her fingers, wondering how it was possible that these hands, this body could be the same flesh and blood that had visited this town a hundred years from now. This couldn't be explained away as a fancy new trick from the brilliant minds at Industrial Light and Magic.

"It might not be such a good idea to drag you into this, Miss Louzana."

"Never you mind about me. Are you running from the law?"

"No, nothing like that."

"Well now, somebody must have set a fire under your feet to make you take off with only the clothes on your back, or rather—lying out on my front porch."

She thought of Michael and his proposal. "There was someone. A man. A friend, really. He wanted to marry me, but I needed time to think about it. Maybe I was scared. . . ."

"Maybe you had good reason if he was raising a hand to you. Is that how you happened across that atrocious bruise on your forehead?"

"I'd nearly forgotten about it." She automatically reached up to hide it. "It must be pretty ugly to look at. Actually, Michael didn't do this. I fell."

"Oh?" Her tone of skepticism was easy to recognize.

"I swear to you that I slipped down a riverbank and hit my head on a rock in the water. Avery found me and took me back to his cabin until the storm blew over. That's God's honest truth!" She jerked her thumb toward the kitchen. "You can ask Av—"

Her mind flashed on his prone body on the table. Realizing her mistake, she dropped her hand back in her lap. "I'm really losing it, aren't I?"

"Losing it? You have a queer way of phrasing words, if you don't mind my saying."

"Not at all," she admitted, reminded of the bewilderment of the long-haired Englishman. "You're not the only one to notice. Looking back, I can see how Avery misunderstood me. We sure butted heads over it, too. But I stood up to him."

With a half smile, she shook her head at her own naïve behavior. He was so big, so intimidating. And he had seemed so indestructible. Until now.

The backs of her eyes burned with unshed tears. "He's going to die, isn't he?"

"With a little bit of prayer, I think the good Lord might see fit to bring him through." Louzana patted Katherine's arm as she rose to her feet.

"I gave up doing that sort of thing when I was five years old."

"That's mighty young to be making such a big decision."

"It's mighty young to lose a mom and dad, too. I was raised by an aunt who didn't believe in anything but hard work. She taught me not to rely on anyone or anything other than myself."

"Maybe it's high time you learned we all need divine help at some time or other. Nothing wrong with admitting it, either. And right now you ought to consider saying a few words—if not for yourself, then on behalf of your man in the other room."

"Please stop calling him 'my man.' " Unable to calm her restlessness, she stood abruptly. "He is not my man, my fella, my husband or my lover."

"I know." The corners of the woman's small mouth tilted upward. "Don't think for a minute I didn't notice your eyes boring into that man's skull when his drawers were off. Right there and then, I knew you were too uncomfortable to be familiar with him in a wifely way. Still and all, there is something between you two. Maybe you just don't know it yet, but I do. I was standing at that bay window when you rode up together."

Katherine looked across the room at burgundy velvet drapes drawn aside by gold satin cords, an elegant visual frame to the delicate lace hanging over the tall, narrow window sashes. Silently, she wound her way around pieces of furniture and stopped beside a large Boston fern set upon a pedestal in the alcove. Folding her arms across her middle, she focused her eyes beyond the open weave of white lacework.

Twilight in the canyon town brought a peaceful quiet to the snow-lined street as lights flickered in windows beneath white rooftops. It was hard to imagine that a brutal fight had taken place out there earlier, let alone that one man's life now hung in the balance because of it.

"Avery never would have set foot in this town if it hadn't been for me," she said quietly, staring at the edge of the porch steps where his fur overcoat lay in a rumpled pile. "He wouldn't have been goaded into fighting. And he wouldn't be bleeding to death on that table. It's my fault. And if he dies—"

"See here, Katherine, you have no call to be blaming yourself for what happened today. Flynt Avery had no reason to believe his life was in danger by coming here. He has never been accused of murder. That is only one of many legends Blackjack LeBouche has fabricated over the years, peppering them with just enough truth to make them believable. He never counted on the reclusive mountain man from Sweetbrier Creek actually coming to town. I think Blackjack had too much to drink this afternoon, and believed his own tales. Maybe he even thought he would make himself a hero by killing Avery."

"Did Avery know about the stories?"

"I think SnowEagle kept him informed. You see, Blackjack has quite a reputation for his stories about the early miners and trappers. After a little liquor, however, he tells lurid tales of promiscuous Wintu girls. Or so I have heard. Closer to the truth is that a few young women vanished. Abducted, some speculate. None were ever found. Not alive, anyway."

Katherine shuddered at their fate, then recalled the white doeskin dress . . . and the infant gown. Was Avery one of those kidnappers? Had he built his secluded cabin to hide himself and the girl from her people? Absolutely not, she decided with a certainty that sprang from deep within some remote part of her.

With conviction, Katherine stated, "Flynt Avery was not one of those men."

"No, dear. But his father was."

Throughout the entire night, Katherine kept a vigil at Avery's side, despite the protests of the two sisters—each of whom took turns reading in the kitchen or dozing in the parlor. Fighting off fatigue, she refused to go upstairs to the room she could not afford, fearful of waking in the morning to learn he had died in his sleep.

Shortly after a brief supper, she had pulled up a chair and perched on the edge of the seat. Holding his hand beneath the blankets, she sought the warmth of his skin and the sound of his soft breathing as her own reassurance throughout the long dark hours. Though the overhead lamp had been extinguished, another one remained lit by the sisters' chair, casting faint shadows across the sleeping face of the legendary recluse.

Katherine studied his decidedly European features. It was hard to imagine this tall blond Englishman as half Wintu, especially when she considered the short, round-faced SnowEagle. And yet, Louzana had sworn that her information about the abduction had come directly from the eighty-year-old holy man himself. Reluctant to give further details, the older woman admitted she and her sister were the only citizens of Dunsmuir who were aware of this truth. Anything else Katherine wished to know would have to be asked of Avery.

If he ever wakes up.

She winced at the thought as the clock in the hall sounded a deep resonant gong once, twice, until it marked the six o'-clock hour.

"We made it through the night."

"Indeed we did." Rita closed her volume of *King's American Dispensatory* and stared pensively at her patient. "I am truly amazed. Most men would not have survived."

Surprised by this admission, Katherine asked, "Don't you believe in your own herbs?"

"Why yes, of course. But a person's body has its own healing power, as well. It seems your man here has more than his share. But then, I should not be the least bit amazed by it. The Indians have strong ties to their spirit world. Some folks joke about the Wintun's belief in gods of the mountain and rocks and animals. But I am willing to bet there is more to it than a good laugh, especially with all the strange things that happen in these parts."

Strange things? Katherine felt goosebumps rise on her arms. What could be stranger than traveling through time from 1996? "Have you ever experienced anything . . . unusual?"

Rita glanced down at the book in her lap as if weighing her decision to answer, then nodded and looked back at Katherine. "Yes. Many times. Lou, too. But we keep it to ourselves, as should you."

"May I ask why you told me?"

"Somehow I felt you would understand."

"Two weeks ago, I doubt I would've believed you. But now. . . ." She slipped her hand out from under the blanket and got up. Pacing the plank floor beside the table, she finally gave in to her own gut instinct to trust the woman. After several moments of starting and stopping and stammering over the right words, she took a deep breath and tried one last time.

"Before Avery found me at the river, I was living in a different time. I don't know how to explain it but maybe these mountains really are the center of a—" She held her hands out, her fingers splayed as if holding a ball. "—an energy field. A cosmic vortex, I think it's called."

Despite the tongue-in-cheek reputation of "West Coast Weirdos" that was unique to California, Katherine didn't really know much about metaphysical concepts, let alone how to explain them.

"Cosmic vortex," Rita repeated, clearly fascinated. "Does that mean you come from up in the cosmos?"

"No. The future. A hundred years from now. *Nineteen* ninety-six." She waited for an expression of disbelief from the dark-haired woman but it didn't come. "I know I must sound crazy to you. If only there were some way to prove—"

"I need no proof." Completely unflappable, Rita stood up, clutching the book in one hand. "I have met enough people in my life to know pretty well right away whom to trust. Made some mistakes in judgment when I was young, but not so any more."

"Then I hope you won't mind if I ask for your help. I can work for my room and board, but there's a lot I don't know about everyday life that you probably take for granted."

"Stay with us as long as you like," Rita offered, adding, "Sister and I would enjoy teaching you. Lou, in particular."

Entering the room with a yawn, Louzana asked, "What about me, in particular?"

"No sense going over it twice, Katherine. Sister and I will chat while you freshen up in your room."

Katherine moved to Avery's side, resting her palm on the center of the blanket so she could feel the rise and fall of his chest. "You'll come and get me if there are any changes?"

"Yes, we promise. Now, scoot. Some of our boarders should be up soon. If you pass any of them, let them know that fresh pastries are being delivered later, which will be available in the dining room with coffee. Meal schedules ought to be back on track by tonight."

Before the clock struck seven, Katherine had washed and changed into a royal blue silk robe from Louzana which was embroidered with Oriental designs. Leaving her bundled clothing untouched on the bed next to Avery's coat, she took the stained red dress downstairs with the intention of cleaning it herself. But Rita intervened, sending it across the street to the Chinese laundry, then muttered plans of purchasing a suitable wardrobe for Katherine before the day was out.

By the time the doctor arrived around nine, Katherine had given up arguing against the unnecessary expense of new clothes, resigned to the fact that both sisters could be as stubborn as Avery when they were determined to have their way.

Anxiously waiting in the parlor with Lou while Avery was being examined, Katherine finally heard murmurs and quickly went to the front hall, pausing in the archway. Dr.

Gill supervised six men as they cautiously moved his patient to a second-floor room across from hers. She barely gave them a chance to place Avery on the bed before she stepped to his side and discovered that the double bed was too short for him. One of the men brought over a chair from the writing desk. He slipped it under Avery's feet, which stuck out through the brass rails at the end of the bed.

Thanking him and the others over her shoulder, she adjusted the sheet and blankets, tucking them through the rails so his feet were covered.

As the men left, Dr. Gill spoke in a gentle tone. "Miss Marshall, I think it best if you prepare yourself—"

"Don't say it. Not in front of him." She spun to face him. "I don't want him to hear you."

"My dear, he is incapable of hearing while unconscious. I am dreadfully sorry but he cannot possibly survive—"

"No!" Her harsh whisper cut him off. "We'll discuss this downstairs in the parlor." She looked to Rita standing in the doorway. "I'll be right back."

After the grim discussion with the country doctor, Katherine walked him to the front door. He promised to return later in the afternoon. After he bid her good day, she headed back up the stairs, each exhausting step more difficult than the last.

The door to Avery's room was ajar. Pausing at the threshold, she saw Rita sitting on the edge of the double bed, her eyes closed. One hand rested on the fresh bandage, directly over the newly sutured wound. For all intents and purposes, the peaceful woman looked as if she were performing some kind of healing meditation. Katherine remained silent, fascinated by this unique nineteenth-century lady.

After a long moment in which Katherine mentally wrestled with whether to leave, Rita opened her eyes. With what seemed like deliberately slow movement, she pulled the blankets up to Avery's chin, then turned her gaze toward the doorway. The serenity in her face awed Katherine, drawing her into the room.

She quietly apologized for the interruption, then asked, "What were you doing just now?"

"A form of prayer, you might say."

"You also might say that your answer leaves room for different interpretations."

Rita gave a single nod of approval and a smile that told of unspoken wisdom. She glanced at Avery, then got up and walked around the chair at the foot of the bed.

Stopping in front of Katherine, the dark-haired woman looked up at her. "I admire you for speaking your mind to the good doctor. I dare say he looked mighty confused in regards to your notion about talking in the presence of your man Mr. Avery. But Dr. Gill has quite a few progressive ideas of his own, what with his funny rail cycle and other forms of exercise. I wouldn't be surprised if your belief will set his mind to thinking a bit differently."

The praise made Katherine become aware of her own strong opinions, formed in a modern culture not yet in existence. "If I'm not more careful, however, the doctor could make a medical discovery before it is meant to happen. Do you realize that I could inadvertently say or do something that could change history? Avery is a perfect example."

"Then again," Rita offered, "you may choose to believe that your arrival in this time was not by accident, but a destiny for you as well as those you encounter here. You have changed nothing that was not already meant to be changed."

The woman reached down and took Katherine's left hand, gently pressing it between her warm palms. "We are all brought into this life for a purpose. I can no more tell you your purpose for coming here than you can tell me mine. But rest assured, young lady, I am certain you are not here to do harm to anyone. So you'd best quit your worrying about such nonsense and start looking for the reason you came to be in our time."

"Yes, ma'am."

"Why, I do believe you sounded just like one of us," Rita remarked with a grin, releasing Katherine's hand. "I must hurry downstairs to help Lou start tonight's diner before she thinks I have abandoned her. What my sister lacks in culinary skills, she makes up for in her teaching abilities."

"I'm not so hot in the kitchen myself," Katherine said, remembering her burnt offerings under Avery's instruction.

"Very well, then, Louzana will sit with Mr. Avery later this afternoon while you join me for a cooking lesson. Meanwhile, I will send her up with a cup of Winterbloom for him and a bite to eat for you."

"Thank you."

After the woman was gone, Katherine stared at the closed door until her attention was drawn to a lingering warmth on her palm. It slowly dawned on her that Rita had touched her with the same hand that had been resting on the bandage when Katherine had walked into the room. Her gaze darted to Avery, then to the door and back to her reddened palm.

She already knew and accepted the fact that Rita was an old-fashioned herbalist. But a healer in a spiritual sense?

Katherine wasn't comfortable with accepting such an extreme concept into her own belief system.

Then again, she wasn't exactly comfortable with accepting time travel either. Yet here she was. She couldn't deny the heat on her hand. It was real. She couldn't deny the chill in the old boarding house. It was real. Why should she deny anything else that was happening around her?

Moving over to the bed, she looked down at the man who had rescued her from certain death at the river. Despite her repeated attempts to escape, he had been determined to take responsibility for her. Now when she had the opportunity to pay back his kindness, she could do nothing but watch over the comatose body of "her man," as the sisters continued to say.

Her man. Two weeks ago, the term wouldn't have set very well in her progressive mindset of the 1990s. But now, oddly enough, it made her feel connected with him in a way that comforted her, giving her a sense of belonging in this era of history. For the moment—however temporary it might be—she was tied to him.

As she sat down next to him, her weight sank into the soft feather mattress until her hip touched his. During the long sleepless night, she had done her best to wash the mud from his long blond hair. In the warmth of the kitchen it had dried, returning to the touchable burnished gold that now spread across the pillow.

Leaning forward, she slipped her upturned hand under the long silken strands and let them slide through her fingers. There was something extremely sensuous about his long hair, something she hadn't noticed in other men she had seen in her own modern-day world. While it wasn't uncommon to see male models and actors with beautiful manes of hair to rival those of their female counterparts, Katherine had never known herself to be influenced one way or the other by the length of a person's hair. And yet, here she was mesmerized by the bearded mountain man.

Her fingers combed through his hair, reaching closer to his head with each movement until her nails lightly scraped against his scalp. She hesitated, studying his closed eyelids, wondering if he could feel her touching him.

Don't stop.

Her hand jerked away, remembering the moment in her car when that same clear voice had told her to turn left onto the dirt road near the river. That previous unspoken command had happened before she had wondered about life in a simpler time. If it wasn't the wish to go back to an innocent era that had brought her back in time, what was it? Why *was* she here?

Mindful of the clear order to continue, she carefully scooted forward, the silk robe sliding easily across the quilt. Using both hands, she slowly massaged his temples, cautious of the bruises from his brawl with Blackjack. Her touch evolved into an intimate caress, tracing each line on his forehead and at the corner of each eye, stroking gently across his closed lids and down his cheeks. She brushed across his ragged beard and down his neck.

Her hands pushed the bedcovers from her path as they moved along his broad shoulders, kneading the firm flesh, discovering another bruise. Inch by inch, she worked downward over taut muscles covered with a sprinkling of dark blond curls. When she reached the edge of the white bandage, she rolled the blanket away, then gasped.

A crimson stain of fresh blood!

Chapter 9

PANIC SET HER heart rate into high gear. Controlling the impulse to run screaming for Rita, Katherine reminded herself that the doctor had reopened the wound. Taking another look at the circle of blood, she realized that it probably wasn't any more than could be expected.

When her body shook from a strong shiver, she couldn't be sure it was from the cold temperature or the renewed fear of losing Avery. Not even Dr. Gill gave her any hope.

Then Louzana's words came into her mind as clear as the night before. *With a little bit of prayer, I think the good Lord might see fit to bring him through.*

Raised in the backlot of the Sodom and Gomorrah of Hollywood, Katherine had grown up without religion. Aunt Lillian had no time or inclination for it, leaving Katherine to formulate her own beliefs. Even though she wasn't sure it would do any good, her mind groped for the right words to form some sort of prayer, any prayer. But nothing seemed right, somehow.

After replacing his blankets, she rose and went to the small writing table that stood beneath the only window. Cinching the silk robe tighter, she stared idly at the view of Mt. Shasta.

Bohem Puyuk—Big Mountain. Even if it wasn't the lodge of the Great Spirit, it did have a majestic beauty that made her think of divinely inspired cathedrals.

She felt self-conscious as she folded her hands, then whispered, "I don't have any fancy speech to say here. But if you're listening, I would appreciate—" She stopped, feeling as if she were presenting a case before a judge without having adequate credentials. With a sigh of resignation, she closed her plea. "Don't let him die."

Time held no meaning for Flynt.

Conversations drifted in and out of his awareness, leading him to wonder if he was dozing off or if he'd been left alone.

Alone and vulnerable.

His thought triggered a return to the ravine in the wilderness. Looking down upon the prone image of his own body on a carpet of pine needles, he heard a twig snap. His gaze was drawn to the crest of the ridge. A cougar emerged from the brush and uttered a loud, blood-curdling cry.

With yellow eyes riveted upon the exposed flesh of his naked form, the cat descended cautiously, moving with a fluid grace that belied its muscular strength. He knew by the size that it was a female, yet she was no less dangerous than a larger male.

Fear crept closer on silent paws. Lowering her small head, she stalked her prey. He watched the scene as a helpless spectator. He tried to yell but his voice made no sound. How could he be seeing this? How could he witness his own physical body lying unprotected on the ground, waiting to be torn and eaten by this predator?

The cougar passed beneath his view, unaware of his watchful presence. He wanted to reach out, taunt her, distract her. Despite his wish, she moved on, closing the distance on her prey.

In her room across the hall, Katherine awoke with a gasp, her heart racing. She had smelled the roasting meat again. She had seen the ceiling of the dim cabin. But the rest of the haunting dream still eluded her.

She lay awake, her muscles tense, her chest tight. Yet she couldn't quite grasp the reason for her anxiety. It was connected to the dream somehow, but she didn't know exactly how. She rolled onto her side and punched down the pillow, then dropped her head into the soft crater. Whatever position she tried, she couldn't settle down and relax. Her mind wandered to thoughts of Avery, realizing this was the first night since her accident that she had slept in a bed without him. Though she chided herself for craving the security of his coat, she groped blindly for the bearskin at the end of the bed, too big and too heavy to hang from the hook on the door or drape on the back of the fragile chair.

Wrapping herself in the familiar comfort, she curled up in the center of the mattress, then squirmed and shifted her hip around an irritating lump inside the coat. Relying on her sense of touch in the darkness, she discovered the outline of a patch pocket on the underside of the bearskin and removed a leather pouch about the size of a baseball. Considering the unwieldy bulk of the fur coat, she wasn't surprised to have missed it earlier.

After lighting the bedside lamp, she untied the leather string and emptied the gold coins into the lap of her new nightgown. Unaware of the actual buying value in the late nineteenth century, she could only guess the pile was probably a small fortune by the day's standards.

Katherine looked toward the door, wondering how the reclusive mountain man had come by such a stash of money. And why did he bring so much on this short trip, especially when he'd planned to return home immediately? Was he worried that someone would find it in his cabin while he was gone?

She picked up one coin, turning it over and over, pondering her suspicions of the Englishman. With a flick of her thumb, she tossed the gold piece onto the mattress, then scooped up the others and returned them to the pouch, which went back into the coat pocket. Snatching up the remaining coin, she blew out the lamp and crossed the hall.

When she opened the door to Avery's room, she spotted Louzana sitting at the desk in a second chair that had been brought into the room. Writing by the low lamplight, the woman whirled about, and clapped her hand to her chest.

"Mercy sakes, you startled the living daylights out of me—especially in that beastly coat," she whispered. "My heart is pounding to beat the band."

"Sorry." The coattail dragged behind Katherine as she shuffled to the bed. Rubbing the coin between her fingers, she looked down at Avery. "I couldn't sleep."

Lou got up from the chair. "Perhaps I could find something in Rita's cupboard to help you."

"That won't be necessary." Katherine gave her a sideways

glance. "I know this may not sound proper but I'm not used to sleeping without him." The implication of a sexual relationship brought an unfamiliar warmth to her cheeks. She quickly added, "I don't mean we—that is, he only had one bed and . . . No, wait—that's not coming out right. We weren't together in a, uh . . . biblical sense. But I . . . well, I miss him—I think. Sort of."

"Why, of course you miss him." Louzana casually stretched her muscles, reaching her hands over her head, then lowering them. "No need explaining it to me, of all people. I already know how it is between you two. Just a matter of time before you figure it out for yourselves. I told Rita, I did. Soon as she explained your situation, I said, 'Those two are meant to be together.' "

"Maybe, maybe not." Katherine shrugged, not ready to relinquish all hope of returning to her own time. "There's no point in both of us watching over him. Why don't you go back to your room."

Louzana walked to the door. "You know where I am if you need anything before morning."

When the latch clicked, Katherine placed the coin on the bedside table and pulled the coat more tightly around her. Looking toward the lamp, she decided against turning down the wick, certain she would lie awake until it burned down and extinguished itself. As she started to draw back the bed-covers, she glanced down at her protective layer of bearskin, then at the bearded Englishman.

With a shake of her head, she let the coat drop to the rug, then slipped between the sheets. Lying on her side next to his warm body, she tucked one arm under her head and stared at his peaceful face. Reassured once more by his steady breathing, she rested her hand on his chest, allowing the slow soothing rhythm to lull her to sleep.

*   *   *

His endless dream continued as Flynt watched from a distance. The female cougar circled his body on the ground, pausing to sniff his ankle, then his hand, and finally his long hair. Terror ripped through him as her mouth opened, revealing sharp fangs ready to sink into his flesh.

Why was he being forced to watch his own mutilation? he wondered in desperation, wishing he could close his eyes yet knowing he could not shut out the macabre scene.

The cougar hovered over his left shoulder. Flynt felt her breath on him. The warm, moist heat made him realize with horror that he would not only witness the attack, but feel it as well.

The jaw of the big cat spread wide.

His scream battled its way up his throat.

"*No—!*"

The muffled, guttural cry startled Katherine from a fitful sleep. It was the middle of the fourth night she had slept by his side, and the first time he'd made a sound beyond a low moan.

"Avery?"

In the dimly lit room, she propped herself up on one elbow, hoping to find his eyes open. But he remained unconscious. His pinched brows reflected his inner struggle against an enemy visible only to him.

"Can you hear me, Avery? It's Kather—"

As she touched his shoulder, his head thrashed from side to side. Yanking her hand away, she scrambled out of the bed and ran for the door. After calling out for the two sisters, she dashed back to his side.

"It's me . . . Kate," she said firmly, trying to break through the barrier of his dark world.

Rita arrived within moments, Louzana following close behind. Despite their disheveled appearance from being summoned from their own beds, they scurried over to Katherine sitting on the mattress next to the sweat-drenched mountain main.

Her two hands were closed around one of his. "He's calmer now," she said, releasing a deep sigh of relief. "But he was having a nightmare."

After hearing the details, Rita calmly nodded.

Katherine asked, "Is it a good sign? Is he coming out of it?"

"We can only hope so."

Louzana offered, "Perhaps I should bring some dry sheets. Between the three of us, we could change the damp linen so he doesn't catch a chill."

"A sensible suggestion," answered the eldest sister, retrieving the hand towel hanging from the side of the washstand. She handed it to Katherine. "May as well fetch some warm water and soap while we're at this. Be back in two shakes of a dog's tail."

By the time the job was over, the light of dawn had crept into the room without further sign of change in Avery. Dejected, Katherine began to wonder if she had merely dreamed the sound of his voice.

Rita paused at the doorway before leaving and lightly shook her finger at Katherine. "Now don't you go losing faith, young lady."

Failing to muster up much of a smile, Katherine politely responded, "No, ma'am. I won't."

"That's a girl," chimed in Louzana optimistically. "I'll spell you at seven-thirty so you can join the others for breakfast."

For the next hour, Katherine continued to hold Avery's

hand, talking quietly to him, hoping he could hear her. A tear etched down her cheek as she traced the crease next to his thumb.

"You've got a long lifeline, Avery," she observed, though she didn't actually know how to read palms. "You still have a lot of years left, Englishman."

The early morning chill of the room drove her to seek warmth under the covers. Pressed against his left side, she glanced at his bearded face, then rested her head on his chest to hear his heartbeat. When the short wiry curls tickled her skin, she felt a sad smile tug at the corners of her mouth.

"For all I know, you could be a cousin to the Queen of England, but I'll always think of you as Grizzly Adams."

"The name is Avery."

His groggy voice brought her head up with a jerk. She gaped at his heavy-lidded blue eyes.

"*Flynt* Avery," he said with great difficulty. "Will you ever get it right?"

Unable to dislodge the answer stuck in her throat, she nodded.

"Where are we?"

"The boardinghouse. You've been here since the fight."

He licked his dry lips. "What happened to the Frenchman?"

"He was released." Katherine could not keep the bitterness from her voice. She had fought nose to nose with Sheriff Murdock over his decision. As a twentieth-century attorney who specialized in contracts in the entertainment industry, she knew how to negotiate amicable agreements between parties. But criminal law was a whole different game of chutzpah that she had never learned to play. Now she wished she had.

Tense and angry, she got up from the bed to get Flynt some water out of the pitcher on the washstand. After pouring Rita's herbal medicine into the empty basin, she refilled his teacup. When she brought it to him, she had regained only a small amount of composure at the injustice of the situation.

"There were too many conflicting reports from eyewitnesses." With her help, he took a sip to wet his mouth. "Some said he pulled the knife from your boot. Others say you did. Most admitted that it all happened too fast to know exactly what happened."

Slowly he formed the words, "Where's my knife?"

"The sheriff returned it. I tucked it inside your coat and put them both under the bed. Maybe you should stop talking until you get some strength back."

"How badly am I hurt?"

"Dr. Gill said it was a miracle you survived. A little higher and the knife would've punctured a major organ. As it was, the blade slid right between your intestines like a greased pig. Doc says you have to be the luckiest guy around."

He smiled weakly, passing the cup back into her hands. "Thank you. Have you been taking care of me all this time?"

"The Walker sisters have really done the work. Rita has been fighting infection with some sort of herbs. They like to let me think I'm helping. But you owe your life to both of them."

"I'll be sure to thank them when we finally meet."

"Until then you should close your eyes."

"So should you," he said as she set the teacup on the bedside table. "You look as weary as I feel. Come back to bed and sleep."

Katherine stared at the space next to him, narrower now than it had seemed when he wasn't awake and staring at her with those blue eyes. Every muscle in her body begged her to lie down on the soft feather mattress. Though Avery was too weak to pose a threat, she considered searching out the coat again. Dismissing the need for protection against him, she compromised by picking up all but the sheet over him and sliding in under the rest of the bedcovers, leaving the linen barrier between them. Lying on her side facing him, she bunched her flat pillow between her ear and her forearm.

His head lolled to the side. In the faint light of the room, she watched his intent gaze travel from her hairline to her chin, then return to her eyes.

"Are you really from another time?"

"Yes," she answered cautiously. "Do you believe me?"

The moment seemed to stretch endlessly before he gave her a solemn nod. Without further comment, he looked up at the ceiling, bid her good night and closed his eyes.

That was it? wondered Katherine, studying his profile. No dubious remarks? No drilling questions? No demand for proof? He had simply taken her at her word.

By late afternoon, Flynt decided he had enough sleep to last him six months. Despite the sharp pain in his gut every time he moved, he found it difficult to tolerate his confinement. He didn't like the weakness that had overtaken his arms and legs in the few short days he'd been laid up. The sooner he was on his feet, the sooner he would regain his strength.

"I don't give a tinker's damn about doctor's orders," he bellowed, snatching the wet rag from Kate. Sitting up with the aid of a considerable number of pillows, he felt a modicum of power in his upright position, as opposed to the helplessness of lying flat on his back. "You are not treating me like an invalid a moment longer. I won't have it, I tell you."

"Suit yourself." She shrugged indifferently while the curve of her lips displayed amusement. "I wasn't exactly thrilled with the idea of giving you this sponge bath, you know. Why did you ask for me, anyway? Rita has been—"

"I know what that woman has been doing," he interrupted, dipping the cloth in the basin on the bedside table. His fist tightened, squeezing out the excess water. He winced from the effort. "And she would keep on bathing every part of my anatomy no matter how much I protested. You, however, have enough good sense to know when a man needs privacy."

"Thank you . . . I think."

"Now if you don't mind, I wish to finish." As she started for the door, he wiped one arm, then paused. "And Kate?"

"Yes?"

"I want my clothes." Her lack of response pricked his curiosity. "My shirt? My trousers?"

She explained about his muddied body lying on the kitchen table and Rita's order to cut the clothes rather than risk moving him. This latest circumstance would extend his stay in bed, which fouled his mood even further.

"There is no point sending you to the mercantile. Nothing will be large enough," he groused. "You must hire a tailor, I'm afraid."

"About the money," Kate stated. "After I found it, I used a little to pay the Walker sisters for our room and board."

"Precisely why I brought it along."

"But you weren't planning to stay. Why did you bring so much?"

"It was my intention to give you some seed money."

"All of it was for me?"

"Still is. Most of it, anyway."

"I can't accept it."

"Nonsense."

"It's too much."

"You now own a modest wardrobe purchased by the two sisters whom you have known for an even shorter time than you have known me. Yet you refuse to allow my financial assistance. Why?"

"Because I've already been enough of an imposition on you without taking your last dime . . . I mean, gold coin."

"I assure you," he chuckled, "I shall not be left destitute. Far from it, actually. Thank you for your concern, however."

"I'm glad I could add a little levity to your otherwise sour mood."

He sobered. "My apologies—for my amusement as well as my rude behavior. I am eager to get back to the cabin. Yola could foal any day now."

"SnowEagle promised to check in on her, remember?"

"Just the same—"

"Nothing is just the same, Avery." She came back to the bed. "Don't you understand? You nearly died! For the time being, you're not taking off into the forest alone."

"I won't be alone."

"Oh?"

"I have Sasti."

"That horse? Spare me the fantasy. He's a dumb animal."

"A highly educated opinion, no doubt." Rubbing his bare chest with the wet cloth unnerved her. He grinned, arching his brows. "From what little you have told me of your life, I hardly consider your expertise to be dependable."

"Flynt . . ." warned an exasperated Katherine. The use of his Christian name gave him pause. He nodded appreciatively, which seemed to further rattle her. Throwing her arms up in surrender, she departed.

He felt no small triumph when she found herself speechless at the end of a go-around with him. Her green eyes fairly flashed with sparks of passion when she held a strong mind about any subject. He could only imagine the same passion in her lovemaking. Such thoughts ignited the familiar flare of heat deep in his loins.

Propped up on the pillows, he raised his knees beneath the bedcovers so as to hide his arousal. In the past few hours, he had admittedly been eager to be on his feet, despite the pain in his abdomen. On the other hand, he had also become increasingly fond of the tables being turned in regard to Kate. For all intents and purposes, she acted as his wife, bringing trays of food and joining him for their midday dinner. While her clothing remained in the other room where she dressed in the morning, she had apparently continued to share his bed, which pleased him.

Even Sheriff Murdock regarded her as Mrs. Avery, though he had been corrected more than once. Still, Flynt could only find errant foolishness in the direction of his thoughts. How could he expect her to be happy in this era of history, let alone with him? She had said earlier in the day that she missed the twentieth century and the amenities which she had once taken for granted.

She wanted to go home.

He wanted her to stay.

They could not each have what they wanted without the

other being denied. So he would leave. The sooner, the better.

"I'm going back with him."

Louzana lifted another plate from the rinse water and swirled the flour-sack towel over it. "Has he asked you?"

"No. And I don't expect he will. But he hasn't recovered—not by a long shot. So he'll need me to look after him. For a while anyway. Meantime, I can try to find the place where—" She stared at the soapsuds encircling her wrists like a bracelet of bubbles. "I won't rest until I know that I did my best to get back to my own time. If I return to the spot by the river where I fell . . ."

"Lord Almighty, Kate." The woman stopped, then blew out a long breath. "I don't know who is the more obstinate—you or that man of yours. Both so determined to run away from the other. Why don't you each set a spell in one place and let nature take its course?"

"That's just not my style, Lou." Kate smiled to herself and shook her head. Even in her own eyes, she had become Kate. Somewhere in the week since Flynt had regained consciousness, the formal name of Katherine had quietly slipped from everyone's vocabulary, much as the Hollywood entertainment lawyer had been relegated to a spot in her memory of Century City high-rise office buildings.

"When I was sitting at the river," Kate said, sliding a plate into the rinse water, "I wondered what it'd be like to come back to a time when life was slower and simpler. I wanted to escape all the complications of my own life—the hectic pace, the dating game, the juggling act. But I never imagined how hard it would be to put all that behind me. I don't want to be a helpless little lady who needs a man to take care of me."

"No one says you have to be." Lou retrieved the rinsed plate as Kate added another to the water.

"And yet that's exactly how I felt when Flynt nearly died—I was scared of losing him because I thought I needed him to take care of me. But I can make it on my own. I can learn to earn a living. Who knows? Maybe I could even find a way to practice law again. That is, if I don't go back to my own time."

Rita listened from the counter across the room while she crushed dried roots in a palm-sized bowl. "Your only reason for accompanying Flynt to his cabin has little, if anything, to do with a concern for his health—am I correct?"

"I'm not exactly heartless." Kate defended herself with a twinge of guilt. "Flynt took care of me when I was hurt, so I'm glad I can return the favor. But that's as far as this relationship goes. Besides, I can't really go forward without trying to find out if I can go back to my old life."

Despite Lou's grumbling, Rita agreed, then added, "You'd best find out for yourself what you need to do. Just don't go getting your feet bogged down in the mud while you're searching for your past along that river bank. Some folks get too fixated on looking back and find themselves stuck, going nowhere."

Kate paused, turning at the waist to look at Rita. "You sounded exactly like my aunt just then."

"She must have been a sensible woman."

"More than a little." Kate turned around to finish the last of the evening dishes. "Being with you two brings back a lot of memories of Aunt Lillian."

"She's probably worried sick about you."

Kate shook her head. "She died a few years ago."

"I'm sorry. Do you have any family at home?"

"Michael and Sunni are as family as family can get." As she talked about the two friends who had become her partners in the Meridian Talent Agency, Kate began to miss them terribly.

Chapter 10

FLYNT STOOD AT the second-floor window of room twelve in the Walker Boardinghouse. It had been two weeks since the fight and a week since he'd been allowed out of bed to sit in a chair. Even though he had only a fraction of his strength back, he was bound and determined to head home today. The spring thaw had melted off all but a little of the snow, leaving the road outside in better traveling condition than the mud and mire of their arrival.

His gaze took in the people moving about Back Street, some to the Wing Sing laundry, others to Lee's Livery, still others traversing the hill that led to the railway station and the main street of business. Due north, the snow-covered slopes of Mt. Shasta held his attention until he heard a soft tap at his door.

"Come in, Kate."

"How did you know it was me?" she asked to his back as he let the curtain fall back into place.

"How could I not? You have hardly given me a moment's peace since I told you I was leaving this morning."

He turned to find her standing in the threshold. With her dark sable hair brushed back, she was modestly dressed in a white cotton blouse tucked into the trim waistband of a rust-brown skirt. For daily chores it was a sensible outfit, to be sure. And yet she could not have looked more breathtaking had she worn a satin gown edged in lace. Taking note of a fair-sized carpetbag clutched in her hands, he made no attempt to hide his frown.

"It seems you decided against my suggestion of staying on with the Walker sisters."

Heedless of his comment, she remarked in awe, "You shaved."

"Why yes, I borrowed a razor and finished that ghastly hatchet job on my beard." Stroking his jawline with the back of his hand, he smiled at her reaction to his clean-shaven face. "I only grow it during the cold winter months. It would have come off soon anyway. You see, Kate? I'm not really that Grizzly Adams fellow after all."

"You can say that again."

He remained silent, gazing at her, studying her, admiring her. Gone was the deathly pale woman with garish cosmetics and painted fingernails he'd found along the bank of the river. In front of him stood a lady. Oh, she still harbored odd mannerisms, but each day brought a new change in her. She had an adaptability he continually respected. Even her pattern of speech began to mirror that of the older sisters, including the soft hint of a southern accent.

Kate Marshall was as much a chameleon as himself, he mused. Despite his reputation as an uncivilized man of the mountains, he too had the ability to alter his image to suit his surroundings. When he visited San Francisco twice a year, he donned the finery expected of him in the city. He even attended the opera and often enjoyed the company of a beautiful woman.

He envisioned Kate joining him on the trip he'd planned for late spring, now postponed to early summer. How he wished to see her in an exquisite emerald gown that would match the color of her eyes. Her long hair would be swept off her slender neck in a luxurious dark cloud of curls. He imagined her slender hand tucked into the crook of his arm as he escorted her through a crowded opera house.

Mentally shaking off such impossibilities, Flynt reminded himself that Kate didn't belong with him in San Francisco any more than she belonged in this time, this century. That is, if her story were to be believed. And—God help him!— he did believe her, which meant he was either as crazy as she, or the mysterious gypsy woman had truly traveled through time.

He eyed her bag once more, then looked into her expressive eyes. He had no business taking her under his wing, yet she stood waiting for his response in patient silence.

"What will you do if I refuse to let you come with me?" he asked.

"I have no idea. Stay on with Rita and Lou, I suppose."

"It would be best."

"Not for you."

"I am in no need of a . . . nursemaid."

"Just like I was in no need of Rick the Rescue Ranger in the midst of a blizzard?"

"It appears pointless to stop you from coming with me."

"Consider it a returned favor."

"Indeed," he murmured, though in his heart he knew the long hours she'd watched over him, taken care of his needs. Her selfless devotion to his health far exceeded the small amount of care he'd given her. A handful of snow on her injured forehead and herbal tea for her headache was nothing by comparison. Yet she insisted upon repaying him, even if it was against his wishes. "Then I suppose it's time to bid the Walkers good-bye and be on our way. Sasti should be saddled and waiting outside by now."

The light in her eyes danced with triumph.

He walked to the bed, then knelt to retrieve his coat from beneath it. When he rose with the cumbersome weight of the bearskin in his arms, his stomach muscles clenched in a painful spasm. He groaned. His legs buckled.

Kate dropped her bag and dashed toward him as he hit the floor with a jolt that ricocheted up his thighs and into his gut. With his fingernails buried deep into the thick fur, he gritted his teeth and leaned against the bed for support.

"Are you all right?"

"Yes," he lied.

Kneeling in front of him, she gingerly pulled the bearskin from his hands and shoved it aside. "Lay down on the bed."

"I *said* I'm fine."

"It won't do you a damn bit of good to argue with me."

She gripped his right arm and tugged him upward and onto the mattress. Flynt tried to take a slow, even breath, but the fire in his belly would not allow him the luxury. Kate hovered over him, her hand touching his cheek, then his brow. Her tenderness melted his stoic facade, just as the warm rays of sunshine outside his window had melted the icicles from the eaves.

"Perhaps I should—"

"Stay in bed another week," she advised, her eyes filled with concern.

"No—!" His vehement response knotted the injured muscles. He grimaced.

"I better get Rita."

Minutes later, Kate returned to the room with the dark-haired sister, who exchanged pleasantries with Flynt in her usual calm demeanor. Taking a seat next to the bed, Rita quickly unbuttoned his new flannel shirt to view the white bandages wrapped around his middle.

She nodded approvingly. "Thankfully, you haven't re-opened the wound."

"I merely picked up the coat."

"You shouldn't be lifting anything heavier than a feather."

Kate added, "Especially that bearskin."

As he indignantly pulled his shirt together, Rita gently shook her finger at him. "You'd best lay low a few more days or you'll be tempting fate with a serious setback. You could possibly bleed internally without knowing."

"Did you hear her, Avery?"

"I have ears, woman."

"Then you'll stay put until you've recuperated."

"I will not take orders from you or anyone else!"

He raised his head from the pillow, only to collapse backward from the pain. Rita slowly moved her head from side to side in grave concern. Kate stood with clenched fists propped on her hips.

"Flynt Avery, you are the most pigheaded, stubborn man in the world."

"Me? You are the one who ran outside in a blizzard."

Rita held up both hands between them as if pushing them apart, halting the verbal sparring match. "Kate, please be a dear and bring him some Winterbloom. You know where everything is."

Flynt asked, "Do you think that's such a good idea?" His gaze didn't waver from the glower in Kate's eyes. "She might use arsenic."

Kate cocked her eyebrows in interest. "Accidents can happen."

Rita appeared amused. "Listen to you two bickering jaybirds!"

The argument came to an abrupt end, both of them murmuring their apologies to their hostess before Kate excused herself to fetch the herbal tea.

"*Mister* Avery," Rita mildly chided. "You are *not* going to bully everybody who's trying to help save your life, especially Kate. She has done nothing but wait on you hand and foot since you were brought in here closer to death's door than most folks ever see. So you'd better start treating her with a tad more respect than I've been witnessing these past few days. As for this silly notion of going home today, you should put that idea out of your head."

Flynt knew the woman was right about his belligerence toward Kate. But damned if that gypsy hellion didn't get under his skin like a prickly thistle. She irritated him every which way he turned—even in his dreams. No longer was he haunted by the vision of the stalking mountain lion. Instead he seemed to be awakened more and more by images of Kate. Erotic images. Images he had no business entertaining, asleep or awake.

"Your concern is duly noted," he responded. "However, I intend to be on my horse no later than this afternoon."

After the midday meal in the dining room, Kate was not surprised to see that Avery had chosen to ignore Rita's advice. Afraid he'd sneak off without her, she waited patiently on the front porch, sitting in one of the rocking chairs. Sasti stood nearby, tied to a hitching rail as a cool mountain breeze ruffled his dark mane and long tail. Draped over the worn saddle was the bearskin coat, which she had taken from his room despite his grumbling protests.

Through the open windows, she could hear a distant conversation between the stubborn mountain man and Louzana, who insisted upon taking only half the amount of money he had offered for room and board during his two-week convalescence.

"You and Miss Rita took good care of me . . . and Kate. I want to pay for the purchase of her clothing, as well."

"Land sakes, Mr. Avery. My sister bought those dresses as a gift. Besides, Kate worked hard and deserved some compensation."

"But it was I who imposed her upon you," he answered in his highbrow British accent.

Imposed? wondered Kate, beginning to feel like an unwanted pile of dirty laundry.

Lou responded, "She was a delightful guest, I assure you."

Thank you, Lou. You're a sweetheart.

"Be that as it may, I take full responsibility for her. She is my burden to bear, not yours."

I'm his what!? Her temper simmered as she heard the thump of his boots on the hardwood floor. When they grew louder, she rose from the rocking chair and reached for the carpetbag at her feet.

He thinks I'm a burden? Her fingers touched the leather handle, then pulled back and clenched into a fist. She thought of Aunt Lillian taking on the guardianship of a frightened little girl who had lost both parents. She thought of her ex-husband escaping the shackles of marriage to a sexually naïve bride. She thought of her dearest friends helping to pick up the pieces from her divorce, saving the agency from ruin.

Leaving the bag in its place, Kate straightened as Avery emerged from the boardinghouse. With a sideways glance, he acknowledged her presence before descending the steps with slow, deliberate movement. She could almost feel his pain in her lower abdomen. How could a man be so incredibly stubborn?

In the narrow shade of the porch awning, he momentarily stared at the coat, then carefully repositioned it in front of the saddle horn. He untied Sasti's reins and led him back to the steps. Despite his injuries, he moved with the familiar rolling gait of his long strides. Kate allowed herself one last look of the burnished blond hair, tied at the nape of his neck. Shadowed from the bright sunlight, he looked up at her and cocked his head.

"Hand me your bag."

She stuffed her hands into the deep pockets of her wool skirt. "I'm staying."

"Whatever for? You were so intent upon going with me this morning."

"I don't want to be a burden." *I wanted to help you,* she was tempted to scream at him. *I care about you, dammit!* But he didn't feel the same. No, he felt obligated to take care of her as if she were a stray dog that had wandered into his yard.

"I didn't mean for you to overhear my discussion with Miss Louzana."

"Doesn't matter now," she sighed. "I'd rather work for my keep here at the boardinghouse."

Avery let the reins drop to the ground and retraced his steps onto the porch. His left hand at his belt buckle might have appeared insignificant if not for his tender state. She glanced down to his hand protecting his stomach from the buckle. How would he ride for miles and miles with that hard metal gouging his gut?

As he walked toward her, she stood firm instead of giving in to the temptation to keep some distance between them. He stopped in front of her, lowering his voice for only her to hear.

"If you don't come with me, how are you going to find out where I found you? You can't go wandering around out there in the woods trying to locate a mysterious portal in time. You need me."

"I do need you," she admitted reluctantly. "And I thought you needed me, too. But I was wrong."

"Very well, then. Good-bye, Kate."

Her gaze met his. Midnight-blue eyes stared down at her. She knew it was a mistake to let him go. He was the only one who could take her back to the one place that might solve the mystery of her arrival in this century, the one place that might lead her back to where she belonged. But what if she went to the spot by the river and nothing happened? What if he was stuck with her forever? His burden.

"Good-bye, Avery. Thank you for . . . everything."

"I will return before I leave for San Francisco."

"You've never set foot in Dunsmuir before now, I don't know why you'd want to come back."

His face lowered toward hers. The scent of shaving soap was new to her but already she recognized the clean, spicy smell and thought of Flynt Avery with the firm jaw and strong chin. "Perhaps I'm interested in your welfare."

"Don't bother. I've been enough of a burden."

She saw a flicker of hurt in his dark eyes, but it was gone in an instant, replaced by a narrowed glare. With his mouth close to hers, he growled, "As you wish."

The warmth of his breath drifted over her lips before he

abruptly stepped away from her and marched to the edge of the porch, his boots hammering the wide wooden planks. Kate winced at the harsh sound, knowing that each angry step had to have cost him a great deal of pain. When he carelessly shoved his foot into the stirrup, she saw him flinch in agony. But he was too proud to heed the warning. Instead, he hiked himself up and threw his leg over the horse, only to collapse on the bearskin with a guttural groan.

"Flynt!" Kate bolted toward him, silently cursing the hindrance of her long skirt as she raced down the steps. At his side, she tried to reach up to him, intent on helping him down from Sasti before he fell off. But he slowly lifted his head and blinked, looking around with glazed eyes. "You should have listened to Rita and stayed in bed. You don't even have enough strength to get on your horse."

He squinted down on her as if trying to focus his vision. "I appreciate your concern, but now that the difficult part is behind me, I shall manage perfectly well, thank you."

His regal air and eloquent tongue diffused her anger. How could she let him go off into the wilderness without her? What if he tumbled out of the saddle? What if something terrible happened and he could not get back on his horse? He'd be lying out there all night long with nothing more than his hunting knife to ward off hungry animals while she sat here at the boarding house pretending his fate didn't matter to her.

Retrieving her bag, she handed it up to him. Taking it from her, he lifted one brow inquisitively. "What am I to do with this?"

"Tie it to the luggage rack," she cracked, bringing Sasti alongside the raised porch to help her mount. With one hand holding her skirt to her knees and the other hand on his shoulder, she eased herself onto the broad rump of the horse behind Flynt.

His head pivoted to the side as he commented over his shoulder, "I am to presume you changed your mind?"

"My lips are sealed."

"That remains to be seen."

His slight chuckle vibrated against her breasts pressed into his back. As her hands slid around his waist, she thought of the stiff bandages wrapped tightly around his torso. Rather than risk disturbing his wound, she hooked her thumbs through the belt loops at his side.

The Walkers chose that moment to come out onto the porch to say a final farewell. Once more, Kate thanked them both for their generosity over the last two weeks.

"Our pleasure," responded Rita with a warm smile.

Louzana reminded her, "You take good care of your man."

Abandoning the impulse to correct the woman, who grinned with impish amusement, Kate returned sweetly, "I will, ma'am."

Avery nodded to them solemnly. "I am indebted to you ladies."

"Poppycock." Rita's brown eyes twinkled. "Lou and I are simply glad you didn't die on us. It would have been the ruin of our good business."

Lou laughed. "After that mare of yours foals, I expect to get a visit from the two of you."

Kate added, "I could use another lesson on housekeeping."

"She will be back as soon as I can convince her that I have mended enough to get along without her."

Kate found herself contemplating the possibility that she might be swept back to her own time when Avery regained his health. If so, she would not see the southern sisters again. The thought saddened her. They were two exceptional ladies with wit and wisdom she admired. Her eyes smarted with held-back tears. Lou met her gaze and softly smiled an understanding smile.

"God be with you," offered the retired schoolmarm, then nodded at Avery. "He couldn't get along without you any more than Rita could get along without me."

"Land sakes, would you look who's talking?" harrumphed Rita.

Kate saw through the good-natured teasing. "Behave, you two."

"Always," vowed Lou, slipping her arm around her sister's waist.

Rita responded in kind. "We'll keep you in our prayers."

Kate and Flynt waved as he turned Sasti toward the middle of Back Street and headed for home.

The journey south to Sweetbrier Creek took much longer than their initial trip into Dunsmuir. Despite his obvious discomfort and Kate's pleas, Flynt refused to stop and rest. At times he broke out in a sweat even as they passed beneath the shade of sugar pines and incense cedar for a mile or more. Yet he pressed on, determined to stay in the saddle. Kate grew more and more worried. There were moments she was afraid he had passed out whenever his head bobbed forward, only to jerk upright with a groan.

Late in the afternoon, Sasti stopped abruptly, growing increasingly agitated.

"What's wrong?" asked Kate, glancing nervously around, recalling dozens of old Westerns with spooked horses. It always, *always* meant trouble. Her neck hair stood on end.

"Bear."

"What?!" she squeaked, her vocal cords hopelessly useless.

He pointed at the soft dirt beside the trail where she saw the prints of bear paws. Huge paws. Enormous paws. It was her turn to break out in a cold sweat. She was a regular contributor to wildlife protection societies, but organ donation wasn't on the volunteer list! Sasti refused to move forward despite Avery's attempts to coax the animal into action.

She offered, "Maybe he knows something we don't."

"Perhaps. But I don't think it's wise to stay either."

When Kate saw a thin column of smoke some distance from the riverside trail, she pointed it out to Flynt. "Couldn't we cut through the woods to see if anyone up there has a gun?"

Avery shook his head. "That cabin belongs to LeBouche."

"The man who stabbed you," she said with a shudder. Just the mention of his name sent the same icy chill down her spine that she'd experienced the few times she'd seen him in town after the fight.

Sasti settled down considerably and started walking again, though not with the same relaxed roll to his gait. She could almost feel the animal's tense muscles beneath her. His ears twitched, his head lifted higher.

Kate kept constant watch on the passing forest of thick trees and dogwood bushes, with white flowers in full bloom. Anyone could be easily camouflaged, hiding out until an opportune moment arose. Was Blackjack watching them now? Were his eyes trained on the two riders? What if he stepped out and showed himself, taunting Avery into another confrontation? This time there would be no one to stop LeBouche from finishing the job.

How she was growing to hate the reality of the "wild and woolly West" that had been romanticized by Hollywood!

This wasn't a John Ford movie where actors used break-away glass and stuntmen. It was the very real, honest-to-God, people-could-get-killed life of the 1890s.

As if Avery sensed her fearful thoughts, he placed one hand on hers where it rested on his hip. "We'll be home soon."

Home.

He made it sound so intimate, so welcoming to her ears. She longed for the safety of the rustic cabin. She could hardly wait to stand on the other side of the barred door, protected from the cougars and bears . . . and Blackjack LeBouche. For the time being, the tiny log house would be her home, but for how long? Until Flynt was well again? A few weeks, perhaps? She could endure the inconveniences and hardships of the nineteenth century for another month, if necessary. Her domestic engineering abilities turned out to be quite adaptable after all. But what if she couldn't get back to her own time? What then? A tight knot formed in the pit of her stomach. Kate swallowed back the lump in her throat.

There was so much she missed, even little things like Starbuck's coffee and Ben and Jerry's Coconut Almond Fudge ice cream. Multiplex theaters and Broadway shows. Washers and dryers. Vacuum cleaners and microwave ovens. Computers and cars. She could give them all up in a heartbeat. But how could she give up her dearest, closest friends in all the world? She wondered what they were going through since her disappearance. There was a strong possibility that they thought she was dead. No, she couldn't accept it, *wouldn't* accept it. Somehow she'd go back to Los Angeles. Somehow she would make it back home.

*   *   *

Sasti carried his two riders into the clearing surrounding Flynt's cabin. SnowEagle rose from the split-log bench next to the door and met them halfway.

"Welcome home to you both."

Kate greeted him with a cheerful hello but Flynt barely responded with a weak gesture of his hand. The Wintu took Sasti's bridle and guided it to the bench. As Kate slid off the horse, her legs buckled. Absently reaching out to steady herself, she jostled Avery. He sucked in a quick gulp of air.

"I'm sorry." She pulled away. "Did I hurt you?"

"No," he answered, handing her bag to her. She dropped it on the bench and reached up to help him dismount. "I need no assistance."

Throwing her hands up in exasperation, she stepped to the ground while SnowEagle kept Sasti still, stroking the animal's nose.

"I heard of your fight with the Frenchman. I trust the Walker woman knew her herbs."

"You taught her well," said Flynt.

"We have taught one another. A lesson you should learn yourself."

"With Kate, no doubt."

"Of course."

Listening to the two men, she hovered close, ready to catch the mountain man if he collapsed, though she knew she'd undoubtedly be flattened by his massive size. Fortunately, Avery managed to inch his way from the back of the horse to the ground, but his attempt to walk unassisted proved fruitless.

Wordlessly, the old man came to his aid. Kate grabbed the carpetbag and moved to Avery's other side to lend her strength as well. Flynt shuffled through the doorway of his cabin and across the shadowy interior. They lowered him onto the bed, which sagged extensively under his weight.

"I should check your sutures," she offered. In preparation for being his only caretaker, she had learned from Rita about changing the dressing with the concoctions she'd prepared.

Flynt sighed heavily, the last of his strength draining from his exhausted body. "Let me be. I'm fine."

"Quit saying 'I'm fine' every time I try to help you."

His eyelids drifted together as he released another lengthy sigh. "Very well. Do what you must."

SnowEagle lingered close by the head of the bed. "You have had a dream that disturbed you," he stated casually. "Tell me of it."

Kate's head snapped up and pivoted toward the white-haired man, her heart lodged in her throat. Her dream! How did he—

Suddenly she realized the question had not been directed at her, but at Flynt, who answered in an exhausted voice. "I am continuously amazed by your insight, old one. How do you know of my dream, yet not its contents?"

"I only know *what* I know without knowing *how* it is that I know. If every secret were revealed to me, I would possess the wisdom of *Olelbis*."

"You speak in riddles. I am tired. My mind is in a fog . . ." His husky voice trailed off. The Wintu leaned forward and pressed his palm to Avery's forehead, then frowned.

"I will bring you stronger medicine," he told Kate, looking down at the exposed flesh and the blackened stitches. "He is still in grave danger."

She didn't like the expression on the ancient face of the shaman. "He *will* live," she stated hopefully, but her own shaky voice was unconvincing. Her fingers trembled as she opened the jar of salve she'd retrieved from her bag.

"A weaker man would not have survived."

"But he *did* survive. He's stronger than ten men."

"So it may seem."

"You've got to believe he's going to make it. You're his great-grandfath . . ." She bit back the word but it was too late. Lou had told her that his young granddaughter had disappeared with the much older Englishman when he'd visited the Cascades thirty years earlier.

He nodded, not appearing surprised in the least. "You haven't learned this from my grandson."

"No, from Louzana. Is there a reason I should not know?"

"None."

She gazed down at the sleeping giant. "Then why didn't Flynt tell me?"

"He keeps much to himself. Too much."

She thought of the trunk of clothes. The infant gown. There was a lot he kept hidden, a lot she didn't know. Yet she knew him intimately, beyond the scope of personal facts and childhood history. Something within Flynt connected her to him, like a lifeline that had been thrown to a drowning victim.

SnowEagle's words broke through her thoughts. "You are here for him."

"Yes, I understand that now." Her busy hands paused in the middle of dressing his wound, her fingertips resting on his warm skin. She momentarily stared at the clean-shaven face of her rescuer, sleeping peacefully after their long ride. "Once he's on his feet again, I'm going to have a hard time saying good-bye."

"There will be no good-bye."

Chapter 11

GOOSEBUMPS ROSE ON Kate's arms. She looked over at the Wintu, his ancient eyes reflecting the wisdom of the ages. "I'm staying here forever?"

He gave neither a nod nor a shake of his head as he turned toward the door. She quickly covered Flynt with the blanket and hurried after his great-grandfather.

"Please, SnowEagle," she begged, following the man walking toward Sasti. "Tell me what you know about me . . . about us."

Taking the reins in one hand, he patted the wide jaw of the horse. "I was told you were coming to save my grandson."

"Are you sure it was me specifically? I'm a lawyer, not a doctor."

He shrugged as if her logical perspective didn't have any basis in the present situation. "We all have helping spirits. Listen to yours. They will lead you."

Kate was losing the thread of coherence—if there ever was one—in their conversation. She had absolutely no idea how to communicate with this Indian shaman who made about as much sense to her as metaphysical philosophers of her own time.

"Listen," he said again. Allowing the reins to drop at his feet, he gestured toward the perimeter of the clearing with a sweep of his arms. His hands gracefully circled back onto his chest. "Then listen here."

Her gaze flickered to the surrounding forest. Bluejays squawked. Smaller birds chirped and sang. Maple and oak leaves rustled in the stiff breeze, filling the woodland air with a hushing sound. The air smelled clean and fresh with the scent of pine warmed by the afternoon sun.

The colors of nature intensified. Azure blue sky. Green leaves of every shape and shade. Gray and mottled brown tree trunks with lichen of a green color so pale that it was almost white. Here and there, carpet swatches of deep green moss crept across rich red-brown soil. Scattered patches of delicate wildflowers grew in pockets of sunlight—blue, gold, purple, red.

The picture of serenity was pristine, yet vibrantly alive with vivid color. Caught in the magic of the mountains, Kate stood in awe.

Listening.

She wanted to believe that somehow she would hear the voice. The voice in her car. The voice in the bedroom of the boarding house. She wanted to believe that she only had to follow SnowEagle's advice and all her questions would miraculously be answered.

But it didn't happen. After several minutes, she shook her head in disappointment. "I don't hear anything."

His small mouth moved into a pixie grin. "But you will." He took the reins again and led Sasti toward the south side of the cabin. "I will tend to the horses before I leave. To-morrow I will return with fish to eat."

"How is the mare?" she asked, certain that Flynt would question her as soon as he awakened.

"Yola is well. Her time is soon. Very soon."

Kate was not about to be the only able-bodied person within miles who could assist in the delivery. Her mind flashed on the image of Prissy wailing to Scarlett O'Hara from the top of the stairs. Her brain cells stockpiled movie trivia, show tunes and contract law—not backwoods birthing procedures for farm animals.

"Maybe you should stick around," she suggested. "Just in case."

"No, I must hunt the medicine plants for Flynt."

"What if it happens tonight?"

"The moon is not full."

"What does the moon have to do with—oh, never mind." Spirit guides or full moons, the man had a different spin on things that she could never begin to understand. She raised her hand in a halfhearted wave. "Tomorrow, then?"

"Tomorrow. Sleep well, *Patit-Pokta*." His final words were unintelligible, spoken in the language of his native tongue but sounding like an endearment. She tested the strange combination of syllables, repeating them under her breath as she went into the cabin.

Flynt continued to sleep as she approached the stone hearth where the kettle hung over smoldering embers. She found a simmering soup that SnowEagle had prepared before their arrival. Hadn't he taken time to eat? With a quick glance at the table, she noticed one bowl with a smidgen of broth in the bottom. He had made more than enough soup for one person, as if anticipating the additional mouths to feed.

How did he know they were coming home today? They

hadn't sent a message. There was no one to bring it. She suddenly remembered his remark about Avery's injury. How did the Wintu get his information if he lived alone in a remote part of the mountains?

Mystified, she pondered the *hows* and *whys* but came up as stymied by the holy man as she was by her own voyage through time. Her analytical left brain demanded logical answers where there didn't seem to be a speck of evidence to follow to an obvious conclusion. Still, she wanted to find out what was happening to her and how she could get back to her own place in history.

Returning to the scene of her accident was the only course to take. There had to be something there that would jog her memory, something that was instrumental in her accidental trip through time. Like Alice's rabbit hole. Or a hidden cave in the hillside. If she went to the riverbank where she'd been found, she could conceivably walk right back through the way she'd come. Would it be as simple as that?

There will be no good-bye.

She glanced at the wounded Englishman as SnowEagle's words echoed in her mind. Finding a perfect little doorway did seem too good to be true. Despite the vivid memories of the last few weeks, she still found herself wondering if she wasn't lying comatose in a hospital bed while her mind played this fanciful game in her head.

Lost among her thoughts in the quiet of the room, she was startled by the groggy voice of Avery calling from his bed.

"Kate?"

The sound of her name created a tender warmth that swirled down through her body to her toes. Comatose or not, she was experiencing feelings unlike any she had felt before. A complicated mix of highs and lows, yearning and repulsion, laughter and anger. He pushed all her buttons—wrong ones and right ones. Even now as he called her name, he had no idea how he had made her heart pound and her palms sweat.

"Kate?" he repeated in a rumbling timbre that brought back the memory of his bathing ritual during their first morning together. She recalled the predatory gleam in his midnight-blue eyes as he mistook her for a hooker. In the days since, there had been hundreds of insignificant little touches that sent fire to the deepest part of her. Yet the closest he had come to her was a kiss in the palm of her hand. The remembrance sent a tingle down her spine.

"I'm here, Flynt." She perched on the edge of the timber bed frame and took his hand in hers. He squeezed it gently, a faint smile on his face. Her heart swelled.

There will be no good-bye.

For a moment she believed it. For a moment she saw the rest of her life stretched out in front of her. For a moment she saw only Flynt.

Flynt squinted at the hazy image leaning over him. How long had he been lying there? He didn't even know if he'd made it home. The miles of trail had become an endless blur of rhythmic rocking on the back of his horse.

And an endless blur of pain.

"Are we home?"

"Yes, you're in your own bed now."

At his temple, he felt the touch of fingertips with a soothing coolness that seeped through his skin, down his neck and shoulders, flowing over his muscles like spring water. Closing his eyes, he drifted with the pleasant sensation, drawn back into a distant memory of his young wife and the caress of her hand on his face.

He spoke to her in her native tongue, pledging his undying love and promising to fulfill her dream of many babies.

"Speak in English, Flynt," came a puzzled female voice that was not Little Deer. His eyelids flew open. It took only an instant to recognize Kate, her brows knitted together. "I don't understand Wintu."

"I am not myself," he explained, unable to share the intimate words to a wife he'd long since thought of as dead and gone. Kate would not understand. How could she? Not even he understood the inexplicable awareness of his wife's unseen presence. Though disturbing at first, he had grown accustomed to the irregular visits, finding a remarkable peace that lingered long after the episodes.

From the day he'd carried Kate into his cabin, Flynt recalled brief instances when he had simply confused her with Little Deer. A glimpse out of the corner of his eye. A shadowy silhouette in the firelight. Had this incident been nothing more than a disoriented state of mind, as well? Perhaps it was, he realized, attributing his dull-witted response to his exhaustion and pain.

"Is SnowEagle here?" he asked.

"He left after taking care of the horses for the night. He'll be back tomorrow."

"Yola? Did she foal?"

"Not yet."

"I need to check on her." Flynt started to rise from the bed. Kate pressed his shoulders back into the mattress.

"You need to get some soup in your stomach. *Then* you need to get a good night's sleep. And it won't do you a—"

"A damn bit of good if I argue with you," he mocked, a slight smile tugging at one corner of his mouth. Though she was clearly struggling to remain serious, a light of humor sparkled in her green eyes.

"You learn quickly, Englishman."

*   *   *

Kate tried hard not to think of her own tired body as she served Flynt, washed the dirty dishes, and prepared for bed. Never mind the amenities of her own modern era, she longed for the conveniences of the Walker Boarding House with its big kitchen sinks and water pump and its indoor bath with the claw-footed iron tub and freshly laundered Turkish towels.

By the time she slipped beneath the blankets, she didn't think twice about maintaining barriers of bedsheets or bearskin coats. She wanted to lie next to Flynt, feel the re-assuring warmth of his body and hear his steady deep breathing. He had been asleep for hours when she quietly positioned herself beside him, barely able to squeeze into the space between his massive body and the outside edge of the bed. She considered climbing over him to take the more secure, wider spot along the wall on the other side of him. But she dismissed the plan as too likely to awaken him. How would she explain herself if he caught her straddled over his hips with nothing between them but his cotton knit drawers?

The sudden image of such a provocative position sent a flash of heat to the surface of her skin. Dousing the fiery thoughts seemed almost impossible. She restlessly shifted to her side, only to find herself with her right knee draped over his thigh and her breasts pressed into his thick biceps.

She held her breath, expecting him to wake up and find her curled around him like a sex kitten purring on the Play-boy channel. Nothing could be further from the truth, of course. She simply did not do the sort of things that turn men into hot-blooded, ravenous Romeos.

The allure of sex and glamour was for the Beautiful Peo-ple in the industry. She was only one of the mundane worker bees doing a job that happened to be a little more fascinat-ing than practicing law in a suburb somewhere—but not much more. Granted, she had a closer view of some of the more wild and risqué lifestyles. But she certainly didn't pick up any tidbits on unleashing her own animal instincts. Hers seemed to have been genetically programmed out, she had decided after her failed marriage. Even though Flynt Avery seemed to trigger some pretty steamy fantasies, she was certain she didn't have the same effect on him.

Well . . . *almost* certain, she thought to herself, remembering his absurd assumption about her profession. The memory brought a smile to her lips.

The first light of dawn filtered into the cabin through the single window, slowly drawing Flynt out of his slumber. He had slept soundly through the night, awakening only once to notice that Kate had joined him in his bed. He gazed down at her now, on her side, her dark hair a soft tumble of sable curls, her lashes long and soft against her cheek, her lips . . . oh, how he wanted to taste those lips.

He lay on his back, watching her sleep, wishing he could sneak into her dreams and steal a kiss. She smelled of womanly scents and sweet, flowery perfume. He noticed the plain cotton gown with simple eyelet trimming the neckline. The top three buttons were undone. Each inhale of breath opened the material and revealed a tantalizing glimpse of the deep valley between her breasts. Each exhale closed it. The sight was enough to beguile him as if he were a curious schoolboy spying through a keyhole into the lady's boudoir.

His hand moved of its own accord, reaching across his bare chest and carefully lifting the blankets from her waist. He folded them back. His palm lightly cupped the gentle swell of her hip. With a sleepy murmur, she slowly shifted, splaying her leg over his thigh. Her knee touched him in an innocent yet intimate manner. As a gentleman, he could do nothing to alleviate his present state of arousal. He could not, would not take advantage of a sleeping woman. Nor could he lie next to her with his pulse pounding in his head and blood pounding through his lower body. He longed to take this mysterious lady into his arms and . . .

And what, he wondered? And enjoy her body as if she were one of the young matrons of San Francisco who were bored with their wealthy old husbands? In all likelihood, Kate was not apt to have the same mutual understanding. Aside from her odd choice of provocative clothing, she was of the most definite mind regarding her moral code. If she took a man into her bed, she would expect him to honor his sense of duty to her. Without a doubt, he knew she would expect matrimony. Was he prepared for such a sacrifice? Could he marry this lady lawyer, knowing she was determined to return to another time period if the opportunity presented itself? Could he begin to allow another woman entry into his life only to lose her, too?

His entire life seemed filled with loss of loved ones and betrayal of family. Too many times he had been hurt by their cruelty or other torturous twists of fate. He couldn't let it happen to him again. He had returned to the seclusion of the Cascades for this reason, to close himself off from the world.

He picked up the edge of the bedcovers and drew them back into place, shielding Kate from his wanton gaze just as he shielded his heart from vulnerability and pain. Even still, he could not quiet the slight regret of his decision. His fingers reached out to Kate, touching the smooth, creamy skin of her cheek.

Her eyelids fluttered open. She gazed up at him with soft green eyes. The longing deep in his loins intensified. He wanted to speak, to cover her with passionate kisses, to whisper her name as he moved inside her. His chest tightened as if an iron cuff were clamped around his ribs, holding him prisoner. It would be so easy to break the promise to himself, so easy to unlock the shackles around his heart.

His hand slid down her throat to the opening of her gown. He watched her eyes widen as he unfastened the fourth button, then the fifth, yet she made not a sound of protest. The sixth. The seventh. Her breathing quickened, as did his. She drew in her lower lip as if struggling with her own inner thoughts. His knuckles brushed against a hardened nipple as he freed more buttons. He slipped his hand under the soft cotton and gently stroked the pebbly circle of flesh. She quietly moaned, parting her moistened lips invitingly.

He carefully slid lower on the mattress, bringing his head down toward hers. She shifted, giving him the freedom to cup her full breast. Another moan of pleasure. His own, he realized, as he bent to claim her mouth with his. His tongue never tasted such sweetness, never experienced such boldness as she matched him with a hunger to mirror his own. The silent language between them urged him on.

It was no longer enough to lie on his back with her body tucked beside him. He wanted to be closer. He needed to feel her against his chest, his belly, his thighs. He wished for her to be wrapped around him, possessing him.

As he twisted and moved to his side, a sharp pain tore through his gut.

Foolish bastard.

He fell back onto the pillow, damning his infirmity, damning himself for succumbing to the weakness of the flesh. His wanton betrayal of propriety deserved punishment.

Kate urgently whispered, "I'm sorry, Flynt. I shouldn't have let you—"

"The blame is not yours but mine. Even if I were capable

of physical exertion—which, it seems, I am not—I had no right to molest you."

"Molest?! You were doing no such thing."

"I took liberties. I had no right."

"Maybe in *this* century. Where I come from, we don't call it molesting or 'taking liberties' when a lady is willing."

"What do you call it?"

"Foreplay—as in 'prior to' the Big Event."

"Rather blunt term. Someone actually named it something so brazen?"

A soft laugh escaped her lips, enchanting him. "I don't think you could begin to realize how brazen Americans have become."

"Colonists were always upstarts."

"Europeans are even more open about their sexuality. You should see the ads that run on British television."

"Ads? Television?"

Kate explained about moving pictures and advertisements that could be viewed in the privacy of one's own home. Flynt found her story to be as fascinating as the novel he'd read which had caused quite a stir among political reformers. He recalled the book's reference to a concert played through a similar device.

He inquired, "Can you access music through a telephone?"

"We can access anything through a telephone—letters through fax machines, e-mail through a computer modem—" She paused, a light flicker about her lips alluding to a perception of humor. "This is all way over your head, isn't it? Actually, we usually access music through radio broadcasts. And we have recorded music on compact discs which can be played anytime you want on your own stereo system—our version of the old phonograph."

"Amazing." He thought of the flat wooden crate shoved beneath the bed where he had stored several volumes of books, wondering if he'd held on to the particular publication he had in mind. "There is an author who wrote a story about traveling through time. Going forward, actually. Until now, I'd quite forgotten about it. Although it has become famous, I had found it a bit too far reaching."

She propped herself up on one elbow, fascination clearly evident in her expression. "May I see it?" she asked eagerly, glancing over her shoulder as if expecting the book to pop out of a wall. Her shoulders sagged.

"I may still have it stashed beneath the bed."

"You told me you had no room for any storage."

"No room for more trunks with blankets and such," he corrected. "If the mice haven't made a nest of them yet, I have a few books hidden in a pine box."

"Why? You could have given me something to read instead of letting me die of boredom while we waited for the snow to melt."

"Quite frankly, I didn't think about them." *No, you were too busy thinking about Kate from dawn till dusk.* "Besides, your days were quite full with domestic duties."

"Quite full," she quipped with a twinge of distaste.

Intent upon bringing a smile back to her morning, he offered, "I might enjoy reviewing the book myself, now that I have a different slant on the subject. I'll pull the box out later."

"You won't be pulling out anything. Rita said—" His fingertips touched her lips.

"Very well. *You* shall pull out the box. Agreed?"

She nodded.

Kate was relieved that they had gotten past the awkward tension following their early-morning interlude, what there had been of it. She should have known better than to let things get carried away. But she'd been caught off guard. Half asleep, drifting in the gray fog between dreams and dawn, she never expected to find Flynt fully aroused and amorous. Wished it? Yes. Expected it? No, never.

A flush of heat crept up her neck, which mortified her all the more. She wasn't the type who blushed. Ever. Yet she felt the telltale sign burning her cheeks and knew he could see it even in the pale morning light. Averting her eyes, she shoved the blankets out of her way.

"I . . . think I'll start breakfast," she said, scrambling out of the bed. As her bare feet hit the floor, Kate glimpsed the clinging knit fabric of his drawers. Flynt jerked the discarded covers over his lower torso, though not fast enough. She spun around and stared at the far wall, feeling the hot flames of desire lick the inside of her thighs.

"Please hand me my pants, Kate."

She strolled to the heart has casually as she could manage on shaky legs. "You should stay in bed. You need your rest."

"I will *not* use a bedpan."

When she realized his meaning, she hastily retrieved his new jeans and shirt from the top of the trunk. "I'll give you a little privacy," she suggested, heading for the door.

Upon her return, she found him sitting in the chair next to the table buttoning his flannel. He looked up as she hurried inside. "What's wrong?"

"Nothing," she answered too cheerfully. "Nothing whatsoever."

He rose to his full height, his left hand braced on the table, steadying himself. "Something frightened you, Kate. I can see it in your eyes. What did you see?"

"I didn't *see* anything." She was telling the truth. It wasn't what she saw that had prompted her dash to the cabin. It was the eerie feeling that a pair of eyes were watching her walk through the clearing. Inside the tiny wooden outhouse she'd imagined all sorts of danger lurking about the mountainside. Remembering the bear tracks, she wondered what wild animal might roam through on its way to the river for an early morning drink of water.

Then she thought of Blackjack LeBouche. Her blood ran cold with the memory of his dark hair and eyes . . . and the darker, evil expression on his face.

She moved toward the hearth, crossing her arms over the bodice of her nightgown as she gazed at the rifle that hung above the hearth. She hadn't paid attention to it before now. It was more like a standard prop on a frontier movie set that displayed all the usual things you'd expect in a cabin. Now, however, she eyed the gun with renewed interest.

"Do you think the Frenchman will bother us . . . I mean, you?"

"No—why? Are you worried?"

"Do you remember threatening to kill him?"

"Said in a moment of anger."

"I know . . ." She turned to face him. "I saw the hatred in your eyes. You would have killed him—"

"He accused me of murdering my wife."

His renewed pain drew her to him. Cautiously, delicately as she could, she asked, "What happened to her?"

He gazed down at her, then shook his head. "Let it be, Kate."

As he started to move away and walk toward the door, she snagged his shirt sleeve. He paused, glancing at her fingertips pinching the red flannel.

She spoke softly, trying to understand the refined Englishman who had isolated himself from civilization. "I only want to help."

"You have done enough already."

"What was her name?"

"You are as tenacious as a dog with a bone."

"Part of my survivalist training as a talent agent. Hollywood does that to you." Her joke was lost on Avery, but the levity of her smile seemed to crack the brick wall he'd erected around his solitude.

"Appeasing your curiosity will have to wait until I come back," he answered, then slowly made his way out of the cabin.

Kate stood staring at the closed door for a long time, her mind filled with a jumble of emotions that were leaping around like spit on a skillet.

The expression popped into her head as if Louzana herself had spoken. Kate smiled at the bizarre predicament she was in. Alice in Wonderland, she mused halfheartedly, shoving her splayed fingers through the crown of her hair.

Kate in the Cascades, she silently mocked.

Several minutes later, Kate had dressed and started the fire to cook their morning meal when the door burst open. She jumped up to see Flynt, wild-eyed and clutching his shirt. Kate ran to him.

"Yola," he gasped. "In trouble."

"So are you, by the looks of it. Get in here!"

"No," he barked, then doubled over.

"Avery, for God's sake, you could be hemorrhaging. Remember what Rita said—"

He swore a blue streak. She gave it right back to him, startling him into momentary silence. After he quickly recovered, he stared at her solemnly. "I don't want to lose her, Kate. Help me save her."

Unable to deny his beseeching gaze, she felt her shoulders sag. "What do you want me to do?"

"Follow directions."

He put his arm around her for support, leaning on her as they walked to the shelter behind the cabin.

"It's a boy!"

"It's a *colt,* Kate."

Flynt leaned his back against the corner of the shelter, watching her with the newborn, its spindly legs wobbling as it struggled to stand on its own. She was an extraordinary woman, absolutely extraordinary. Though she had initially balked at his directive to reach inside for the hooves, she had done it—and done it as well as could have been expected of a squeamish city girl.

"He's a*dor*able." She fairly glowed with the flush of excitement, despite the bloody mess she'd made of her new blouse and skirt. Turning from the mare and her foal, she gazed at him with emerald green eyes moist and bright. "Isn't it a miracle, Flynt?"

"Yes, it is indeed." His heart warmed.

The small enclosure grew darker as a figure stepped into the doorway, drawing their attention. SnowEagle moved toward them, passing behind Sasti. The indifferent sire chewed lazily on his feed.

Stroking Yola's forehead, the Wintu smiled at the new mother. "You made this old man look a fool. The moon was not full last night."

Flynt grumbled, "You are not the only one to feel foolish. I was forced to sit here like a helpless child while Kate saved the two of them."

"You coached," she pointed out, defending him from himself. He shrugged off her comment, knowing it was Kate alone who had done the work.

"The ordeal is over and it appears Yola is quite well, considering the circumstances. Perhaps we should do something about cleaning you up."

She glanced down at her arms and clothes, her face registering the appalling sight. "Oh, good God!" Her nose wrinkled as she pinched the material between her fingers, pulling it away from her body. Even her long hair had not escaped untouched. "I'm a disgusting mess."

SnowEagle spoke. "A worthy price to pay for the joy of bringing this new life into the world."

She hesitated, glancing at the big-eyed colt already nursing from his mother. Her disgust melted into a grin as she looked down at her hands in awe. "I really did it, didn't I?"

"You really did," echoed Flynt.

Chapter 12

THE REMAINDER OF the morning passed with a peaceful sense of quiet comfort. While Flynt rested and Kate cleaned herself up the best she could, SnowEagle pan-fried three large brown trout he'd caught earlier. After their meal, the Wintu prepared his medicinal plants, administered to Flynt, then helped his grandson move outside so Kate might thoroughly bathe in privacy.

Chirps and whistles and melodious notes of songbirds contributed to the serenity of the woods. As the two men sat in companionable silence on the wooden bench in the sun, Flynt heard the scurry of mountain quail within the underbrush. He tilted his head backward against the rough log wall of the cabin.

"It feels good to be home," he sighed.

Speaking in the Wintu language, SnowEagle answered, *"Olelbis* answered my prayers and I am grateful."

"You knew about the fight with LeBouche, didn't you?"

"The night before you left, I sensed danger. Yet I knew

nothing more. In my sleep, I entered the spirit world and saw through your eyes all that you have seen. Now tell me your dream and I will help you to understand the wisdom of it."

Flynt described with detail about the dead fawn that had changed its shape into the image of his own body.

"What do you understand of this dream?"

With a sign of sadness, he answered. "The fawn was Little Deer. Somehow I have known all along that she is dead."

"And in her death was also the death of your own spirit which you saw lying on the forest floor."

Flynt bowed his head, realizing the significance of those words. After a moment, he looked up, holding back the latent sorrow. "Then what is the meaning of the mountain lion?"

"Is it so difficult? Think hard."

After a length of silence in which birds called and the wind whispered, Flynt said with bewilderment, "Kate?"

The holy man nodded, pleased. "She is the *patit-pokta*."

"Cougar-woman?" Flynt pondered this insight.

"She has the teeth of a predator, but she has come to protect you. She has been led to you—to keep watch over you, to save your life."

"And she has," responded Flynt, recalling all she had done for him since the stabbing.

"There is more . . . *much* more for her to do."

"How much more? What is going to happen to her?"

"I only know that Kate will not let any harm come to you."

"Will she be safe from this harm? Tell me she will not be hurt or killed trying to protect me."

"She is strong. Stronger than she imagines."

"You are not answering my question."

SnowEagle rose to his feet, turned and placed his hand on

Flynt's shoulder. "You know that I hold nothing back from you. Do not be so quick to feel betrayed. There are those of us who want only to help. You have only to let us."

"You speak of Kate?"

"I speak of Kate."

As if hearing her name had summoned her from the cabin, Kate opened the door and stepped outside. Flynt eyed the red calico dress, noticing the tight bodice that outlined her rounded breasts. It was clear she was not bound into ribbed stays or any other sort of undergarment. Nor did she have shoes or stockings on her bare feet. The hem was too short, exposing her slender ankles. It stirred unwanted memories of touching her at the riverbank, kneading her flesh for any sign of broken bones. He remembered his own physical response—as inappropriate at the time as it was now.

Toweling her wet hair, she seemed oblivious of his discomfort with her revealing attire. She pressed the ends with the cloth in one hand while carrying a brush with the other.

SnowEagle smiled at Flynt as if reading his thoughts. "I must be leaving now."

"Already?" she asked, disappointment on her face. "You don't need to rush off, do you?"

"It is time for me to go." His gaze shifted back and forth between Flynt and Kate, amusement in his dark eyes. "I will bring more food tomorrow."

After SnowEagle departed into the woods, Flynt watched Kate standing before him as she silently began brushing the snarls from her hair. She muttered an oath. "I'll never get these tangles out."

"Allow me to help."

She pivoted at her waist and stared at him with a perplexed grin.

"Is there something offensive about brushing a lady's hair in the twentieth century? Is it not done?"

"No . . . I mean—yes, it's done. I just never—"

"Then you are about to." His eyebrows lifted expectantly as he held out his palm. "The brush?"

She plopped it unceremoniously into his hand. "I'll get the stool."

"That won't be necessary." He carefully shifted to one side, moving one leg over the bench and straddling it. Patting the sent in front of him, he beckoned her to sit.

Kate eyed it dubiously, then walked over and sat down, her back straight as an arrow. He began at the ends, carefully brushing the tangles out inch by inch until the bristles glided effortlessly through her hair. With each slow, methodical stroke, the bristles lightly scraped her scalp. Soon her spine relaxed, losing its stiff posture. She tilted her head back, her eyes closed.

"Mmmm," she moaned contentedly. "This is heaven."

He couldn't agree more.

Her dark brown hair was all but completely dry, with glints of red and copper highlights reflected in the bright sun. And yet he didn't want to stop. Even as he grew tired and his stomach muscles began to complain of sitting up too long, he didn't wish to quit.

"Isn't the warm sunshine great?"

"Tremendous," he observed, watching her spread her arms out and arch toward the midday sun. She twisted around and gazed over her shoulder at him. The tiny buttons of her dress pulled tightly across her bosom. The discomfort in his belly moved downward into a throbbing ache in his groin.

Taking the brush from his hand, she sweetly smiled, thanked him, and hopped to her feet before he could blink.

Had she given him half a chance to gather his wits about him, he would not have allowed such an easy escape. He would have taken her in his arms and kissed her senseless.

His gaze followed her to the doorway, thoroughly enjoying the subtle sway of her hips. He could watch her for hours, mesmerized by every movement of her body.

"Avery?"

"Hmmm?"

She hooked her hand on her hip in a haughty pose. "Are you listening to me?"

"Why yes, of course . . . you were saying?"

"You look like you're about to fall over into the dirt. You need a nap."

"I do not," he growled. He did not appreciate being treated like a schoolboy, most especially when his wayward thoughts were infinitely beyond the mind of a ten-year-old.

"Cranky, aren't we? A sure sign, if there ever was one." She offered her shoulder to lean on but he refused it. Still, she kept close watch on him as he shuffled into the dark cabin and over to the bed.

"You'll need help with your boots," she informed him with a tone that brooked no argument. After completing the task, she started to move away, but this time Flynt was a tad quicker. He had intended to set her straight about ordering him about. But as he grasped her hands and drew her near, he realized his disadvantage. Sitting on the edge of the bed frame with his feet planted wide, he was in no position to anger the spitfire standing between his legs and looking down at him with wariness in her eyes.

His irritation vanished.

"I don't know what I'd have done without you today." His gaze traveled over her face, noting the glow of her skin, the slight almond shape of her eyes, the gentle slope of her nose, the fullness of her lips. "I simply wanted to say . . . thank you."

He leaned his head toward hers, giving her ample time to turn aside if she so chose. She didn't, which encouraged him enormously. Their lips met in a coy touch, then another. He knew he would not be satisfied with only one taste of her. Yet he held back, unwilling to shatter the magic of the moment by asking too much of her. He felt her hands trembling and wondered if it was his own fingers that shook with trepidation. Could he give her what she wanted, what she needed? A home, a family, a sense of security in this foreign time?

She swayed into him, her slender back arching. Her lips pressed against his mouth, then parted tentatively, inviting him. She was a shy seductress with the tip of her tongue, engaging him in a slow-moving parry that was full of intimate suggestion. His hands cupped her bottom, pulling her into the apex of his thighs. She murmured a soft kittenish sound in her throat. He groaned, shutting out all thought, all worries, all concerns. The pain of his injury faded, receding further and further into the back of his mind as his desire escalated.

He broke off the kiss and inhaled deeply as if it were his last breath. The clean scent of her hair filled his nostrils, drawing him down into its silken warmth. He nuzzled her ear, then kissed her neck.

"God help me." The rasp in his voice betrayed his tenuous thread of control. "I cannot stop but I don't dare go on."

Kate stepped back, her breathing as ragged as his own. Her pink lips were dark and swollen from the bruising he'd given them. His fingertips touched them. "Forgive me."

"There is nothing to forgive," she whispered in a manner that heightened his arousal. With a sly smile, she moved out of the circle of his arms and gathered the bedclothes into her arms, then spread them out at his feet. As he watched with increasing curiosity, she repeated the procedure with his own bearskin coat.

After smoothing out layers of bedding, she rose to her feet and turned to him, boldly taking his face in her hands and rekindling the tantalizing fire in his mouth. Little bit by little bit, she deftly disrobed him until his bare backside perched on the edge of the bed. Only the cotton bandages remained wrapped around his middle. He was naked as the day he was born, yet she remained fully clothed—a rare turn for him, which he intended to remedy. He attempted to reach for the top button of her bodice but she snatched his hands and shook her head, smiling silently. Smugly.

Her gaze pointed to the blankets on the floor, then back to him. He gave a nod of acquiescence and reclined on the soft fur. Without allowing as much as a single touch from his hand, she unbuttoned each button with a deliberate pause after each. Slowly, her bodice opened into a deep vee to her waist, revealing the plump curve of her breasts without giving him the entire view. He had never witnessed such an artistically seductive performance. Only as her dress slithered down her bare thighs did he see the slight quiver in her hands.

Glancing down at him, she gave him almost a sly smile.

He reached up to her. "Come here."

She knelt at his side. His hand slipped behind her neck and drew her down. As she leaned over him, he kissed her long and languishingly. He started to lift her, to coax her on top.

She lightly pushed herself away. "Don't exert yourself."

"Too late."

"Lay still. I'm taking over."

"Not likely."

"My way or no way."

He stared at her in good-humored disbelief. This was not a nineteenth-century lady, he remembered belatedly. Though uncomfortable with the idea of playing the submissive role, he complied with a small amount of challenged pride. "As you wish."

"That's more like it."

She slid one leg over his hip and straddled him, and almost immediately he became entranced with this new and enchanting temptress. She was bold and wild one moment, sultry and saucy the next. Time and again she took him to the very edge of his control, then brought him back. Now as she poised herself on the tip of his manhood, he could feel her dewy moistness. He feared he would explode the moment he entered her. But again she slowed her movements, lowering herself by tiny increments. When she had taken his full length into her, she tightened around his thickened flesh, then released. Tightened. Released. She had no need for outward movement. Her feminine muscles gripped him stronger and stronger. His hands clutched her thighs. His eyes closed as he allowed himself to feel the exquisite pleasure she was giving him.

"Dear God in heaven, Kate. What are you doing to me?" His hips lifted toward her.

"Don't . . ." she pleaded as her own primal rhythm set in motion. He halted his own movement, clenching his jaw as the pressure built inside his loins. Each time she plunged him deeper, each time she tightened around him. The moment of her own fulfillment came. She cried out as a warm wetness surged out of her body, triggering his own release. The power, the momentum was not his own but hers. Exquisite pleasure. Exquisite torture. For one brief instant, his entire being entered her, became a part of her. For a fleeting glimpse in time, he knew euphoria. It was a heaven that he never wanted to leave.

But just as quickly, he plummeted back into his own body, tumbling to earth. Depleted of all strength, he lay motionless except for his labored breathing. When Kate collapsed next to him, it was all he could do to turn his head and kiss her temple.

"You are a magnificent little wench."

Kate smiled slowly to herself, then chuckled softly. Something deep inside her had been building up to this moment with Flynt. Though she would deny it to her dying breath if anyone asked, she had known since that morning that she would lure him into bed and make love to him. It had been in the back of her mind when she had pulled out the new jeans she'd hidden in the bottom of her borrowed bag. Stopped by a tingle of mischievous desire, she had changed her mind and found the red dress that the Chinese laundry had cleaned. On yet another whim, she vetoed the Victorian underwear which would have taken her forever to put on, never mind getting them off at the right moment. Without the layers of lingerie, she was surprised with the snug fit. The dress had shrunk. The fit was even tighter than before. All the better, she decided as she walked outside with her towel and her brush.

Kate felt a small amount of satisfaction that Flynt had so readily offered to brush her hair. If he hadn't, she would've asked anyway. Lord, she was shameless. What had come over her, anyway?

Never in her life had she done most of the things she'd just done for Flynt. And *to* Flynt. Undressing him as if she were some sort of dominatrix? Stripping as if she were Gypsy Rose Lee? And the rest . . . Holy smokes! But damned if it didn't turn him every which way plus inside out.

Katherine never would have done this.

But Kate would!

She felt as though she had uncorked a vintage champagne that had only gotten better with age. Her head lolled to one side to gaze at Avery. He had awakened a part of her she had never known existed. Was it him? Or was it the crazy idea that she was caught in a science-fiction fantasy that had unleashed her inhibitions? If none of this was real, what did it matter if she allowed herself to be swept away with passion? Whether she had traveled back to the past or lay comatose in a hospital, she could enjoy exploring these feelings for Flynt. No business calls would interfere. No approval—or disapproval!—from friends. No blood tests for sexually transmitted diseases. And no body clock ticking away, asking if this was the right man, the future father of her children.

Children.

She was twenty-eight years old with distant dreams of motherhood still hovering somewhere out there on the horizon. Babies simply weren't an option in her busy life. Certainly not while she was lost in this time warp.

What if . . . ?

No . . . uh-uh. No way. She couldn't possibly get pregnant, especially since she hadn't had her monthly cycle since she left home. Rita had supplied her with the necessities, telling her how women dealt with the inconvenience in the 1890s. But she hadn't had any use for them yet. Actually, she'd begun to think it was the one blessing in this whole nightmare! Obviously she was under extreme stress from her backward leap of the century, or else she was dreaming this whole experience. Either way, she was more than happy to shut down the menstrual system for the duration of the trip.

So much for birth control, she thought to herself with a grin.

Flynt drifted in and out of sleep, vaguely aware of Kate lying with him on the floor of the cabin. He rolled onto his side, careful of his wound, and tucked his arm around her middle. She made a soft, contented sound and scooted her backside against him. He smiled into her hair, pressing his lips into the back of her head. He couldn't remember the last time he had felt this peaceful. . . .

The dream sneaked into his netherworld of pleasant rest. He saw the distant figure of his body and approached it on silent feet. The tawny mountain lion appeared on the ridge above the ravine. She stealthily crept through the woods, passed beneath his vision and approached the prone figure on the forest floor. Flynt watched her circle, sniff, circle again. He could hear her loud, rumbling purr from deep within her throat. She opened her large mouth. Fangs glistened.

NO!

He tried to scream but emitted no sound. In horror, he watched her lower her head. But then she did the most amazing thing—she licked his whiskered cheek like a mother with a cub. He was astounded by the sight of it as he saw this wild beast recline next to his body. With ears and eyes alert, she kept watch.

"You were smiling in your sleep," Kate told him later while she prepared potatoes for their supper. She had dressed in a more utilitarian skirt and blouse, though still without shoes.

"I was dreaming."

"About me, I hope."

"Apparently—if I am to believe SnowEagle."

She looked up from the table where she sat in front of a wooden bowl, butchering the potato instead of peeling it. "You spoke to him about it?"

"Yes." He explained about the dream and also its interpretation. "Today I dreamed it again. This time, however, I didn't awaken when the cougar opened its mouth. Instead, I saw it guarding me—just as SnowEagle had explained to me."

Kate appeared skeptical. "And that was supposed to be me?"

"He even called you '*Patit-Pokta.*' "

When Flynt spoke the Wintu words, she fumbled with the potato, dropping it onto her lap.

"What's wrong?" he asked.

"You told him the dream this morning while I was in here taking a bath?"

"Yes."

She repeated each syllable of the words with great care. "What does it mean?"

"*Patit* is the Wintu word for mountain lion or cougar. *Pokta* is woman. He called you Cougar-Woman."

"Flynt, he called me that *yesterday*. How could he have known about your dream if you hadn't told him yet?"

"He shared my dream. He also saw the fight in one of his visions." Kate looked at him with disbelief. "SnowEagle is a descendent of deeply spiritual people. He is as much a part of the ancient myths and legends of these mountains as the animal spirits he believes in. His power is great but it is still very much a mystery to me."

"He isn't the only one who is a mystery." She left the table and came over to the bed, sitting at his feet. "When you brought me here in the snowstorm, I wondered what kind of man would live alone in the wilderness in the twentieth century. Maybe it's more acceptable in these days, but somehow I still sense that you weren't cut out to be a hermit. Who were you before?"

Flynt grew uncomfortable with her pointed question. He wanted to evade it but found it impossible to uphold the cool indifference he had always conveyed to outsiders. Kate was not an outsider. Not anymore. He studied the curious concern etched into the tiny lines across her forehead.

"I have never talked about my life with anyone," he cautiously admitted.

"Not even your wife?"

"Not even I knew the truth about myself until . . ." He shook his head slowly. It was too complicated to explain all that had happened to him back then. Within a few short days he had lost so much, and been betrayed as well. He tightened his grip on the anger and pain that had long since been buried. "Little Deer didn't live long enough to find out about me."

"But *I'm* here now." Kate touched his leg in a gentle reassurance of her presence. "I want to know all about you."

Did she really? he wondered. Would she feel the same about him when she learned about his past? Or would he be rejected again? He stared at her hand resting on his denim jeans. "No, you're better off not knowing."

"Won't you let me be the judge of that?"

"No. It's best if I—"

"—keep the secret?" she interjected. "Neither one of us knows what the future holds. I may be going back to where I belong any day now, possibly any minute. You're getting better so you won't need me much longer."

I DO need you! The realization darted through his mind,

yet he remained silent, unable to voice his feelings when he could lose her in the wink of an eye.

"But what if I *don't* leave, Flynt?" The notion lifted his spirits. "What happens to me . . . to *us?* How can I have a relationship with you when I don't even know who you are?"

"You need only to know who I am today. My actions tell you of the man I am, not my past."

She shoved herself off the bed and threw her hands up in the air. "Fine! Shut me out," she fumed, her arms akimbo. "Maybe I should just go back to kitchen duty and forget I asked."

"Perhaps you should."

She marched back to her post, muttering under her breath in disgust. "Men . . ."

Women! he responded in his head. Why must they meddle in affairs that are not their own? Why must they poke and prod for every tidbit, every detail? Never satisfied to leave well enough alone.

"I am going out for some fresh air," he groused, lowering his legs to the floor. "I will be checking on the mare should you be in need of me."

"I won't need anything."

Except a full accounting of my sordid past, he thought bitterly, walking slowly to the door.

After Flynt satisfied his concern for Yola and her colt, he gave Sasti proper attention, then wandered to the uphill path leading from the rear of the cabin. He didn't venture far, only a short distance so he would be within the sound of Kate's call. There was a fallen log on which he had often sat during the months following his wife's disappearance, unable to deal with the empty cabin that had reminded him too much of her.

His pant legs brushed through low-growing five-finger ferns and young shoots from sprouted acorns. The warm spring weather had melted all but a few remnants of snow under the protective shadow of the sugar pines and Douglas fir. A carpet of dense clover surrounded the log, much of it in blooms of white puffballs. He lowered himself to the ground and used the thick oak log for a backrest. Allowing the sights and sounds and smells to soothe his soul, he sat silent and listened. In the distance, the faint trickle of Sweetbrier Creek came to him through the trees. All around were the conversations of birds he had come to recognize over the years—little towhees and juncos, musical warblers and thrushes. His gaze roamed the secluded haven, settling upon a nearby rock where a chipmunk paused, blinked, and scampered off. It reappeared an instant later, an acorn in its jowls. Flynt smiled at it before it darted away once more. He waited for its return but it didn't come back.

He sighed heavily. Would he one day find himself sitting here after Kate left? Would he wait for her return as he'd done with Little Deer? He thought of those weeks after her disappearance when he'd wondered if his wife had been taken away by white men like his father. He thought of his father, the noble Englishman who appointed himself guardian of a young half-breed Wintu girl of thirteen. Lies and deceit—all of it.

Flynt had struggled to put the pieces of his shattered life back together when he had lost all hope. Everything had come tumbling down on him like a house of cards. Years of deception by his father had left him dazed and confused. His only solace was the knowledge that he had begun a new life in the Cascades with the young wife that he loved. But when he had lost her there seemed to be nothing left to live for.

Flynt heard a twig snap. His head jerked around.

Kate.

Dear, sweet, wonderful Kate, he mused with affectionate sarcasm. Sweet was hardly the temperament he had encountered nine times out of ten. Nonetheless, his response to her presence was as sweet as any he could well imagine.

She spoke in a hushed tone as if his sanctuary were as sacred as any cathedral. "I was worried."

"I must not have heard you call."

"I didn't."

"How did you find me? Has SnowEagle taught you a few tricks?"

She approached, a tender smile on her lips. "Just luck."

He gazed at the sensible black shoes she'd acquired through the Walker sisters' generosity. "I was thinking about my past."

"I'm sorry if I stirred up bad memories." She knelt beside him. "I have no right to ask. You have no obligation to me. If I can't go back home, I'll go to Dunsmuir to live with Rita and Lou. And if we're meant to have any sort of relationship, we'll start fresh and do it proper—the way people do in the nineteenth century."

"Twice you have referred to a 'relationship' as if there is something other than marriage under consideration. With me, they are one and the same. If you want to be courted, please say so."

She smiled, then pulled it back with little to no success. "Yes," she answered with a small modicum of seriousness. "If I stay, I would like to be . . . courted."

He felt a grin tug at the corners of his mouth. "Isn't that rather like closing the barn door after the horse has run off?"

"You could say that."

"I believe I just did."

Her guileless expression positively enamored him. Dropping her gaze, she quietly admitted, "I just don't want to end up a wife by default."

Wife? Yes, he had offered as much. And she deserved as much. But by default?

"If—and I do mean an emphatic *if*—I were to marry you I certainly would not do so out of some misguided sense of duty."

"I'm not so sure."

He reached up and smoothed his fingertips across her furrowed brow. "I could never take the sacred vow of marriage unless I could solemnly promise to love, honor and cherish my wife. This is my sense of duty that I carry with me."

"Your parents must've been proud of you."

"Wherever would you get such an idea?" he scoffed. "It is in spite of my parents that I have become who I am."

"And who is that exactly—the recluse or the gentleman?"

"Both," he snapped, then checked his temper. He looked at her warily. "You have made your point. I will tell you about my past. And you will understand what makes me such a puzzle today."

Chapter 13

As Flynt sat with Kate next to him in the woods, he revealed the story of his father, a wealthy world traveler who sought adventure and prosperity to add to his riches in Britain, where his arranged marriage had produced two daughters. In his mid-forties, he traveled through the Cascades with a company of hunters, staying at an inn near Soda Springs. He was introduced to SnowEagle, one of only a handful of Northern Wintun Indians remaining in the upper reaches of their territory. Often accompanying the shaman was his daughter's child, a girl of thirteen. The Englishman befriended her, teaching his language to her. His stories of London captured her fancy. When his extended visit ended, she left with him.

Kate asked, "Your father didn't kidnap her?"

"She went willingly. You see, she was half white. Her father was a trapper who had abandoned her and her mother when she was small. She wanted to see the white man's world. She wanted to fit in with her father's people. I imagine she expected to be taken into my father's house as his ward to be raised with his two daughters and introduced into polite society. Instead, he ensconced her in a modest house far from his own family yet close enough for his regular visits. Within a year, I was born. He convinced her to relinquish me to his lawful wife to be raised as his proper heir rather than a bastard. No one knew of the arrangement. Not even I was aware that my father's wife was not my real mother. I never saw the half-breed girl. She died in childbirth two years later."

At eighteen, Flynt had voyaged to America with his father, who sought new medicinal herbs to patent in England. Without knowledge of his own mixed blood, he felt mysteriously attracted to the quiet Wintu, especially the old shaman. He quickly learned to communicate with them and adopted their spiritual teachings. His father berated him for his fascination, warning him not to become too enamored with the exotic heathens, especially a particular young woman.

"Satisfy your curiosity with her," his father had said to Flynt at the time. "But you are forbidden to marry her."

The girl of whom he spoke was not yet fourteen, four years younger than Flynt.

He said to Kate, "We were friends and nothing more. I was appalled by my father's suggestion. I had no knowledge that he had bedded my mother at that same young age."

Returning to England, he spent a full year trying to find his niche in his father's vast business ventures, but grew disillusioned with his life in London, often dreaming of the Cascades and longing to return someday. He held back from Kate the details of his randy forays into British society. An eligible bachelor amid smitten young ladies was a lethal mix, made all the more dangerous by marriage-minded mothers in pursuit of a wealthy match for their daughters. No, Kate did not need to hear about those conquests and narrow escapes. Nor the dalliances with wedded socialites; he had found trouble among them, as well.

He bypassed the sown wild oats and told her of his return to California at the age of twenty-three. "SnowEagle welcomed me, as did the dear young friend who had grown into a woman in my absence. She had not chosen a husband but had waited for my return. The shaman blessed our marriage but soon came to me with a vision of great sorrow on the horizon."

Kate spoke up. "Are his visions always right?"

"I have never known him to be wrong, though sometimes he may not have all the information to interpret it entirely. With Little Deer, he told her about our baby before she knew of her condition. But he took me aside and warned me of an unknown danger that loomed like a dark cloud over my wife and child."

"He didn't know what it was?"

Flynt shook his head. "Several months later I received a delayed letter summoning me to England by request of my father's company. He had died suddenly, leaving no one at the helm except his tyrannical widow and bickering daughters. Little Deer was in no condition to travel, awaiting the birth of our child. I feared for her safety, as well, imagining the dark cloud of danger that SnowEagle had prophesied. But I felt a certain obligation to make arrangements for the company to continue until I could return to England with my family in two to three months.

"I left Little Deer in SnowEagle's care and went to San Francisco where I had acquaintances with legal expertise. Through their law firm, I received a solicitor's letter informing me that my stepmother intended to protect the

Avery holdings for the rightful heirs—her two daughters. This letter also revealed my illegitimate birth by the Wintu girl."

Flynt told Kate that he made arrangements with allies to thwart his stepmother's manipulative efforts until he could arrive. But when he returned to his cabin in the Cascades, he discovered his wife had disappeared. After eight weeks of searching, he was told by SnowEagle to stop, that Little Deer would not be found. Numb with grief and exhausted from his endless wandering through the mountains, he reluctantly left for England to fulfill his duties to the companies in his name.

In 1886, he came back to Northern California on the newly completed Southern Pacific Rail Road. During his two-year absence, he had fought for and won his financial inheritance, then transferred his assets to San Francisco, investing in numerous business ventures. He was intent upon escaping the ugliness of civilization, but he still returned twice a year to meet with his associates and purchase supplies for his reclusive livelihood in the mountains.

"There you have it, Kate—I am nothing more than the bastard son of a rich Englishman and his half-breed mistress."

"Do you think I hold it against you for something your father did? Or for the fact that you are one-quarter Native American?"

"Is that what you call Indians—Native Americans?"

"It's considered 'politically correct' but some choose to be known as Native Indians or Native Peoples. Unfortunately, there's still poverty and unfair treatment—to a lesser extent, but it's still there. But the renewed pride in their cultures has brought about the National Museum of the American Indian, a part of the Smithsonian."

"You seem quite knowledgeable."

"Far from it," she confessed. "I was invited to a seminar at the Southwest Museum a few years ago. Two of my clients helped organize a program, 'Native Americans in the Media,' and thought I'd find it helpful. It opened my eyes."

Flynt looked at her for a long time. "So it is respected to be of Native American heritage?"

"Revered by many, actually. People visit places such as Arizona and New Mexico to learn more about the spirituality of various tribes. There's quite a number who want to understand their connection to the earth, to nature, to other living things. They are finally realizing that Native Americans have had the inside scoop all along. Some Indians resent it, saying whites are stealing the sacred traditions. But some see it as an opportunity to educate the rest of the world. Like SnowEagle has been teaching you."

"It's different—he knew I was one of his own. He had sensed all along that I was his great-grandson."

"Somehow I think he would have taught you anyway. He could have rejected you because your father took your mother away from her people."

"He saw her leave. He knew it was her choice, the path she was meant to take. The Wintu do not carry animosity. They see deeper meanings and seek peaceful methods to solve their differences. Negotiation. Bartering their possessions. It is not about hatred."

"No wonder they've practically vanished."

"Not entirely vanished. They live in small numbers. Or marry into the white culture or into other tribes like the Shasta or Modoc, who used to be their enemies." He thought of her answers and grew puzzled. "You do indeed come from a different time and place if you say that there is no shame to be Indian."

Her hand reached up and stroked his chin. "I wish you could come back with me and see it. You'd be fascinated by everything that has changed in a hundred years. Cars. Airplanes. All the big, tall buildings and—"

"What's wrong?"

"Did you say you have all your money tied up in businesses in San Francisco?"

"Yes. I have invested in a few lucrative establishments."

"Sell them," she said emphatically. "Or else move them to another city."

"Why in thunder would I want to sell my perfectly fine business ventures?"

Kate warned him about the earthquake and the devastating aftermath of fire that would happen in 1906. "You could lose everything if you don't do something about it now."

"I have already lost all that mattered to me once before in my life. And it was not money. I could lose all of my assets tomorrow and it would not change how I live. But I am beginning to wonder if I lost you tomorrow, if you returned home as you so desperately hope to do—" He gazed at her. The words stuck fast in his throat as he realized how long it had been since he spoke the feelings of his heart. "I wonder . . . if I could endure losing you."

Kate leaned forward and kissed his lips. He slipped his arms around her waist and gently pulled her onto his lap. He had not meant to be swept away once more, yet he saw it happening and was loath to stop it. He unbuttoned her blouse and chemise, then dipped his head to suckle her breast. The sound of her groan hardened his shaft, pressing it against the confines of his trousers. He slipped his hand beneath her skirt. His fingers skimmed up her bare thigh.

Finding no evidence of underdrawers, he lifted his head

and looked into her green eyes with a wry smile on his face. "You shameless wench."

She laughed at her own bawdiness, then gasped in delight as he caressed the soft folds of her femininity. He covered her mouth with his own as he continued to touch and tease her intimately. Soon he felt her body reach its zenith of sexual pleasure. She cried out his name. He wanted nothing more than to be inside her at that moment. But he held back, eager for the day when he could utilize all his strength and more.

She kissed him then with a lazy passion that spoke to him of her sated appetite. As her tongue did delicious things to his mouth, she shifted around on his lap until her knees were tucked neatly on either side of his hips. Her hand wandered to his waistband, unfastened it and freed him.

"You needn't," he offered, though he prayed she would.

"Shhh."

She touched him and stroked him. His fingers squeezed her buttocks, kneading the firm flesh. She rose on her knees, bringing her breasts to his mouth. He caressed one rosy nipple with his tongue, circling it. Then taking it between his lips, he tugged gently, eliciting her moan of approval.

In their quiet wooded sanctuary, on a bed of clover, Kate made love to him for the second time that day.

The following afternoon, Flynt awoke from a short rest to find the cabin empty. He found Kate outside with the new mother and foal. She was dressed in a pair of new denim jeans which fit snugly across her hips. The only concession to her femininity was the long-sleeved yellow cotton blouse. Though unadorned with lace or other frills, it was tapered from her full breasts to her narrow waist, accentuating her womanly curves.

He watched her with the frisky colt, both seemingly fascinated with the novelty of one another. The little one's ungainly antics prompted laughter from her that absolutely charmed him. One particular moment of amusement got the better of him and he snickered. Her head twisted around and she saw him standing there. Though she scolded him for sneaking around behind her back, she didn't mean a word of it—not from the way her eyes twinkled and danced.

He came to her side, walking a tad more ably than the day before. Kneeling with caution for his wound, he kissed her lightly, resisting the temptation to start another romp. Then he turned his attention to the colt, stroking the chestnut coat.

"What are you going to name him?"

"I avoid names. 'Boy' or 'Girl' has always sufficed in the past."

"She's had others?"

"Of course. I keep them only until it's time to sell them."

"Then you'll be selling this one, too?"

"I must," he answered, "I have no need for a corral of horses to feed."

"Then why do you keep Yola?"

"Purely sentimental, I'm afraid. She was my wedding gift to Little Deer."

"Oh."

"Now I have spoiled your good spirits. Perhaps I should consider selling her, as well. She could go with her colt."

"You wouldn't do that to Sasti."

He grinned, shaking his head at her concern for the beasts. "You may very well have a valid point. Sasti would be miserable indeed if I sent away his lady love. It might break his heart."

"Quit teasing me," she said, nudging him with her shoulder. He teetered, and lightly fell to his side, feigning hurt. "Are you all right?"

Flynt snagged her about the waist and pulled her down to him. She squawked in protest but quickly gave up her fight when he cupped the back of her head and brought her closer for a kiss. Their playful interlude was short lived, however, as the curious colt poked his velvet nose in their faces.

"Cut it out, Romeo," pleaded Kate with a laugh, pushing herself off Flynt. "Romeo—there's a name for him!"

"You can't possibly be serious."

She beamed at him innocently. "I guess not."

In the waning hours of the afternoon, Kate read aloud from the book Flynt had mentioned reading a few years earlier. The title, *Looking Backward,* was enough to send an eerie quiver down her spine. In the story, the nineteenth-century narrator awakens to find himself in Boston of the year 2000. As she read his fascinating depictions of a futuristic American utopia, she often paused to explain to Flynt the inaccuracy regarding the socialist government. However, other seemingly insignificant details to the story were surprisingly prophetic. She had to keep reminding herself that the Bellamy novel had been published in *eighteen* eighty-eight.

"He actually talks about credit cards!" she mused, explaining the slight difference between the author's version and the real thing in the late twentieth century. "You would think he might have actually gone into the future himself."

"Perhaps he did."

She glanced at Flynt, wondering if he was humoring her. He was eyeing her with a gleam that quickened her pulse. Lord, he was more irresistible than chocolate. Thoughts of the book vanished as she gazed at him resting on the bed, his blond hair tied back. She recalled the way it had looked in the woods when they had made love—loose and flowing over his broad shoulders. When he had dipped his head, his hair fell across her breasts in its own intimate caress.

Putting the book aside, she got up from the chair by the table where the lantern had aided her reading. Going to his bed, she felt the unmistakable stirring deep inside. "At the rate we're going, you will never regain your strength."

"On the contrary," he said, taking her hand as she stood beside him. He kissed her palm, then drew her down next to him. "You are just the tonic I need for a hasty recovery."

Kate let her body melt against him. If this was a dream, she never wanted to wake up. It was too wonderful to believe that she'd actually found peace and contentment in a rustic backwoods cabin, let alone in a whole different century. For the first time in her life, she felt genuinely alive, not just existing from day to day. Flynt only had to look at her and her skin tingled, her body craved his touch.

A light *tap-tap* at the door made her jump. She scrambled out of the low-slung mattress, buttoning her blouse and cursing her clumsy hands. His chuckle brought her head up. "Quit laughing," she muttered.

"It's only SnowEagle."

"Only?! I don't want him to think—"

"He won't *think*, he'll *know*."

Flynt was undoubtedly right. The clairvoyant shaman probably had them pegged for lovers from the day he walked into the cabin and saw Kate for the first time. Walking toward the door, she smoothed her skirt and combed her fingers through her hair the best she could. With her hand on the latch, she glanced back at Flynt.

"Do I look presentable?" His mischievous gleam sent a ripple of desire into her lower belly. "I shouldn't have asked."

True to his word, SnowEagle had returned with more fish to fry for dinner. Kate welcomed him into the cabin, taking the string of trout from him as she thanked him.

"I cleaned them for you," he told her, giving her a wink. "To save you the trouble."

"Bless you."

Flynt had remained in the bed, but propped himself against his folded coat. "What is that bag you're carrying?"

His great-grandfather lifted the black bag from his left side and handed it to Kate.

"My purse!" She lit up like a five-year-old at the sight of saltwater taffy. Depositing the fish on the trestle table beneath the window, she quickly took the satchel. "Where'd you find it?"

"Under the bushes at the riverbank."

"Thank you so much." She fairly glowed with gratitude, then turned toward the bed. "Look, Flynt!"

He watched her bring the black leather bag over to the bed and turn it upside down, dumping the contents onto his lap. A thick book landed on his thigh.

"Ow!"

"Sorry. That's my organizer. My whole life is packed into this thing."

She picked it up and yanked open the flap with a ripping sound. But upon closer examination, he saw that nothing had torn. On the contrary, there was a fuzzy square of cloth on one side and a stiff nubby swatch on the other. He touched them inquisitively.

"Velcro," she said, then pulled out several small cards. "Credit cards."

Flynt took one and studied it. *Looking Backward* had depicted the purchase of merchandise with a credit card, and here in his hand was just such a item from the future.

"Positively amazing." He touched the raised letters of her name and a series of numbers, then turned it over and over.

"And here's my driver's license. See . . . my picture, my name, my birthday, my height, my weigh—oh, forget that. It's wrong anyway."

She rummaged through the organizer, showing both Flynt and SnowEagle the odds and ends of her life. A flat pad was described as a "solar calculator" which functioned as an intelligent adding machine through the use of a "photocell," whatever that was. Most of the gadgets held little or no meaning for Flynt. SnowEagle was amused by the pocketknife on her key ring, however. At least it was something useful. Not like a list of addresses of people who did not yet exist. Not like a calendar with appointments a hundred years away.

When Kate flipped to a section of small, colorful photographs, she pulled them out and presented them to Flynt.

"This is my family—my best friends, actually. Sunni is the woman on the left. Michael is the man on the right."

She had spoken of Sunni and Michael a few times during their conversations at the boarding house. In the picture, Sunni wore an extremely short skirt and a tight blouse—if it could be called such a thing. Her golden hair was a voluminous cloud of soft curls. And her eyes were shadowed with the same sort of cosmetics that he'd seen on Kate when he'd found her.

"So this is Michael," he finally said, gazing at the handsome dark-haired gentleman. "He's the one you're supposed to marry?"

"No. He's the one who asked. I didn't give him an answer."

"He's quite dapper. Is this the style of men's clothing in your time?" His finger tapped the image of Michael in a suit.

"For those who can afford it. It's Armani."

"I thought you said it was Michael."

"The suit is an Arman—never mind." She took the pictures from him, shuffled them and handed one back. "That's the three of us at the beach."

He jerked his head back at the sight of the near-naked bodies, one of which was Kate's, though she was more modestly covered than her friends. He scrutinized the scraps of shimmery pink cloth discreetly placed over minute portions of Sunni's anatomy, while Kate wore a clinging black fabric that clothed her from neck to thigh. This was straitlaced Katherine, the attorney? Next to her stood Michael in brightly colored baggy pants that were cut short. His arm was draped protectively around Kate's waist.

Her betrothed, he told himself with no small amount of jealousy. Despite Kate's denial, he suspected that she would undoubtedly return to the twentieth century and accept his proposal of marriage. And there wasn't a bloody thing Flynt could do about it. Resisting the urge to crumple the glossy paper in his hand, he wished he could give her a reason not to return to Michael, who could offer her the one thing the Avery fortune could not buy—her own life one hundred years in the future.

He went through the half dozen color photographs one by one. Seeing these snippets of her life, he began to realize all that she had left behind. How could he expect her to give up so much to stay here with him? Even if he bought a grand home in San Francisco, it would not have the inventions she was accustomed to. She would not have the freedom to dress as she pleased, without the restrictive attire of today's fashions. Nor would she mold herself into the acceptable role of submissive and fragile society matron. He would be fooling himself to believe she would be happy with him. Handing the pictures back to her, he turned to SnowEagle, who had been curiously inspecting a foldaway brush.

"Would you be willing to show Kate where you found her purse?"

The old man paused in toying with the brush. "If she wishes."

Kate quickly leaped into the conversation, giving Flynt a quizzical look. "I'd rather not bother SnowEagle. It's a long way—"

"You can ride Sasti."

"But I have fish to fry."

"I'm capable of cooking."

"But you shouldn't be left alone. Not yet."

"What harm can come to me in my own cabin?"

Uncertainty flickered across her face. "I won't leave you."

"Go."

"What if—" Her green eyes shone bright with sudden tears. "What if something happens while I'm there? What if I'm taken home?"

"That is what you want, isn't it?"

"No—I mean, yes!" She got up and paced the floor like a nervous cat. "You aren't fully recovered and besides—"

"Kate?"

She stopped in midstride, pivoting toward him. "Yes?"

"Let SnowEagle do as I asked. If you are meant to return to your own home, it would be best for both of us if we did not try to prolong the inevitable."

Her chin wobbled as she tore her gaze away.

SnowEagle rose from the chair he had occupied during their discussion. "I will saddle Sasti."

When he departed, the cabin fell into silence. Kate kept her back to Flynt, her head bowed. He picked up the black leather bag next to his leg and quietly refilled it with her personal items.

"You'll need this," he said finally, holding it out to her.

She slowly turned around as she scrubbed a stream of tears from her cheek. The sight of her sorrow mirrored his own. The piercing pain in the center of his chest was infinitely worse than the stab of the hunting knife he'd taken in his gut.

"Come kiss me good-bye," he gently commanded.

"SnowEagle said there would be no good-bye."

"All the more reason to say it."

"Saying good-bye will keep me here? That makes about as much sense as a rooster crowing at the moon."

A small grin crept across his mouth. "Let me guess—that would be something Miss Rita would say."

She gave a soft, short chuckle. "Miss Louzana, actually."

Flynt levered himself out of the deep mattress as she came across the room. He wrapped his arms around her and held her tightly. Her cheek pressed against his chest. The crown of her head tucked perfectly under his chin. He drew a deep and difficult breath, holding the scent of her in his lungs until he couldn't hold it any longer. His spirits, which had soared so high less than an hour earlier, now plummeted mercilessly.

I love you, Kate. The poignant words echoed in his mind but he could not speak them aloud. He would sooner die than capture her heart and tether her to a time that was not her own. Keeping her here would be too cruel, like caging a mountain lion. In his dreams he had seen her again as the cougar watching over him in his sleep. It was time he woke up and sent her on her way.

In the language of his great-grandfather, he murmured to her the thoughts of his heart. She lifted her head and leaned back, looking up at him with question in her eyes.

"Tell me what you said." The sweet plea in her voice curled around his soul with the tendrils of a morning glory.

"It was merely a Wintu blessing, wishing you a safe journey, Cougar-Woman."

As her gaze scrutinized him for a long moment, he hoped she could not see the lie that it was. He lowered his mouth to hers, kissing her tenderly. She responded with a hunger that he had no hope of satisfying.

With tremendous effort, he pulled away. "SnowEagle will be waiting for you." *So will I. Come back to me, Kate.*

"I don't know how to thank you—"

"You already have. More than you know. Go now."

"Good-bye, Flynt." She reached up to his cheek, wiping a wayward tear. He turned his head and pressed his lips into her palm. For an instant he held his breath, his eyelids squeezed tight, gathering his strength to let her walk out of his life.

He finally opened his eyes and gazed down at her. "Good-bye, Kate."

At the river, Kate stood on the crest of the embankment with SnowEagle. There were spots of snow where there hadn't been before. Wildflowers sprung up in random places but not in a pattern she could recognize from her first visit. And the surrounding trees seemed just as thick and just as tall as she remembered him. But then, she really hadn't paid close attention to such things when she had parked her car and wandered through the woods. She looked down the slope to the water's edge, searching for the familiar boulder.

SnowEagle asked, "Do you recognize anything?"

She shook her head. "The river is higher and much faster than when I was here."

"The snow is melting."

"I think I see the rock I sat on." She pointed to a ruffle of white water where the river rushed over and around the granite. SnowEagle nodded.

She felt an odd prickly sensation at the base of her neck. Turning quickly, she glanced in all directions, then realized the shaman was observing her queer behavior.

"I can't seem to shake this feeling that somebody is watching me. Not all the time but just now. . . ." She looked over her shoulder. "Do you feel it?"

Before the Wintu could reply, a sound in the bushes drew their attention. The Frenchman stepped into view with a rifle cradled in the crook of his elbow.

Kate tensed as her stomach lurched.

Chapter 14

"BONJOUR, MES AMIS," he greeted, a sickeningly sweet smile lifting his black mustache. A classic Tarantino slimeball, she thought, wondering once again if this wasn't all a nightmare that she'd formulated from her Hollywood backlot upbringing.

SnowEagle responded to Blackjack with a calm demeanor and a few French words, which surprised Kate. LeBouche, too. His eyebrows shot up, then dipped into a scowl.

"Where is *Monsieur* Avery, eh?" He fingered the trigger of his rifle as he craned his neck to scan the vicinity.

Thank God Flynt didn't come with us, she thought with an inward sigh of relief. She eyed the weapon, wishing she had something for protection against him. An Uzi came to mind, despite the fact that she'd never in her life advocated violent resolutions.

"Flynt is fishing downriver," she said, hoping her lie would keep Blackjack away from the cabin.

"And you are alone, *n'est-ce-pas?*"

"No, as you can plainly see."

"Bah! This old Digger Indian? You need a proper chaperon."

"And I suppose you're offering your services?"

"That is exactly what I think."

"No thanks," she answered without hiding her hatred for the man. "I'm doing just fine."

His eyes narrowed. "Behave, *mon chou,* and you will not be hurt." He waved the serious end of the barrel at the Wintu, motioning him to move off. Stark fear sliced down the center of her body. When the shaman did not go, Blackjack strode toward them. His dark glare left no doubt as to his malevolent intentions. Kate stepped backward, slowly shaking her head.

Run!

The voice in her head catapulted her into action. She bolted into the woods, drawing him away from SnowEagle. But it wasn't the old man that Blackjack wanted. She knew in her gut that he was chasing her down. Swatting branches out of her way, she crashed through the forest, wishing for a pair of running shoes instead of the stiff work shoes.

Don't look back.

But she did. The Frenchman was gaining on her. Pouring all her strength into a last-ditch effort, she sprinted toward Sasti, snatched his reins and stabbed the toe of her shoe into the stirrup. Clutching the saddle horn, she yanked herself upward.

Her head jerked back. Blackjack had grabbed her by the hair, pulling her down from the horse.

"*No*—!" she screamed, struggling against him. With his tight grip on the hair at the base of her skull, she couldn't turn and fight. Sasti nickered and shied away from the skirmish.

Blackjack yanked her around to face him. His eyes burned with anger. Winded from his pursuit, he spat words in rapid French. Cursing her, no doubt. She didn't need a translator. He was telling her exactly what he planned to do to her.

"I swear to God you're going to pay for this."

He laughed at her insipid display of courage. "I pay for nothing. I never paid for that Digger wife of the squawman."

"Y-you did this to Little Deer?"

"*Oui*. She was very good. But too fat—" He glanced down her body. "—not like you, *mon petite*."

"She was eight months pregnant, you son of a bitch." She tried a quick knee to the groin, but he was quicker than her, shoving her away from him. She stumbled backward, landing on her backside on a pile of dried leaves and pine needles.

He pointed the rifle at her chest. "Undress."

She froze.

"*Maintenant!*"

"Okay, okay," she said hastily, tugging at the laces of one shoe. The new leather was stiff and tight and didn't want to loosen under her fumbling fingers. When he made a threatening step toward her, she worked harder and got the shoe off. The other one proved just as stubborn but finally gave way. "Did you kill Little Deer, too?"

"She . . . fell into a ravine. Perhaps you will, too." He watched her hands move to the top buttons of her blouse. Her fingers shook so badly she didn't think she could manage.

Please God, just let me get out of this alive!

His expression changed to a puzzled frown as she peeled her shirt off her shoulders, revealing her white lace bra rather than a Victorian camisole. She unfastened her jeans and slipped them down her legs. His eyebrows darted upward at the sight of her bikini briefs. Pine needles pricked her buttocks through the satin. She had a sudden image of herself lying on this bed of pins with the Frenchman on top of her. Revulsion and fear gripped her. She let her hands drop to her lap, refusing to finish the job.

"*Refusez-moi?*" he said in disgust at her lack of cooperation. "*Quel dommage*—What a pity. I take you anyway."

Blackjack came toward her, unbuckling his belt with one hand as he kept steady aim with the other. She felt the now-familiar tingling on the back of her neck. With a furtive glance, she sought a pair of watchful eyes upon them. There was no one, she realized with a sinking feeling of despair.

Averting her gaze from the gun barrel leveled on her, she focused on some pale pink flowers blooming next to a rock. In all the years she'd lived in crime-infested Los Angeles, she had always been cautious, always careful, always grateful that she had not been a victim of violence. Her less fortunate friends had told her that it was simply a matter of time. Now it was about to happen a hundred years in the past with a celluloid villain in a pine-scented forest among the pale pink flowers.

And there wasn't a damn thing she could do about it. Not while there was a gun to her head.

Cold steel touched her temple. She flinched. He chuckled, pressing harder with the muzzle of the rifle until she was forced onto her back. Keeping her head turned aside, she refused to watch him standing over her, his feet planted between her ankles. Out of the corner of her eye, she saw him kneel.

The gun barrel touched her chin, skimmed down her neck, over her bra and navel. It rested there as his fingers traced the delicate elastic lace trim of her panties. Her breathing became shallow. Her heart slammed against her chest.

With a jerk of his hand, the cloth ripped. "*Bon!* You make this easy for me, *oui?*" he murmured, drawing the rifle lower on her belly. She heard the clink of his belt buckle as he opened his pants.

She squeezed her eyes shut. *No . . . dear God, no . . .*

The sensation of cold metal suddenly vanished from her skin as she heard a gasp of surprise. Her eyelids flew open. The man stared straight ahead in wide-eyed terror, his skin ghostly white. The rifle dropped to the ground beside her. Shaking his head violently, he crossed himself, babbling in French. In the next instant, he was scrambling away on his hands and knees. Half sobbing, half screaming, he managed to get to his feet after three bad falls, pull his trousers up from his ankles and run hysterically into the woods.

Curbing her own impulse to jump into her clothes and hightail it out of there, Kate was scared to attract the attention of whatever was out there. She lay motionless for several moments, wondering if it was a bear or mountain lion. She listened, hearing nothing more than the distant wail of the distraught Frenchman crashing through the bushes. If a wild animal had been a few yards away, why didn't he use his rifle?

She slowly rose up on one elbow, then cautiously peered over her shoulder. Whatever he'd seen—it was gone. She collapsed onto her back. Her eyes stared at the blue sky overhead as tears of relief trickled down into her hair. She didn't know how or what had saved her, but she was grateful just the same.

On the highest branches of an evergreen, a branch dipped and swayed. She squinted, focusing her gaze on the treetop. The white crest of a bald eagle caught the light of the late afternoon sun. The enormous predator swiveled its head back and forth, surveying its territory. It looked downward in its search for food.

"Don't even think about it," she muttered to the bird. Wiping her face dry, she chuckled morosely to herself at the absurdity of her comment. To a damn eagle, of all things. But at least she was alive to laugh at herself.

After Kate quickly dressed, she realized Sasti had disappeared and assumed the horse had instinctively headed back to the cabin. Wasn't that the standard M.O. in Westerns?

"Trigger always stuck around for Roy," she groused under her breath, kicking a stone with the toe of her shoe. Such perfect little scenarios only happened in Tinseltown, and then only after twenty-one takes.

Accepting the fact that they'd have to hike to the cabin, she went back toward the riverbank in search of the shaman. SnowEagle sat cross-legged with a wad of moss pressed to his temple.

"His gunstock," the old man explained as Kate inspected the bloody cut. "He knocked me out."

"The horse is gone. Can you walk?"

"I can walk. Where is the Frenchman? Did he hurt you?"

She gave him a brief run-down on the close call with Blackjack, leaving out the seedier details.

"I am glad you are safe."

"That makes two of us," she answered, scanning the area for her purse, which she'd lost in the confusion. She retrieved it and helped SnowEagle to his feet. "Come on. We've got to get home before it gets too dark to find our way."

*   *   *

When SnowEagle and Kate emerged into the clearing of the cabin, Sasti was coming toward them with Flynt in the saddle. He stopped the horse in front of them and quickly dismounted, still showing favor to his injuries. Kate kept a steady hand under the old man's elbow, but held her other hand out to Flynt.

"I was on my way out to look for you two," he said, as her arm went around his waist and she hugged him. His tender embrace restored a small sense of security. She felt safe again. "I was resting and didn't realize Sasti had returned without you until I came outside just this moment."

He pulled back and held her at arm's length, scanning her from head to toe. His gaze darted to SnowEagle holding the lump of moss to his temple. "What happened?"

Kate touched his arm in an attempt to calm him. "If you'll quit babbling for a second, I'll tell you."

"I do not babble," he barked. She couldn't get angry with him, knowing his temper stemmed from worry.

"No, of course you don't," she placated. "Let's go inside."

On the way into the cabin, SnowEagle spoke in Wintu that she couldn't understand. But the red-faced anger from Flynt was evidence enough that he had learned of the attack. He slammed the door wide open, yet controlled his temper long enough to help Kate see the shaman to the single chair.

"LeBouche!" Flynt rounded on his heel and came at Kate, grabbing her by the shoulders. She let her heavy bag fall to the dirt floor. "What did he do to you?" His voice was rough and ragged with the strain of holding back his rage. "Tell me, Kate! Did he violate you?"

"No."

His midnight-blue eyes were dark with fury. His gaze narrowed. "The truth, dammit! You're holding something back—I can see it."

"I'm not holding anything back," she lied, unwilling to reveal the knowledge of his wife's fate at the hands of the Frenchman. "He tried to rape me but—"

"I swear to all that is holy I will kill the bastard!"

"Flynt, you're hurting me!"

Instantly, his fingers loosened their grip and he pulled her into his arms, apologizing profusely. She finished explaining, "Something scared LeBouche so bad that he dropped his gun and took off running."

"Where is it?" he asked, leaning back to see her face. "Did you bring it back with you?"

"I was in too big of a hurry looking for Sasti and SnowEagle." *Not to mention getting dressed.* Flynt didn't need to know how far the rape attempt had progressed before it was interrupted. He was already mad enough to commit murder—with good reason. Her sudden thought startled her. She of all people knew damn well that killing Blackjack would not be considered justifiable homicide. In a courtroom, Avery would not stand a snowball's chance in hell, as Lou was known to say.

"You will not go back there without me, do you understand?"

Kate stepped back, rubbing her sore arms. "LeBouche won't try anything again. I doubt he'll ever set foot within a hundred yards of that place after what happened today."

"Nor will you. Not unless I accompany you."

His brusque, authoritative manner was understandable, considering the circumstances. But it ruffled her feathers all the same. Little by little, she felt like her independent identity of the twentieth century was slowly eroding away. Soon she would be barefoot and pregnant—God forbid!

"I will not end up as a porcelain doll kept safe and out of harm's way on a curio shelf," she stated to Flynt, then glanced around the shabby interior. Maybe there wasn't a curio shelf. And maybe she would end up looking more like Raggedy Ann than a delicate figurine. But it didn't change the way she felt about her personal freedom to come and go as she pleased.

Kate sat down on the short, stocky storage barrel that Flynt often used for a seat at the table. Close enough to SnowEagle to inspect his wound, she reached up to lower his hand but he did so on his own.

"The bleeding has stopped?" he asked, but it was more a statement than a question. The injury had looked far worse at the river. Now it seemed to be little more than a scratch.

"Yes . . . yes, it has." She studied the cut with awe. "But all the same, you should probably spend the night here. That was a nasty blow to the head."

"It is not necessary," answered the shaman. "I wish to return to my own bed. You do not need an old man underfoot."

"You won't be in the way. And you haven't eaten—"

"I shall leave after I eat."

Kate couldn't change his mind. After a meal of trout she had prepared by lantern light, SnowEagle went outside with Flynt. The tedious chore of cleaning up the sparse dishes seemed to take forever. Nothing about this life came easy. She had realized it soon enough. It was one thing to read about all the backbreaking work of a frontier woman while sitting in the comfort of her living room sofa. It was something else altogether to put every waking minute toward cooking and cleaning just to survive.

The lamp flickered shadows across the log walls as she dried her hands on a dingy towel. Her nails were filed down to nothing. Her skin was rough and red from daily chores.

She looked about at the crude accommodations which had been barely tolerable her first two weeks. Whenever the dirt and mud had started to drive her nuts, she had promised herself that a hot bubble bath was waiting for her at home. She had played the same fantasy with the food and cooking, vowing to treat herself to the most elaborate dinner at her favorite restaurant when she got back to Los Angeles. She'd managed to get through those weeks by remembering the inconvenience was only temporary. But now . . .

She plopped onto the seat of the chair, letting her hands hang limp between her knees. The trip to the river hadn't accomplished anything. There was no evidence of a passageway to the future. She had not been taken back. Perhaps she never would be.

There will be no good-bye.

SnowEagle had been right. Part of her was glad. The part that didn't want to lose Flynt. Her gaze fell to the floor beside her where they had first made love. The memory stirred the embers of feelings for the man who had been an intimidating Grizzly Adams only a few short weeks ago. Now she didn't want to imagine her life without him. But a part of her couldn't imagine living out the rest of her years in this cabin, either.

Taking a good hard look around, she wondered if she was strong enough to make it through the day-to-day trials and hardships of living in this century, especially in these rugged Cascades. She was spoiled and soft from all the amenities of her modern life. She would be lucky to last ten years.

Or less, if Blackjack ever caught her alone again.

The image of the attack came back to her with startling clarity, more vivid than the reality itself. The leer. The chase. The mouth of the gun barrel as big as a cannon. Reliving the terror, she cupped her hand over her mouth to hold back the choking sob. She began to rock forward and back. The chair creaked. She touched her temple where the cold steel had pressed against her skin.

Why was it coming back to her? Why now? She'd made it back to SnowEagle without falling apart. Together, they had walked all the way home without her losing it. She had cooked dinner and sat through the meal and felt only a peaceful sense of calm. The whimper seemed to come from somewhere else, yet it was her own voice emitting the anguished murmur of frightening despair.

"I can't do it." Her voice was reedy and thin. "I can't hold it together anymore."

"Kate?" She felt the warmth of brawny hands on her shoulders.

"I'm losing my mind. None of this is real, is it? *You're* not real."

"I *am* real—I assure you." He came around to her side and lifted her to her feet. She stared up into his blue eyes filled with worry. Her fingers touched the shadow of the day's growth of his beard. How could she feel him? How could she be experiencing any of this? For a while she had pretended that she could handle the strange and bizarre experience. Go with the flow. See where it would end. But this feeling of helplessness that engulfed her now was more than she could bear.

Her fingertips rested on his lower lip. He kissed them. She lifted her gaze to his, her throat tightening as if a noose were closing her windpipe. "I'm scared, Flynt."

"There's no need. I'm here with you. Forget about LeBouche."

She shook her head. "You don't understand . . . It's not just him. It's everything. It's this place—"

"We'll get another place. More suitable. A house. In the city, if you would prefer."

"But I don't fit in."

"I know it feels that way now. But think of yourself in a foreign country. You will adapt, I know you will. Look at how much you have already learned from me, from the Walker sisters. They said themselves that you are quick-witted and easy to teach. You can go back to them for more lessons."

"I was crazy to say all those things about moving in with Rita and Lou."

"I think so, too. You belong here with me."

She abruptly moved away. "I don't belong here at all."

"Nonsense." He stepped toward her. "You let me decide."

"I don't *want* you to decide what's best for me. That's the problem. I'm used to deciding for myself what I need to do, when I come and go, where I live, how I live, who I see. Do you have any idea what a culture shock this is for my brain? I don't know the first thing about taking care of myself in the nineteenth century where women were used up and worn out by the men who decided their fate."

"Then we shall make our home in the city where you'll not need to do any physical labor. You shall wear the finest French fashions, have tea with your society ladies and attend the opera."

She rolled her eyes heavenward. "You just don't get it, Avery."

"Apparently not." He looked bewildered.

Her shoulders slumped. "All those novels I've read about strong women who overcame all odds with sheer will and determination—that's not me. I keep falling down hills and getting myself in deep—" She bit back the last word. "Never mind."

Flynt went to the bed, retrieved the bearskin and let it settle on the floor next to the dark fireplace. The fire for their supper had burned down, leaving nothing but warm ashes. Taking a seat in the vacated chair, he shucked his boots, then his shirt. Kate eyed his silent ritual with suspicion.

"What are you doing?"

"Getting ready for bed." He came up to her, took her hand and led her to the pelt on the ground.

"I've just spilled my guts to you, and all you can think of is going to bed? What is it about you men, anyway? A woman gets too emotional and a man suddenly thinks the only solution must be sex? Is it a genetic guy thing?"

He chuckled, then leaned over and nuzzled her neck.

"Flynt!" admonished Kate, backing away. Her frustration escalated. "I can't believe you're doing this!"

He grinned impishly. She told herself not to fall for that little-boy smile. Not this time. After all, she was trying to make a point. He was not going to treat her like his Neanderthal bride. Uh-uh. Not her.

He took a step. She sidled away. He retreated.

"Good," she stated smugly. "This is exactly what I was talking about. . . ."

Her eyes watched him shed his jeans. He was definitely not playing fair. She tried not to appreciate his well-endowed physique as he walked to the trunk in the corner and casually dropped his pants on the closed lid.

Damn his hide.

Ignoring her, he grabbed a pillow and the remaining covers from the bed and brought them over to the bearskin. He stretched out on his back, propping his head up slightly. Only then did his gaze return to her. "Now then, what were you talking about—exactly?"

"I'm not coming down there."

He glanced at his arousal. "More's the pity."

"Why are you doing this to me?"

"To you?" The flat of his hand clapped against his chest in feigned modesty while the rest of his anatomy was exposed for all the world to see. Her, at least. "It is *you* who does this to *me*."

"That's a crock!"

"Crock, you say?"

"Knock it off, Avery."

"I may need your help to do so, I'm afraid." He lay there watching her with an impossibly devastating gleam in his eyes. Her insides heated up thirty degrees.

"Why can't you take me seriously?"

His facial expression suddenly sobered. "That is the crux, my dear Kate. I *do* take you seriously. For as long as you are here—and I do pray that will be a long, long while—I intend to show you exactly how deeply serious I am about you. Now be a sweetheart and come down here so I can make you feel safe and warm and thoroughly loved. Then perhaps you will know that you do indeed belong here . . . with me . . . for however much time we have together."

Kate felt her heart melt to her toes. Never in her life had she heard such beautiful things said to her. Not by anyone. "Oh God," she murmured, more to herself than to him. "You *are* too good to be real."

"As I said before—I *am* real." He held his hand out to her. "Let me show you."

Chapter 15

ONE WEEK SLIPPED into two, then four, then eight. The month of June brought warmer weather and the end of spring. With his full strength restored, Flynt set out before dawn to hunt deer with the rifle he'd kept over the mantel. In the tradition of his great-grandfather's people, he went to the river, to a place shown to him years ago that was considered sacred. He knelt in front of a granite rock, took a worn charm stone from his pocket and offered prayers to *Olelbis* for success in his hunt. The Wintu respected all life and could not take plant or animal without permission. When he finished, he bathed in the frigid waters, cleansing his body.

By midday, Flynt had shot a fine buck on the west ridge of the canyon near a small meadow. It would provide enough meat for SnowEagle as well. He rode Sasti to the bark house near a tributary and found the old man outside sitting cross-legged, a pipe of wild tobacco in his hands, his eyes closed. Quietly dismounting from the horse, Flynt lingered in the distance, reverently waiting for a sign to come forward. Previous visits had taught him that SnowEagle would not be surprised by the unexpected arrival of his great-grandson. On the contrary, the shaman would come out of his prayerful trace knowing that Flynt was nearby.

Today was no different.

SnowEagle opened his eyes, took a deep breath and said aloud, "The deer has died for you today as you have asked of it."

"Indeed, he has honored me," Flynt answered, stepping out of the forest shadows. He led Sasti forward with the carcass draped over the animal's rump. "There is enough for you."

After words of gratitude to the spirits of the mountain and sun and beasts of the forest, the two men began to prepare the meat, working side by side. After several minutes of talk about daily activities and other such mundane topics, SnowEagle began to speak of the knowledge he had received upon two separate occasions, one of which had been that morning during Flynt's arrival.

"*Patit-Pokta*—she is here to help you."

"As you have said already." Flynt drew his knife from its sheath.

"But she is on her own vision quest, as well. And she is not alone. The spirit of Little Deer is with her."

Flynt's head snapped up, surprised to hear the Wintu speak the name of the dead. "Are you saying my wife has come back?"

"Your wife has led this woman to you—to help all of you."

"I have often felt that the ghost of Little Deer has walked these mountains. I have even thought that I could feel her near me."

"That is because you did not destroy all of her belongings as is our way. You should have burned the clothing as I had instructed you to do.

"Now you say that her spirit has guided Kate to me?"

He nodded. "I tell you this because she is with *Patit-Pokta*, protecting her."

"Where was she when LeBouche attacked?" Flynt whisked his sharp blade through the flesh of the deer as if it were the throat of the Frenchman. "The bastard nearly raped Kate."

"But he was frightened off."

"Little Deer?"

Again SnowEagle nodded. "I do not know if he saw her image or something that she knew would terrify him. I do know that it was her doing."

They worked in silence as Flynt mulled over this information. His hands stilled. He stared at the crimson blood on his fingers. "I have no reason to believe this—but for a long time I have felt that my wife died at the hands of another. Since the fight with Blackjack I have imagined that it could well have been a man such as him. The attack on Kate has made me dwell even more on this possibility."

"And if you are right? What will you do with this knowledge?"

His jaw clenched. His wet fingers curled into a fist. "It has been all I could do to keep my promise to Kate these last few weeks. I have found myself consumed with rage when I think of that man's hands on her. If it was he who killed Little Deer—and with her, my child—I am not certain that I could keep from killing LeBouche the next time we meet."

"Be careful of what you say. Words have power—silent or spoken. Harm that is given comes back."

"If that is true, why did Blackjack get away with stabbing

me? Why was he still a free man to accost you and Kate at the river? Where is his punishment?"

"It is not for you to tell *Olelbis* how or when the Frenchman should answer for the hurt he has caused."

"It is not easy for me to let go as it is for you. I was raised to believe in 'an eye for an eye.' I was raised to believe in justice. It's difficult to choose not to seek revenge."

"You were raised in another world. Yet you have chosen to live in this one. Your ancestors are my ancestors. You seek their wisdom through me. I tell you that their wisdom is already in you. Their peace is already in you."

"I feel none of it."

"Even with your woman?"

The turnabout by his great-grandfather unnerved Flynt. He went back to his task, muttering to the shaman that there were some privacies best kept to himself. Not that he was embarrassed to speak of his intimacy with Kate. But he was reluctant to admit that his vengeful thoughts against Blackjack could be so easily put aside if the motivation suited him. If he could forget about such hatred while making love to Kate, he would have to face the fact that he was capable of disposing of his need for revenge altogether. And that in itself was the rub. Damn it all, he could not yet let go of this festering obsession.

"I will finish our work," stated SnowEagle, sitting back on his heels. "It is time for you to go."

Flynt looked up, puzzled. "The job will be done in half the time with both of us on it. I am in no hurry to leave." This was but a half-truth, for his mind was nearly always wandering back to the cabin with thoughts of Kate waiting for him there.

"Take only enough for one meal. Come back tomorrow

and I will have your share ready for you. Do not use an open fire. Not tonight. Cook inside."

He pondered the explicit instructions. If he had heard them from anyone other than SnowEagle, he would have called him a fool for telling him to roast the meat in the hearth during the warm months of the year. "I will do as you say but may I know why? What is the significance? What have you been told?"

SnowEagle motioned to the heavens. "On this day the sun stands longest of all other days." The Wintu attached their own mystical interpretation of the change of season, known to Flynt as the summer solstice. "This is a day of change. I have told you of Little Deer. She is with your woman now. She is watching. She is not alone. Our ancestors stand with her—people and animal spirits, both. Remember this tonight when you are with *Patit-Pokta*. Go now. Take your meat. Prepare it as I have said. Tomorrow I will see you again."

At the cabin, Kate had spent the better part of the day doing some major spring cleaning. After dragging the tables outside, she'd scrubbed them down with a stiff brush and let the sun bleach them dry, then brought out the mattress and bedclothes and aired them over pine boughs. Except for the bed frame and humpback chest, she had emptied the cabin and swept it clean with a poorly constructed broom made of three freshly cut pine branches.

Taking a much-needed break, she sat on the bench in the sun and read a few chapters from another novel. In the past several weeks, she had completed only four more books from the crate under the bed. Each precious moment she could capture for a few pages were few and far between. There was always something to be washed or roots to dig or berries to pick. Her days were full and she often collapsed into bed bone tired.

Twice she had sneaked off to the river by herself when her nerves were raw and homesickness pressed heavily on her heart. She missed Sunni and Michael terribly and worried that they were sick with grief. Each time she went to the river, she had left a message for Flynt written with the pen and notepaper from her purse and discreetly placed for him to find if she didn't return. Each time she had sat at the water's edge, torn between her desire to stay with him or go back to where she belonged. Each time she had grown anxious with the same sensation that she was being watched.

Blackjack LeBouche had not been seen in the weeks following the attack, leastwise not by Kate, Flynt or SnowEagle. The rifle had disappeared from the place where it had been dropped, Kate had noticed, unable to tell Flynt without revealing that she'd gone against his orders. He'd be mad or hurt or both—any way she looked at it, she didn't have any explanation for her impulsive behavior on those two occasions. Only that she couldn't bear the sadness of losing her friends. Would he believe her? Or would he think she simply didn't want to spend her life with him? She didn't know and didn't want to take that chance.

Kate realized her mind had been wandering when she attempted to reread the same page for the third time. Giving up on the book, she went back to the task of putting the cabin back in order. As she dragged the battered dining table inside, she worried about Flynt hunting alone. She hoped that he would find only a deer. The thought of him running into LeBouche made her shiver with dread. She had talked him out of going after her attacker. But if the Frenchman confronted Flynt, there would be more at stake than personal revenge for the stabbing.

As she stood back and surveyed the day's work, she gazed upon the dark walls and wished there were at least one hanging picture, if not two or three more windows. Without a spray bottle of Windex at her disposal, she could do little to the single window but wipe it with a damp cloth. To her disappointment, everything looked much the same as before she'd started. There had to be something she could do to add a little softness, a little touch of homeyness to the bleak, rustic interior. A swatch of lace on the mantel? A square of calico draped diagonally across the table? She went to the chest in the corner. In the two-and-a-half months since her arrival, it had remained closed. She didn't recall any table linens or doilies, but then again, she hadn't been seeking them either. It wouldn't hurt to take another gander at the inventory.

Take another gander? She smiled at the Rita-ism as she lifted the lid of the trunk and took out piece after piece of clothing. Certain words and phrases of the two sisters had popped into her thoughts and conversations with Flynt over the weeks since her short stay at the boarding house during his recovery. She was surprised at how many times she'd caught herself using folksy witticisms instead of her own contemporary phrases.

The yellow gingham dress captured her interest, unlike the first time she'd seen it. She held it up to her shoulders and glanced down at the narrow cut of the waist. It would probably fit now. The hard work and backwoods cuisine had whittled off ten pounds, if not more. She didn't have a bathroom scale, of course. But her jeans were loose and her bra was on its first hooks instead of last. On a whim, she changed into the dress and found that it fit nicely, although the skirt ended several inches above the floor. She'd gotten thinner but not shorter.

Her fingers skimmed along the lace stitched into the front

of the dress in two parallel lines, accenting the slender silhouette. For at least the hundredth time she wished there were a nice, big mirror. Aside from a small pocket one in her purse and a slightly larger one that Flynt brought out for his morning shave, she had not seen herself since leaving Dunsmuir. At times she was actually grateful for the mixed blessing. But once in a while she felt a tug of vanity, wondering if she'd changed and how much so.

She removed the gingham and put it to one side, hoping she could manage the simple task of letting out the hem. She picked up her jeans to step into them, then paused, her eyes on the open trunk. Leaving the pants on the bed, she knelt on the floor and retrieved the white leather dress. She touched the glass beads and white shells sewn into patterns.

Tempted to try it on, she glanced over her shoulder to the closed and barred door. Should she dare? She held it up to herself as she'd done with the cotton dress. Would it fit? It appeared so. She wondered what the buttery soft leather would feel like next to her bare skin.

Her curiosity won out. She took off her bra and her mended panties. Then she slipped the white beaded dress over her head. It slid smoothly over her breasts and hips with room to spare. Not much but enough to be comfortable. *Very* comfortable, she decided. The sleeves were short, edged with fringe that reached her elbows. The bottom of the dress was also trimmed with fringe which brushed her knees.

More than ever, she wished for a mirror to see herself in this beautifully ornate Native American dress. How did she look? she wondered. If it were 1996, she would feel ridiculous. But this wasn't and she didn't. Still, she wanted to see it on. She went to Flynt's shaving supplies and pulled out his rectangular mirror. The light was dismal. She moved to the front of the worktable, closer to the window. Holding the mirror out at arm's length, she tilted it up and down, turned herself side to side. But all she captured were shadowy glimpses. Disappointed, she dropped her hand to her side and started to return to the corner of the room.

Go outside.

The hairs on the back of her neck stood on end. Goose-bumps rose on her arms. She felt unseen eyes watching her . . . again. Slowly, she turned her gaze to the divided window panes, expecting to see a face peering in through the glass, hoping there wouldn't be. Her heart picked up its pace, thumping inside her chest.

Go outside, repeated the silent command. Her bare toes curled into the floor as if she could dig in and hold on to the spot where she stood. The sensation of being observed had always happened elsewhere, never inside the cabin. And never had it coincided with the strong, distinct voice in her head.

How could she convince herself that both of these strange things were nothing but her imagination on overdrive? How could she dismiss them as weird woo-woo stuff that wasn't real? She was living in the nineteenth century, for heaven's sake! And if she could make love to a man born in 1862, then why shouldn't she accept that some invisible being was communicating with her through thought waves?

"And maybe I've been abducted by aliens and all this time-travel experience is a brain-wave experiment," she grumbled aloud, more than a little tired of the bizarre and unexplicable twists and turns. This was the kind of stuff that writers pitched at studio execs: "*Quantum Leap* crossbreeds with the *X-Files*—Scully meets Mulder in a past life!" She didn't believe it could really happen. But she couldn't deny that it was happening to her either.

Fed up and frustrated, she glanced around, then upward. "All right, you win. I'll go outside."

Kate emerged from the cabin feeling much like a novice actress stepping out from stage left for an audition. The moxie was all there, brave and daring for the discerning eyes beyond the footlights. But her stomach felt like an animated commercial for stomach acid. As casually as she could manage, she walked a little to the left, avoiding the stones under her tender feet, looked about, then walked to the right.

"Anything else?" she asked, a bit louder than she'd intended. Feeling foolish, she listened for the voice. Nothing. She waited. Still nothing. The forgotten mirror in her hand caught the afternoon sun filtering through the trees, bouncing a white light into the woods. The reflection startled her at first, causing her to wonder what or who was in the shadows beyond the clearing. But almost immediately she realized the cause. She toyed with the mirror for a few moments, like a puppeteer with a marionette, pirouetting the reflected light from rock to limb. It reminded her of Tinkerbell. She grinned, then set the mirror on the bench and stepped back to get a look at herself.

As Sasti ascended the narrow woodland path toward the cabin, Flynt caught a glimpse of white through the thick greenery. Holding on tight to the wrapped venison, he coaxed the roan into a quicker pace, all the while straining his eyes to see beyond the screen of shrubs and bushes and low branches. When he came upon the open space, he saw an image that could only have leaped forward from his memory.

The white doeskin dress. He had purchased it from a Hupa woman for Little Deer as a wedding dress. Though it was not of her own Wintun people, it was a magnificent garment which had suited her well for their marriage ceremony among her small tribal family. He could not believe his eyes then or now.

"Little Deer?" he called in Wintu, remembering SnowEagle's words of her presence here. She whirled around at the sound of his voice.

"Flynt, you scared me to death," gasped Kate. Her right hand snatched something from the bench and held it behind her. "I didn't expect you."

"Apparently so."

"Please don't be angry about the dress." She backed toward the door. "I was looking in the trunk for a piece of material I could use for a tablecloth, and I came across this and—" She shrugged innocently. "I guess my curiosity got the better of me."

After dropping to his feet in front of her, he kissed her soundly on the lips, then pressed the wrapped meat into her free hand. "Take this inside while I stable Sasti."

She glanced at the leather-wrapped bundle, then up at him. "You're not mad? About the dress, I mean?"

Had it not been for the visit with his great-grandfather, perhaps he might have been a bit put off by the disturbing sight. If Little Deer was a spirit-helper to Kate, it should not surprise him that she'd been led to put on the dress that Little Deer had worn as his bride. "I admit that I was a trifle startled but now that I have had the opportunity to appreciate it on you—no, I am not angry."

Her mouth fell open in a perplexed little O that simply looked too irresistible. He could not keep from kissing her. As he did so, his hands drifted to her waist and gently pulled her against him, pressing the wrapped meat to her breasts. He didn't mind at all. Nor did she, for there was little clothing between them to hide the secret of his arousal.

She smiled into his lips and murmured, "Before or after dinner?"

"After—" He took the object in her hidden hand. "—I see this." Grinning victoriously, he pulled his shaving mirror out from behind her.

"You sneak!" Kate yelped, her face pinkening.

"Caught you, Narcissus."

She tried to grab the mirror but he held it high, well out of her reach. "You tricked me. That's not fair to kiss me senseless when you didn't really mean it."

"Oh, you can be sure that I meant it." He laughed, then stole yet another kiss—a quick one this time. She jumped back and bumped into the door frame. "And what were you doing with my mirror, may I ask?"

"You know good and well what I was doing with it. I just wanted to see what the dress looked like on me."

"Quite exquisite, actually. You may take my word."

"I don't have much choice, do I?"

"If you would like a larger mirror, I could arrange to order one in Dunsmuir. Perhaps the mercantile would have one in stock."

Kate sobered immediately. "You're not going back there because of me. Not again. I don't want to be responsible if anything happens to you."

"You were not responsible the first time."

Her gaze dropped from his. Clutching the bundle to her bosom, she started to turn away. "I'll go change back into my own clothes."

"No!"

She flinched. Her head pivoted. She looked at him with eyes wide and filled with unspoken questions.

"I didn't mean to snap at you that way. The dress . . ." He

recalled SnowEagle's words of this special night. "It holds great meaning for me."

"Which is why I should take it off."

He shook his head, his gaze taking in the softness of her hair, the green of her eyes, her full lips, the stubborn tilt to her chin. He loved this woman as he never thought he would love again. His heart constricted in his chest.

"It was a gift for my bride," he said, reverently touching a shell on her shoulder. Emotion tightened his throat. "I want you to wear it."

"As your bride?"

He nodded. "For as long as we are together."

"What if I am gone tomorrow?"

"Then we will have tonight."

Her eyes were bright with moisture. She leaned into him and lifted herself onto her toes to offer her mouth to his. She tasted good, inviting.

"Does this mean yes?" he asked after their lips parted. One corner of her mouth tilted upward in a saucy but uncertain smile. "Well?"

"I . . ."

"Is it so difficult a decision?"

"As a matter of fact, it is."

"It needn't be."

"For you, maybe. You haven't had your life disrupted, your entire world turned upside-down."

"Oh no?" Having Kate enter his life had done exactly that.

"I don't want you to marry me simply because I'm living with you. No one is forcing you to make an honest woman of me."

"Precisely. I do not feel the least bit coerced. Marriage

seems the logical progression of our . . . 'relationship'—as you would say."

"Logical?" Her dark brows arrowed upward. He saw the flash of ire like sparks of light from cut emeralds. Next, she would lambaste him with her refusal to be a liability to him—a burden. Why couldn't she see that he only wanted to take care of her, give her a name in this time period which had no record of her birth? Why couldn't she see that he only wanted to do right by her? Any other woman he'd known would have been joyous to accept his proposal of marriage.

Kate was *not* any other woman he'd known, he reminded himself—which was exactly why she'd stolen his heart. Sasti nudged him from behind. As he turned toward the horse, he tossed out, "This discussion is not yet finished." Then, with a softer tone, he added, "Don't be angry, Kate."

When Flynt returned several minutes later, he found Kate sitting at the dining table inside the cabin. The bundled meat was on the workbench against the wall. She didn't glance up when he walked past, but continued cleaning potatoes and roots to go into the kettle. He went to the hearth and set the sticks for a fire. After a number of weeks cooking over an open fire, his actions went unquestioned, which was not like Kate. In silence, he finished the task and prepared the meat to roast.

Afterward, he announced, "I'm going to wash up." As he started for the door, she popped up from her seat.

"I'm done here. You can use the table."

He had been bathing outside since the weather had turned warm. Therefore, he recognized the offer as a veiled truce.

"Thank you, but I'm likely to make a muddy mess of things. Why don't you find something for that tablecloth you mentioned earlier." He brought out his large hunting knife. "Use this on one of those nightgowns in the trunk. It'll have to do in lieu of scissors."

Kate stared at the weapon in his palm, the handle turned toward her. When she didn't take it, he placed it on the table in front of her.

"Put it away." Her voice was a gravelly whisper. "I can't look at it without seeing it in Blackjack's hand and your blood dripping from it." Her head turned aside, then tilted upward. He noticed her eyes were red-rimmed.

She had been crying.

Damn you, Avery, for being every kind of fool.

He sheathed the blade and came to her side, dropping to one knee. "We have a continuous way of mucking up matters between us, haven't we?"

A sad smile answered him. "Can't live with you, can't live without you."

"Indeed—my sentiments exactly. With you, I find myself playing either a fool or a rake. Never any middle ground."

Her hand cupped his cheek in a tender fashion. "How is it you can put up with me?"

"Dearest Kate." He grinned and kissed her palm. "I need only ask myself how would I ever cope without you. Had I been thrown into another world which is not my own, it would be no easier for me than for you now. You have a right to your moments of despair, your bouts of indecision and confusion. When we discuss Bellamy's novel, I imagine myself as him and I wonder how I could keep from going mad."

"Not you." She stroked his long hair, smiling at him. "Not after the way you pored over all the stuff in my purse. I think you'd be fascinated with all the inventions we've talked about."

"Like a kid in a candy store, I believe you've already said."

"More like a kid in a virtual-reality booth."

Kate saw his bafflement and explained the technology in simplest terms, which wasn't hard considering that her concept of VRT was limited to a clip from a television newsmagazine with Stone Phillips. But she enjoyed the way his dark eyes lit up as if she were a storyteller of mythic proportions. Yes, she could definitely see him exploring the latter part of the twentieth century with her.

"You'd fit right in," she assured him, her fingers combing through the burnished gold at his temple. "You wouldn't even have to cut your hair."

"This is the fashion? What of those photographs of Michael?"

"In my neck of the woods, it's common to see any length."

"Your 'neck of the woods'? You are sounding more and more like a close cousin to Rita and Louzana every day."

"Funny how I find myself missing those two sisters almost as much as I miss Sunni and Michael."

Flynt lost some of the starlight in his midnight-blue eyes. "If you were to go back, would you marry this Michael fellow?"

"No," she answered honestly. "I left L.A. to do some soul searching about Michael and me. Maybe he and I were together in another life. Maybe we were siblings in the twelfth century. Maybe we were married in the colonial days. But we weren't meant to be more than friends this time around. Not for me, anyway."

"Reincarnation? You? When did this belief come about?"

"Somewhere after I fell down the rabbit hole."

She continued to touch the silken strands of his hair, letting it glide between her fingers with a sensuous stroke of its own appeal. She had never known the intense interest that some women had for long hair on men. Not until she had met Flynt. The memory of his thick blond hair cascading over her bare breasts sent a ripple of desire to the pit of her belly. She gave him a sweet but smoldering look. "Make love to me."

"After dinner."

"Now."

"On one condition . . ." He drew her hand from his hair and brought it together with the other one. All the playfulness left his expression. "Say you will marry me."

Chapter 16

SOMEWHERE INSIDE KATE was a little girl who wanted to leap to her feet, throw both her arms up like Rocky Balboa and shout, "Yes!" But the older adult balked, grabbing the hyperactive, naïve little kid and stuffing a sock in her mouth. Why couldn't she accept his proposal, albeit a little less eagerly? What was wrong with making a commitment that she'd already made in the flesh? Her body ached for his touch. Even now as he waited for her answer, she longed to feel him against her.

She recalled the March afternoon when she had sat at the river contemplating Michael's marriage proposal. "Right before I came here, I had been thinking about the days when kids grew up in the same town and married each other. There had been no viable alternatives for a girl to consider. But here I am back in the good old days with a perfectly wonderful man who wants me, and all I can think about is whether or not there are any options I've missed."

"Have you come upon any?"

She shook her head, then gave a halfhearted, self-mocking laugh. "I keep thinking of Deborah Kerr in *An Affair to Remember.*"

"A book?"

"A movie—one of those talking motion pictures I told you about. A wonderfully sappy, three-hankie tearjerker. Even though she loved Cary Grant, she wouldn't allow herself to be a burden on him. But he loved her too much to let her go."

"Rather like us, wouldn't you say?"

"But do you?"

"Do I what?"

"Do you love me too much to let me go?"

"I assume it is quite obvious."

"Then say it." Were all Englishmen so closemouthed about their feelings or was Flynt Avery the only one?

"Say that I love you? Is this why you couldn't agree to marry me—because I'd forgotten to say something so pointedly evident?"

"Yes, dammit."

He clicked his tongue in admonition. "Let's not become hostile over a mere oversight."

"Oversight?" Even as she stiffened, she saw the twinkle of mischief in his eyes. She tried to pull her hands from his grasp but he refused to release her.

"I love you, Katherine Marshall." The rich resonant timbre of his voice filled the small, quiet cabin with a warm hum. "And I pledge my undying devotion to you throughout all eternity—this life and the next, together or apart. I ask for your hand in marriage. If you accept, I will consider us husband and wife in the eyes of God from this moment onward."

Her hands would have been shaking if he hadn't had a

strong grip on them. She swallowed hard, trying to dislodge the lump in her throat. This was the moment she had waited for her entire life. The first time around for her had been more like an agreement of merger between two like-minded studio executives. Her first wedding had been a production number to rival Andrew Lloyd Webber. Her own vows had been a hollow reading from a dead script, only she just didn't know it until it was too late. This time was different. This time she heard the intensity of his emotion beckoning her heart. This time she heard the music in her ears when there was no music at all.

"I love you, Flynt Avery." Her voice was wobbly and unsure but she was never more sure of anything in her whole life. She nervously cleared her throat and tried again. "I take you as my husband from this day forward, through this century and the rest. I will love, honor and cherish—"

"Obey," he corrected.

She whispered conspiratorially. "That part was axed with the women's movement."

Flynt grinned. "I see."

"You distracted me. Where was I?"

"Doesn't matter. You've said the important part." He bracketed her face with his large hands, drawing her to him. "Congratulations, Mrs. Avery. You may now kiss the groom."

"Could we make that Ms. Marshall-Avery?" kidded Kate.

"Utterly ridiculous," he murmured against her mouth, then pressed his lips to hers. She opened to him and their tongues parried seductively until she was breathless.

"Now?" she asked.

"After—"

"Don't you dare say 'After dinner.' "

"Not at all. But I should wash off the sweat and grime.

Dressing out a deer doesn't lend well to a romantic ambience."

She wrinkled her nose. "What an appealing thought. Go, then. Get cleaned up. And scrub under your fingernails, for heaven's sake."

"I won't be long, I promise." After a quick peck on her lips he dashed out the door, leaving it ajar.

As the low fire crackled beneath the venison, Kate went to close the door. She caught sight of Flynt heading in the direction of Sweetbrier Creek, casting a long shadow in the late afternoon sun. His lengthy strides gobbled up the ground with powerful strokes. He was a magnificent study of muscular proportion. Broad shoulders. Lean hips. Long legs. And hands that could make her body melt into a puddle of hot butter.

After he disappeared into the woods she closed the door and leaned against it, tilting her head back. It had all happened so fast—the proposal, her acceptance, their vows to one another. Yet she didn't feel the slightest twinge of regret. She smiled to herself in giddy disbelief. She cupped her hand over her mouth. Lord, it was crazy. It was nuts. But damned if his words didn't make sense. *Live moment to moment.* And that's exactly what she intended to do.

Her body flushed with the heat of wanting him.

On an impulse that she didn't question, she took the freshly aired bearskin from the bed and laid it out on the floor near the hearth. She wanted to see him in the firelight. She wanted to look into his eyes when he made love to her.

She began to undress, then remembered his request to stay in the ceremonial gown. Stretching out on the fur pelt, she waited for him to return, luxuriating in the anticipation. She listened to the spit and crackle of the fire, the pop and sizzle of meat juices dropping into the embers. Outside, the birds added their own distinctly different sounds. Her hearing seemed fine-tuned to a crystal clarity. All of her senses seemed sharper—sight, smell, touch. It was as if someone had turned everything up a notch—colors, sounds, textures. Even her own heartbeat felt strong and loud in her ears.

When Flynt came through the door, she had already heard his approaching footsteps. She could have sworn she had felt the vibration through the ground beneath her, but she dismissed the notion as too far-fetched.

Holding his chambray shirt in his hand, he was bare-chested, the top half of his summer-weight drawers hanging down over the waistband of his trousers. The scars from the stabbing marred his smooth skin with angry red marks. Droplets of water clung to the smattering of dark blond hair on his chest, which rose and fell in rapid breaths.

"You ran?"

"You didn't think I'd keep you waiting, did you?"

"On our wedding night? I certainly hope not."

He removed his boots and shed the rest of his clothing, then approached the edge of the bearskin and knelt in front of her. When he leaned over to kiss her, his hair fell across her cheek. It was damp from his quick bath and felt cool to her burning skin.

"Aren't you a bit too warm here by the fire?" he asked as his lips brushed hers.

"*A bit* doesn't begin to describe how hot I am. But it has nothing to do with the fire."

She heard him snicker while his kisses traveled down her neck and his hand traveled up her thigh. He found the sensitive nub that made her gasp at his touch, wanting more. But he toyed with her, sliding his fingertips down her other leg and back up. Now and then he skimmed the delicate folds of her womanhood, causing her to moan breathlessly, hoping he would quit teasing her body, yet loving every caress.

His hand wandered over her hip, to her waist, down her belly. She arched toward him, silently begging him to release her from the tempest churning through her lower body. His mouth descended on hers as if he instinctively responded to her thought, deftly manipulating his fingers with a rhythm and precise pressure that escalated her to the epitome of pleasure. The explosive release mushroomed outward from the point of his touch, rippling through her in a sonic wave that sounded like the cry of her own voice.

She had not been aware of her grip on his shoulders until she dropped her hands back down onto the fur beside her head. Drifting in a daze of contented bliss, she smiled up at Flynt, feeling the sweet pulsing ache between her legs. "Your turn," she purred.

"My pleasure."

Lord, how his grin could mesmerize her. She propped herself on one elbow and pressed his shoulders onto the bearskin. Playing his own game on him, she skimmed her fingertips across the less-than-intimate places on his body, avoiding his sensitive scars. Little by little, she added a light brush or gentle caress of his arousal that stoked his fire. However, his patience quickly wore thin. He took her hand, guiding it downward. She wrapped her fingers around his swollen member and had stroked him only a few times when he groaned, "Enough."

A sudden urgency came over him. He seized the bottom of the doeskin dress and brought it up over her head, then tossed it carelessly aside. Kate sucked in a breath as he gently pushed her onto her back. His dark eyes held a primal gleam. Predatory. In that one instant, she knew her power over him. It electrified her. She gave back that power and let him take her with raw force. Each time he plunged into her, she heard his exertion in his bestial noises, felt his powerful thrusts against the wall of her womb. Their coupling was savage, almost brutal. Their sweat-sheened naked bodies bucked against one another.

Kate squeezed her eyes shut, feeling the tension building with each thrust. Her legs widened to take more of him. Panting wildly, she cupped his buttocks, pulling him into her.

On the brink of ecstasy, she felt the nape of her neck prickle. The intense aroma of meat triggered her memory. Her heart leaped to her throat.

Her dream!

"Ohmigod," she gasped, realizing this was the dream she had tried so hard to remember. The room swirled around her in a dizzying kaleidoscope. Her head thrashed side to side. She frantically pushed against Flynt's shoulders.

"No . . . Kate . . . Don't. " He pounded into her with each word, then let out a guttural sound as he rocked against her in the final explosive throes of climax. When his lengthy release was complete, he collapsed in exhaustion, gulping deep drafts of air.

She wrapped her arms and legs around him, holding him inside her and closing her eyes tight. It had all come back to her now. She clung to Flynt, afraid to let him go.

"Kate, you're trembling." He began to lift himself off her but she wouldn't release him. "What's wrong?"

She shook her head, unable to articulate anything just yet. Everything was so jumbled, like an odd echo of words and movement and thoughts and sensations. She was acutely aware of every nerve ending that sent signals to her brain. The smell of the meat. The view of the ceiling above. The touch of his moist skin beneath her fingertips and against her belly and thighs. The fullness of his thick flesh still inside her.

And the feeling of being watched.

Déjà vu. All of it. The aroma had triggered the buried memory that had haunted her from that first night in Dunsmuir. There had always been the scent of meat that niggled at the back of her mind. And there had been that one night weeks ago when she'd seen something familiar in the dark ceiling. But the rest of it had escaped her, no matter how much she'd tried to recall the details.

"Kate, you're as white as a sheet. What happened? Did I hurt you?"

She released a shaky breath. "No. . . ." She hugged him to her. His male musk filled her nostrils with the familiarity of his intimate presence—calming her, soothing her, making her feel safe and secure. How could she have dreamed of this man while she was in another time?

He withdrew from her and rolled onto his side next to her. His palm cupped her cheek. "Forgive me for taking you so."

She reached up and covered his hand with her own.

"You didn't do anything wrong. I didn't know I could drive a man wild like that," she admitted, trying to put him at ease about her own sudden change of mood. "I've never experienced anything so hot and wild. Except in a recurrent dream that I couldn't quite remember until now."

"I like your sort of dreams." He smiled, then leaned over and kissed the tip of her breast. A quiver rippled through her. His eyebrow winged upward in a seductive query. "Ready again? I am not quite recovered but there are ways . . ."

His hand drifted down her rib cage. She stopped it at her belly and felt a flutter inside. "Yes, I want you. I don't think I'll ever get enough of you. But not right now. Not just yet."

A slight frown of concern wrinkled his forehead. "If this dream troubles you so much, it may help to talk it out."

She explained all that she could remember—before and after she had arrived in the nineteenth century. When she had finished, Flynt offered, "So you had experienced a prophetic dream. A rather nice one, I might add. Such things are not unusual, especially after you have lived in these mountains. SnowEagle has them all the time."

"But he's a Wintu shaman."

"He would tell you himself that we all have the ability to some extent or another. We simply don't train ourselves to remember them."

She gazed up into his eyes. "What if all of this is a dream, Flynt? What if I am really lying in a hospital bed in 1996 and everything I have experienced is all a fabrication of my mind?"

"We have been through this before." He kissed her forehead. "If this is all in your head, so be it. But I refuse to stop believing that you are here with me. I am determined to live each moment as if it is our last. So should you."

Kate stared up into his midnight-blue eyes. A feeling of completion and rightness enveloped her in a warm glow that seeped into her bones.

"I love you, Katherine." His voice was barely above a whisper. She lifted one finger and traced the edge of his jaw, affirming his very real presence.

"God knows how much I love you."

Flynt slowly smiled. "I do believe he does."

The cooking fire had died down to embers, prompting him to slip into his trousers so he could fetch more wood. Kate got up and draped the dress over the open trunk, then pulled out the white shirt she had first used as a pajama top.

She put it on and padded to the table to put the vegetables on to cook.

When their supper was finally ready, they sat on the bearskin on the floor and ate. The room had grown exceptionally warm. Kate watched Flynt push a lock of damp hair from his sweat-beaded forehead. She plucked the front placket of the shirt from her chest as a droplet of sweat trickled down the valley between her breasts.

Twilight gave way to evening and darkness descended upon the cabin. Flynt lit the lantern on the table and put a small amount of fuel on the dying log. Then he joined Kate on the floor, lying down behind her with one arm propping him up and the other wrapped around her middle. They watched the flames lick at the dry wood.

He nibbled her right earlobe, distracting her as he unbuttoned her shirt and tugged it off her shoulder. He kissed her there while helping her withdraw her arm from the sleeve.

"I intend to make this official, you know," he murmured, his hands doing wonderful things to her. "A minister. A ring. We shall leave for Dunsmuir in the morning. The Walker sisters will be delighted by our news." She remained silent except for a heavy sigh. "Don't worry about LeBouche. I will be extra careful."

Her hand rested on his arm. "How did you know what I was thinking?"

"How could I not? You have made it quite clear how you feel about returning to Dunsmuir." Silencing further discussion with a distracting caress, he continued his slow exploration of her body, culminating in a soft and gentle joining of their souls. The tenderness of his lovemaking brought tears to her eyes. Afterward, he carried her to the comfort of the bed to sleep.

*　　*　　*

Several minutes after Flynt had brought the blankets back to cover her and had slipped in beside her, the darkened cabin slowly grew brighter as if the wick on the lantern had been turned up. Kate leaned up on one elbow to look in the direction of the table where the lamp had been set. Flynt followed her gaze. The soot-rimmed glass globe emanated only a soft glow. Behind it, however, was an iridescent glow that lengthened in height and width, spreading out around the bed in a half circle.

Hair-raising goosebumps climbed her arms and up her neck. She whispered to Flynt, "What's going on?"

"Shhh," he soothed. In her left ear, she heard a soft, high-pitched whistle. When her hand gripped his forearm, he carefully peeled away her fingers. After a long moment, Flynt murmured, "Breathe, Kate."

Until his command, she hadn't realized that she'd been holding her breath. Closing her eyes, she inhaled, then exhaled. Two more times she did it, feeling a little more calm each time.

"I'm going to sit up and face them," he warned her in a low voice.

"Not me—I'm naked!"

"I don't think they care."

"They?" she asked, belatedly realizing he had already spoken of the light as "them."

"Here." He plucked her shirt from the bedpost, where he'd hung it when he'd retrieved the blankets. He handed it to her and shifted his position with slow and deliberate movement. She followed, sitting on the edge of the timber frame.

Kate saw the dim outline of a figure in the middle of the semicircle of light. The image was grainy, like a bootleg copy of a film from the thirties. Other shadowy shapes wa-

vered in and out of her vision. She could barely make out a
few shapes, some human, some animal. When she tried to
focus on them, they disappeared. Her fear had gradually dis-
sipated as she turned her gaze back to the central figure. Little by little, it became more visible.

It was a woman. Though the apparition appeared translucent, the dark log wall in the background helped to clarify
her features. Kate could see three dark lines on the woman's
chin.

"Do you see her?" she asked Flynt in a hushed whisper.

"No. I only see a glowing light."

"She has black hair. And three long marks on her chin."

"Tattoos."

"And she's wearing—" Kate glanced to the open chest.
"That dress, Flynt. It's the same one. I think it's . . ."

"Little Deer."

"You can see her now?"

"No," he answered quietly with disappointment in his
voice. "But I sense her presence as I have in the past."

"Why can't you see her and I can?"

"Perhaps SnowEagle knows. The Wintu believe we are all
guided and protected by helping-spirits."

"And Little Deer is mine?" asked Kate skeptically, watching the ghostly woman in front of them.

"So says my great-grandfather. There are others, too."

"We've been performing in front of an audience?" she
groaned, her gaze flitting to the inconsistent images that
flanked Little Deer.

"SnowEagle told me that this was a special night. It's the
summer solstice—a time of great importance to the Wintu."

"I bet she's upset with you for taking a new wife."

"Does she look upset?"

Kate studied the woman in front of her. "Actually, she has one of those Mona Lisa smiles as if she knows something."

"I don't doubt."

Flynt spoke in the language of the Wintun people. Kate picked up a familiar greeting she'd heard between him and his great-grandfather, but the rest of his words escaped her.

Tell my husband I am safe.

The familiar voice in her head startled Kate. Little Deer had not opened her mouth, yet the message came through loud and clear—just like all the others.

She angled her head to look up at Flynt. "She said to tell you she is safe."

"You heard her?"

"It's not the first time," she admitted, explaining the bizarre verbal command in her car at the river. "I didn't know who or what it was until now."

His dark eyes clouded as he stared down at her. "She was with you in the future. It was Little Deer who brought you here."

Kate looked at the young Wintu woman who lifted her hands, striking a pose that brought back a vague feeling of recognition. Slowly the memory crept to the forefront of her mind.

"I—I've seen you before, haven't I?" she said to the wavering image. "You were in the woods when I started to leave the river. That's when I fell."

Little Deer nodded.

Abruptly, Kate launched to her feet. The front plackets of the shirt flapped open but she ignored them. She turned to Flynt, reaching out for his hand. "What if she's come to take me back?"

His fingers tightened around hers. "Is that what you want?"

"No . . . yes. Oh, Flynt—you know how much I want to go home but I don't want to leave you." Her other hand cupped his cheek. "I can't go without you."

"You may have no choice."

Keeping a firm grip on his hand, she turned to Little Deer, who shook her head solemnly before Kate could ask for him to go with her.

Your work is not done. But soon I will return.

"What work?" The apparition began to fade away. "Don't go!"

Little Deer drew a small shadowy figure from among the nebulous semicircle of light. It was a dark-haired boy of three or four. She nudged him forward. His dark eyes captured her heart. Midnight-blue. Kate felt a strange yearning deep in her soul. She reached out to him. As his tiny hand rose toward hers, the room began to darken until only his youthful shape was silhouetted in a bright glow. Then he was gone.

While firelight danced on the surrounding walls, Kate sat back on the bed frame, staring down at her fingertips, wondering whether or not she had felt the touch of the little hand. It had seemed so real, yet she couldn't be sure.

"What did she say?" asked Flynt gently.

"I have work left to do. But she didn't elaborate." She pivoted and gazed into his blue eyes. "I . . . think I saw your son."

"My . . . son. Are you sure?"

She nodded tentatively. "She brought him out as if she were showing him to me. But I'm not sure why. She didn't say."

There was a certain sadness in his eyes before he looked away from her. She rested her hand on his shoulder.

"You asked her about the baby, didn't you?"

"I did. And I wish now that I hadn't. It brings back nothing but painful memories." He pushed himself to his feet and walked toward the workbench. Leaning his palms on the wooden top, he hung his head between his shoulders. Kate went to him. She slipped her arms around his waist and pressed her cheek against his broad back.

"I'm sorry you didn't get to see either of them. He was a beautiful child, Flynt. He had your eyes—that's how I knew. They looked right into me like they were the eyes of an old soul. Like SnowEagle." She told him of the peculiar longing for the boy, of how Little Deer had pushed him toward her, of his hand reaching out to her.

Flynt slowly turned and gazed down at Kate, silently studying her. His expression vacillated between deep thoughtfulness and a curious bewilderment. "Did he come toward you?"

She nodded. "But then he disappeared—" She snapped her fingers. "—like that."

"He is still here."

"He is?" She glanced back over her shoulder. "Do you sense him like you had sensed Little Deer?"

He shook his head. "I think she showed you our son."

"Haven't you been listening to me? That's what I just said—I saw your son."

"*Our* son—yours and mine. She has brought him back to me tonight."

"It's not possible," she stammered. "I can't be."

"I believe you are."

"But Little Deer told me I had work yet to do. Certainly this isn't what she meant."

"Why not? Isn't it quite a task to carry a child, to give birth?"

"Yes, but—" Kate shoved herself away from him, her

stomach churning with panic and disbelief. There had been absolutely no sign of a menstrual cycle since early March, three weeks before she'd left Los Angeles. It had been nearly four months. Surely she was not capable of conceiving a baby. "Just because a couple of ghosts make an appearance in the night, doesn't automatically translate that I'm pregnant, Flynt. I think you've been up in these mystic mountains too long. We *both* have."

"Very well, then. We shall move as soon as possible."

"You're jumping the gun a little, don't you think? Sure, I'd like to live somewhere with a few modern conveniences—even by your standards here in the nineteenth century. But what about SnowEagle? You can't just leave an eighty-year-old man out here in the wilderness alone."

"He would enjoy San Francisco."

"He'd shrivel up and die if he didn't have his mountains."

"Then we shall build a house in Dunsmuir." He crossed the floor in two strides and took her into his arms. "I won't make the same mistake twice, Kate. This time my wife and child will have the best of care."

"But Flynt, I'm not pregnant."

"If you are not—though I still say you are—then you will be." He brushed his lips across hers. "Soon. Very soon."

Flynt awakened before daybreak, his body tired but his spirits uplifted. He felt like a puffed-up rooster about to crow at the rising sun. He climbed out of the low-slung mattress and heard a soft feminine whimper of disapproval. Grinning to himself, he imagined her lithe little body stretching like a contented feline.

Patit-Pokta. She was his Cougar-Woman, most definitely. In his dreams he saw her tawny coat as she lay next to him in the forest, guarding him, protecting him. In his sleep he had reached out to stroke her fur, only to feel the slick, smooth skin of a woman beneath his hand. He could not say which pleased him more—the presence of the cougar in his dreams or the presence of Kate in his bed. Asleep or awake, he felt overwhelmingly grateful to have been rescued from his solitude and loneliness. Before she came into his life, he could not even say that he had existed for the last eight years. He had been nothing more than a hollow shell.

He slipped into his clothes and quietly left the cabin to see to his animals and his own morning ritual. Yola was doing well, as was her colt. Sasti had acquired an odd paternalism that vaguely amused Flynt. As he let the three out of the shelter, his roan acted a tad more frisky than was his normal. The young colt kicked up his heels and raced around the clearing that was growing lighter as dawn crept in on soft shoes.

Flynt watched the mare go about nibbling sweet grass and clover, almost indifferent to the two males in her life.

Rather typical, he observed as the colt and stallion strutted and pranced proudly for recognition.

"We men are all fools for love," he murmured, leaving them to their posturing while he washed at the creek.

Chapter 17

A SMALL AMOUNT of hazy morning sunlight filtered through the window when Flynt returned to the cabin, allowing him to find his shaving supplies without the need of a lantern.

"Flynt?" Kate's sleepy voice drifted across the room and wrapped around him like a long swath of Oriental silk. He considered following it back into the warm confines of the bed and her body. He set the shaving mug and brush on the table, telling himself that he would see only to her question and not to his own needs. Sitting on the frame of the bed, he gazed down at her heavy-lidded eyes and tousled dark hair.

"Did you sleep well?"

"When did you let me sleep?"

He chuckled quietly. "The last ten minutes that I've been outside should have left you quite rested."

Her smile widened as her eyes drifted closed and she snuggled into the mattress. "Give me another hour. Between your insatiable appetite and that weird woo-woo visit from the netherworld, I haven't had a moment's rest."

Kate's peculiar vernacular never ceased to amuse him. "And what 'weird woo-woo' might that be, if I may ask?"

She popped one eye open. "The visit from Little Deer."

"Say again?"

"Little Deer? The light show? The boy?"

"I haven't the foggiest idea what you are talking about."

A frown wrinkled her forehead. "You don't remember."

"It must have been another of your dreams."

"No . . . at least I don't think so. Damn," she muttered, turning her head into the crook of her arm. "It was so real. Just like everything else in this God-forsaken place. I'm losing my mind, Flynt. I can't tell what's real and what's not."

"Come now, Kate. There's no need to ruin a perfectly wonderful honeymoon with melancholy over a mere dream." He pulled the blanket from her shoulder. "Time to get up. I promised you a trip to Dunsmuir today. And a legal marriage ceremony, as I recall."

She rolled onto her back and stretched with a frustrated groan. He held back his own groan as his gaze settled on the dusky pink circles on her firm, round breasts. He could not keep from wanting her or from touching her. Her breathing quickened.

"Will we be checking into the honeymoon suite at the Walker Boarding House?" she asked with a coquettish smile. He was pleased with himself for turning her mood so quickly.

"If they have one."

"We'll have to be extra quiet."

"A pity," he said, arousing her as well as himself. "Perhaps we should give ourselves one last chance to make a bit of a ruckus. What do you say?"

"I say you're shameless."

"Now isn't that the pot calling the kettle black?"

Two hours later, Flynt led Sasti from the stable, saddled and ready for the long ride. Yola hadn't been ridden in so long that he didn't wish to put Kate on her, even if the colt had to trot along with its mother. Instead, he intended to ride double.

"We'll stop along the way to see SnowEagle. If he will agree to take care of the animals, we will stay longer so you can have a few extra days to visit with the Walker sisters."

Wearing the yellow gingham dress she'd hemmed that morning, Kate clutched both hands around the leather handles of Rita's valise, which appeared to be stuffed full of her necessary items for the trip. After he swung up into the saddle, she handed up her bag and used the bench as a step to climb up behind him. She put her arms around his waist and laced her fingers together over his belt buckle. Flynt felt the softness of her breasts against his back and tried not to think of their long and amorous night together. Instead, he thought of the long and amorous night that awaited him at the end of their journey north.

With a subtle press of his knees, he turned Sasti toward the trail that led down the mountainside. A few feet from the edge of the clearing, five horses emerged from the same path, each with an armed rider. He recognized only Sheriff Henry Murdock from the brief interrogation regarding the fight with LeBouche.

"Avery," greeted the lawman with a nod, a rifle draped across his forearm. Then to Kate, "Ma'am."

Flynt didn't hear her response before he answered, "Good morning, Sheriff. Is there trouble?"

"Yep, I'd say there's a peck of trouble. Where were you yesterday 'bout noon?"

Kate tightened her hold around his waist. "You don't have to tell him."

"I have no reason not to," he stated, keeping his eyes on the sheriff. "I was hunting on the other side of the canyon. The west ridge. I took down a sizable buck near one of the meadows."

"Anyone see you?"

"I was alone."

"Too bad. You wouldn't happen to have anything to show for your efforts now, would you?" The sheriff stood up in his stirrups and tried to get a good look around the clearing.

"I took the carcass to the old Wintu, SnowEagle. We dressed it out at his lodge a few miles from here. I had planned to retrieve the rest of it today."

"No deer, huh? Now that certainly don't look good for you."

Kate spoke up. "Are you implying there has been a crime committed and you suspect Flynt? If so, he has a right to have legal counsel present during any questioning."

One of the other men remarked, "What have we got here—a lady lawyer?"

"As a matter of fact—"

Flynt jerked around and muttered under his breath, "Quiet, Kate. You have nothing to substantiate your background *here.*"

"I will not be quiet." Her measured words were delivered in a low threat. "Not if they're a lynch mob."

Sheriff Murdock overheard her. "I guarantee you that we are not a group of vigilantes, ma'am."

"Then state your business."

"We're here to escort Mr. Avery back to town to stand trial for murder."

"Murder?!" echoed Flynt and Kate together.

"Blackjack LeBouche brought his wife to Dr. Gill's late last night. She'd been beaten within an inch of her life. Before she passed out, she told her husband that her and their eleven-year-old boy were attacked on their homestead around noon."

Kate asked, "Did she specifically state that it was Flynt Avery?"

"No, ma'am. But her description couldn't fit anyone else—big, giant mountain man with long blond hair. Blackjack says Avery here threatened revenge. Some folks in town might be inclined to agree, seeing as how they saw that brawl on Back Street."

Flynt shifted in his saddle. "What did the boy say?"

"Boy's dead. Throat slit, says LeBouche."

"Where was the Frenchman when all this happened?"

"Sitting behind some unlucky hands at a card game in town. Got plenty of eyewitnesses, too. He didn't leave the table until after supper time."

Kate interjected, "He still could've done it. You said he didn't bring his wife to the doctor's until late last night."

"We'll let a judge listen to both sides. My job's to take your mister in and lock him up."

Flynt maintained a calm facade despite the seething anger beneath the surface. A child butchered. A woman beaten and unconscious. How could anyone think him capable of such a heinous crime? Yet he had no alibi. And plenty of motive, if some people were to be believed.

"I only request that I be allowed to make a brief stop to speak with SnowEagle about caring for my horses while I'm gone."

From behind him, Kate added, "You could show them the deer you shot—what's left of it anyway."

The sheriff shook his head. "Won't make much difference at this point. Even if you were with the old man the whole day, not too many folks put much stock in the words of a senile old Digger Indian."

"Don't call him that," snapped Kate. Flynt placed his hand over hers. Murdock looked a bit wary-eyed at her.

"Would you mind getting down off the horse, ma'am. We've got to take him in."

"Yes, I *do* mind. I'm going with him. And I'm going to make damn sure he gets a fair trial."

The lawman appeared to be weighing his options.

Flynt advised, "I should tell you, sir, that when this particular lady makes up her mind about something, she's not one to easily reckon with." Murdock's eyebrows arched with a distinct dislike of any challenge to his authority. "But I promise she will be on her best behavior—and will hold her tongue."

"She better," he warned. "We've got a long ride and I'm in no mood to listen to an ill-tempered, foul-mouthed woman for the duration."

"I beg your—" Her words were cut off by Flynt elbowing her lightly in the ribs.

"Behave, dear Kate," he cautioned with mock sweetness, certain that he felt the daggers of her glare stabbing the back of his skull.

Rita and Louzana Walker were waiting outside the jail when Kate and Flynt rode into town with the sheriff and his citizen deputies. She didn't know how long the sisters had been standing there by the door, but Kate was grateful to see their two familiar faces after passing by the curious stares of several dozen townspeople. The sisters came forward to the edge of the wooden boardwalk as the riders dismounted.

"Good afternoon, Henry," greeted Lou solemnly.

" 'Afternoon, Miss Louzana, Miss Rita." Murdock was polite, yet stuck to business as he thanked the men and asked one of them to take his horse and Sasti to Lee's Livery, then motioned for his prisoner to head up the steps.

"May I have a moment, Sheriff," asked Flynt, handing the carpet bag to Kate. "I'd like to say good-bye."

Struck by the finality of his words, Kate glanced up at him, searching his face for some sign of hope. SnowEagle's remark came back to her—*There will be no good-bye.*

The lawman tilted his head toward the jail. "You can do that inside."

Kate took his arm and walked with Flynt up the stiars. They paused beside the two sisters. Louzana sniffled, dabbing her nose with a purple handkerchief. Rita remained stoic, reaching out and taking the satchel from Kate. "We'll be right here. Take your time."

Sheriff Murdock didn't leave them alone until he frisked Flynt, confiscated the hunting knife and led them both into a cell. "I'll be back in five minutes."

Kate flinched as the iron door clanged shut. Neither of them spoke until the footsteps died beyond the outer door. She glanced at the bars on the window, then at the pathetic excuse for a bed that was at least a foot shorter than Flynt. It looked like every jail cell in every Western she'd ever seen. But this one had the added realism of dank air, musty blankets, and an empty pisspot in the corner.

Flynt took a step toward her and enveloped her in his long arms. "I had rather hoped to shield you from this scene. It would have been better to have said our good-byes outside in the fresh air and sunshine."

There will be no good-bye.

She pressed her cheek against his broad chest. "I know you didn't do it."

"As do I. But it'll take some doing to convince a judge, I'm afraid."

Leaning back from him, she looked up into his midnight-blue eyes. "You can't be punished for a crime you didn't commit. I won't let it happen."

"This will not be the first time in history that the wrong man hung for someone else's offense. Nor will it be the last."

Wrong man hung... Wrong man hung... Wrong man hung...

The words reverberated in her brain, growing more and more familiar. In her mind's eye, she saw big, bold letters spelling it out—WRONG MAN HUNG! A headline from a yellowed newspaper popped into her head. Names fell into place as she recalled bits and pieces from the article about a mistaken execution. A wealthy recluse. A gambler. His murdered wife and child.

She gripped the front of his shirt. "Blackjack did it, Flynt."

"We *think* he did it. We don't know with absolute certainty."

"I *do.* I saw a clipping from the *News* in a museum before I came back here to 1892. He confessed, Flynt. He had murdered his own family in a drunken rage."

"That is why you are here then, isn't it?" he asked, gazing down upon her. "Who better to defend me in court than you?"

"No—I specialize in contract law, not criminal law. Negotiations, not cross-examinations."

"I believe you are the only one who can exonerate me,

Kate. I'm convinced of it. You were brought here to save my life."

"I don't know the first thing about working within the confines of the nineteenth-century judicial system."

"You'll find a way."

Kate wished she could feel as optimistic as Flynt appeared. At least a spark of hope had returned to his eyes. But she wasn't so sure she was the best attorney his money could buy. And he had plenty of money to bankroll a dream team of legal counsel.

If she didn't get him off, he was going to die by the hangman's noose. If she succeeded, her mission would be accomplished and she'd probably be taken back to 1996. Either way she would lose Flynt forever. But she'd rather live without him in the future, knowing she had won him a acquittal and spared his life.

"We're going to need more help if we expect to win this case. Your business partners in San Francisco should be contacted. They can round up the best lawyers in the city. You can afford it, right?"

"That's my girl!"

"Girl?"

One corner of his mouth lifted in a moderately apologetic grin. "Pardon me, counselor."

"That's more like it." Her hands snaked around his waist as she pressed her body against the length of him. "Our legal interview is now concluded. You may kiss your . . ."

"Lady lawyer?" he offered, bringing his face close to hers. "Or were you about to say 'bride'?"

"No, not at all," she lied, wondering how it was that he could pick up on her thoughts. She chided herself for feeling a twinge of disappointment about their wedding plans. There were more important things to think about—like

Flynt's life. "My status as your bride isn't exactly official. Not yet, anyway."

"Perhaps not in the eyes of the law. But in mine, you are." He dropped his mouth to hers, kissing her deeply, passionately. The sound of the sheriff's return startled them. As the lawman walked toward the jail cell, Flynt hugged her tight and whispered in her ear. "I'm going to miss you every moment we are apart."

Kate held him close, tears close to overflowing. "I love you, Flynt."

Murdock seemed to be making an extra effort to be noisy—rattling keys, banging them against the bars, clearing his throat with a loud cough. By the time he opened the iron door, Flynt had stepped away from Kate, distancing himself from her.

"May I come back at dinner time with a tray for Flynt?" she asked.

"Fine by me." The sheriff stood back, allowing her space to exit.

She turned toward Flynt, who had his right hand wrapped around one of the window bars, gazing out at the Walker Boarding House. "I'll be back in a few hours."

He didn't look back at her but kept his eyes on the outside world. "I'll be watching for you."

With a heavy heart and leaden feet, Kate had to drag herself out of the jail cell. The two sisters' eyes were on her as she stepped onto the boardwalk. Lou immediately came up to her and put her arms around her.

"We're so sorry, sugar."

Kate returned the hug but refused to give in to a display of emotional tears. "I suppose you know about the murder," she said to them both. They each nodded as Lou stepped aside, but kept her arm around Kate's shoulders.

"First, let's get you settled in, then we'll talk," offered Rita, gesturing with a tip of her head toward the boarding house. "We have a room ready and waiting. Room twelve."

"Flynt's room overlooking the street?" she asked, her gaze darting to the second-floor window.

"Is it, sister?" Rita asked Lou, then answered herself. "Why I do believe it is. Well then, you'll feel right at home."

The three women crossed the dusty dirt road and mounted the corner steps to the Walkers' wraparound veranda. Inside, at the foot of the stairs, Kate thanked them both and took the valise from the older sister's hand.

Lou gave her a gentle squeeze before dropping her arm to her side. "Why don't you lie down and rest awhile before joining us for tea. You're looking a mite peaked."

She nodded. "Maybe for a few minutes."

"Take as long as you need. We're certainly not going anywhere."

Kate started up the stairs, then paused with her left foot on the first tread. "I promised Flynt I'd bring his supper to him. Would it be too much trouble to make up a tray?"

"Not in the least," announced Rita.

"Of course," added Lou. "How about enough for two, then you could join him."

"No, that won't be necessary. I don't have much of an appetite."

"Nonsense." Rita frowned at her. "You must keep up your strength. Get on up there now. If you happen to doze off too awfully long, we'll be sure to wake you in time to take some food to that man of yours."

"Thanks, Rita." Smiling at the motherly nature of the two ladies, Kate felt as if a quilt of comfort had been wrapped around her soul. "You too, Lou."

"Our pleasure," they answered in unison.

As she wearily plodded up the first flight of stairs, she felt their eyes on her, watching her in silence. She went to her door on the second floor and reached for the antiquated iron key that had been left in the keyhole. Snippets of whispers floated up the stairwell as she opened the door. She hesitated, her fingers wrapped around the cool brass knob.

". . . Shh, she'll hear you."

"I've half a mind to tell her."

"You wouldn't."

"She'll know soon enough."

"You can't be sure."

"The proof is in the pudding, Lou."

Their conversation faded away as if the two women were headed in the direction of the kitchen. Kate's stomach knotted. What proof? What did Rita want to tell her? Was it information about Blackjack and the murder?

A young family emerged from a door down the hall. The tall, slender father held a wide-eyed toddler in his arms as his expectant wife walked alongside. With a rosy complexion, she could hardly be a day over eighteen. "I wish you'd stop fussin' so, Tommy. I got three more months of carrying this baby but you act like it's three days."

"I should stay with you, honey. I don't need to go on this trip."

"Don't you dare use me for an excuse. It's my fault you didn't—" The wife stopped short when she saw Kate. "How d'ya do, ma'am? You must be the lady my aunts have been telling me about."

"Yes . . ." Caught off guard, Kate wasn't exactly sure what the sisters had been telling the young mother. Dropping her hand from the doorknob, she smoothed the skirt of her dress. "Yes, I'm Kate Marshall. Excuse me if I seem surprised. I wasn't aware of a niece."

"Not by blood, just by love. I'm Charlie—Charlotte, actually. This here's my husband Tommy Morrison and our daughter Mary."

Little Mary wriggled in her daddy's arms as he offered a hand. "Pleased to make your acquaintance, ma'am."

She accepted his handshake, then smiled at the cherub face of his daughter. "Hi there, sweetie."

Mary chirped, " 'Lo."

A delicate little butterfly of envy fluttered somewhere in the vicinity of her heart. When her glance inadvertently fell upon the rounded belly of the young mother, she felt gossamer wings fanning a tiny spark of a secret longing. She tried to file away the errant thought and offered her congratulations on the impending addition to their family.

Charlie beamed. "We're hoping for a boy this time."

Kate thought of the dark-eyed boy that had touched her last night. *In a dream,* she reminded herself harshly. It was only a fanciful dream. "I hope you get your wish."

"Me, too," offered Tommy.

As he put his arm around his wife, Kate recalled the conversation she'd had with Flynt about kids growing up in the same town and marrying without all the qualms of doubts and options. And here they were standing in front of her—two young people who were in love and forging a future together.

"Well," sighed Charlie after a brief lull that became an awkward pause. "We've got to get to the station before the train pulls in. Tommy's going to St. Louis about a job prospect."

"I only wish the timing were a little better."

His wife looked up at him. "You'll be back in no time. Meanwhile, Aunt Rita and Aunt Lou are going to spoil Mary to pieces."

"They better not let you lift a finger."

"Would you listen to this man?" she asked Kate, clicking her tongue. "Dr. Gill told him I'm as healthy as a horse but he acts like I'm as sick as a dog."

"You *were* sick as a dog for four months."

"I'm past that stage now. And I'll do my share of washing dishes if my aunts allow it."

Kate had a hunch neither Rita nor Lou would allow Charlie to do a single task while under their watchful eyes. "You have a safe trip, Tommy. It was nice meeting you."

"You, too. I wish you the best of luck for your Mr. Avery."

Her smile faltered.

Nudging her husband, Charlie gave him a mortified stare before turning to Kate. "We didn't mean to upset you. If there's anything we—that is, I can do while Tommy's gone . . ."

"Thank you, but I'm sure everything's going to be fine. Things have a way of working themselves out somehow."

"You sound like you've been around Aunt Rita for a while."

"Not long enough, I'm afraid."

"I feel the same way." Charlie rubbed her stomach in that unconscious way that expectant mothers do.

Mary fussed, ending the conversation and sending the three on their way to the depot. None too soon for Kate. She had become more and more aware of her own jealous green-eyed monster.

Dropping the carpetbag onto the bed, she went to the window and pulled back the lace curtains. But her interest wasn't drawn to the picturesque scene of snow-covered Mt. Shasta in the distance. Her gaze went immediately to the jail on the corner of Back Street and the road leading down the hill toward the Southern Pacific rail yard. There was no sign of Flynt in the window toward the back of the brick building.

She stared at the darkened cell and felt a chill of fear. Flynt appeared at the bars, almost as if he sensed her presence in his old room. She wiggled her fingers at him. He returned a half wave. Flattening her palm on the center pane of glass, she watched him mirror her gesture and imagined the warmth of his touch bridging the distance between them.

"I . . . love . . . you." She formed each word so he could see her mouth clearly. He nodded, pointed to his heart, then pointed back at her. She forced a smile of encouragement. Their silent moment of communication was interrupted as a couple of barefoot boys in baggy overalls carted an empty wooden crate up to the jailhouse window. They had come to see a rare sight in Dunsmuir—an honest-to-goodness, real-life prisoner.

He won't be a prisoner for long, Kate thought to herself, vowing to do everything in her power to see that Flynt would soon walk out of that cell a free man.

Out of the corner of her eye, she caught sight of the Morrisons walking away from the boarding house, heading down the long series of wooden steps that flanked the Chinese laundry and Bilicke's Mt. Shasta Hotel. Tommy fretted over his expectant wife's every move, hovering close enough to offer his free hand to help her down the stairs.

Kate abruptly dropped the lace curtains and turned away from the window, battling the envy that had never been a part of her nature. Trying to think of something other than the young couple, she grabbed the carpetbag from the bed to put it away in the free-standing closet. But her mind drifted back to Charlie and Tommy.

The quintessential little family knew where they fit in and where they were headed. Unlike Kate, who was torn between two time periods, there was no limbo for either Tommy or Charlie. They would have their brood of children and raise them in a white clapboard house—be it in Dunsmuir or St. Louis. In sixty years, they would sit on their front porch rocking in their rocking chairs with dozens of grandchildren and great-grandchildren.

Kate wouldn't have such a life. She'd be lucky if she could save the man she loved from being hung. That was all she could think about now. Maudlin thoughts of babies and fifty-year anniversaries weren't going to do her a damn bit of good.

In a huff of self-recrimination, she marched to the mirrored wardrobe and stowed the bag. Closing the door, she did a double take at the full-length image of herself. For the briefest moment, she hadn't recognized the thin woman in the old-fashioned yellow dress. Staring at her sunken cheeks and the dark circles under her eyes, she understood why Lou and Rita were so concerned. Even her skin looked pale and sallow compared to Charlie's soft pink glow.

Wishing the Maybelline goddess would drop a bag of cosmetics in her hands wasn't going to make it so. Kate reached up and pinched her cheeks to bring some color to them. The realization of her desperation slowly dawned on her as she lowered her hands and gazed down at them.

"What am I doing?!" she muttered in disgust, then glanced up at her reflection. At twenty-eight years old, she was considered an old maid in this century. The last thing she needed was broken capillaries to accentuate her fading beauty. "You're losing it, Katherine Marshall. You're losing it big time."

"Are you out of your mind, Kate?" Lou set her hands on her hips, standing in the middle of the kitchen. Rita stirred a pot of soup on the stove. Kate had left earlier without taking the time to rest as she'd promised. Instead, she had freshened up and paid a visit to Dr. Gill to see about the condition of the beaten woman. "What kind of fool puts herself right into the thick of the worst possible mess she could imagine?"

"If only you could have seen Gert LeBouche, Lou."

"I don't need to see that poor soul. Whatever possessed you to go to the doctor's in the first place?"

"I had to find out if she had regained consciousness yet. I was hoping to talk her into testifying on Flynt's behalf."

"Then why in heaven's name do you need to go through with this wild-eyed scheme of yours? Just wait 'til that woman wakes up."

Rita spoke quietly over her shoulder. "I happen to agree with Lou on this one, Kate, though Lord knows we rarely stand on the same side of the fence on any two occasions. What you plan to do is downright dangerous."

"I know, I know." Kate threw up her arms in exasperation. "But if Gert doesn't make it through the night, I'll have lost my only chance on this. I don't see how I have much choice."

Lou tapped her toe impatiently. "I'll bet a hole in a donut that Flynt doesn't have an inkling about any of this. Might I be right?"

"I'll tell him after it's all over."

"When it's all over," Rita warned, wiping her hands on her apron, "I don't want to send my poor sister Lou over to that jail cell to tell your man that you got yourself killed trying to lure the real murderer into a trap."

"Me?!" Lou scowled at Rita. "What about you? Who says I'm going to be the one to break that kind of tragic news?"

"Stop! Enough squabbling." Kate held up her palms in

surrender. "I'll go over there myself right now. Are you two satisfied?"

"Not unless you abandon this crazy idea."

"I can't, Lou. Please try to understand. I've explained everything to you both. I know I'm here to save Flynt. I've got to do this, even if it means I'll be taken back to my life in the future. I can't stand by and watch him die."

"But you can defend him in a court of law." Lou was not about to back down.

"Too risky. If this trap doesn't work tonight, I may still have to represent Flynt, even though I'm not qualified to be his defense attorney. Let's worry about that tomorrow, okay?"

Neither sister looked the least bit convinced, which did nothing to bolster her own confidence in her scheme to force Blackjack into showing his hand.

Chapter 18

FLYNT HAD SPENT the better part of his time pacing the floor of his jail cell, except for the brief visit with the two ten-year-olds at his window. One was the brother of the little town crier who had run along the boardwalk announcing his initial arrival with Kate. Neither boy had believed that the legendary Sasquatch had come to town that day. Despite Avery's size, he was clearly not the seven-foot hairy giant of trapper lore. Fortunately, the scruffy fellows also didn't accept the rumor that Avery was a murderer. Their youthful opinion of his character had been a small boost to his sagging morale.

Considering the cruel twists and turns in his life eight years earlier, it was a challenge to keep his spirits from plummeting before he had his moment in court. Would fate deal him yet another harsh blow? Would this one prove insurmountable? He had overcome his father's death and his stepmother's betrayal. He had barely managed to endure the loss of Little Deer. But this murder charge . . . If he could not convince the judge of his innocence. . . .

Flynt shut his eyes to the pessimistic suppositions, blocking the emotional tumult in his mind. He went to the window and rested his forearms between the bars, letting his hands dangle outside. A gentle breeze touched his face, bringing with it the scent of the canyon. Pine and cedar mingled with the smell of smoke from coal-burning engines down at the roundhouse. A strong savory aroma of food also told him it was nearing dinner hour at the hotels and homes within the two-block town.

His stomach rumbled, reminding him that the last full meal he'd eaten had been breakfast with Kate. He leaned his forehead against the iron bars, thinking of her. His mind's eye leaped from one memory to another like a fickle frog leaping lilypads. He remembered how he'd slung her over his shoulder and carried her back to the cabin—and her slap that had followed! He recalled her upturned bottom in white cotton drawers the day she had refused to wear the gingham dress and had gone digging through the chest for the most ridiculous—and tantalizing!—outfit to wear. His thoughts leapt forward to the joy and awe on her radiant face at the sight of the newborn colt. Then, backward to her atrocious attempts to cook for him. He had been lucky to survive.

The irony of his last musing was not lost on him. He *had* been lucky to survive her cooking. And he'd been lucky to survive the fight with LeBouche. Would he be so lucky again? Or had his luck run out?

He spotted Kate just then, and his anxiety faded for the moment. She had come from the back porch of the boarding house with a covered tray in her hands. Concentrating on the placement of her steps as she crossed the rutted street, she was not aware of his eyes on her until she was midway across. When their eyes met, her lovely face lit up with a heart-stopping smile that gentled his restless spirit.

Minutes later, as she entered his cell under Sheriff Murdock's scrutiny, Flynt had to quell the desire to put the tray aside and hold her in his arms. They both looked to the lawman, who lingered with his grip on the open door.

"Might she keep me company while I eat?"

"I don't see why that's necessary. Besides, she might have brought a weapon to pass along to you when my back's turned."

Kate set the dinner tray on top of the woolen blanket spread across the mattress, then held her arms out straight from her sides. "As you can see, I have nothing to hide."

It was true. The tight-fitting bodice of her yellow gingham molded to her womanly curves in such a manner as to leave nothing to one's imagination, let alone hide a knife or pistol.

The sheriff's eyebrows drew together. "There's other places—"

"If I'd had anything strapped to my legs when I came in here, I would've been walking like a bowlegged cowboy." When she saw he wasn't convinced, she remarked with petulant exasperation, "You don't believe me? Fine—then take a good look."

She hoisted her shoe to the edge of the bed frame, and yanked the hem of her skirt clear up to the top of her bare thigh, thoroughly shocking the startled lawman. She dropped her foot to the floor and gave him a quick glance of her other leg in the same manner. Had it been any other woman, Flynt might have been appalled. But her photograph in a bathing suit had shown him a woman from an entirely different culture with its distinctly unconventional perspective, one that he found rather advantageous at this particular moment. And quite amusing, as well. Murdock's slack-jawed expression was quite priceless.

"Satisfied?" she asked smugly, standing there with her arms folded across her chest as if she were a prim and proper schoolmarm in that pretty little dress. The sheriff blinked several times as if he weren't altogether sure if he'd seen what he just saw. Flynt bit the inside of his cheek to keep from breaking into an all-out grin.

"I'm going to be right outside that door," warned Murdock, hiking his thumb over his shoulder.

"I'll be sure to holler when I'm ready to leave." Kate's politeness could have been regarded as genuine sincerity or masked condescension. The sheriff appeared to regard it as a truce.

He nodded to them both and left.

Flynt walked over to her, shaking his head in disbelief. "Any other tricks, my dear lady?"

"None you haven't already seen." She stepped into his embrace and met his kiss with an ardor that created lustful thoughts he had no business entertaining under his present circumstances. His palms skimmed the length of her slender back and settled on the delectable curve of her bottom. The heat of wanting her grew hotter. He moved his mouth from her lips to her chin, down her neck to the edge of lace at her collar. His tongue traced a line to her earlobe where he nibbled gently, eliciting a quiet moan from her.

"Dear God, how I want you right now." The husky timbre of his voice betrayed his weakening restraint.

"Then take me, Flynt."

His chuckle rumbled in his chest. "You are *extraordinary,* do you know that?"

Her breathing ragged, she whispered impatiently, "Quit the pompous British commentary, Englishman."

"You're serious then?"

"What do you think?"

"I think we have a problem with locale."

"I don't care." Her fingernails raked across his shoulder blades. Her feverish words tumbled out in a mad rush. "This might be the last I'll see of you—" She faltered, then added, "*Tonight,* that is. I'll see you tomorrow, of course. And—"

His suspicion roused, Flynt pulled away. "What are you planning to do, Kate? *Tonight,* that is." He echoed her own words but with a different connotation.

"I—I'm not sure. Exactly. There's Lou and Rita. You know we really haven't had much of a chance to catch up on things. I suppose the three of us will sit around talking until all hours."

"Why do I have this notion that you are not telling me the whole truth?"

"I don't know why." She frowned, stepping back. "But you sure know how to kill a mood."

"Kate . . ." cautioned Flynt.

"Your supper's getting cold."

"Something is amiss. And I demand to know what it is."

"The only thing 'amiss,' as you say, is that you are locked up. And I'm going to get your charges dropped if it's the last thing I do."

"Are you speaking as my attorney or my lover?"

"One and the same."

"No, my attorney would not do anything in foolish disregard for her safety."

"I already did something foolish when I let you talk me into representing you." She dropped her head back and stared at the ceiling. Silence hung heavy in the room that grew dim with the approach of evening. "I don't want to fight."

"Neither do I. We're both a bit on edge from all that's happened today."

She gave him a sideways glance with a small smile. "It doesn't help matters when we didn't get a great deal of rest last night."

"Are you willing to tell me about the dream yet?" He had inquired of it during breakfast, but she'd evaded his question.

"It was nothing." She shrugged. "Just a dream."

"So was the one you'd had before you came here to 1892—the one of us making love."

After a pensive nod, she seemed to come to a sudden change of heart and shook her head. "That was different. That was just a—Never mind. It doesn't matter anyhow. What matters right now is your case. In fact, I really should be going. I need to knock on some doors to find some friendly witnesses."

"Must you do so now?" he asked, curious about her quick turnabout. Only a minute earlier she had desperately wanted to be in his arms. Now she acted as if she couldn't wait to get away. Why had she thrown herself at him, almost in desperation? And why was she so nervously intent upon conducting business during everyone's dinner hour? "Can't your work wait until morning?"

"There isn't time, Flynt. I have to start to prepare and I can't waste a minute. Every person who saw that fight with LeBouche must be questioned. We need to find anyone who will testify to seeing him pull your knife. If we can prove you had no intentions of killing him that day in the street, maybe we'll be able to cast a shadow of doubt upon your intention to kill his family. But that's only the beginning—"

He held up his hand. "You have made your point."

"Sheriff?" she called out at the bars. "I'm ready."

Flynt stepped up behind her, grasped her shoulders and kissed her behind the ear. "When we have seen our way clear of this bloody mess, we are going to spend two months in a glorious hotel suite overlooking San Francisco Bay. The best the city has to offer."

She pivoted about and gazed at him, touching the edge of his jaw with her fingertips. "I can't wait," she said softly, then brushed her lips against his as Sheriff Murdock came through the outer door.

Close to midnight, Kate lay motionless in the pitch-black darkness of a room that had recently been occupied by the unconscious wife of Blackjack LeBouche. The badly beaten woman had been moved to another part of Dr. Gill's house. His family had been sent to the neighbors, removing them from danger.

Kate hoped the scheme worked as well as it always did in the mysteries and whodunits she'd seen. It was too late to wonder if she'd made the right decision. The doctor had already passed along news that Gert LeBouche was steadily improving, though in reality her condition had sadly deteriorated over the course of the evening. He had been dismayed by the woman's decline, fearing that the loss of her only child had undermined her will to live. He had told Kate and Sheriff Murdock that it was only a matter of time before Gert slipped away.

Only a matter of time. . . .

Kate had never been so aware of the passage of time. She had sneaked back to the Gills' after dark, which had been close to nine. At ten, she had heard a clock mark the hour with deep gongs. By then the switch had been completed and she had begun the long wait, hoping Blackjack had taken the bait. The eleven-o'clock hour had been announced by the clock with no sign of the Frenchman. She prayed that he would be desperate enough to do something to turn the tide in his favor. In an odd way, she knew that same sense of desperation as she put herself in grave danger. Blackjack, however, would be out to save his own neck. Kate was out to save Flynt's.

Would he even show up? She hoped so! She also hoped that he'd make some noise, some slight sound announcing his entrance, to give her enough warning to call out to the sheriff waiting down the hall.

The escalating tension in her body tightened her muscles and shortened her breath. She could hear herself in the still of the night. Paying close attention to the sound of her breathing, she slowly inhaled, then exhaled, trying to relax and stay calm yet alert. She could not let something as seemingly insignificant as a shallow breath give an intruder cause to suspect a trap.

The distant gong of the clock startled her, even though she'd been expecting it. Her nerves were strung as tight as a piano string, as Rita would have said.

Then she heard something.

Or at least she thought she'd heard something—the slightest indecipherable sound. But it was lost in the lengthy toll of a dozen deep chimes. Could she have imagined it? Had her mind formulated ideas of evil out of simple bumps and creaks and other noises that houses tended to make?

Suddenly a hand clamped down over her mouth. *"C'est moi*—it is me, Gert."

The room was too dark to see him, but there was no doubt that it was Blackjack. Despite the terror that gripped her, Kate kept silent, determined to give him ample opportunity to incriminate himself.

He murmured in a mixture of French and English, his accented speech interrupted by an occasional broken sob. The man was distraught with grief and bitterness.

"Jacques would be alive now if he didn't try to stop me from hitting you. He knew better, the stupid boy. So what if I knock you around? Don't I always make it up to you? I always make love to you after, yes? Jacques should not have attacked me—his own papa. It was not my fault, *ma chérie.*"

Kate had the confession she needed. All she had to do now was knock his hand away and scream like hell.

"Je t'aime beaucoup. Go with God, my love."

The pillow under her head was abruptly snatched away, then dropped on her face as he slid his hand from her mouth. She tried to cry out but her shriek was muffled. The scent of antiseptic permeated the linen pressed to her nostrils.

Her arms flailed. Her legs kicked. The Frenchman fought her. She tried to toss her head to the side but it was pinned against the mattress. Her open mouth sucked dry cloth against her tongue as she struggled for air.

A harsh whisper came to her ear. "I cannot let you live, Gert. You cannot tell them I killed my own son!"

Kate felt the pressure of his hands pushing down on the pillow, one on each side of her cheek. She scratched at his wrist and forearms. But he only cursed her efforts. She frantically reached up and gouged at his face with her thumbs, mentally aiming for his eye sockets. Hit or miss, she had nothing to lose.

"Aaugh!" His anguished howl filled the room. His hands let up, giving her a split second to shove the pillow off her face. Gasping for breath, she let out a strangled cry for help.

The sound of heavy footsteps pounded in the hall, growing louder. The door flung open and slammed against a bureau, sending a vase crashing to the floor. Light spilled in from the hallway, silhouetting the sheriff with his gun drawn. Blackjack stumbled toward the window, one hand over his eyes while the other flailed blindly in front of him. Shards of porcelain crunched beneath the soles of his shoes.

"Don't take another step, LeBouche," ordered Murdock. The doctor stood behind him, gravely watching the whole scene.

Blackjack whimpered, "I only came to see my wife. And this woman, she attacked me!"

"You dirty son of—" Kate sat up too quickly. Her head spun. "You came to *kill* your wife and I'll testify to that fact. Word for word."

A low-pitched whistle entered her left ear. The room seemed to tilt. She gripped her hands to her skull and leaned over, propping her elbows on her knees.

Dr. Gill came to her aid. "You better lie down."

"I've just got to get a little oxygen to the brain cells," she muttered, belatedly realizing how strange she must have sounded to the men.

Sheriff Murdock kept his aim on the Frenchman but spoke to Kate. "I don't know how in blue blazes you knew LeBouche would come here tonight, ma'am. But I'm grateful all the same. I'll take him down to the jail now."

"I'm coming with you." She started to push herself off the bed but the doctor grasped her arm.

"You best give yourself an hour or so before you traipse off into the night," advised Dr. Gill. "I'll escort you to the boarding house after you've rested from your ordeal."

"I don't need to rest. I need to see Flynt." The odd ringing in her ear added to the irritation.

"Sheriff, if you intend to release Mr. Avery based upon this lady's testimony here in this room, would you make sure he gets over here straightaway?"

"That I will." Murdock turned to LeBouche, who was still babbling about his innocence and rubbing his watery eyes. "Get a move on, Blackjack."

After the lawman left the room with his prisoner, the doctor insisted that she lie down and rest, then excused himself to check on Gert. Kate tried to follow orders, knowing that Flynt would come to her as soon as he was a free man. But instead of relaxing, her inexplicable anxiety grew. She told herself there was no reason to worry. The sheriff had as much as said that Flynt was no longer a suspect. Still, she couldn't deny the sense of urgency she felt about seeing him again.

Alone for only a few minutes, she finally gave in to her gut instinct and got out of bed. Her equilibrium had improved enough to allow her to sneak down the back stairs and out the kitchen door. By the time she reached Back Street, she attributed the slight dizziness to her winded dash to the jail. The low-pitched whistle had subsided, though she couldn't be certain when it had stopped.

It is time. The familiar voice lifted the hair on her neck, unleashing a wave of goosebumps down her arms.

In the distance, a glowing ball of light moved toward her. She quickened her pace. A few yards from the sheriff's office, she recognized the wavering image of Little Deer from her dream. Instead of the initial fear she'd experienced at the riverbank, she felt a sense of peace and comfort. The young woman held out her hands. Kate looked beyond her to the front door of the jail.

It is time, the spirit repeated.

"Not yet," pleaded Kate, hiking her skirt higher so she could lengthen her brisk stride. The thought of leaving Flynt sent panic through her. "Just give me a few more minutes. Let me say good-bye."

There will be no good-bye.

She broke into a run but her feet grew heavy. Her legs slowed as she pressed against a force greater than her own strength. With a desperate cry, she lunged forward, reaching out to the fading image of the past.

Flynt awoke from a fitful sleep, unaware he'd drifted off on the uncomfortably short bed. He had dreamed of the cougar again. She had risen from her place at his side and walked a few yards, then paused and looked back at him. He had sensed her reluctance to leave. He had wanted to go with her. After she'd turned away and disappeared into the forest, the cougar's bloodcurdling scream had pierced the eerie silence.

He had been lying awake when Sheriff Murdock brought in Blackjack and put him in the adjacent cell. The lawman explained the heroic trap set by Kate as he escorted Flynt to the front office.

"She's waiting for you at Doc's place. Big fancy house up the street from Bilicke's. Can't miss it."

"Why is she still there? Is she hurt?"

"Just a bit shook up is all. She wanted to hightail it out of there but Doc insisted she stay. He's not one to mess with."

"Neither is she."

"You got that right." Murdock handed over the sheathed hunting knife. "No hard feelings, then?"

"You were merely doing your job, Sheriff."

After Flynt found the house he was escorted by the doctor to an empty bedroom. "Where is she?"

"I—I don't know. I left her here while I was checking on the other woman. She must've slipped out."

Flynt ran back to the jail, then to the boardinghouse, heading straight toward the back porch when he caught sight of the light burning in the kitchen. He burst in, praying that he would see Kate sitting with the Walker sisters. But Rita and Louzana were alone.

"Kate's missing," he barked with unintentional harshness. "Have you seen her?"

"Land sakes—no!" Lou clapped her palm to her bosom.

Rita came to her feet. "Not since she left for Dr. Gill's around nine."

"Why didn't you stop her?"

"We talked till we were blue in the face," answered Lou.

"You should've locked her in her room."

"She's a grown woman," argued Rita with an even tone. "I gave her my advice but she chose not to heed it. You can holler all you want but it's not going to solve the question of her whereabouts."

Reining his anger, Flynt put his hand on the doorknob. "I'm going back to the doctor's house. She might be lying in the dark somewhere and I ran right past her."

Rita stepped forward. "Why on earth would she be lying in the dark?"

"If she fainted from all the excitement—"

"Kate wouldn't faint," Lou piped up.

Rita grabbed his arm to keep him from dashing out the door. "What excitement?"

"The Frenchman nearly killed her, thinking she was his wife."

"Kate was right?" asked Lou, coming across the room, wringing her hands.

"It appears so," he offered. "Now you must excuse me, ladies. I don't want to waste a minute more."

"No, of course not. Go-go-go," shooed Rita.

Lou called out as he ran the length of the back porch, "Take a lantern."

He backtracked only long enough to take from her hand the lantern that she'd gotten out of a nearby storage room off the kitchen. "Thank you, ma'am."

Lou responded, "We'll be here waiting."

"And praying," added Rita.

When word of Kate's disappearance circulated through the noisy saloons, many patrons left whiskey bottles and card games to join the search. The small railroad town came alive with flickering lamplight and torches moving up and down the streets, through yards, between houses. One careless drunk accidentally touched off a small brush fire with his torch, both of which were quickly doused by an alert citizen. By daybreak there wasn't a soul still in bed. Some women left their children with other mothers and went out beating the bushes. One man brought out his sorry-eyed bloodhound that stopped in the street in front of the jail and bayed like a lunatic.

"Blue never done nuthin' this crazy before," the owner complained, tugging on the hemp rope tied around the neck of the stubborn dog.

Someone groused, "What about the time he chased a damn skunk into Van Fossen's drug store?"

Flynt walked slump-shouldered past the exchange and headed toward the front steps of the Walker Boarding House. Miss Louzana had been pacing the porch for at least two hours.

"She's gone back," she said as he closed the distance between them. Hearing her confirm his thoughts was almost too much to bear. He sank down onto the railing, his head hanging.

"I think I've known it all along," he admitted reluctantly, unable to lift his gaze from his boots, planted wide on the worn wooden planks. He didn't wish to see his own sadness reflected in her eyes. His chest felt hollow and sunken, making each breath an effort in labor.

Across the way, a ruckus started around a side window of the jail. Angry shouts drew a crowd, bringing people from all directions up and down the street. Despite the pale light in the sky, many still carried torches and lanterns.

"Now what do you suppose that's all about?" asked Lou.

Flynt straightened to his full height and stared at the growing throng. "I don't like the looks of this."

Rita came out the door, wiping her hands on her apron. She reached around behind her waist and untied the strings. "I've been watching out the kitchen window. Called one of the Branstetter boys over to ask about the fuss. He says the Frenchman's been shouting out the window at folks."

"He was drunk when Murdock dumped him in his cell."

"Maybe so," answered Lou, "But that was some hours ago." She asked her older sister, "What's he saying that's stirring up everybody?"

"Claims the murder charge can't be proven without Kate's testimony."

Lou shook her head in disgust. "He's right, y'know. What a shame. What a cotton-pickin' shame."

Flynt moved toward the steps, keeping his eye on the action across the street. "You aren't the only one who feels that way, Miss Louzana."

Sheriff Murdock emerged from the jail with a rifle in his hands. "If none of you see fit to keep searching for the woman, then you can go on back to your own homes."

"Blackjack says you gotta let him go. That true?" yelled a man.

"Can't have a trial without a witness to his confession."

Heated shouts echoed angry sentiments. Flynt glimpsed more than a few weapons among the milling crowd. "You two better go inside. Stay away from the windows, too. There very well might be bullets flying."

Rita spoke from behind him. "And just where do you think you're going?"

"Sheriff Murdock can't handle those men all by himself." He went down the corner stairs and out into the street.

"We're takin' LeBouche, Sheriff," announced another man. "Now get out of the way."

"You're not taking my prisoner." Murdock stood his ground, his finger on the trigger of his rifle. "I'm telling you to go home. You're all fine, upstanding citizens of this town. You God-fearing folks don't want blood on your hands. This man isn't worth it."

"He is so!"

"He killed his own boy!"

"Doc says the wife's gonna die, too!"

"Blackjack did it!"

Sheriff Murdock shook his head. "We don't have a witness."

"Dr. Gill heard that Marshall woman. He believes her. That's enough for us!"

The lawman called out over the shouts and noise, "Judge can't use secondhand testimony. All Doc's got is one person's word against another. And that one person happens to be missing. Now I'm telling you for the last time—"

Flynt wove through the sea of vigilantes and approached the boardwalk in front of the jail. Murdock mistook the advance as a threat and leveled the barrel of his rifle. "That's far enough, Avery."

"I don't want this any more than you do, Sheriff. I came to see if I could help."

"That man in there tried to frame you for murder and

nearly killed your lady friend. If anybody wants to see him hang, you'd probably supply the rope yourself."

Flynt didn't care for the ring of truth in the lawman's words. How often had he contemplated revenge? If Murdock learned of the earlier attack on Kate at the river, he would have yet another reason to be suspicious of Flynt.

"I swear to you, Murdock, I have no desire to see it end this way."

Someone called out, "Hang LeBouche! Hang LeBouche!"

Flynt turned around to face the crowd, holding his hands up to stop the grisly chant that only got louder and louder. The men pressed forward as women hung back, adding their voices.

"You can't do this," he yelled at the seething crowd. Then he felt the crack at the base of his skull.

Stunned by the blow, he blinked once before the butt of a shotgun slammed into his tender gut. Pain shot through his body. He doubled over. Struck in the back, his legs collapsed under him. His knees hit the dirt as someone else's knee caught him under the chin.

Everything went black.

Chapter 19

Rᴇᴛᴜʀɴᴇᴅ ᴛᴏ 1996, Kate stood in the small museum, gazing down into the glass display case. The front page headline of the *News* declared, Lᴇʙᴏᴜᴄʜᴇ ʜᴜɴɢ! The yellowed article described the angry vigilante hanging. The last paragraph mentioned the release of Flynt Avery, as well as the curiosity regarding the whereabouts of his mysterious female companion. Relief that he had survived mingled with the pain of losing him. If only she could have some small clue about the fate of her mountain man. Had he lived out his life in solitude? Did he find someone else to love?

Her mind drifted back to the moment she knew she'd never see him again. She had lunged toward the melting image of a historical town from a century ago. But as she'd landed on her hands and knees, her palms scraped along the hard black asphalt of Dunsmuir Avenue. The soft dirt of Back Street was gone. Crying tears of frustration and heartache, she stood up in the deserted street and went to the sidewalk, where she found a pay phone. Placing a collect call to Michael, she woke him in the middle of the night.

"Thank God you're alive!" His voice was choked with emotion as he spoke rapidly. "It's been a living hell these past three months, not knowing if you were dead or alive. Even our private investigator came up empty. Are you all right? Where have you been?"

"I . . . don't remember anything before I woke up in the center of town a few minutes ago." Lying didn't come easy for her, but she wasn't ready to reveal her bizarre supernatural experience. She might never be ready. Knowing her purse was at the cabin, she told him it was missing, which was one concession of truth. "But I have a spare set of keys hidden in the Lexus. If I can find my way back to where I left it, I should be able to get—Damn, I don't have any gas cards."

"You don't have a car either. The police impounded it."

She'd learned the authorities had found not only her car but blood on the boulder at the riverbank. An explanation about her three-month disappearance would be expected as well as proof that she was the missing Katherine Marshall—neither of which she could provide.

"I still have a key to your condo," Michael offered. "I'll go by and get some identification for you. Do you still save all your old driver's licenses?"

"In the file cabinet."

"And to think I used to tease you about squirreling away those damn things. Looks like they'll come in handy. I'll fly in to the closest commercial airport and rent a car. With any luck, I'll be there by this afternoon."

"I'll be waiting at the police station."

Her entrance in the old-fashioned yellow gingham dress

had startled the night-duty officer, who brought in the chief. After extensive questioning, she had held to her story of amnesia but managed to avoid a medical examination for her head injury. Accompanied by a female officer, Kate had spent the remainder of the night in the Traveler's Hotel, located in the same block as the old Walker Boarding House. But sleep had eluded her, as haunting memories kept her wondering if it had all been a delusion.

Now, standing in front of the display case of the museum, Kate realized her journey to the past had been as real as the gingham dress that was packed in the trunk of the Lexus along with the other things she'd worn her last day in 1892. After answering a million questions, she managed to get her car released from the police. Michael had also brought with him a change of clothes when he'd stopped at her condo for her ID. She glanced down at her cream-colored tailored slacks and matching sleeveless vest, which seemed to belong to someone other than her.

"Katherine?" Michael came up behind her, placing his hands on her shoulders. She turned around, masking the disappointment of hearing the formality in her full name. She'd grown accustomed to the shorter nickname. It suited her. Or it had suited her in the past, she reminded herself, realizing that the life she'd lived a century ago was part of distant history that needed to be put away on a shelf like an old diary. The same for her abbreviated name. With her return to her present-day life, she would also return to the use of Katherine.

"I'm ready to leave any time you are," she said, her back to the ancient newspaper clipping. He had indulged her insistence upon visiting the museum, never questioning her reasons. She was grateful for his silence, unable to explain why she needed to see musty old antiques before heading home to Los Angeles.

"Are you sure you don't want to wait until tomorrow morning to get a fresh start?"

"I'd rather not." The thought of spending one more night in the canyon town only made her think of Flynt. She couldn't do it. "We can stop somewhere for the night after we return your rental car in Redding."

He didn't make any move to exit the museum. Instead, he stared at her with gentle brown eyes. "God, I missed you."

"I missed you, too." She leaned into his tender embrace, wishing she could have fallen in love with him but knowing now more than ever that there was only one man who would own her heart.

JUNE 23, 1892

Flynt stood at the window of room twelve in the boarding house, gazing at the snow-covered peak of Mt. Shasta, tinged pink and lavender by the setting sun. The back of his head still smarted from the pistol-whipping he'd taken in the dawn-lit street. Somewhere in the woods behind the jail and the houses uphill from town, Blackjack LeBouche had been hung from an oak tree. Flynt hadn't been there to see it. Even if he'd been conscious, he wouldn't have chosen to witness the macabre execution. As it was, he'd found himself lying in the dirt and looking up into the concerned face of Rita Walker. He'd soon learned the sheriff hadn't fared much better. Louzana and Dr. Gill were seeing to Murdock, who had taken a bullet in the shoulder when someone tried to wrestle his rifle from him.

From his second-floor view, he watched a wagon coming

out of the livery and heading north. The town was quieter than most days, he noticed. Not many people on the street. Whenever a few met, their expressions were grave. A pall had settled over the canyon. Perhaps justice had been served but there was no pride in the manner in which it had been doled out, no celebration over the death of the murderer. Word came back that LeBouche had made not one but two last-minute confessions. The Frenchman had admitted to killing his son as well as Little Deer eight years earlier.

At least Flynt could lay to rest the mystery behind the disappearance of the first woman he'd loved. The same could not be said about Kate, the second woman he had loved and now lost.

A profound emptiness chilled him to the bone despite the warmth of midsummer. With numbing grief, he walked over to the bed, sat on the edge of the feathered mattress, and drew his knife from its leather sheath. He laid the glistening steel blade on his open palm, staring at the sharp point.

"Mr. Avery?" Rita tapped at his closed door. "Flynt?"

"Come in."

"I don't mean to disturb—" She gasped at the sight of his weapon openly displayed. "Tell me you weren't contemplating using that on yourself."

"I am."

"Lord Almighty, son. Kate wouldn't want you to take your own life. Neither do I, if that counts for anything."

"It does, Miss Rita." He attempted a smile but fell short. "Let me assure you I have no such intention of taking my life."

Without speaking another word, he reached behind his head, grasped the leather strap that tied back his hair, and cut off the thick ponytail. He gazed down at the blond shank clutched in his fingers. Kate had loved it long and flowing.

She had loved the feel of it brushing against her bare skin. His vision blurred as tears stung his eyes. The dark cloud of grief descended upon him, heavier than ever. He forced himself to look at the older woman.

She seemed to know exactly why he'd done what he'd just done. "My heart goes out to you, Flynt. If there's anything I can do . . ."

"Will you cut off the rest? Not all of it. But I want it short. The shorter the better."

"I understand. Let me get some scissors."

AUGUST 4, 1996

On a smoggy Sunday afternoon in Los Angeles, Katherine chose to beat the August heat in her air-conditioned condo, poring over contracts that needed her attention. Sunni popped by unannounced. Both she and Michael had been making little out-of-their-way visits over the past several weeks, checking in on Katherine, making sure she hadn't disappeared again. Whether it was for their own peace of mind or for Katherine's own safety, it didn't really matter. It was endearing. After all, they were her only family.

Sitting cross-legged on her new sofa, her bare feet tucked beneath her flowing cotton skirt, Katherine sipped a cup of herbal tea while Sunni drank high-octane iced coffee across from her, enveloped in the squatty fat-boy chair with its huge soft arms and wide seat. She wore her usual trend-setting attire that showed off her best assets. Katherine admired the Sharon Stone moxie of her best friend. Sunni did whatever she chose, wore whatever struck her fancy, and said whatever was on her mind. And no one batted an eye, least of all Katherine. She loved being back with Sunni.

But it didn't make up for the hurt of losing Flynt.

Sunni gave her a hard, studied look. "You're not seriously considering selling your share of the agency to Michael and me, are you?"

Katherine put down her cup and saucer on the coffee table next to the paperback classic *Looking Backward* and a slender booklet by Peter Knudtson detailing the lives of the Wintun Indians.

Her fingertips brushed a piece of lint from the scarred surface of the old yellowed oak table that had been cut down from an antique kitchen table. It had reminded her of the one in the cabin. One week after her return, she had called her decorator and replaced every piece of chrome and glass with natural woods and soft fibers. Her office had received the same makeover. Katherine herself had given her Nordstrom's personal shopper free rein to create a new wardrobe that was less tailored, less . . . Hollywood.

She picked up a wheat cracker from a china plate. "I'm not sure I belong here any more. I've been thinking of moving to a small town, maybe open a private practice. Family law, that sort of thing."

"You've been back barely six weeks. How could you uproot yourself so soon after—well, your . . . ordeal. What's your therapist think of these changes? Have you told her about your spending spree?" She gestured to the surrounding living room that had been transformed from cold, clean high-tech to warm, plush Ethan Allen country-modern, which included an antique humpback trunk similar to the one in Flynt's cabin.

"I didn't go back to her after my first visit."

"Why not?" Sunni leaned forward, plunking her empty glass onto the tabletop. "You've been through a traumatic experience that was so bad you've blocked it from your memory. How could you quit seeing your shrink?"

"She can't help me remember anything." *Not when I already remember every last detail.*

"She might help you understand why you've gone from techno-lawyer-in-chrome to nature-woman-in-earth-tones. I've never seen this kind of abrupt change."

"Are you kidding? This is Hollywood, where plastic surgery and sweeps week can alter facial structure just to boost ratings! Why should a little redecorating make you so nervous?"

"Because it's not the same Katherine Marshall who came back to us. Even Michael is concerned."

"Old news, Sunni." She reached into the wooden bowl on the coffee table which contained a mix of raisins, nuts and granola. Scooping up a handful, she settled back into the overstuffed couch, picked out a piece of dried apple and popped it into her mouth. "Michael has been over here at least three times a week, hovering over me, worrying that the fall I took at the river has caused brain damage, and pleading with me to see a specialist."

"And begging you to marry him?"

"Not begging. But he's persistent."

"Well?"

"Well what? I can't possibly marry Michael." *I'm in love with someone else.* She shook off the sudden approach of tears. Her gaze dropped to the trail mix in her cupped palm. She nibbled a little more. Sunni got up from the chair and came over to the sofa, dropping down next to Katherine.

"What the hell happened to you up there in the mountains?" she asked softly.

A flood of memories washed over her. Hundreds of images in the span of a few seconds. She wanted to spill everything, but she couldn't expect Sunni to believe it any more than the psychotherapist, who had talked of delusional dreams that the mind creates to protect itself from traumatic reality.

Avoiding Sunni's eyes, Katherine grabbed another handful of granola. "People change," she answered evasively. "I just happen to have taken a little longer than most. Call me a late bloomer, if you will."

"See? The way you talk now—it's . . . different somehow. With a vague accent. That's exactly what I'm referring to!" Sunni pointed her finger.

Katherine abruptly pulled back, a startling memory flashing in her mind's eye. A rifle pointing at her. Blackjack. The cold steel on her belly. The rip of cloth. Fear stole the warmth from her body. She felt the blood drain from her face.

"Katherine?"

A hand touched her shoulder. She jerked away. "No—!"

She lunged to her feet and took a half dozen steps before she realized she had no need to run. No forest surrounded her. No sounds of birds and rushing water. Only the hauntingly beautiful music of Suzanne Ciani filled the air. Her compact disk *Dream Suite* was playing on the stereo. The current track had become a familiar favorite, poignantly entitled " 'Til Time and Times Are Done."

Turning back to Sunni, she sighed. "Forgive me—I tend to be a bit jumpy these days."

"No need to apologize," responded her friend, patting the cushion next to her. "I want to help, Katherine. Talk to me. What set you off like that?"

"Your finger." It sounded so ridiculous now. "It was like a gun in my face."

Choosing her words carefully, she sat down and explained

bits and pieces of her three-month disappearance. She couched her story in the present time period, hoping to convince Sunni that Flynt Avery and the Frenchman were reclusive rivals in a remote region of the Southern Cascades.

Sunni learned only of the rescue at the river, the knife fight and the attempted rape. "It sounds like *Deliverance* of the nineties," her friend commented afterward, shock and horror written across her delicate features. Unaware of the intimate relationship with Avery, she asked, "Where are they now? Did they kill one another? Is that how you finally escaped?"

"Blackjack is dead." Strung up by vigilantes, according to the yellowed newspaper clipping in the museum. "As for Flynt . . ." More than one hundred years had passed since she'd seen him in his jail cell. "He's gone, too."

She felt Sunni's eyes riveted on her, scrutinizing her. She tried to refrain from squirming in her seat like a cheating student under the glare of an all-discerning teacher.

"Tell me about this guy Avery."

"Flynt?" she asked with a casual voice that sounded a little too weak. Katherine noticed her hand was empty and reached for her teacup but changed her mind when she felt the slight tremble of her fingers. She didn't dare try to pick up the fragile china and risk dropping it on the floor. Her hand moved past the saucer to the wheat crackers. "He was quite the gentleman, actually. Once I got to know him, that is. At first I thought he was some sort of long-haired British rocker who had run away to play Grizzly Adams."

Sunni snapped her fingers. "British! That's where your accent came from."

"Me? An accent? I haven't!"

"Listen to yourself! And you've picked up words and phrases, too. Very refined. Almost snooty."

"Nonsense." Katherine dismissed the notion with a flip of her hand which held the half-eaten cracker. Sunni snatched it away and held it out, shaking it at Katherine as if it were a scolding finger.

"You've got to quit eating all the time. I know you lost some weight but you don't need to pack it on quite so fast."

"I'm not. I've only gained back ten of the fifteen pounds I lost."

"The rate you're going, you'll put on another ten by the end of this month. And ten by the end of the next. Get a grip, girl. It's like you're completely out of control. I see you eating all the time."

"I didn't know you were keeping track."

"How can I not? You have bowls of this rabbit food everywhere. The fridge at the office is packed with sprouts and mineral water. What happened to your M&M fetish?"

Katherine grew annoyed at the cross-examination. She rose from the sofa. Too quickly, she realized too late. The head rush that followed made the room spin. Sunni leaped up and steadied her, then eased her back down onto the couch.

"Lay down," insisted her friend.

"I'm fine. Really I am." Where had she heard those words before? From Flynt, of course. The backs of her eyeballs smarted with stifled tears. "I jumped up too fast, that's all."

"Maybe, maybe not. I don't suppose you saw a doctor for a physical since your accident."

"No. And you're starting to sound too much like Michael now."

Sunni knelt on the floor, her pale blue eyes serious. "When he came to get you in Dunsmuir, why did you refuse a medical examination?"

"I didn't need one. By then it'd been three months since

my fall. It was pointless to spend thousands of dollars on tests when I hadn't had any problems in all that time."

"You'd said you didn't remember anything about those months you were missing. But now you suddenly, somehow, recall *almost* getting raped. Are you telling me the truth?"

"Yes," she answered, feeling guilty for omitting the rest of the real story.

"Are you sure? Think back . . . Maybe you blocked the worst part of it. Could you have actually been raped?"

"No!"

"How can you be so certain, especially with amnesia? A doctor *should* have seen you. For God's sake, Katherine— you could have contracted a disease. You need to see a doctor. Get some tests. Let's hope you're not HIV-positive. Or pregnant."

There was no chance of either one, but Katherine couldn't explain her theory on the improbability of viable sperm that was over a century old. Nor could she say that the AIDS epidemic had yet to invade the populace of the 1890s. The only thing she could say in her defense was that the likelihood of conception was remote, given the lapse in her cycle while she was gone.

"Stress," she related. "I still haven't gotten it back."

"All the more reason to make an appointment tomorrow morning—first thing."

"I'll be all right, Sunni. Quit mothering me, please," she gently begged. "This whole experience *has* changed me. And I have the decorator's bills to remind me. But new furnishings didn't quite fix what's wrong with me, with my life. I thought it would but it didn't. I'm feeling lost . . . restless. There was something about the mountains that connected me to the bigger picture."

She thought of SnowEagle and his wise words of advice,

his teachings of the spirits within the animals and rocks and plants and people. He had spoken of the cycle of birth and life and death and rebirth. He had taught her to listen with her heart, listen to the wisdom within. Little by little, she had begun to believe that her new life with Flynt had been her own rebirth, the new beginning she had looked back upon when she'd sat at the river the very first time. Now, however, she felt trapped between two different centuries, unable to be the new Kate she'd left behind and unable to continue her present-day life that belonged to another Katherine who had ceased to exist.

Sunni spoke with bewilderment in her voice. "I just don't get it. You've worked so hard to keep this agency on its feet. And now you sound like you're going to throw it all away— for what? For some nebulous idea of a perfect world in small-town America? It's not there, Katherine. You may as well face it. Stay here. Stay with the agency. It's your security."

Katherine turned her head away and stared at the soft forest-green floral fabric on the back of the couch. The banked tears finally overflowed as her mind filled with memories of Flynt and their unfulfilled plans to live in Dunsmuir. Perhaps that era in time hadn't been perfect. Perhaps it had had a wild streak every now and then with gamblers such as LeBouche. But she thought of the Walker sisters and their boarders. She thought of Dr. Gill and his wife. She thought of the pine scent and pioneer spirit. Even though she'd hated the drudgery of living in the cabin, she might have adapted to the quiet busyness of living in the tiny railroad town. Anything would have been better than living without Flynt.

"I need to go back, Sunni." *To 1892. To Flynt. To the woman named Kate that I found in myself back there.*

"To Dunsmuir?" she asked, unaware of the full meaning of Kate's words. "Why?"

"I . . . I lost something."

"The police have promised to notify you if your purse or clothes are found."

Katherine slowly sat up, then gazed beseechingly at her lifelong friend. "Please try to understand. I don't think I can go forward with my life unless I go back up north. I've got to resolve some issues."

"I'm going with you."

"No, you don't need to go."

"I *want* to go. Besides—the last time you took off, you were missing for three months! If I go, I can keep tabs on you."

AUGUST 7, 1892

Flynt sat cross-legged on the ground, facing SnowEagle in front of the Wintu's bark lodge. His great-grandfather had been smoking a pipe of *lol,* preparing himself for the trance. Flynt never ceased to feel great awe and privilege whenever he was in attendance during the shaman's sacred time with the spirit world. Soon the old man sucked in a quick breath, a sign that the helpers from the other side had come to speak.

"The prophecy in your vision," began SnowEagle in his native Wintu dialect. "It is still unfolding. It is not yet complete. You will unite with the Cougar-Woman, but not in this lifetime."

The mountain spirit favored Flynt's decision to leave the Cascades. He had told SnowEagle that he needed to seek a new life in another place. With thoughts of Kate's prediction about San Francisco, he planned to reinvest his financial assets elsewhere, perhaps Los Angeles. This time together would be their last, for his great-grandfather had insisted that this was a journey for Flynt to make alone. As a parting gift, he had offered nearly all his worldly possessions to SnowEagle. Although the Wintu had refused the cabin, he had accepted Yola and the colt. Flynt would ride Sasti to Dunsmuir to catch the train, after which SnowEagle would claim the horse from the livery on Back Street.

As the wild tobacco-induced trance continued, the shaman advised, "You will find your peace where the sea meets the shore. Like Dunsmuir, it is a young town not far from the city of Los Angeles . . . Santa Monica. There are cliffs there. Know that *Patit-Pokta,* where she is now, goes to this place to walk along the water and think of her time here with you at this river. When you find the cliffs, you will sense her presence on the same sand more than one hundred years from now."

SnowEagle had just confirmed the feeling which had been gnawing at Flynt for weeks, feelings he had not been able to put into words. He realized now that his trip to Los Angeles was his only way of getting as close to Kate as possible, as close as the expanse of a century would allow. Living where she would one day live, walking the same ground she would one day walk, viewing the same sights of ocean and hills—these things would draw him nearer to her and comfort him.

When the trance was over, the two men rose to their feet. They clasped hands in farewell, then stepped toward one another and gave a brief but affectionate embrace.

"I wish you would change your mind and come with me."

"I am old, my son. My work here is nearing an end."

"I could stay until then."

SnowEagle shook his head. "We each have different journeys that we must take alone. Yours has come sooner than mine. You cannot refuse to accept this destiny any more than I can refuse mine."

"But what if—"

"When I am called to join the ancient ones, I will no longer be here to see what happens to this body. It does not matter, young one. Go now, you have a great deal of travel ahead of you."

"Thank you for all you have given me, Great-grandfather."

"It is you who have given to me as well. Remember that you are guided by *Olelbis* and your spirit-helpers. Stay open to them. They are there for you."

"I will."

Chapter 20

AUGUST 17, 1996

By THE THIRD week of August, Katherine had already postponed her trip to Dunsmuir with Sunni twice before she'd finally freed up five full days from her busy schedule. Although Michael had wanted to join them, she'd convinced him to hold down the fort, promising to check in every evening so he wouldn't worry.

"I'll worry anyway," he'd told her in her office the day before she'd left town. "I love you, Katherine."

"I love you, too, Michael. But not the way you want." *Not the way I love Flynt.*

The long drive to Northern California on I-5 seemed to take less time with the conversation going almost nonstop. By evening they entered the mountains north of Lake Shasta. Sunni was at the wheel, which suited Katherine just fine. She didn't want the responsibility of keeping her eyes on the road. She was too distracted by the familiar sight of

Mount Shasta and the smell of the pines. Her hands soon became cold and clammy. Her stomach grew queasy.

She rolled down the window to let the refreshing wind blow across her face. The fragrance of the forest filled her head with memories. They passed a freeway sign for Sweetbrier Creek. She thought of the cabin near the gurgling stream.

I miss you, Flynt, she said silently toward the wooded ridge. *God, how I miss you.*

The moon was full and bright in the starry night sky when they pulled into the parking lot of the Railroad Park Resort south of Dunsmuir. Katherine had made reservations there because of its close proximity to the familiar territory surrounding Sweetbrier Creek.

The young clerk cheerfully greeted the two women as they approached the front desk. "You must be the Marshall party of two," she said. "We were expecting you around six. I was hoping you didn't take the wrong exit. People get lost real easy up here when they don't know the area."

"Yes, I've heard," answered Katherine. She filled out the reservation slip and pulled a credit card from her wallet. It was brand new, one of the handful she'd replaced after her return to Los Angeles. The others were with Flynt. Or had been, anyway. By now they were long gone. Just like the man. Her fingers shook. The card dropped onto the counter. "I'm so sorry. Here—" She slid the plastic toward the clerk who smiled back at her.

"Happens all the time. It's a long drive from anywhere to get to here. By the time some guests show up they're tired and cranky and practically fall asleep on us before we can show them to their caboose."

Sunni piped in, "Caboose? We're sharing a *caboose*?"

Katherine chuckled with the clerk. "Don't look so

stunned, for heaven's sake. The converted cars are the drawing card of this place."

"What's the bed—a luggage cart?"

"Our beds and mattresses are as real as our vintage railroad cars," said the clerk with a wide grin, grabbing a pair of keys and leading them toward the door. "If you want a bite to eat, there's not much open down at this end of town at this hour. But the Hitching Post ought to suit you just fine. I'll draw you a little map to show you how to get there."

"I already know the way." Katherine thanked the woman.

By the time they were shown to their caboose and left alone for the night, Sunni had developed a definite expression of skepticism. "Is she for real?"

Katherine smiled, remembering her own disbelief when she'd encountered the open friendliness of the small-town residents—from the waitress at the roadside diner to the Walker sisters a hundred years ago.

"Get used to it," she told Sunni. "I think it's catching. Probably some kind of government experiment with their drinking water."

"Are you serious?"

"Absolutely not." Katherine hoisted her suitcase onto her bed. "It's nothing more than down-home hospitality."

"Yeah right. And I'm the Pillsbury doughboy."

"I didn't believe it either at first. But it's the genuine real thing. Kind of nice, I think."

"Is this why we're here—for you to scope out the town as a place to live?"

"Not exactly." Without Flynt, she couldn't imagine herself living out her life alone in these mountains. The memories were too raw, too fresh to expose heerself every day to the sight of places they'd been together. No, she was hoping for answers. But not to put down roots.

She rummaged through her folded jeans and sweaters for an unopened bag of granola. She tore off a corner and shook a few pieces into her mouth.

Sunni grabbed the cellophane pouch. "That's your third since lunch," she reprimanded.

"Would you please quit doing that?" Katherine retrieved the goodies with a peeved snatch of her hand. "My stomach's a little unsettled from all the mountain driving."

"You've never been carsick in your life."

"I've never ridden with you on winding roads before."

"Spoken by the person who rode every roller coaster at Six Flags Magic Mountain three times in one day."

"Not one of them was driven by you, I might add."

"Whoa, back the truck up, princess. *I'm* the one who has PMS down to an art form. But right now I'd say you got it hanging in the Louvre."

"I wish this was something so simple. At least it would explain why I think I'm going crazy."

"What happened to the doctor's appointment?"

"After this trip," she hedged, closing her suitcase. "I promise."

"I'm making the appointment and driving you there myself."

At six-thirty the next morning, Katherine was dressed and on her way out the door of their shared room. Her hand was turning the doorknob when Sunni grumbled, "You're not going anywhere without me."

"Playing bodyguard, are we?"

"Damn straight."

"Go back to sleep," Katherine softly suggested, making an effort to soothe ruffled feathers. "I was only going to take a short walk. I'll bring back some coffee for you."

"Give me five minutes." The covers flew off her bed and her feet hit the floor. Padding across the carpet wearing the football jersey of a former lover, Sunni muttered a few choice epithets that she rarely used.

Katherine sighed, knowing how much she'd tried her friend's patience. She couldn't blame her for being grouchy, but the stubborn determination to play watchdog amazed Katherine.

So like Flynt. The voice in her head startled her. She hadn't heard it in weeks. She hadn't heard it since leaving Dunsmuir.

Sunni paused at the bathroom door. "Are you all right? You look pale."

"I just need a little fresh air. I'll wait for you outside."

"Don't go far."

"I won't, Mother."

Sunni gave her a cocky grin. "You better mind me, child."

As Katherine stood in the morning sun and took a deep breath of pure mountain air, she couldn't help but wonder about the voice in her head. She would never get used to the distinctive timbre or the suddenness of it. Yet it never actually frightened her. Not like the creepy feeling of being watched by invisible eyes. That memory still lifted the hairs on the back of her neck.

After breakfast, Sunni insisted on stopping at the small police headquarters to see if there was any new information about the missing purse or clothes. Katherine suspected an ulterior motive, however, when Sunni asked the officer on duty for detailed directions to the site along the Sacramento River where the Lexus had been found in March. Clearly, her friend was taking precautions against getting lost. Just in case of such an event, she even arranged to check back later so the authorities would be aware of their whereabouts.

"I'm not taking any chances of a repeat performance of your disappearance last spring," she later told Katherine as they drove south on the main street to catch the I-5 on-ramp.

There were no long, meandering side trips like the one Katherine had taken during her first visit to the river. They followed the hand-drawn map without so much as one peep from the peculiar voice that had told her to turn onto the rutted dirt road.

As she parked the car, she wasn't surprised by the feeling of *déjà vu*. This time, however, she'd worn clothing more appropriate for traipsing around the woods. Her jeans and hiking boots were a far cry from the gauze skirt and designer boots that had disappeared into history. She led Sunni through the trees, following the rushing sound of the water. At the crest of the riverbank, she glanced around.

Everything was as she remembered. The granite rock was not only visible again but the water level had dropped even further, leaving the small boulder high and dry among tiny pebbles and smooth stones.

She told Sunni a little bit about her first visit here, omitting the apparition of Little Deer. She pointed toward the water. "I smacked my forehead on that boulder, but it was halfway under water at the time. When I woke up, I was in Flynt's cabin."

"Is it near here?"

She nodded, looking over her shoulder in the direction that SnowEagle had taken her. "Near enough. The hike is strenuous if you're not in shape because it's mostly uphill from here. It was downriver some, too."

"Was? You mean it's gone?"

"Yes—I mean no . . . it's probably still there." Realizing how hard it was to sidestep the truth of her journey back in time, she grew increasingly uncomfortable. If she wasn't more careful, she would trip herself up and Sunni would find out the real story. Though she was fairly sure the cabin no longer existed, a sense of curiosity pushed her to investigate. If there wasn't a trace of it left, she would claim that she'd lost her bearings in the woods, that the cabin was probably located on a different ridge.

But it was there.

Someone had kept it up, though not recently from the looks of it. The clearing had grown over with meadow grass and some small saplings. The outhouse and animal shelter were both gone. Katherine didn't talk about the colt she had helped deliver. She remained silent, unable to speak with the avalanche of memories.

The door of the cabin yawned wide. The glass window was completely gone, leaving a gaping hole. Inside, the far corner of the roof was missing. Filtered sunlight illuminated the empty room. Her eyes were drawn to the fireplace where the thick wooden mantel looked chiseled and worn from abuse. She walked toward it, but Sunni grabbed her arm.

"It looks ready to tumble down on our heads," she warned, dropping her hand. "Better not tempt fate."

Katherine wanted to laugh out loud. Tempt fate? She wanted to curse fate, yell at it, demand that it own up to the cruel trick it had played on her. For a split second, she almost ran up to the hearth to grab a loose stone, to let it tumble down on her, to let it take her to wherever Flynt had gone.

Sunni's fingertips touched Katherine at the elbow. "This place is too depressing for me. I'll wait for you outside."

Katherine slowly nodded, vaguely aware of her friend's presence. "I won't be long."

Several minutes later, she dragged herself away from the roomful of bittersweet memories. She walked out of the cabin to find Sunni standing in knee-high weeds, her head tilted back as she stared into the azure blue sky. Her friend silently motioned her over with a wave of her arm, then pointed at the tree tops.

"Look at that," she whispered in hushed awe.

Katherine craned her neck, squinting from the bright glare of the September sun. Then she saw it.

A bald eagle—majestic and proud.

"Isn't it spectacular?" asked Sunni.

"I wonder if it's the same one I saw back in March. There was one at the river . . ."

Katherine suddenly recalled a number of other times she'd seen one. The day Flynt had been stabbed, an eagle had circled overhead as she and Lou followed Flynt's body into the boarding house. The day Blackjack had attacked her, she'd looked up to see those eyes staring down upon her. And the last time was on her final trip to Dunsmuir with Flynt. Escorted by the posse of deputies, they had been following the river north when she'd caught sight of an eagle overhead, staying with them for the better part of an hour.

Somehow she didn't think it was just a coincidence any more. Yet she didn't quite believe the niggling thought in the back of her mind.

It couldn't be, she rationalized.

Why not, Kate? You traveled through time, didn't you?

Yes, but . . . SnowEagle?

She felt the telltale prickle on her neck. She glanced around, sensing an eerie shift in the light breeze. Beyond the doorway of the cabin stood a shadowy, indistinct outline that could have been a figure of a woman or a trick of the light filtering through the far corner of the roof. Katherine felt her pulse quicken.

Sunni quietly asked, "Isn't he incredible?"

Katherine looked up at the bald eagle, bewildered by the sensation of someone watching her. Was it SnowEagle? Was it Little Deer? Or was it a spirit of the *Bohem Puyuk*—the Big Mountain the shaman had spoken of? Whatever it was, Katherine felt a certain sense of closure, of farewell to her past in the Cascades.

SEPTEMBER 26, 1892

Flynt sat at the base of the cliffs and looked out upon the moon glistening off the waves rolling into shore. Saddlebags at his feet, he had left his bay gelding at the rooming house and walked the mile or so to the bluffs.

The peace he sought still eluded him, despite his regular visits to the ocean over the last few weeks. The salt-tinged air did little to lift the melancholy that had grown darker with each month since Kate had vanished. It was worse this time than it had been with Little Deer. Perhaps the confrontation with his stepmother in London had been the distraction he'd needed back then, forcing him to deal with financial matters until his heart had started to heal from the loss of his first wife. With Kate, Flynt had no such distraction. He had expedited his affairs in San Francisco, encouraging his business partners to relocate in Southern California. Eager to follow his money and loyal to his friendship, all but one had moved to Los Angeles. They were now busy with reinvesting his assets into recently discovered oil fields, buying land from Long Beach to the valley of the Mission of San Fernando. Delegating the negotiations, Flynt held no enthusiasm for multiplying his fortune.

It seemed that the only motivation to get out of bed each

morning was the daily walk to the beach, often late at night when no one visited the stretch of sand beneath the bluffs. The solitude comforted him, though only a small amount. The rhythmic roll of waves crashing along the shore soothed the ache in his chest. But the sadness still remained.

He reached for the saddlebags and withdrew the black leather bag which went with him everywhere. He had been through its contents hundreds of times, touching the items she had once touched. It was pure torture and he knew it, yet it was the sweetest torture all the same. He pulled out a card with her photograph. He didn't need to look at it to know it was her license to drive, having committed to memory every location of everything in her organizer-book. His fingers closed around the plastic card.

In his mind's eye, he saw Kate laughing. He smiled to himself as he stared out at the Pacific Ocean. He imagined her here in 1996, wondering if she had found laughter in her life or if she was as bereft of joy as he. Michael was there for her, however. Perhaps she had decided to put her past behind her and look to her future with the young man who was her lifelong friend. Kate had once denied the possibility. But Flynt doubted she could have known what her true feelings would be after she'd returned to her own place and time.

In a strange way, he hoped Michael had stepped forward to take responsibility for Kate. She would need him now, though she would be reluctant to accept help from anyone. But he hated the thought of her facing her future alone. Unlike Flynt, she had more than investments to burden her. If what Rita had suspected was indeed true, his lady lawyer was now an expectant mother.

His fist clenched tight around the card in his hand as he sent out a fervent prayer for his woman and child, hoping beyond hope that both were safe and well. The misery of losing Kate was compounded by the notion of her carrying his illegitimate child—the shame she would endure, the fear and loneliness of facing the birth without him. He could only wish that her friend Michael would hold compassion in his heart for her.

He stowed the card in its slot in the book, then put the book into its bag, and returned it to his saddlebag.

Why did she have to be taken from him, Flynt asked for the thousandth time. Why was he spared from the hangman's noose only to die a slow death of despondency?

His throat constricted as he battled back the sob in his chest. He pinched the bridge of his nose and fought hard against the sting at the back of his eyes. He had no idea how many nights he had sat in this same spot, unable to keep the tears at bay. Tonight would be no different.

It is time for your grief to end.

His head jerked up at the words spoken clearly in his head.

From the white crest of a wave illuminated by the moon, a shimmery ball of light moved toward him. He watched it grow larger as it approached. The ghostly image of Little Deer hovered several feet in front of him, her arms reaching out.

An initial onslaught of falling pebbles startled him from his vision. He grabbed the bag and dove for safety away from the base of the cliff. The eroded bluff gave way, pelting him with rocks and stones. Knocked to the ground by the landslide, he felt a peculiar peacefulness descend upon him along with the soil and debris. A sense of resignation passed through his mind, as if he were putting down a crippled horse that had no strength to recover. His own will to live wasn't strong enough to repair the shredded remnants of his heart.

Drifting in a dark void, he heard a sharp reprimand.

"You could have gotten killed by that landslide," a man's voice barked from some distance away. "Get the hell away from the base of those bluffs!"

Flynt blinked his eyes, slightly disappointed that his life had been spared once more. Staring into the heavens above, he could see only a small handful of stars dotting the night sky. Hearing a low hum of indeterminable cause, he slowly sat up and glanced around, seeing unfamiliar buildings and artificial lights.

Recalling Bellamy's novel and Kate's own stories of the future, he leapt to his feet, his heart pounding with excitement. Could this be? Did he dare hope? Or was it a dream? He remembered that Kate had often asked the same question of her own experience in the past. He chuckled, recalling the countless times she had wondered if she was lying unconscious in a hospital and merely dreaming of her journey through time.

Now that he looked around him, he could only assume that the apparition of his deceased wife had been more than a mere vision, more than a trick of his mind. SnowEagle had told him that Little Deer had been instrumental in Kate's appearance as well as her disappearance. If this was real, he prayed that he had been taken to the era in which Kate now lived. He desperately hoped that the year was 1996.

SEPTEMBER 27, 1996

Kate sat at her desk at the Meridian Talent Agency, her elbows propped on the green felt blotter, her forehead cupped in her palms. "I still can't believe it."

Sunni came around behind her and gently massaged her shoulders. "You still have time to do something about it."

"No!" Her head shot up. Sunni tugged her backward in the executive chair, then swiveled it to face her.

"Katherine, don't put yourself through this nightmare. You've already been through enough. You don't need to be so damn noble about this . . . this—"

"Baby."

"No, this tragic mistake," she corrected. "This product of rape."

"It wasn't rape," admitted Katherine, sagging deeper into the soft upholstery. "It's pointless to continue this charade any longer. Sit down. I have quite a story to tell you."

After a long and difficult explanation to her friend, Katherine sighed heavily. "You probably think I'm crazy. *I* think I'm crazy!"

Getting up and pacing the floor in long-legged strides, Sunni let loose a string of epithets, adding, "I don't know *what* to think!"

The intercom buzzed. Katherine reached for the button but her friend beat her to it. "Hold all calls, Valerie. Katherine is *not* to be disturbed until further notice."

Katherine muttered sarcastically, "Oh, now *that* didn't just set off an alarm through the office staff. You definitely missed your cattle call in the theater of melodrama."

Sunni blithely apologized but pounced right back onto the subject of discussion. "We're going to bring Michael in here and tell him the whole scenario. Once he's over the shock, he'll throw that marriage proposal at your feet again. And this time you're going to accept."

Katherine rolled her eyes in disbelief. "I'm not dropping this bomb on Michael. Why should he be expected to take care of me? I'm not helpless. I'm not a fallen woman from the nineteenth century. This baby is mine and I'm not getting rid of him."

"Him?"

"It's Flynt's son," she blurted out, remembering the little boy with midnight-blue eyes who had appeared with Little Deer. Counting back the days, Katherine knew without a doubt that she had conceived their son that night. And for one brief moment, she had been given a chance to see him, to touch him. "I'm going through with this pregnancy and I'm having this baby."

A commotion in the hall interrupted Sunni's response. Doors slammed at regular intervals, each one louder than the last. Katherine came to her feet as the door of her own office flew open.

Valerie's voice carried into the room, "Sir, I can't let you go in there. I insist you leave."

The receptionist was hidden behind a tall broad-shouldered gentleman who stood almost as tall as the doorway. Although his dark blond hair was cut relatively short, he held an uncanny resemblance to Flynt Avery. Had the same forces that brought her back to the future granted her a real-life image of her mountain man?

Sunni broke the momentary stun of silence. "Val, get Michael in here! Mister, I don't know who in the hell you think you are but I suggest you leave. Now!"

Flynt stared at Kate surrounded by her own world and felt a sudden dread. What if she resented his imposition into her sophisticated life of this future time? Unable to risk the possibility of rejection, he simply held up her leather bag.

"You seem to have forgotten something." *Me, perhaps?*

Her green eyes appeared uncertain and confused. Slowly, she came around her desk and walked toward him as Sunni stepped into her path.

"Katherine! What are you doing?"

Without taking her eyes from Flynt, Kate gently moved her friend aside and approached him. Her hand seemed to rise of its own accord, reaching toward his face.

"Are you—?"

"I am, Kate."

"Oh God . . . Flynt . . . ?" Her eyes filled with tears. She touched his cheek as his own vision blurred. "I—I thought I lost you. I thought you were dead."

"I assure you, *Patit-Pokta,* I am very much alive." He covered her hand with his own, then turned his head and kissed her palm. "I am yours, if you will have me."

She mutely nodded, stepping into his arms. He dropped his mouth to hers, reveling in the feel of her, the taste of her. He would never have his fill of her.

Epilogue

NEARLY THREE MONTHS later, Kate and Flynt were curled up on the floral sofa watching *It's a Wonderful Life* for the fourth time in as many weeks. When the phone rang, she appeared somewhat perturbed.

"Who could be calling us on Christmas Eve?"

"Perhaps it is the security office phoning about a visitor. Michael or Sunni?"

"They know better than to pop by unannounced these days," she answered with a mischievous twinkle in her eyes. Despite her delicate condition, she continued to prolong their honeymoon. The official wedding had taken place at the old cabin after some creative footwork had produced his credentials of identification.

"Send him up, Howie," she said into the receiver, then cradled it. "It's a special delivery for me."

When the doorbell rang a few moments later, she left Flynt humming "Buffalo Gals" with Jimmy Stewart as she opened the door to a uniformed courier. Returning to the couch with a large envelope, she passed in front of him to take her seat next to him. But Flynt gently pulled her onto his lap, then shut off the VCR, pretending to be as curious as she about the package. Though he didn't dare spoil the surprise, he was eager to see if his arrangements had met with success. If not, he would still be the happiest man alive.

Beneath his hand on her stomach a ripple of movement broadened his smile. She had told him of the peculiar visit from Little Deer six months earlier, which he'd thought was merely a dream at the time. Now, however, he didn't doubt for a moment that she had been given a glimpse of their son. He could hardly wait for the day he would see the child, too.

As Kate withdrew a sheaf of papers with a small envelope attached, the baby kicked her. Out of the corner of her eye, she caught the proud grin on Flynt's face and recalled the time she couldn't imagine him as a father. She was wrong about a lot of things back then.

He nudged her impatiently, drawing her from her daydream. She silently skimmed the legal jargon on the letterhead of the Wells Fargo Bank, glancing at him nervously with disbelief.

"You drew up a will in 1892, leaving all your assets in a trust at this bank?"

"I did. Open the note addressed to you."

Inside the small envelope was a handwritten letter. . . .

My Dearest Kate,

I pray this letter will one day find its way into your hands. I cannot begin to describe the pain of losing you. Have you safely returned to your life in 1996? Are

*you well? I ask myself these questions every night as I
fall asleep and every morning when I awake.*

*After you vanished, Rita revealed to me her suspi-
cions about your condition. I hope it is true—that you
are with child. I only wish I could be there, Kate.
When you read this letter, I will be gone. Upon my
demise, however, I have arranged for you to be the
beneficiary of my estate. This inheritance should be
enough to keep you and our son or daughter in good
stead.*

*Since I cannot be with you, this is my way of reach-
ing over the century that separates us and letting you
know that I will always love you.*

> *Eternally Yours,*
> *Your husband Flynt*

"But how did you—? Why today?" asked Kate tearfully.

"I didn't know I would be taken to the future. I can only
assume that I was declared dead after a sufficient number of
years. As for today, I had your organizer-book with me, so I
used this address and chose a date you might be at home this
year. Until this moment, I wasn't sure if my arrangements
would succeed."

"*Succeed* is an understatement!"

Kate was astounded not only at the amassed fortune but at
the prime real estate held in trust. Though Flynt was equally
stunned at the cumulative value, he would have been content
even as a pauper. Now, more than ever, he finally realized
that wealth can't be measured by the size of a man's fortune
but only by the love in his heart.

. . . With a tear for the dark past, turn we then to the dazzling future, and, veiling our eyes, press forward. The long and weary winter of the race is ended. Its summer has begun. Humanity has burst the chrysalis. The heavens are before it.

—EDWARD BELLAMY
Looking Backward

Dear Readers,

While reading the *Dunsmuir Centennial Book,* I came across the brief history of Louis Napolean Girard: "In the early 1890s, the family [of Louis Girard] moved to Castella, where he was town constable. While he was constable, a woman and her child were fatally stabbed by her husband. The wife dragged herself to the Girards' home where she died on the steps. Louis jailed the man. When the news spread to the newly growing Dunsmuir, a lynch mob was formed and they came to Castella on a handcar. They tied Constable Girard, took the prisoner, and hanged him on a tree in front of the schoolhouse."

As with most writers, I began to wonder, "What if . . . ?" What if there were an innocent man who was accused of such a crime? What if a woman saw the newspaper clipping about his mistaken execution? From these questions came the story of Flynt Avery and Kate Marshall in *This Time Together.*

Dr. Benjamin Gill was hired by the Southern Pacific Company to be the town's first doctor. He is the only real-life personality that was used in the writing of this book. Rita and Louzana were fictionalized characters whose boardinghouse was in the approximate location of an actual rooming house owned by two sisters, Mertes Elgie Neher and Augusta Mertes Sheafor, along with their mother, Margaret Schmidt Mertes. Except for Mrs. Sheafor's teaching background, similar to Louzana's, these historical figures of the town were not the same characters depicted by the Walker sisters. As for Mertes, she married Doc Gill's son in February 1900. Now, how's that for an honest-to-goodness happy ending?

Sincerely,

Susan Leslie Liepitz

TIMELESS

Four breathtaking tales of hearts that reach across time—for love...

Linda Lael Miller, the *New York Times* bestselling author, takes a vintage dress-shop owner on a breathtaking adventure in medieval England—where bewitching love awaits...

Diana Bane unlocks the secret love behind Maggie's taunting dreams of a clan war from centuries past...

Anna Jennet's heroine takes a plunge into the sea from the cliffs of Cornwall—and falls back in time, into the arms of a heroic knight...

Elaine Crawford finds time is of the essence when an engaged workaholic inherits a California ranch—a place she's seen somewhere before...

___0-425-13701-5/$4.99